Pieces of Silver

Pieces of Silver

Pamela Oldfield

G.K. Hall & Co. • Chivers Press
Thorndike, Maine USA Bath, England

This Large Print edition is published by G.K. Hall & Co., USA
and by Chivers Press, England.

Published in 2000 in the U.S. by arrangement with
Piatkus Books, Ltd.

Published in 2000 in the U.K. by arrangement with Piatkus.

U.S. Hardcover 0-7838-9146-6 (Romance Series Edition)
U.K. Hardcover 0-7540-1490-8 (Windsor Large Print)
U.K. Softcover 0-7540-2379-6 (Paragon Large Print)

G.K. Hall Large Print Romance Series.

The text of this Large Print edition is unabridged.
Other aspects of the book may vary from the original edition.

Set in 16 pt. Plantin by Rick Gundberg.

Printed in the United States on permanent paper.

British Library Cataloguing in Publication Data available

Pieces of Silver

CHAPTER 1

'Get up, damn you!'

Sprawled in the aisle, one arm thrown out. Looks as though he's thumbing a lift. Just his bad luck to hit his head on the pillar. Nasty, that. Serves the blighter right though. He had it coming to him. Still, better get out of here before someone comes. Out of here and out of Canterbury.

'Not dead, are you, old chum?'

'Course he's not dead. But he is still. Eyes staring. Mouth open. Couple of teeth gone. Damn! A warning. That's all it was meant to be. A warning that a gentleman shouldn't behave like that. Hardly cricket. Hardly *Fellstowe*! If only he hadn't fought back. Tidier with his fists than I remember.

He's *not* dead.

But if he is, God will have noticed! Not a sparrow and all that.

'Get up!' Nothing. 'D'you hear me? I'm on to you! *Get up!*'

Unconscious? Yes, that's it. He'll come round at any minute. So maybe this is a good time to go. He'll wake up in his own time and — And what? Would he take it like a man and keep quiet or would he go to the police? Tell them he'd been attacked and left for dead? That could be very awkward for his family. Nasty scandal in all the newspapers. He wouldn't want that.

If push comes to shove I'll say he was still breathing when I left him. But where to hide him so he won't be found too soon? Can't leave him in the middle of the blasted aisle. Between the pews? Behind the altar . . .

Footsteps!

'God Almighty!'

Someone's coming! Quick! Get back to the door and close it . . . Too late! It's an old woman. Head her off.

'Er — sorry madam. Can't let you in at present.'

'But I'm already in!'

Pulling off knitted gloves. Grey hair. Sensible shoes. Everyone's granny.

'I mean, no further. Can't let you in any further —'

'Why not?'

Why couldn't he let her in? Because there's a man sprawled in the aisle! 'Er — repairs. Yes, undergoing repairs.' Look at the nosy old bat! Eyes everywhere. Just my luck. Mustn't let her look down the aisle. Don't groan, old chum, for God's sake!

'The vicar never said anything to me about repairs.'

'Well, maybe he forgot. It hardly matters. You can pray outside, can't you? God is everywhere. That's what they say, isn't it?'

'Are you all right? You look a bit flustered.'

'I'm fine, thank you. But I must insist you say your prayers or whatever outside.' If she saw too much he would have to deal with her. She was peering past him.

'I don't want to say any prayers. I'm Mrs Bly, the cleaner. Polish the pews, dust the window sills, mop over the floor. I'm a bit late actually —'

A cleaner? At this time of night? 'Not this evening, madam.' Convince her. Ah! Inspiration. 'Unless you like rats.'

'Rats?' She actually shuddered. Backing away.

'And mice. I'm a rat-catcher.' Fingers crossed.

'Rat-catcher? You said you were doing repairs.'

Play it cool but get rid of her. Get her out. Could she have seen anything? Curiosity killed the cat. 'The vicar didn't want it known. Might deter the congregation.' She's retreating, thank God.

'Deter them? I should jolly well think it would! Not that I've ever heard any. Rats. I mean. Although now I come to think of it I have heard the odd scamper. I thought it was mice. I bang my broom around to frighten them off.'

She was close to the door now. Go, Mrs Bly. Go. You won't regret it. Pulling on her gloves, squeezing plump fingers into white cotton.

She said, 'Well, you're welcome to them. Rats! Ugh! Makes my flesh creep just to think about them.' She hesitated. 'But when am I going to get my cleaning done? We've got a wedding tomorrow afternoon. The Ropers' daughter. Mrs Belling'll be in first thing to do the flowers and —'

Smile. 'First thing in the morning, madam. That's what the vicar said.' Why didn't she just clear off? 'He said to tell you to come back first thing in the morning.'

'The vicar? I thought he was away.'

'Er — Well, somebody did. Chap in black.'

'The rector? Mr Fellowes?'

Smile and nod. For God's sake *go!* At any moment a badly beaten man might come staggering up the aisle. Blood-stained clothes. Missing teeth. Probably give her a heart attack.

She said, 'Well then, it'll have to be the morning but it's most inconvenient. I've promised my neighbour — Oh well!' Turning to go. Turning back. *Now* what?

'Where's your dog?'

'Dog?'

'Rat-catchers always have a dog.'

He thought rapidly. 'Modern methods, madam. This is 1935. We use — er — gas. Yes, gas the little beggars. Much quicker.'

'Gas? I've never heard of that.'

'More humane. All God's creatures, aren't we.'

'I suppose so. Right then, I'm off. I'll come

back first thing in the morning. There won't be anything — you know, nothing *dead?*'

Mouth suddenly dry. 'Dead?' Heart thudding. 'Oh! You mean rats and mice!' Deep breath. 'Not so much as a whisker. All cleared away neat and tidy.' He tried another smile. His mouth felt stiff but he must have succeeded because she smiled back. He gave her a little salute, touching his forehead with the forefinger of his right hand. 'I'd better make a start!'

She laughed. 'No peace for the wicked!'

He closed the door behind her. Thank God for small mercies!

Back to his victim. No pulse. No movement. The hands were limp and a small pool of blood had seeped from his left ear. He wouldn't be staggering anywhere.

He was dead.

James Moore entered the dining room with one minute to spare. Dinner at Grange Park was always at eight o'clock and all members of the family who were present were expected to be there on time. It was one of the things Clarice fussed about — like never bringing friends home without prior warning and waiting for Agnes to bring the post in in the morning. She was fond of reminding them all that there were standards to be maintained. Women smoking was another thing she could not abide and for that reason Harriet, her husband's sister, had stayed away for years.

James took his seat at the top of the table with his back to the portrait of his grandfather. Similar sombre pictures hung on the pale walls, strategically placed between the wall lights. Deep red velvet curtains added to the tone of the room which was elegant in an old-fashioned way.

James Moore was tall with prematurely white hair and a fashionably large moustache. He smiled at his wife across glittering silver and glassware and realised, not for the first time, that age was catching up with her. A few lines around the eyes and grey in her hair. They were both past their prime and the children were adults. Soon he suspected that he and Clarice would no longer be needed and the thought depressed him.

He said wistfully, 'I thought Dulcie was going to try to get home for dinner tonight.' Dulcie was his favourite and he had never hidden the fact.

'Well, she hasn't tried hard enough, has she? Not even for some decent cooking.'

His wife's tone was sharp and James regretted his words. He knew that his constant concern with his daughter's welfare irked his wife. *He* called it concern: *she* called it fussing.

He said, 'I don't know how they manage. Harriet was never a great cook and —'

'A *great* cook? Your sister couldn't boil an egg.'

He bit back an answer, refusing to be provoked. His sister Harriet was always a source of friction between them. In her younger days she had been a stalwart member of the Suffragette movement. Clarice abhorred their aims and made a great show of never using her vote.

Now she tutted irritably. 'Dulcie's just as bad. Not an ounce of domesticity in her. God help her husband — if she ever finds one which I doubt! No man will ever measure up to Teddy in her eyes. He's her hero and always will be . . . Oh James!' She smiled suddenly. 'Do you remember that terrible concoction she gave us once?' She frowned. 'Something foreign made with lots of beans. Something French — sounded like casserole but — Oh yes! *Cassoulet!* That was it. It was awful but we had to eat it because she was so proud of it.'

James, feeling wicked, said, 'Cassoulet. That was it. We all had terrible wind afterwards and —'

'James! Please!' Clarice blushed.

'Well, we did, dear. Then to please her, we said how good it was —'

'And were terrified she might make it again.'

They both laughed. James reached for the cruet and fiddled with the pepper pot until Clarice tutted.

He said, 'They're probably dining at the County Hotel!'

'Don't be silly, James. Harriet only goes there for special occasions. I can't see why they are so devoted to the place after that waitress spoiled Dulcie's blouse. I much prefer the Fountain. At least they train their staff properly.'

'It was an accident, Clarice.'

'It was gross carelessness. Stupid woman. The stain never came out. Tomato soup, of all things. I could have told her. There's something in tomatoes that —'

To deflect one well-worn story he revived another. 'Harriet does so love her oysters.'

'Oysters! I've told her so many times that shellfish are not to be trusted. I knew a man once — my uncle's gardener —'

He finished the familiar tale. 'He ate some mussels and they poisoned him and he died.'

She was not amused. 'Well, he did, dear.'

'I've eaten oysters,' he insisted.

'More fool you then! And her!'

Give up, James, he told himself. You're on a losing wicket. Clarice had never liked Harriet; had never tired of criticising his sister's independent life style.

Clarice said, 'Your sister never did get her priorities right. Can't stand men or animals and won't ride. Let's hope it doesn't rub off on Dulcie.'

He glanced at the clock. 'She only said she *might* manage it. Teddy's late too.'

'No doubt your daughter has found something better to do than spend a few hours with her family.' She lowered her head a little, looking at him over the top of her spectacles.

James ignored the sharp words for he understood the pain that lay behind them. Their daughter's defection to Harriet's house had been a great blow. Logically, of course, Harriet's house in St George's Terrace made perfect sense because Dulcie worked in Canterbury. Grange Park was several miles outside the town on the London Road which meant a long bicycle ride, sometimes in inclement weather. He sighed. They missed Dulcie more than either of them would admit.

Agnes came into the room, saw that Teddy was absent and looked at her mistress for guidance.

'We'll give him another minute or two, Agnes. If he's not here then you can bring in the soup.'

James leaned back in his chair and sighed. 'This blasted wedding. Annabel and young Brayne. Teddy's been unsettled by it.'

Clarice fussed with her table napkin. 'He's had plenty of time to get used to the idea. And if you ask me he's better off without her. Annabel Roper broke his heart and I for one will not forgive her.'

He groaned inwardly. Here we go again! 'Look, for the last time — they weren't officially engaged.'

'Don't argue, dear. It was an understanding. It amounts to the same thing.'

'I sometimes wonder if he still loves her —' He fell silent. This was an argument he could never win.

Clarice tossed her head. 'I give him more credit than that, James. Teddy is not a fool. When

Annabel threw him over for his best friend he should have come to his senses. I hope he has stopped moping over her.'

'He didn't *mope,* dear, surely.' Did men mope? Women, perhaps, but not men. Not Teddy.

Clarice shrugged. 'Well what would you call it? He went off to Cornwall without a word to anyone. Frightened us all to death and then came back days later looking ill and unhappy. She dabbed at her mouth with the table napkin. 'Maybe you'd prefer the word "pine".'

'That's what dogs do, isn't it?'

'Don't quibble, James, please.'

'It was years ago. Three or four years. He ought to be over it by now.' But then again, maybe not. Teddy's way was to suffer in silence. He had been a moody child, difficult to understand. Impossible to get close to. Only Dulcie had managed it. James had always envied his children their easy relationship. He said, 'I asked him something about the estate yesterday and he almost snapped my head off. Not like him to —'

He stopped as Agnes reappeared. He took out his watch and registered surprise. 'Twenty past!' he said. Before his wife could speak he said, 'Give him five more minutes.'

For what seemed an eternity they sat without speaking as the minutes passed. At half past eight Agnes brought in a tureen of vegetable soup and served two helpings. James watched her leave the room. Agnes. Small, birdlike. Totally loyal. Once she had been the children's nanny, young, pretty and desirable. Not that she had allowed anything of *that* sort. Over the years, when the children no longer needed her, she had replaced the housekeeper. She would be with them now until she died.

'He's never late,' Clarice said. 'Something must have happened to him. If not, then it's most inconsiderate of him.'

James tried to hide his unease. His appetite was fast disappearing. He was a peace-loving man and they had recently fought a losing battle with Dulcie over her so-called career. A *lady journalist* on Wilfred's newspaper. It was quite absurd — but then his half-brother never could resist Dulcie. Nobody could. They had finally surrendered and were now enjoying peace of a sort. He hoped they were not now going to clash swords with Teddy. Sharing a family crisis with Clarice was not for the faint-hearted.

He smiled. 'You know what they say, dear. "Don't trouble trouble 'til trouble troubles you!" '

'Oh don't be trite, James!'

'I mean it, dear. Tomorrow Annabel and Clive will be married and it will all be over. Not even Teddy would pine or mope for another man's wife. He is much too sensible for that. I do wish we had accepted the invitations but as usual your argument won the day.'

'I should hope so, too. Go to the wedding indeed!'

'It was an olive branch, Clarice.'

'I don't care what it was.'

'Refusing has made us look petty-minded.'

'Petty-minded?' Her voice rose. 'Their daughter insults our son and they have the nerve to invite us to the wedding! Wild horses wouldn't drag me to set foot in St Alphege's church. Poky little place. I can't think what they're about, holding the ceremony there.'

'You know very well what they're about. It's the church where her parents were married. And her grandfather's buried there. Annabel told us that —'

'I don't want to hear about Annabel, James. Clive and Annabel can tie the knot wherever they like but I shan't be there to see it. There's something about that girl's eyes. Almost a cast.'

'Some people find that attractive.' He couldn't resist it. When Teddy had been courting Annabel, Clarice had approved. Now she could find nothing good to say about the girl.

'Attractive? Don't talk such nonsense. It's a flaw and you know it. She's not in the same league as Dulcie when it comes to looks.' She stirred her soup thoughtfully then glanced quickly at the grandfather clock. 'It really is too bad. What on earth is he up to?'

They ate their soup in silence. He loved vegetable soup the way Agnes made it. Thick and floury and full of flavour. Nursery food, he called it. It comforted him and reminded him of his own childhood.

Clarice looked again at the clock and then, pursing her lips, at James.

'Don't blame me!' he protested.

'I'm not blaming you, James.'

'Of course you are. I know that look. You're trying to make me feel responsible for Teddy's lateness.'

'Now you're being ridiculous!' She snatched up the bell and rang for Agnes who cleared the table in a nervous silence. When they were once more alone Clarice went on relentlessly. 'And asking Teddy to be best man! "Let bygones be bygones" indeed.'

'Oh not all that again, please Clarice!'

'It has made us look such fools!' She adopted a shrill tone. "My dear! Have you heard? Annabel Roper's jilted Teddy Moore for his best friend"!' She took a large mouthful of wine which went down the wrong way.

'You're exaggerating, Clarice,' he said when she stopped coughing.

He almost winced as her eyes narrowed. 'There was no way Teddy could be Clive's best man but you didn't have the strength of will to argue with him. You left it all to me.'

'Because they had once been such good friends.'

'Friends? Who needs enemies with friends like that?' Clarice's jaw was clenched and the familiar, tell-tale red was spreading across her neck. 'The trouble —'

She broke off as they heard the front door open and close. There was a mutter of voices.

James said, 'Ah!' and smiled. Saved!

Agnes came in with a loaded tray and said, 'Master Edward's back. He doesn't want any soup so I'll go ahead with the lamb, shall I?'

Clarice nodded, her eyes on the door which led into the hall. After a moment or two Teddy came into the room. Clarice stared at him open mouthed. James, too, was disconcerted by his son's appearance. Dishevelled was the appropriate word. His face was very pale and his dark hair was tousled. He was still wearing flannels, sandals and an open-necked shirt. He was breathless as though he had been running.

'Teddy!' cried Clarice. 'Whatever has happened to you?'

Without meeting her gaze he said, 'Nothing. I don't want to talk about it. OK?'

'OK?' Her voice rose. 'No, it is not *OK*. You're twenty minutes late for dinner and —'

'So I'm late, I'm sorry. D'you want me to grovel?'

His attitude was aggressive but his voice was rough with emotion.

James felt his throat tighten. 'Something's happened. What is it? You can tell us.'

'It's nothing!'

Agnes produced creamed potatoes, lamb in garlic and runner beans. She watched Teddy from the corner of her eye and James saw that she, too, sensed that something was wrong.

Clarice said, 'Where have you been?'

'That's my business.'

'Teddy!' Clarice glanced from her son to her

husband and back to Teddy.

'I don't want to talk about it. OK?'

'Don't keep saying "OK"! You know how I detest this awful slang —'

'That's it! I'm not hungry.' Teddy threw down his napkin and stood up.

James put out a restraining hand and caught his son's sleeve as he made to pass him. 'Please, Teddy. You must eat. If you don't want to tell us we won't press you. Sit down, please Teddy.' He gave Clarice a warning glance. She looked frightened and he suddenly pitied her.

Teddy hesitated then reluctantly returned to his seat. In silence he offered the food to his mother and then to his father. He served himself then stared at the food on his plate as though he didn't know what to do with it.

James said gently 'You can trust us. We only want to help — if we can.'

'I tell you I'm O — I'm fine.' He stabbed half-heartedly at a piece of lamb. 'It's nothing to worry about.' He looked from one to the other. 'For heaven's sake! I'm a grown man. I don't have to share everything with you, do I? Aren't I allowed a life of my own?'

They stared at him, startled by his intensity. James put a forkful of food into his mouth, chewed and tried to swallow it. It felt unmanageable.

Teddy pushed back his plate and reached for the decanter. Red wine splashed on to the damask cloth. 'It was something I — It didn't turn out quite as I expected but —' He shrugged and then drained the glass.

James struggled to think of something to say that would defuse the situation but his mind remained infuriatingly blank. He watched his son refill his glass and his anxiety grew. Teddy was not greedy where food and wine were concerned. He had always been a boy of quiet, moderate habits. His school reports from Fellstowe had been neither good nor bad. Although not so bright as Dulcie, he had done slightly better than her outside the classroom, enjoying running, jumping and tennis.

As the silence lengthened James stole a glance at his wife. She, too, was toying with her food. The colour had faded from her neck and she looked suddenly older. He was assailed by a sense of helplessness. His son needed help and his wife needed reassurance and he was powerless to offer either. He no longer understood his own children or felt able to help them. At moments like this he knew what agony it was to be a parent.

Teddy choked down another mouthful and then looked up. 'Well, let's talk about something else, shall we. Surely my problems pale into insignificance beside the dead in Quetta and the demise of the French franc!'

'Quetta? Oh, *Quetta*! That was too dreadful!' Clarice clutched at the proffered straw. 'Twenty thousand dead. I always think an earthquake must be terrible. Like a volcano. I mean not exactly like it but an act of God. So random. So unpredictable. So —' She faltered to a stop. To James she said 'Don't you think . . .' Then stopped again.

'Yes. Quite frightful.' He looked at Teddy who was drinking his wine thirstily, his fingers gripping the stem of the glass. 'And the franc. Yes. The poor old franc has certainly taken a dive.' He sounded unnaturally hearty and despised himself. 'Perhaps your mother would like some more wine,' he suggested pointedly.

'Would you, Mother?'

'No — er, that is, yes. Why not!'

She was thoroughly flustered, thought James, and that made him more nervous. Teddy was his heir and would one day inherit the estate in Cornwall: would marry, hopefully, and raise a family to carry on the family name. Until now James had never had the slightest doubt that his son would play his part admirably. This new Teddy was a bit of a shock. Turning up late to dinner without changing his clothes was bad enough. His defiant manner and the drinking were more worrying.

He asked, 'This isn't about the wedding, is it, Teddy?' The words tumbled out before he could stop them and he saw Clarice's shocked expression.

Teddy tensed. 'Not exactly. No.'

Clarice said, 'We do know how you feel, dear, but in the —'

'That's just it, Mother, you don't.' His hand

tightened around the stem of the glass. Suddenly it broke. With a muttered curse, he dropped the two halves of the glass and wine spread across the cloth like blood.

Clarice stared. 'Teddy!'

He said, 'You don't understand how I feel. How could you understand?' He began to mop the spilt wine with his table napkin. 'You don't even *know* me.' Dropping the napkin, he sucked his hand. 'Damn!' He looked from one to the other. 'You don't know what I've done and I hope you never will.'

Clarice said, 'Your hand!'

James said, 'What you've *done?*'

'Oh, for God's sake, don't fuss!'

James felt his throat tighten. Didn't *know* their own son? What on earth did he mean? He cleared his throat. 'Look here, old lad, whatever it is you've done — or whatever has *happened* — we're on your side! Your mother and I are behind you one hundred per cent. We all make mistakes. We all do things we wish undone. But it can be sorted out somehow. Your mother and I —'

He caught Clarice's eye and saw gratitude. So he was on the right track; saying the right things. That was a relief anyway.

Teddy had wrapped a handkerchief round his hand and he now pushed back against his chair so fiercely that it toppled over. In the ensuing silence he righted it. 'Thanks, Father. And you, Mother.' His attempt at a smile was heartbreaking. 'I can deal with it. Don't worry about me.' He walked to the door. 'I mean it. I'll be OK.' He hesitated. Glanced at the clock. 'I have to go out again.'

The door closed behind him then opened again as Agnes came in with the tray. She looked after Teddy and then at her mistress.

Clarice said, 'He's not well. Not hungry.'

Her face fell. 'I made a rhubarb pie. His favourite.'

James, who had risen to his feet, sank back on to his chair. 'Save some for him,' he suggested. 'He might fancy it later.'

They watched her clear the plates, ignoring the disappointment on her face as she saw how little they had eaten. She had also registered the speed with which the decanter had been emptied and pointedly suggested opening another bottle.

'No thank you,' Clarice told her, trying unsuccessfully to hide her mortification. 'But I think —' said James, 'that we will require a brandy later.'

Clarice hesitated, then nodded.

'We'll take it in the drawing room with our coffee, Agnes,' he said. A stiff brandy, he told himself. Very stiff.

Another family crisis was almost certainly upon them.

Early the following morning the sound of a bicycle bell alerted Teddy to the fact that his sister was making one of her flying visits. From behind the curtain he watched her arrival with affection tinged with dismay. Although four years separated them they had always been very close. She adored her big brother, convinced that he would never willingly put a foot wrong. He, in turn, had revelled in her admiration. In return he had been protective, indulgent, a constant champion. He grinned, remembering the horror with which he had first set eyes on her — a screaming infant in his mother's arms: a red-faced girl child with hair like white silk. His immediate suggestion that his mother should 'put her back in her cot' had been greeted with great amusement by the doting adults. Hardly an auspicious beginning, he thought, watching her prop her bicycle against the clipped yew beside the steps.

Dulcie was everything he could never be. Where he was introverted, she was outgoing. Where he trod carefully, she rushed in. He kept his thoughts to himself, aware always of a certain darkness in his soul. Dulcie was an open book, an impulsive scatterbrain.

His smile broadened as she looked up at his window, shading her eyes to wave a greeting. Her pale gold hair picked up the sun and she looked particularly young and vulnerable — although looks could be deceptive, he reflected. He was suddenly reminded of the day she had jumped from the first floor of the old barn at Sparks Corner after he had expressly forbidden it. Stubborn as a mule, determined to prove herself as brave as any boy, Dulcie had built a pile of straw and had launched herself on to it from the upstairs window. Even with a badly sprained ankle she had been entirely unrepentant.

Now, in spite of his unhappiness, he felt briefly the familiar glow of delight at her appearance and, waving, returned her greeting.

'Come down!' she mouthed and then he heard her shouting a greeting through the letterbox to Agnes.

Teddy hesitated. Since last night he had remained in his room, unable to join his parents at the breakfast table. He had pretended a sick headache. In fact he had more than a sick headache — he had a hangover, brought about by a bottle of red wine which he had slowly consumed throughout the long, sleepless night. Now he felt like death. Remorse and grief weighed on him. No, he decided, he would not go down. Dulcie would have to come up to him. He tightened the cord of his dressing gown and waited for her footsteps on the stairs.

He heard Agnes greet her and then her mother and then the voices withdrew into the drawing room. No doubt she was being informed of last night's débâcle. He sighed. What an appalling mess it all was. A disaster. In retrospect it seemed to be the nightmare he had been waiting for all his life. He moved to stand in front of the mirror, staring with distaste at his reflection. A younger, male version of his mother stared back. Dark hair. Brown eyes. Thin features which on his mother looked elegant. On him they produced a slightly saturnine appearance. At least he had cleaned his teeth and taken a bath but he still looked grim. Dulcie would see through the sick headache but she would not pry further — unless Mother had primed her to find out what was wrong. It would almost be a relief to confide in Dulcie but that would be unforgivable. And a betrayal of sorts. There was nothing anyone could do to help him now.

He combed his hair and straightened the collar of his pyjamas. You're a bloody fool, Teddy! he said to himself. His reflection did nothing to refute this statement and he turned away in disgust.

Footsteps on the stairs. A knock at the door.

'Who is it?' he said, for no better reason than to delay the moment when he must face her.

'Me, of course.'

She came in. Slim, very blonde, touchingly pretty with a creamy complexion and huge blue eyes. Considering her looks it was incredible that she wasn't vain, he thought. Her looks had never interested her. Young men falling beneath her spell had provoked either amusement or irritation.

She threw herself on to the middle of his unmade bed and regarded the room with disapproval. Teddy saw it through her eyes. The windows, closed against the summer air, curtains pulled against the bright sunlight. His clothes strewn around, an empty bottle on the bedside table. A shelf full of mementoes of school — his grey Fellstowe cap, his tennis racket, a few well-worn books and the tuck box Agnes used to fill for him. Always a slab of gingerbread, a box of dates, chocolate and butterscotch.

And on the far wall, the dreary picture that great grandfather had left him — three Highland cattle wading in a stream. His mother insisted he display it but he'd always hated it. One day, he'd told Dulcie, he would smash the thing. He smiled. She had been so thrilled at his daring.

'What are you grinning at?' she demanded.

'You always make me smile!'

She liked that. 'I could make you a Bloody Mary,' she offered. 'You look as though you could do with one.'

He sank into the ancient sofa which had seen better days and which his mother was waiting to throw out *when* she could persuade him to part with it.

'I feel like hell,' he said and was surprised by a deep, shuddering sigh.

'You look it. Poor old thing.'

'I suppose they told you.'

'Every sordid detail!' She laughed. ' "He came to the table without even a wash and he looked dreadful!" So you've fallen off your pedestal!'

'With a vengeance,' he agreed. And from a great height, he reflected. If she only knew the half of it. But she didn't. Only Annabel knew and she was hardly likely to tell anyone. At the thought of her he closed his eyes against the painful memories.

Dulcie looked at him. 'They said you cut your hand.'

He held out his hand, revealing the small wound which was already healing.

'Oh good. Not too bad,' She gave him a long look. 'Don't tell me about it — unless you want to.'

'I *can't* tell you. I wish I could.' In a way it was the truth.

'That's that, then.'

He could sense her disappointment. 'Are they very upset?'

'Stewing in their own juice. I think that's the most apt description. Puzzled and hurt and worried but not angry . . . You aren't ill, are you? If you've been given so many months to live I want to know.'

'It's nothing like that, I promise you.' Better if it had been, he thought. Solve a lot of problems.

'Then I won't ask.' She slid from the bed and crossed to the windows to fling them open. 'It's called fresh air. It gets into your lungs and does you good.' To demonstrate, she took a deep breath. Turning she asked, 'Come for a walk?'

He shook his head.

'A swim, then. The chap's been to clean the pool.'

He groaned. The thought of bobbing around in the pool made him nauseous. He said 'Too cold. It's only June.'

'It should be flaming.'

'Well, it's not. Forget about me. Tell me your news.'

Dulcie sighed. She drew up one leg and clasped her hands around her knee. 'I wish I had some. Some good news, I mean. Still the same old rubbish — mothers' meetings, hundredth birthdays, funerals, weddings — Oh! Yes, I almost forgot in all the excitement. You'll never guess whose wedding I'm covering this afternoon.'

Oh God! He stared at her transfixed. 'Not — Annabel's?'

'The same. Ghastly, isn't it? I wanted to do the story of the jail break. You have heard, I suppose.'

'Jail break? No.'

'That man that escaped from the prison yesterday. The man you used to go to school with. Remember? Albert Parker. Manslaughter. Born and bred in Canterbury, I'm afraid. It's nothing to boast about.'

He frowned. 'I remember. Nasty piece of work. Big man. Not bad looking.'

She shrugged. 'He might *look* OK on the outside. He's pretty rotten inside. I went in this morning determined to argue with Cobsey. I mean I've been there nearly a month and I still don't get a sniff of anything remotely interesting. Cobsey does it on purpose. He hates me.'

'The boss's pet!' He was astonished that she'd lasted a month. She had never seen the seedy side of life. How on earth would she cope? He wondered if their uncle had told Cobbs not to give her any unpleasant assignments.

She grimaced. 'Something like that!'

'Poor man. You can't really blame him. He is the editor, after all, and it must be galling to have someone dumped on you like that.'

'It's not much fun for *me!* Being a junior reporter is boring with a capital B.'

'Well, you've only got a few more months to go and your probation will be over. It might get more interesting.'

'It won't. Cobsey will see to that. He's hoping I'll give up in disgust but I won't.'

'Think yourself lucky that you've got the job at all. How many lady journalists do you know? You're a rarity.'

'Then I should have rarity value!' She sighed. 'Mother would love it if I gave up and came home.'

Teddy suspected that it was his mother's opposition to the idea that had finally persuaded Wilfred to give her the job on the *Standard.*

'Still, an escaped convict is hardly the job for a woman.' Teddy realised his mistake before he had finished the sentence.

Dulcie sprang from the bed and towered over him, hands on her hips. 'Not you too!'

'Calm down. I only meant —'

'I know what you meant! You meant that a weak woman can't cope with a story about an escaped convict. You're every bit as bad as Cobsey. Worse, in fact, because you're my brother and supposed to be on my side!'

Teddy looked into the furious face. How did she manage to look angry and attractive at the same time, he wondered. He could see why poor old Gerald had been smitten but he had stood about as much chance as a snowball in hell.

'I'm sorry, Dulcie. I just don't like the thought of you getting yourself into any danger.'

'Well, Annabel's stupid wedding should be harmless enough!' She subsided, her anger gone as swiftly as it had come. Suddenly she gave him a wicked grin. 'I'm terribly tempted to sabotage them. To write something scurrilous about the wedding — or camp it up a bit. I could lay it on with a trowel so that everyone would laugh. Annabel would never forgive me but who cares? I've never forgiven her for what she did to you.'

Teddy said slowly 'I wish you would, Dulcie . . . I have, you see. I just couldn't go on hating her.'

Her expression changed. 'Oh Teddy! You don't still love her?'

He couldn't answer which was answer enough. For a long time neither of them spoke.

'You do,' she said.

He nodded.

'She doesn't deserve it.' Dulcie frowned. 'She must be an idiot, to choose Clive instead of you. He's such a —' She slapped a hand to her mouth. 'You don't still like *him* too, do you? He was so sneaky. You can't still like Clive!'

He hesitated. 'Hardly.' And Clive could

hardly like *him!* Not after last night.

'Well, that's a relief! I could strangle the wretch.'

Aware of her scrutiny, Teddy turned his head slightly, afraid that she would read the expression in his eyes. In an attempt to change the subject he said 'So, tell me about your escaped convict.'

'He's not mine. Cobsey said he couldn't give the assignment to a woman. Gus was positively beaming when he passed me on his way out of the office heading for the police station. Gave me a wink and thumbs up. This Parker strangled another man years ago. He was sentenced to eighteen years but he's escaped. Got out the day before yesterday by hiding in a laundry van. It looks as though someone helped him to escape. The police are talking as though they're going to catch him but I should think he'd be miles away from Canterbury by now.' She sighed. 'I could have written it just as well as Gus. It's not as though they're asking me to *catch* him. Just write up the facts in an interesting way. Nothing dangerous in that.'

'Do you *want* to write about a murderer?'

'I want to write about anything that's going to make headlines!'

'Your turn will come.'

'Thanks for the platitude but I know it won't. Cobsey will keep fobbing me off with boring stuff like Annabel. Sorry but you know what I mean — and then at the end of the six months he'll tell Uncle Wilfred I'm no good. No experience, he'll say. And I'll be out on my ear.'

'Out on your ear?' He smiled in spite of himself. 'What a dreadful phrase. I hope mother doesn't hear you talking like that. I got a wigging last night for "OK"!'

She grinned. 'She'll have to get used to the new me. Blame it on to the *Standard.* It's Gus, actually. He's a bad influence.'

He grinned. 'And how's the white monster? Still wrecking Aunt Harriet's home?'

Now she laughed. 'The white monster, as you so rudely call him, is fine, thank you. Poor Max. He's just boisterous.'

'Max? Is that what you're calling him?'

'It was Harriet's idea. And he's not wrecking the house. Just chews up the odd slipper. All puppies do that sort of thing.'

'He's hardly a puppy!'

'Some dogs mature later than others. Anyway, he's stopped nipping ankles. I've started training him.'

'That should be worth watching!' he said, grinning. 'The phrase "the blind leading the blind" springs to mind!'

Dulcie's look was frosty. 'For your information, Teddy, he *is* improving. He sometimes sits when he's told and he knows what "Fetch!" means.'

'He may *know* what it means but does he obey? Does he fetch it?'

He watched her struggling with the truth.

'Sometimes. Mostly. Sometimes he doesn't. Depends what he's thinking about,' Her tone was withering. 'Do *you* do everything you're told? Are *you* good all the time?'

The words hit a nerve and he was suddenly consumed with guilt. He had behaved very badly indeed and he was never going to forgive himself.

She said 'Well, *are* you?'

He shook his head, unable to answer. Who was he to criticise Dulcie who was white as driven snow by comparison.

She said, 'Cats don't do what you tell them. Horses don't. Not always. So why should dogs be expected to jump to attention?'

As the silence lengthened her expression changed. Her eyes narrowed and she stared at him. As ever, Teddy knew exactly what was going through her mind. They had always exchanged confidences and they trusted each other implicitly. Now, for the first time, he was hiding something and that hurt her. So be it. In a way he was shielding her because if she ever *did* know what he had done, her pain would be a hundred times greater.

'So do you want a Bloody Mary?' she demanded. 'You'll have to make the effort, Teddy. Unless you want Mother up here, clucking over you. Or worse still, Agnes!'

'I'm feeling better already!' He managed a smile.

She regarded him sadly. 'I'm not fooled, Teddy.

I know you've got troubles. If you need me —' She shrugged. 'You know what I'm trying to say.'

'I know and thanks.'

'And you'll come downstairs?'

'Are you staying for lunch?' He hoped so. Her presence at the table would ease matters.

'Can't I'm afraid. The wedding's at two and I want to take a quick look inside the church beforehand. I've never been inside St Alphege's. A quick recce of the church and write a description. Then I'll go back at two. Find myself somewhere to sit where I'll be unobtrusive during the ceremony. I don't want the ushers asking me which "side" I'm on. But I'll be here for another half an hour.'

When the door closed behind her he stared at it. Had he said too much? Maybe not. So she was covering the wedding. That could be interesting. He stood up and began to dress with desperate haste. Annabel's wedding. Annabel and Clive.

Oh God!

Earlier the same morning, in another part of Canterbury, Ellen Bly hummed cheerfully as she approached the church. Nice to think there was now no likelihood of a chance meeting with a rat. And no more scamperings in dark corners. She'd make the cleaning last so that she could have a word or two with Mrs Belling when she arrived to do the flowers. She'd tell her about the humane way they killed the rats. She'd nip home for a bit of dinner and then be back in time to watch the wedding. One of these days she really would treat herself to a little box camera. The town was full of visitors snapping away and she'd like a penny for every time someone took a photograph of the cathedral.

It never did any harm to have a bit of a chat with Mrs Belling because she was one of the women who worked on the altar cloths. The sewing group. She would try and slip in a mention of her own talents because she was a neat hand with a needle and thread even though she said it herself. Presumably repairing valuable altar cloths and robes paid better than cleaning. It would be a step up, too, and she wasn't averse to bettering herself.

She unlocked the door and stepped inside the church, sniffing cautiously in case any gas still lingered. It smelled exactly the same as usual — the familiar mix of stone dust, woodworm, candles and flowers. Today she had brought a tin of lavender wax which she had paid for out of her own pocket. It was a little something she always did for weddings. An anonymous gift to the happy couple. The lavender wax smelled so much nicer than the cheap polish they provided.

Inside the church she paused to admire it, her own kingdom for two hours a week. The early morning sunshine streamed through the coloured glass of the windows, highlighting the motes of dust which were never still. The vaulted roof was shadowed, the empty pews waited, the altar never failed to impress her. Now the church was silent but later it would come alive. The Wedding March, the choir and the bells pealing. She did love a wedding — all the excitement and beautiful hats and so many smiling faces.

'This won't do, Ellen Bly!' She drew off her gloves. She would wear her old ones while she worked. Taking off her jacket she laid it with her gloves on the last pew and made her way towards the vestry. There, in the cupboard, she found bucket and mop and dusters. For nearly an hour she dusted and polished and finally she filled the bucket with water and prepared to mop the stone floor.

She had just started to mop round the altar when she noticed a dull red stain creeping up the lower edge of the altar cloth.

'Oh my giddy aunt!'

She looked at it with horror. The vicar wouldn't be very pleased when he saw it. Her first thought was that no one could blame her for the mark. She would make that quite clear. Her second thought was that, whatever it was, there was no time now to wash the cloth, dry, iron and return it in time for the wedding. Even if it was her job which it wasn't. The laundry was responsible for all the church linen including the choirboys' vestments. Muttering to herself, she lowered herself to her knees and picked up the edge of the altar cloth.

'What on earth — ?'

The red stain was fresh. Still wet. Looking down she saw a small red puddle. Beyond it she saw a man's head.

Holding her breath while her heart raced, she lifted the cloth.

And saw the body.

Her scream echoed alarmingly within the four stone walls adding to her fear. Still screaming she scrambled backwards and fell awkwardly. She went down heavily, clutching at the table to save herself and pulling candlesticks, pitcher and brass plates with her. Freed from the shadow of the altar cloth, the young man's body was more visible. For a long horrified moment Ellen Bly stared down into the vacant face and then, resuming her screams, she stumbled up the aisle towards the door.

Chapter 2

Dulcie heard the screams before she reached the church door. Startled, she pushed it open and stepped inside and immediately collided with an elderly woman who was rushing out.

'Wait,' said Dulcie. 'What's the matter?'

The woman clutched at her with trembling fingers. She was chalk white and breathless and her plump frame quivered with fright. 'Back there! It's terrible!' Her voice shook. 'Oh Lord! I never thought to see such a dreadful thing. Never!' Clasping her hands, she pressed them to her mouth. 'It's a dead man! It is! If you don't believe me —' She swayed back, leaning against the door, gasping for breath.

Dulcie put an arm round her shoulders. 'It's OK. I do believe you.' She didn't, of course, but she wasn't going to say so. Drunk, maybe. 'Take your time. I'll come in with you and you can show —'

'Go back in there? No. I can't! He was *bleeding!* The vicar will be so upset. All over the altar cloth — this big red stain!' She staggered back, staring into Dulcie's face. 'I'll never forget it.'

Her mouth trembled and tears sprang into her eyes. 'I can't go back. I can't!' She laid a hand over her heart. 'O-oh! I think I'm going to faint.'

Her eyes rolled and she slumped forward with a little moan. Dulcie caught her awkwardly as she fell, lowered her carefully to the ground and propped her against the door frame. Reluctant to leave her alone, Dulcie hailed the first passer-by — a young man pushing a bicycle.

'Excuse me, but would you wait with this woman, just for a moment. She's not feeling too well.'

As the man moved cautiously forward, Dulcie took her chance and hurried into the church. If the blood was on the altar cloth she had a good idea where the wounded man was to be found. As she hurried inside her excitement was tempered by guilt. The death of a fellow human being was a terrible thing and she ought to be saddened by it. She was, to some extent, but overwhelmingly she was excited by the prospect of a 'scoop'. To be first on the scene was something to write about — something Gus would have wanted to do. And she had pipped him to the post.

Her excitement vanished, however, as soon as she saw the lifeless figure which lay under the altar. Her guilt vanished with it. The man was slim, well dressed — and so helpless. Unexpectedly, the sight brought a lump to her throat and tears pricked her eyelids. In his rumpled clothes, he looked like a child abandoned in sleep, careless of the world. Her heart ached for him, whoever he was. He was somebody's son. Somebody's brother, maybe. She tried to imagine how she would feel if Teddy were lying there, lost to them forever, beyond all help and comfort.

'I'm so sorry!' she whispered. She knelt beside the crumpled body. His face, pressed against the floor, was turned away from her. The back of his neck was young, with dark hair that curled softly into his collar. Blood from his ear had congealed on his shirt. She laid a tentative finger against what little she could see of his neck and found it disturbingly cold.

'What happened to you?' she whispered.

Only he knew but the secret might have died with him. It was not a natural death, she was sure of that. If he had been taken suddenly ill he would hardly have put himself under the altar. Nor was it the natural choice for a suicide attempt. He had died at the hand of an assailant. She realised suddenly that the journalist within her was beginning to replace the caring fellow human and guilt returned. To assuage it, she hastily closed her eyes and said, 'Please God, be with this unhappy soul.'

From outside the church there came the sound of shouting followed by a blast on a whistle. Someone had called the police. Footsteps sounded and the the church door creaked on its hinges. Quickly Dulcie stood up, distancing herself from the body.

'Over here!' she called.

Turning, she saw a young policeman walking quickly down the aisle. 'I'm Constable Stanley. The ambulance is on its way,' he said.

'He's already dead.'

He looked nervous. 'Strewth!' He stood beside her, staring at the body, apparently rallying his thoughts. 'You sure?'

'See for yourself.'

He knelt beside the still figure, hands hovering uncertainly. 'You didn't move him?'

'Of course not!'

'You found him just like this?' He took out a notebook and pencil. 'And there's no pulse?'

'The cleaner found him. She's the lady sitting outside. She fainted.'

'I'm not surprised!' He stared helplessly at the body. 'Isn't he breathing?'

'No. He's cold. Obviously dead.'

Glancing up, he took exception to this. 'You an expert, then?'

Dulcie said nothing. She wanted to take out her own notebook but she didn't want him to know that she worked for the *Standard*.

He wrote something in his notebook and said, 'I've sent someone for the vicar. He'll know what to —' He stopped abruptly, having almost admitted that he did *not* know how to proceed. He stood up and walked slowly round the body, regarding it from all angles. Then he took a watch from his pocket, studied it and put it away. 'Eleven minutes past ten!' He wrote it down then glanced at Dulcie. 'And you are?'

'Dulcie Moore. I live at St George's Terrace with my aunt Harriet Moore.'

'And what are you doing here?'

She hesitated. 'There's going to be a wedding later today. I was checking the flower arrangements.'

He looked around. 'There aren't any flowers.'

'I know. I — I suppose I'm too early. Just as I arrived the cleaner rushed out screaming and collapsed into my arms.'

At that moment a man in a dark cassock appeared at the end of the aisle and hurried towards them.

The policeman brightened. 'I'm Constable Stanley. Are you the vicar?'

'The rector. Fellowes is the name.' He was stout with greying hair. 'The vicar is away but is expected back in time for the wedding. What's this about someone collapsing in the church?'

Recovering his composure, the constable shook his head, 'I doubt if there'll be a wedding here today. Not with all this.' He waved a hand in the direction of the dead man. 'Dead body,' he explained.

'Good gracious me! Oh dear!' As the rector knelt, a few feet from the body, he made the sign of the cross. As he did so several people appeared in the church doorway. The constable rushed up to them, waving his arms officiously.

'No sightseers!' he told them. 'There's been a — an incident. Suspicious circumstances. This is a crime scene and I must ask — I must *insist* — that you leave at once.'

Grumbling they withdrew. All except one. A formidable lady with an armful of flowers and foliage. 'I'm afraid I must be allowed in,' she told him. 'I'm Mrs Belling. I have to arrange these flowers. The wedding's at two and —'

'Sorry. Not even you, madam.'

Her voice rose. 'I shall speak to your superior, constable.'

'You do that, madam. He'll be here directly.'

Muttering, she allowed herself to be pushed outside with the rest.

Dulcie looked at the rector. 'Will the wedding be cancelled? Can they do that?' Incongruously, her first thought had been that this news would please Teddy. Now Annabel and Clive would have to delay the wedding. Perhaps it was an omen.

'Oh dearie me!' the rector muttered, ignoring her questions. 'Poor young man. What a terrible, *terrible* thing to happen!' He began to gather up the fallen altar cloth and the church plate.

The policeman called to him sharply. 'Don't touch anything! Unless you want your fingerprints all over them.' He turned to Dulcie. 'I think you should go now. We shall have to tell the bride and groom their wedding's been cancelled. A pity but there it is. Can't have dozens of guests tramping over the clues.'

Dulcie said, 'Well, good luck!'

She walked out of the church and into the

crowd that had gathered outside. In answer to their demands for information she said, 'There's a dead man. The police are monitoring events.' Monitoring events. It sounded rather good, she thought as she pushed her way out on to the street. She would use it in her article. She retrieved her bicycle and set off towards the office. Looking at it sensibly it did seem that circumstances had conspired to help her. She would produce a piece of dazzling copy and would leave it with Cobsey. With any luck he would realise her full potential and give her some interesting work to do. It was an ill wind that blew nobody any good!

Annabel stood in her bedroom and looked at her wedding gown which lay across the quilt. At the head of the bed, propped against the ornate woodwork of the bedhead, a once fluffy rabbit shared pillow space with a puppy-dog 'nightie case'. The ivory silk of the dress glowed richly, the white ribbons caught the sun. Small white pearls decorated the neckline. Irrationally she felt that she hated it. Thank goodness the lace veil would hide her face. Her eyes were red rimmed from weeping and her face was pale. No one would notice walking *down* the aisle but once in the vestry she would have to throw back the veil. Then her distress would be obvious to everyone.

She sighed deeply. Perhaps a few charitable souls would put it down to 'nerves' but the rest would whisper. They would wonder what she had to cry about and, even as she forced a smile, they would see through the pretence. And Clive —*poor* Clive! He didn't deserve this. He was the only person who had acted throughout with total integrity. She and Teddy could make no such claim. She picked up the circlet of flowers which would hold the lace in place and touched the delicate wax petals.

'Serves you right, you stupid creature!' she told herself and the bitterness almost shocked her. In a few short hours she would marry Clive even though she knew she could never make him happy. Because she found herself in an impossible situation. She could tell him the truth, call off the wedding and break her parents' hearts as well as his. Between bouts of weeping, she had wrestled with the problem but had found no solution. Because there was no way out of the maze she had created for herself. She had hurt and betrayed the two men she loved best in the world and her punishment had already started. Last night had been horrible. Disastrous. Teddy had behaved abominably but some of the blame for what happened was hers.

Brushing tears from her eyes, she moved to the dressing table. She sat down carefully on the stool which her mother had covered in pink velvet as a surprise for her thirteenth birthday. Her body ached and her mind was a whirlpool of misery. This was her wedding day but she felt sick both in body and mind. Slowly she allowed her gaze to survey for the last time the room which had seen her childhood come and go. Her grandmother's sampler hung over the bed. 'Home Is Where The Heart Is.'

'Dear God help me!' she whispered. 'I know I've sinned. I want to put things right but what can I do?'

On the window sill she saw the carved wooden elephant her father had brought home after his African safari. And beside it the New Testament the church had given her when she was confirmed. So many gifts. So much love. And she had repaid it by letting them all down.

She had brought this disaster on herself by her inability to see where her true future lay. She had broken Teddy's heart by her sudden change of allegiance and now she must pay the penalty. If she didn't she would break Clive's heart. No matter what she said or did now she could never undo the damage.

Only a miracle could save them and she could hardly expect God to arrange one for her. People who behaved as badly as she did could expect no favours.

'Oh Lord!' Her mother was coming up the stairs. Hastily, Annabel pulled her face into a semblance of a smile. There was a tap at the door.

'Annabel, dear. Are you coming down?' She wore a blue silk housecoat and no make up. Her dark hair, hardly tinged with grey, hung loose down her back. The hairdresser was coming at ten o'clock. 'You must eat something, darling. It's getting so late. It's your favourite — scrambled eggs with smoked salmon. A special treat. I've tried to keep it hot but it will be spoilt if you don't eat it soon. Scrambled egg goes so rubbery when it's overdone.'

Her mother's plump face was bright with excitement and Annabel knew what a great day this was going to be for her. Her only child getting married. And to dear Clive. The four children had grown up together — Annabel, Teddy, Clive and Dulcie. It had been her mother's oft expressed wish that Dulcie should marry Clive and Annabel should marry Teddy. Sadly for her mother, Dulcie had shown no interest in marrying anybody, let alone Clive.

Annabel smiled. 'Give me two minutes. I'll come down.' What would she say if she knew?

Her mother peered at her. 'Not tears, darling?'

'Not really. Only —' She searched for something convincing to say. 'Only for what I'm losing. My home. You. Father.'

'Oh you silly darling girl!' Her mother rushed to hug her. 'You're not *losing* us! What a thing to say. We'll still be here. Any time you want us. Oh, don't let such foolish ideas spoil this wonderful day.' Releasing her she stared with reverence at the wedding dress, clasping her hands in front of her heart. 'Oh that beautiful dress. I can't wait to see Clive's face when he sees you. His darling bride!'

She clutched Annabel to her again, her smile

shaky with emotion. Suddenly she drew back. 'And you do think my hat — Oh I know it's foolish of me to go on about it but I do want everything to be perfect for you. I keep wondering —'

'It's lovely, Mother, really.' Annabel wanted to scream. To plead. To blurt it all out: I *can't* marry Clive! She said 'It suits you. Honestly, Mother. And the roses are exactly the right shade. Would I lie to you?'

'But your father says —'

Annabel stood up abandoning the idea of two more minutes of solitude. 'He was teasing you, Mother. You ought to know him by now. And even if he wasn't, what does Father know about clothes? Come on. Let's go down and eat.'

Taking a deep breath she held her mother's arm and led her out of the bedroom and down the stairs.

Clive's mother sat on the sofa, her face hidden in her hands. Opposite her sat her husband, whisky in hand. A Siamese cat, sensitive to the charged atmosphere, watched them suspiciously.

'He can't have gone,' Nora insisted. 'He wouldn't do that to us, Charles. Not Clive.'

'Then where is the silly bugger?'

'Charles!'

Her heart wasn't in the small reprimand because she recognised the suffering in his voice. It echoed her own, 'He must have had an accident.' She wanted to believe it. A small accident. Nothing serious. Just enough to explain why his bed had not been slept in. He had gone out for a few drinks with friends. A stag night, he'd called it, and he said he would be back by eleven at the latest and they had gone to bed believing it. This morning the nightmare had started.

'Dammit, Nora!' Charles thumped the table so fiercely that Nora jumped with fright. 'He can't do this to us. I'll wring his neck if he — if he's let that girl down.'

'I do *wish* you'd ring one of his friends. I know it means letting them know he isn't here but —' She swallowed. 'If he's not going to turn up, everyone's going to find out eventually.'

Charles drew a deep breath. 'I could ring Douggie. The best man ought to know.'

He finished the whisky in two gulps and set down the empty glass. They moved to the telephone in the hall and Nora looked up the number in the book. She read it aloud while her husband waited for the operator. A few moments later Charles was through to his son's friend.

'Look, Douggie — um — sorry to bother you but what time did Clive leave you last night? . . . Clive. Yes.' He frowned. 'Didn't show up? But that's impossible! I mean — Well, we know he left here to . . . Not at all?'

Nora whispered, 'What's he saying?' but Charles shook his head, concentrating on the unwelcome information. '. . . Well, thanks anyway. No, no! Nothing's exactly *wrong*. I can't explain just at the moment but . . . Look here, I may have to ring you back . . . Yes, a little problem . . . I'm so sorry. So frightfully sorry.' He hung up and turned to his wife. His face was ashen. 'He — Douggie says he didn't turn up. They had a few drinks, waited until eleven and then went home.' He sat down heavily, staring with unfocused eyes. 'Just didn't turn up!' He looked up. 'What on earth can it mean?'

Nora put an unsteady hand to her head. 'I can't believe it. Not our Clive! Oh Charles! What shall we do?'

'Where *is* he? That's what I want to know.'

Nora drew a long breath. Shock and worry were taking their toll and she longed for a small brandy to fortify herself for whatever lay ahead. But her husband had already started along that road and if she encouraged him, there was no knowing where it would end. She couldn't risk him turning up drunk at the wedding. If there ever *was* a wedding. She was beginning to doubt it. If their son had jilted Annabel Roper it would be the talk of Canterbury and they would never be able to hold their heads up again. In which case she, too, might turn to drink.

The fingers of her husband's right hand drummed on the hall table and it was all she could do not to slap them. Couldn't he see how irritating it was? There were times when she wanted to scream at him. Now was one of them. She needed support, not this cold, helpless despair. Why couldn't he put his arm round her and say the right things? If there were any right things to say at such a time.

'Shall we have a pot of tea?' she suggested.

'Not for me.'

Suddenly the idea no longer appealed to her either. 'We shall have to tell the Ropers sometime,' she said. 'If he doesn't come home.' An image of her son lying drunk in a ditch rose, spectre-like. He would never have drunk that much — unless his friends had spiked his drinks. But they couldn't have done that because he hadn't turned up. Her mouth twisted bitterly. Charles's friends had made him drunk the night before their wedding. She had never forgiven them. He had been so ill the next morning. Hardly able to get through the ceremony. Men were such fools . . . Stag night! What a crass phrase. It summoned up horrid visions of stags in the rutting season. Animals fighting each other for the females. She shook her head. Clive wouldn't fight anyone. He was the mildest of men. Her legs felt weak. 'I must sit down,' she muttered and made her way back to the sitting room. As she sank down on the sofa Charles trailed in after her. He took his glass, refilled it and sat down in a nearby armchair.

'The Ropers!' whispered Nora. 'They'll have to cancel everything. The service. The reception. They'll have to send back all the presents.' Her voice was rising and she knew that she was not far from hysteria. The Ropers would never speak to them again. Nobody would. And what of Clive? Would he ever come back to face them? The thought that she might never see her son again weighed like lead somewhere in the region of her stomach.

'We could ring the hospitals again,' she said.

'It'll do no good.'

'Well, you suggest something then!' It was so like him, she thought furiously. No ideas of his own. He simply sat there, swilling whisky, pouring scorn on her ideas. She looked at him with distaste. A weak man. They had been married thirty-one years and it had not been wildly successful. Certainly not a love match. Her parents had been wrong. His money had not compensated for the lack of affection. But she had tried to forgive him. He had given her a son. Her beloved Clive. Now it seemed that he might have been taken from her by this cruel twist of fate.

Her husband turned bleary eyes towards her. 'He'll turn up!' he said 'and when he does I'll give him a large piece of my mind. And if he offers me the slightest argument I swear I'll knock his ruddy block off!'

'Don't be ridiculous!'

A ring at the doorbell startled them.

'It's the police!' she cried. 'Something has happened to him. Oh my God!'

'It could be anybody.'

'It's the police!'

They listened as the maid hurried to answer it.

A moment later the rector was ushered into the room and she let out a long sigh of relief. Anyone was better than a policeman.

He was looking very nervous, she thought

fearfully. Had he somehow got wind of their predicament? Somehow she managed a smile. 'Mr Fellowes. How nice to see you. Is this —'

He interrupted her. 'I'm afraid something rather dreadful has happened. I hardly know how to tell you this but —' He drew a deep breath.

'Is it about Clive?' she cried, her terror returning.

'Clive? Your son? No, Mrs Brayne.'

He looked surprised at the question and she took heart.

'It's about the wedding. I'm afraid there has been a most unfortunate occurrence. You've probably heard. An — an accident, you might say. Someone has been injured — well, more than injured actually, all rather nasty — and the police suspect foul play. I'm not at liberty to divulge anything further — the police — you know how they are. Not that people won't talk. They will.' He shrugged. 'They've cordoned off the entire church — graveyard and all — and no one can use it until further notice. I shudder to think what the vicar will have to say when he knows. He's on his way back from Sussex — the funeral of an old family friend. Died very suddenly — heart, they think. But there'll be nothing he can do to persuade the police. Either we must borrow another church — if one has a vacancy which I very much doubt — summer weddings being so popular — or your son's wedding will have to be indefinitely postponed.'

Nora closed her eyes. The rector's rambling

made no sort of sense but she had grasped the all-important fact. For some reason their son's wedding could not go ahead. Clive or no Clive, there would be no wedding. She looked at her husband and saw her own relief mirrored there then uttered a silent prayer of thanks.

Charles said, 'Borrow another church? Have it somewhere else? Good Lord no! No, no, no! Sorry, rector. Couldn't possibly think of such a thing.'

He looked to her for corroboration and she said, 'Oh no, Charles. It must be St Alphege's.'

The rector nodded. 'I do see your point but — Well, it's all so terribly inconvenient — I mean cancelling a wedding! Hardly the way we like to treat valued members of our congregation but —'

Charles held up a peremptory hand. 'No "buts", Mr Fellowes. It's *our* church. That's how we look upon it. We were married at St Alphege's and my son will be married there. We'll just have to postpone it until such time as we can get in. No one's blaming you. Damned awkward but these things happen.'

The rector's surprise was obvious: his gratitude doubly so. Nora fought back hysteria. Mr Fellowes had no doubt expected a huge outcry and in the normal way that is exactly what he would have encountered. She gave him a shaky smile and blinked back tears. He had no way of knowing how convenient the cancellation was.

His face cleared. 'Well, that's jolly understanding of you. To take it like that, I mean. Who could have thought — That is, I'm not allowed to say too much but — Well, what a day this has been! Talk about Thomas à Becket!'

They offered him a sherry but he said he was on his way to the Ropers to break the news to them. They watched him pedal away, black skirt flapping.

They looked at each, unable to believe their good fortune.

Nora said, 'God moves in a mysterious way!' and began to laugh. She went on laughing until the laughter turned to tears. She sobbed 'Hold me! Please! Just hold me!' but instead he poured her a brandy and refilled his own glass.

It took a second brandy to bring her round. Eventually they set about organising the telegrams which just might stall the guests. After much heart searching they wrote: PROBLEM AT CHURCH STOP DEEPLY REGRET WEDDING POSTPONED STOP MORE LATER

Three hours later, still with no word from Clive, Nora suddenly collapsed.

Her husband drank another brandy and sent for the doctor.

Jack Spencer, tired and disillusioned, was preparing to go off duty when the young constable found him in the locker room. Nobody knew quite how Blake had been allowed to join the force. He was two inches too short.

'Guvnor wants you,' he told Jack.

Jack removed his helmet. 'I'm off duty, Blake. Gone home. You didn't find me.'

'But I did!'

Jack rolled grey eyes despairingly. 'But the guvnor doesn't know that, does he?' He had been up most of the night since the prison break-out, reading up the file of the original case and then checking known contacts of the escaped prisoner. Now he ran a hand through his dark hair. More than anything, he wanted to go home.

He hesitated. 'Know what it's about?'

The day had been wasted chasing false leads in search of the escaped prisoner. Parker's girl-friend had assured him that she had seen him briefly and that he was planning to leave the country. Jack felt certain that the man would not be hanging around in Canterbury. In view of this, he had promised himself a few hours' sleep and then he would write his overdue letter to Judith. It had been more than a week and she claimed to set such store by his letters. He produced his cycle clips. 'You didn't find me.'

The young constable grinned. 'Please yourself — but you might be sorry! Suspicious death. Could be murder!'

Jack's head jerked up. 'Murder? Never!'

'Could well be. Stanners got called to this church and there's this old woman who's fainted clean away and this other young woman and this body. Dead as a doornail. And where did they find him? Only under the blinking altar. True as

I'm standing here. Like a sacrifice, in a way.'

'A sacrifice would be *on* the altar, surely.'

'Trust you!'

Jack was intrigued. Canterbury was hardly a turbulent town and murders were rare. If there *was* one he wanted to be in on it. Tossing his cycle clips back into the locker he straightened up. The sleep and Judith's letter would have to wait.

Blake said, 'Remember me, won't you — if you need anyone.'

'I'll think about it.'

Upstairs he made his way to the room at the far end of the corridor. It bore a small plaque. Detective Inspector Frank Berridge. Jack knocked.

'Come in!'

The detective inspector was nearing retirement and showed signs of strain. His thin face was lined but his ruddy complexion made him look healthier than he was. Thirty-five years in the force and poor health had taken its toll of his energies though not his enthusiasm.

'Ah, Jack. Glad we caught you before you went home. Nasty business this.' He pointed to a chair and Jack sat down. 'I'm taking you off the Parker case. He'll be out of Canterbury by now. Out of *Kent* if he's any sense. Let someone else look for him. We've got something else to worry about. Suspicious death so far. Young chappie dead in St Alphege's church. Know it?'

'Is it the one off Palace Street, sir?'

'Good man. Someone had hidden him under the altar, would you believe!'

'So Blake says. Bit weird, isn't it?'

'Exactly! And no ID so far.' The detective inspector picked up a ruler and fiddled with it.

'Probable cause of death, sir?' Jack asked hopefully. A shooting would be very acceptable. There was something solid, something *prestigious* about a shooting. The newspapers would be full of it. He saw himself being interviewed, well dressed but modest, revealing little but managing to suggest a cautious optimism. This might just be the break he'd been waiting for. Accidental shootings were not uncommon, of course, since shotguns were the norm among the huntin', shootin', fishin' types. Farmers, too, could easily get a licence to keep down vermin. Stabbings were messy. Poisonings very rare. They'd had a stabbing in Canterbury a couple of years back but that had been before his promotion to detective sergeant and he hadn't got much of a look in.

'Jack!'

'Sorry, sir. I was just thinking.'

'You're not here to think. You're here to *listen*. I said it looks like a bashing, Jack. A bit of GBH that went too far. No need to look so disappointed. What d'you expect — Al Capone?'

Jack rearranged his expression. The guvnor didn't miss a trick. 'Couldn't have been an accident then? Got drunk, fell down and split his head open?'

The detective inspector shrugged wordlessly.

'Suicide?'

'Hardly. He was moved. And a few blood splashes on a pillar in the aisle.'

'Any motive?'

'Not robbery. There was money in his pocket.'

Jack's mind was beginning to move. 'Anyone been reported missing locally?'

'Not that I know of. Ask at the desk.'

'Could it have been more than one assailant?'

The shoulders lifted in another shrug. 'Who can say? Don't rule anything out at this stage, Jack. We've sealed off the area, of course. Not the easiest thing with a church but we had no choice. Vicar's a bit uncooperative but I daresay that's understandable in the circumstances. Had to cancel a wedding. Some poor sods' happiest day up the spout!'

'Tough luck. Still, they can't blame us, sir. We didn't murder him.'

'They can't blame us but they probably will.' He shrugged again.

'Any sign of a weapon?'

'Not yet. And nothing yet from pathology. You can chase that up, Jack. Also talk to the woman who found the body. Name of Bly. And another woman who saw it. The usual performance, Jack.'

Jack was thinking. 'They couldn't have met by accident at that time and in that place. Must have been arranged. Odd, don't you think?'

'Very odd.'

Jack leaned forward, elbows on his thighs, hands steepled under his chin. 'If they knew what time the church would be locked up they must be local. Or one of them must.'

'Tricked the other into a meeting? Anything's possible.'

Jack tried to hide his growing excitement. Maybe at last Fate was smiling on him.

'I'll need some help, sir. Door to door etc.'

'You can have Blake and Stanley. Stanley found the body. He's got the details.'

'Blake? He's useless, sir. No experience. Not a lot up here.' He tapped his head.

'Then this is a chance to put something there!' He glared at Jack. 'It'll be your good deed for the year.'

'Right, sir.' Jack had learned when not to argue. It came with the territory. He brightened suddenly. 'And can we have a room, sir?'

'*If* it's murder you can. See how things go. If you haven't sewn it up in twenty-four hours ask me again.'

Jack recognised the tone of dismissal and stood up. 'Just one thing, sir. Are we going to keep this one? I mean —'

'I know what you mean, Jack. You mean, are we going to let our chaps slog their guts out day after day doing all the leg work and then, when it gets really interesting, send for some berk from Scotland Yard who will take all the credit?'

Jack laughed wryly. 'That's about it, sir.'

The detective inspector shook his head. 'Probably, Jack. That's the way the world wags. If we don't crack it promptly we'll have to ask for help. A drawn-out murder hunt's a costly business. We both know we can't afford to go it alone. Not enough manpower, for a start. But I'm calling it a suspicious death and that'll give you a chance. You just might get lucky.' He collected some papers together, shuffling them into a neat pile. 'Do your best. I don't want the bastards down here any more than you do. I'll back you for a couple of days but after that —' He threw his hands wide in a helpless gesture.

'Right, sir. Thank you. I'll get on to it right away.'

He turned to leave the room.

'And Jack.'

'Sir?'

'We all need the odd hour of sleep now and again. Get a few hours' kip in first.'

'Yes, sir,' said Jack.

Grinning, Jack closed the door behind him. He wasn't such a bad guvnor but with the threat of Scotland Yard hanging over him and a chance to make a name for himself, Jack was wide awake. Sleep was the last thing on his mind.

Chapter 3

That evening Dulcie sat in her aunt's comfortable sitting room, her slippered feet curled beneath her on the sofa. Her face wore a disgruntled look and she sipped her tea absentmindedly.

'It's totally unfair,' she insisted. 'I was there and I must know more than Gus about everything. But I get Annabel's cancelled wedding.'

Her aunt smiled. 'It could make a nice piece. How do you feel when your wedding is cancelled due to a murder? Quite interesting. The women readers would lap it up.'

Harriet was an older version of Dulcie. Slightly taller and with deeper blonde hair, she was still attractive at fifty-five, though, like her niece, set no store at all on her looks. She did, however, feel a permanent resentment that she had been born female. Had it been otherwise, she liked to tell people, bricklaying would have been her chosen occupation. She had taken Dulcie's side against James when they wanted to send her to a Swiss finishing school to study cookery and household management. For this she had earned Dulcie's undying gratitude. When the latter decided to live in the town, a spare room in her aunt's house had been the obvious choice. James and Clarice, reluctantly bowing to the inevitable, had agreed that their daughter should live with a relative rather than lodge with strangers.

Dulcie groaned. 'But I don't want to interest women. I want to interest everyone. Murder is of interest to everyone. I was the second person to see the body — third if you count the killer. Gus has missed all that. What made me more furious was that Cobsey made me hand over my notes and Gus looked so horribly smug. I could have slapped him. I just hope he can't read my writing. If he asks me I shall pretend I can't read it either.'

She poured a second cup of tea for each of them.

Harriet said, 'What about Clive? Are you going to interview him? He might be just as upset as Annabel.'

Dulcie blew on her tea to cool it. 'Apparently not. Cobsey rang them but Clive's father answered the phone. It seems that Clive's mother has been put to bed and is under doctor's orders to rest. The shock of it all, I suppose. He said Clive was in no mood for interviews and slammed down the telephone.'

'That was then. Now it's now!' Harriet winked. 'Nothing to stop you turning up on the doorstep as a friend of the family. Clive has never fallen out with you, has he?'

Dulcie was considering this idea when the doorbell rang. This was followed by a furious barking from the kitchen. On the way to the front door, Harriet shouted 'Stop it, Max! D'you hear me?' The noise continued unabated and her aunt's head appeared round the door.

'That animal's got to go,' she warned.

Dulcie was still smiling when Harriet came back into the room followed by a stranger — a man in his thirties wearing a dark suit.

'This is Sergeant Spencer —' Harriet began.

'Detective Sergeant Jack Spencer,' he corrected her.

He was staring at Dulcie, disconcerted. The way all men do, Dulcie thought, irritated. She was more than just a pretty face. But no one would give her the chance to prove it.

Harriet said, 'I've explained that you're my niece.'

Dulcie regarded the policeman without smiling. For a moment neither spoke.

Suddenly he smiled. 'I'm sorry to disturb you but I'm investigating a suspicious death. I understand from Constable Stanley that you were in the church moments after the body was discovered. I'd like to ask you a few questions, if I may.'

Dulcie said, 'Of course.' She regarded him approvingly. He was not exactly handsome but certainly personable, stockily built with dark brown hair and grey eyes. The dark suit flattered him and he wore it with an air of authority which she admired. The level of her interest surprised her. She had thought growing up with a brother had rendered her more or less immune to the opposite sex. Certainly the thought of marriage did not hold her in thrall as it did many young women of her generation. Children had no place in her scheme of things either. Her ambition was to make her mark as a journalist. If she was honest, she also wanted to prove herself capable of independence. If she was *entirely* honest, she desperately wanted to impress Teddy.

The detective took out his notebook. Harriet, waving him to a chair, went into the kitchen to fetch another cup and saucer and replenish the tea pot. Dulcie, a little excited by the novelty of the situation, tried hard to appear unruffled.

'Now, Miss Moore, according to Constable Stanley, your first words were "Over here!" and "He's already dead".'

She nodded.

'Already dead?'

'The constable said he had sent for an ambulance. I thought perhaps the constable imagined the victim simply unconscious.'

'But you *knew* he was dead.'

'Yes, I did.'

'How did you know?'

She stared at him. How had she known? 'Er — I suppose —'

'Did you see his face?'

'No, I didn't. He was lying sort of face downward. I saw his back.'

'Did you examine him, perhaps? Try to rouse him?'

Dulcie felt rather flustered by the line of questioning. She had seen herself as something of a heroine, calm and resourceful in a crisis. Now she was being forced to doubt the wisdom of her actions 'No. I didn't touch him. At least — I think I did just touch him. I touched the back of his neck.' She looked at the detective earnestly. 'He looked so pathetic, lying there and in a way he —' She stopped abruptly, frowning. In a way — what? She had almost said that the dead man reminded her of someone. But that was impossible. 'He looked almost childlike,' she improvised. 'And he was very cold.' She thought about it. 'And the cleaner had already told me he was dead.'

'I see. The cleaner knew he was dead. Had *she* touched him? Moved him, perhaps?'

Dulcie sensed his irritation. 'I doubt it. She was terrified. She said "There's a dead man" or something like that. Maybe she said "a dead body". I can't remember. She said he was bleeding. I remember that.'

He wrote busily then laid the notebook aside and accepted his tea and a custard cream. Dulcie caught her aunt's eye. Harriet raised her eyebrows and made an imperceptible nod in the sergeant's direction. Of course! This was her chance to find out more about the murder. A chance that Gus would miss. But would Jack Spencer reveal any juicy details?

She said quickly, 'Was it really murder, Sergeant?'

'Detective Sergeant.'

'Was it really murder, Detective Sergeant! I mean, in a church of all places. It's bizarre.'

'Too early to say for sure, I'm afraid, but it's beginning to look like a distinct possibility. If it was an accident, of course, it might be manslaughter. Too early to say.'

Aha! So they suspected murder. She pressed on. 'Do you know who he is — or rather, was?'

This time he gave her a straight look. 'I'm sorry, Miss Moore, but I'm the one asking the questions.'

'Oh! Sorry.' He wasn't giving much away and she wondered briefly whether or not she should flutter her eyelashes at him. But would her aunt ever forgive her? Harriet was entirely scornful of such behaviour and Dulcie was, in fact, of the same mind. Except today when it might prove useful. On reflection she decided against it. Detective Sergeant Spencer might just be proof against her charms and that would be mortifying.

He asked for a little more milk to cool his tea, swallowed a few mouthfuls and picked up notebook and pencil. 'Do you know St Alphege's church well, Miss Moore?'

'Not at all.'

'You don't worship there?'

'No. Although I did know there was going to be a wedding. I was sent to cover it for my —' Blast! It had slipped out. 'For my newspaper.'

That surprised him. 'For your *newspaper?* You

can't mean you're a reporter?'

Harriet could stay silent no longer. 'Why not? A woman can cover a story as well as a man. Maybe better.'

He glanced at her. 'Have I said they can't?'

Dulcie thought she detected a hint of steeliness in his tone. This was food and drink to Harriet, she thought, with affection. Her aunt loved an argument. If it developed, they might prove to be a well matched pair.

Harriet said sharply 'You certainly implied it.'

'You imagined that I did, madam.' He turned back to Dulcie, effectively dismissing Harriet. 'And your newspaper is — ?'

'The *Canterbury Standard.* I was there to make a few notes about the church in advance. Flowers and suchlike.'

This was the appropriate time, she thought, to tell him that she knew the bride and groom, that the family had been invited to the wedding and declined. So why did she hold back? Perhaps because it hardly seemed important. Or because he had almost snubbed her aunt. Perhaps because *'I'm the one asking the questions'* still rankled.

'Miss Moore, had you ever seen the deceased before yesterday?'

'Of course not.'

'So you *did* see his face.'

'No. He was turned away from me.'

'So if you didn't see his face, how can you be sure you've never seen him before?'

Harriet snapped. 'What is this — an interrogation?'

He ignored her.

Dulcie was beginning to feel rattled. Speaking slowly, as though to a child, she said. 'What I mean is that as far as I know none of my friends, relations or aquaintances — casual or otherwise — are missing, so are unlikely to have been murdered in St Alphege's church.'

'Do you have many relatives in Canterbury, Miss Moore?'

'My parents, my brother Teddy and, of course, my aunt.'

'And your brother — does he work in the town?'

'No. The family owns a small estate in Cornwall and he manages that. He's away a lot.'

'Is he away now?'

'No.'

'So when did he come back?'

'A couple of days ago.'

Her thoughts spun. Teddy was in no mood to answer a lot of silly questions. He already had something on his mind and this policeman was not going to add to his worries. 'I hope you are not about to interrogate my entire family,' she snapped. 'Just because, by the merest fluke, I was at the scene of the crime when the body was discovered —'

Harriet chimed in at once. 'This whole thing is becoming ridiculous!' She glared at Detective Sergeant Spencer.

He, in turn, gave Dulcie a frosty look. 'Of course not. Although if at any time, for any reason, I should decide it was necessary, I most certainly would interrogate your family. I'd interrogate the King if I thought it necessary.' He switched his gaze to Harriet. 'And murder, Mrs Moore, is never —'

'Miss Moore!' she said triumphantly. 'My fiancé died in the war.'

'*Miss* Moore. I beg your pardon. I was going to say that murder is never ridiculous. A man has been killed and it is my job to find who killed him and bring him to justice. I shall have to *question* a great many people. It's called an investigation.'

Dulcie was tempted to say, 'Why not arrest me and have done with it!' but intuition warned her that this man was not to be trifled with. And, somehow, he still impressed her.

He added a few words to his report then stood up. He slipped the notebook and pencil into his pocket and said, 'I won't take up any more of your day, ladies.' As he turned to go he glanced across at Dulcie. 'And a word of warning, if I may, Miss Moore. People who commit murder are not nice people and I suggest you give up any notion you might have about pursuing your own enquiries. You might bite off more than you can chew.'

She stood up. 'I'm a journalist, Detective Sergeant Spencer. I too have a job to do. I shall do it to the best of my ability. Murder or no murder.'

His expression defied interpretation. 'As you

wish,' To Harriet he said: 'I can see myself out.'

Harriet was still smarting. She said, 'Better come with you. You might steal the silver!' Her short laugh suggested that he should take the remark as a joke.

Dulcie watched the detective's stiff back as he made his exit without further comment. Slowly she sat down, waiting for the opening and closing of the front door that would tell her that Jack Spencer had gone. Maybe her aunt's last jibe had been a mistake. A serious misjudgement on her part. Detective Sergeant Jack Spencer appeared to value his dignity.

Harriet came back into the room, 'Of all the arrogant, overbearing men — !' she said. 'Let's hope that's the last we shall hear of him!'

Dulcie nodded but she didn't share her aunt's optimism. For reasons that escaped her, she was suddenly filled with vague misgivings. This is the *start* of something, she thought, not the *end*.

The following morning Charles Brayne, sprawled in an armchair in the library, had drunk too much by the time Detective Sergeant Spencer arrived on his doorstep. Not enough actually to look drunk but enough to be a little muddle-headed and getting worse. He told the maid to show the man into the drawing room and rushed into the bathroom to comb his hair and wipe a damp flannel over his flushed face. He took the stairs carefully and tried to think what the man could want. The vicar had already broken the news about the cancelled wedding so it could hardly be that.

Outside the drawing-room door he paused to take several deep breaths and to reflect on the fact that he would have to face this alone. Nora had taken to her bed, something she often did in times of trouble. She had perfected the art of collapsing, he thought bitterly. He wished he could do the same. Go to bed and stay there until this damned awful mess was over.

He went into the room, hand outstretched. Sunshine streamed in through the French windows, warming the cool green of the walls and the deeper green of the somewhat austere suite.

'My maid tells me you're a chief inspector,' he lied. Flatter the man. It paid dividends. 'How can I help you?'

He waved a hand to indicate that they should seat themselves either side of the fireplace where the empty grate was hidden by a tapestry firescreen — a flowery piece of Nora's handiwork which he particularly detested.

'It's detective sergeant, actually, sir. Detective Sergeant Jack Spencer. I'm heading the enquiry into the suspicious circumstances of a man's death. The man in St Alphege's church, to be exact. The rector has told you what happened, I understand.'

Charles nodded his head and, instantly regretting the movement, said, 'That's right. Most unfortunate day to choose but the poor blighter didn't ask to die. Just one of those things.'

The detective looked round the room. 'Your wife is welcome to join us, Mr Brayne. You're all involved to some extent. Your son's wedding and so on.'

'My wife is confined to bed, I'm afraid. Doctor's orders. She's a rather frail soul. Can't take the knocks, I fear. Easily overwrought. She'll be fine in a day or two.' *If* their son condescended to put in an appearance. She'd be out of bed like a shot then, he reflected sourly. Meanwhile she would hide under the bedclothes, feigning sleep, leaving her husband to cope alone.

The detective smiled. 'I really came to apologise about the scene of crime procedure. The vicar did plead your case most earnestly but there is no way we can allow the public to go traipsing around what appears to be a murder scene. We must keep the area intact until all the tests are complete. Footprints, fingerprints, hair, mud from the shoes, anything that might give us the first clue.' He smiled. 'Er, your son, sir? Wouldn't he like to join us? It must be a blow, having your wedding cancelled at a moment's notice.'

Charles was drunk but not too drunk. He recognised the question as an important one and wondered how best to answer it. Be vague. Say as little as possible. 'He's not here at the moment. Er — Just popped out.'

'There's no hurry, sir. I can wait.'

'He might be some time. I'm — I'm not at all sure where he's gone.' He saw the policeman's eyes narrow slightly. 'That is, I know he won't be long.'

'But you don't know where he is.'

'No,' He searched his mind for a suitable place. 'Maybe gone round to his fiancée's house. Annabel's. Console her. Something like that.' He immediately realised his mistake. Suppose the wretched man had already been to the Ropers?

'Ah yes! That's quite likely in the circumstances. Poor young woman. I really am most sorry for them. I shall be calling on her when I leave you.'

'You will? Oh!' That was damned awkward. What the dickens was he going to say now?

'But he said nothing when he left the house? Your son, I mean.'

'Nothing.' Not quite true, of course. He said, 'Cheerio. See you later,' but that was yesterday.

'What time was that — approximately?'

Hell and damnation! 'I didn't see the going of him, I'm afraid, Inspector. My wife — when she wakes up — probably could be more helpful.'

'But he was here first thing?'

Now the blasted detective was leaning forward like a dog scenting a rabbit. Charles swallowed hard, desperate not to make matters worse. He was aware that the longer he said nothing, the more suspicious it would appear. 'My son would have slept in his own bed.' Oh Lord! What on earth made him say that? 'What I mean to say is, that he was naturally upset and probably wandered off to think things over. He may not have gone to see Annabel — in fact, now I come to think of it, I doubt that he would. That is, he may have set off to see her and then . . .' He put a hand to his head which was thumping painfully. He closed his eyes for a moment.

After a long silence the detective said, 'Mr Brayne, I'm not sure that you're being totally honest with me.'

Charles opened his eyes. Just like Nora to abandon him to this wretch and his blasted questions. 'I am!' he insisted. 'Trying to, anyway, for what it's worth.' This was all Clive's fault. Disappearing without a word. Worrying them to death.

The silence lengthened. Then the policeman said, 'Mr Brayne, did your son sleep here last night?'

'Of course he did!' How was he supposed to answer?

'You're quite sure?'

'I — We assume he did. He went out to a — a stag night with a few friends. No doubt he came back late — after we went to bed.' Although he didn't actually make the rendezvous. Never did meet up with his friends. Still, no need to tell the policeman everything. Bile rose suddenly in his throat and he swallowed hard. What he needed was another drink. If only this blighter would sod off he could pour himself one but he was damned if he was going to offer one to his tormentor.

'Did you see your son this morning?'

God! He was a persistent blighter. 'I didn't. No.' At least *that* wasn't a lie.

There was something about the man's expression and something about his tone of voice which worried Charles.

The man frowned. 'You didn't see him this morning — the day he was going to be married? *Before* you knew that it had had to be cancelled. Doesn't that seem — Well, a bit odd?'

Charles leaned forward and put his head in his hands. He felt ill. Damned police, sniffing around at a time like this. It was so unfair. His wife and his son remove themselves, leaving him to take the heat. Damnably unfair. He came to a sudden decision. He would tell him the truth and to hell with it all. Everyone would know sooner or later. Annabel and her damned parents had already been on the blower, demanding to talk to Clive. Why should he have to lie to save their skins. He thought of his wife sleeping peacefully upstairs — and his son, God knows where. But at least they didn't have to put up with this malarkey.

He cleared his throat. 'Look here, Inspector or whatever you are.' He stared at the man opposite him and wished he hadn't drunk so much. The outline of the policeman's head was ever so slightly blurred round the edges. 'I haven't been entirely truthful. All very difficult . . . As parents, I mean . . . Have you got a family?'

'No, sir.'

No. He wouldn't, would he. Too smart to tie himself down. 'My son. Clive — he's a decent enough lad. Bit of a Mummy's boy but . . . none the worse. Nothing a bit of responsibility won't cure. See what I mean. It's not that he's weak exactly. It's really —'

'Your son, sir. Could we stick to the point. Did he or didn't he come home last night?'

Well, this was it. He'd done his best but the law was the law. 'No, he didn't. But there's no law against that, is there? He's a grown man.'

'It's not that, sir. It's just that — how old is your son, Mr Brayne?'

Charles was vaguely aware of a change in the policeman's expression and a shift in his line of questioning. So Clive had jilted Annabel. He wouldn't be the first man to do so. Wouldn't be the last, either. It wasn't a criminal offence, was it? . . . If only he could think straight. He felt queasy. And getting worse.

'Clive? How old is Clive? He's twenty-four. Birthday last month. 2nd of May.' To his surprise he felt a rush of tears and blinked fiercely. Twenty-four. Just a boy. Too young to wed, dammit! He should have waited . . .

'And his colouring, sir?'

'Colouring? *Colouring?* Dark curly hair. Brown eyes.' He took a deep breath. 'If you want the truth, we think he's jilted her. There. Now you know.' He lifted his head with an effort and realised suddenly that he was crying. 'Skipped off,' he mumbled. 'Moonlight flit. Jilted the poor girl.

Oh God!' He fumbled in his jacket pocket for a handkerchief and blew his nose. 'You can see my problem.'

To his surprise the policeman said nothing. Instead, he leaned forward, reached out his hand and rested it briefly on his knee. Not such a bad chap, then, after all. A spark of humanity. Charles drew a long, shuddering sigh.

'Mr Brayne, I don't want to alarm you but has it occurred to you that your son may have been involved in — in some kind of accident? Do you have a photograph of him?'

It took a moment or two before he could consider this request. His insides churned. A stiff whisky would put him right. 'Would you like a drink, Inspector?'

'Not on duty, sir, thank you. The photograph — of your son?'

Think. Think! Did he have a photograph of Clive? 'Of course we do . . .' He stood up unsteadily and put a hand to his head.

'A recent one, sir, if that's possible.'

Charles tried to study his expression but the face was indistinct. But there was nothing wrong with his hearing and he detected a certain — a certain what? He breathed heavily, searching for the right word . . . Kindness! That was it. 'Why?' he demanded. His suspicion grew. 'Why d'you want —' A terrible idea was forming at the back of his confused mind. An idea so terrible . . . 'What d'you mean? Tell me!' But did he want to know? It couldn't be — not Clive. 'A recent photo?' he stammered. Fear sharpened his wits. He straightened up suddenly. 'Why?'

The detective stood up slowly. 'I'm sorry, sir. I don't want to worry you. It may be nothing. A coincidence. The photograph, sir?'

Oh God! This man thought that — he definitely couldn't take any more of this without a drink. Stumbling slightly, he made his way to the sideboard and, holding the trembling bottle with two hands, poured himself a large whisky. He swallowed it in three gulps and immediately felt better.

'Photograph. Right.' He moved like an automaton. The album was in the sideboard. With shaking hands he turned the pages as the detective stood up to take it from him. 'That was taken last year when they announced their engagement. That's my son. That's Annabel. A pretty girl — young woman rather. That's Clive. Twenty-three then, of course. Too young really. Takes after his mother . . .'

He fell abruptly into the dark silence of knowing. Soon the policeman would tell him. He would be kind but he would tell him. That it was his son Clive who had been found dead under the altar. Clive who had caused the wedding to be cancelled. His mouth twisted hysterically and he almost laughed. In a way Clive *had* jilted Annabel.

He felt himself sway.

Closing the album, the detective took hold of his arm to steady him. 'Please sit down, Mr Brayne. I think I may have some very bad news.'

Charles sat down, his legs shaking under him.

'I think you should accompany me to the — to the hospital, Mr Brayne. I'm deeply sorry. You may have to — that is, I may have to ask you to — to —'

'I know.' Poor blighter. Rotten job.

'To identify your son. Do you have a telephone? Right. Then with your permission I'll send for a taxicab.'

Charles brushed a hand across the tears which now streamed down his face. 'He took after his mother,' he said.

And then the black despair closed in.

Dulcie arrived at Grange Park just after eleven and found the family gathered in the drawing room. They looked shocked and drawn and Dulcie knew at once that they had heard the news. Petals had fallen from the roses on the window sill and none of the windows had been opened.

'Agnes told us,' her mother explained after a perfunctory kiss of greeting. 'The butcher's boy told her. Apparently it's all over the town.'

She sat down again. James, beside her on the buttoned sofa, shook his head. 'It's beyond me. It really is. That nice young man — For heaven's sake! Who'd want to kill Clive? What's he ever clone to anyone? Harmless as a fly! I don't know what this country's coming to and that's a fact.'

Dulcie sat on the arm of Teddy's chair. He looked at the end of his tether, she thought. His face wore a haunted look and there were dark shadows beneath his eyes. She tried not to think that now that Clive was dead Teddy might one day win back Annabel's affection. It was not a thought she was proud of but it lingered in her mind in spite of her efforts to erase it.

Dulcie leaned towards Teddy and slipped her arm around his shoulders. 'I'm so sorry,' she said. 'We'll just have to remember the fun we had when we were all children. Try and forget the last couple of years.'

He didn't answer.

Her mother sighed heavily. She had been crying and her face was blotched. She wiped away a stray tear. 'I keep wondering what he was doing there at such a time. And what this other man was up to? A church is such a strange place to meet up. Was it arranged, do you think? I mean, did he know this other man?'

Dulcie shrugged. 'That's for the police to discover. I hope this detective sergeant knows what he's doing. He looked terribly young to be in charge of a murder.'

Her father glanced at her sharply. 'You've *met* the man?'

'Detective Sergeant Jack Spencer.' She wondered why she enjoyed repeating his name. 'He came to Aunt Harriet's last evening to ask me about when I saw the body. Only I didn't know it was Clive then. I hadn't seen his face. Poor Clive. I forgive him for all the sneaky things he did now that he's —' She stopped, guiltily. There was no need to spell it out. She had been angry when he had set his cap at Annabel but now she remembered how defenceless his body had looked. No wonder it had looked vaguely familiar. Probably the hair. As a little girl she had envied him those dark curls, hating her own smooth blonde locks. 'I was going to visit Annabel today but now, of course, I don't like to intrude.'

Her mother said, 'A funeral instead of a wedding. Poor Annabel. I can't help feeling sorry for her. And for Clive's parents, of course. What must *they* be going through!'

James snorted. 'You were not so charitable a few days ago.'

'Well, of course I wasn't. I didn't know this was going to happen.' She looked at Dulcie. 'Men! They don't understand these things. Especially your father. Actually I don't see why you *shouldn't* visit poor Annabel. She might like someone her own age to talk to. You were always so close until — Well, you know what I mean. You two girls always had your heads together, exchanging confidences. Inseparable. Couldn't you make it up? She's suffered so much.'

Dulcie hesitated. 'I'd like to think I'd be welcome . . . I might go. They can only turn me away.'

Teddy said suddenly, 'I'll be away tomorrow, maybe longer.'

'Teddy!' Dulcie was shocked. 'You must stay for the funeral, surely.'

'It's not possible. There's too much to do.

Jennings is going downhill fast and I must support him.'

Dulcie thought, 'He won't catch my eye!' Why not?

Her father said, 'It can wait, surely.'

Teddy rushed on, ignoring the interruption, his face set. 'I've advertised. I'm sure I told you. I want Jennings to give the new chap the low-down on the estate while he still can. I'm seeing a man in London. Name's Coil. Dennis or Donald or something.' He took a quick breath. 'Trained in Penrith under Hugh Ross. Highly recommended. Then there's the audit still to check and a chap coming over at the weekend to discuss an autumn shoot. The group from Germany. Remember?'

They stared at him, disconcerted. Clarice glanced surreptitiously at Charles. Dulcie was becoming increasingly nervous.

'The four from Munich?' she asked, feigning interest. 'Three men and the woman who nearly shot you?' It was a humorous story, one which Teddy had told many times over the dinner table. Now nobody laughed.

Teddy nodded.

Clarice looked troubled. 'I can see you're busy dear, but I do think you should reconsider. If you don't go to the funeral it will look as though you don't care. And the police will want to talk to all his friends. Known contacts, as they call it. They always do. Won't it look a bit odd if you've gone away?'

'I can't help that, Mother.' His tone was sharp. 'You have to realise that there will be a post mortem and an inquest. It will probably take a week or more. I can't hang around Canterbury waiting to be asked a lot of silly questions. Nor for Clive's funeral. He's dead. He's not going to miss me.'

Charles reddened angrily. 'Teddy! That's damned hard, isn't it? What the hell's got into you?'

Dulcie cried, 'Father! Leave him alone! If he says he can't be at the funeral, then he can't. I'm sure he'd stay if he could.'

She waited for him to agree but he was silent.

Clarice said, her voice shrill, 'Don't interfere, Dulcie. And don't speak to your father in that tone of voice. Charles is quite right. Teddy *should* pay his last respects and what's more to the point, Teddy knows it.'

'For Christ's sake!' Teddy muttered.

Briefly he caught Dulcie's eye and she read his mute apppeal for help. If only she knew what to do or say, she thought miserably.

Clarice seemed to regret her outburst. She leaned across and took Teddy's hand in hers but he immediately withdrew it. 'Teddy, *please* dear. You can't just walk away when your best friend — Well, your oldest friend — has been murdered.'

He looked at her, his face haggard. 'I'll write to them. And to Annabel.'

Dulcie bit back angry words. Couldn't her

parents see how *thoughtless* they were being? Teddy was seriously troubled and they were only concerned with appearances. How would it *look* if their son stayed away from the funeral. If only Teddy would confide in *her*. She had probably been waiting all her life for Teddy to *need* her but he was shutting her out. Was it just the wedding? That was cancelled now and Annabel was free from her engagement. Perhaps he felt guilty because of the way it had come about — almost as though he had willed something awful to happen to Clive. Reluctantly she saw it through the eyes of Detective Sergeant Spencer. Would he regard Teddy's absence with suspicion? The answer had to be 'Yes'.

Her mother was crying softly; her father was making no effort to comfort her. Dulcie, still smarting from her rebuff, decided she had had enough. She stood up. 'I think I will go across to Annabel's. I might be of some comfort. She'll either want to see me or she won't.' Her conscience pricked her. Her reasons for going were very mixed and her job with the *Standard* was definitely a factor in her decision. 'I'll give her our commiserations, shall I?'

'Of course, dear,' said Clarice. 'If there's anything we can do to help. Anything at all. That poor, dear girl!'

James rolled his eyes but Dulcie let it pass.

Teddy said, 'Take care, Sis!'

Startled, she looked at him. He hadn't called her that for years. During her tomboy years she had jibbed at the name Dulcie as altogether too feminine. To her mother's horror, she had tried to convert her family and friends to 'Sis'. It had long since fallen into disuse so what on earth had prompted its use today, she wondered. She smiled at her brother. 'And you,' she said.

The farewells over, she retrieved her bicycle and free-wheeled down the gently sloping drive. Her face was drawn into a frown as she tried to analyse the recent conversation. She felt deeply apprehensive. Teddy's uncharacteristic behaviour troubled her. She thought she understood him but perhaps she had been fooling herself. Lulling herself into a false complacency. He was big brother, best friend and confidant rolled into one. She had always believed the bond between them would last a lifetime. Now something — or someone — had come between them.

Teddy had a secret he would not share.

At the Ropers' home, Dulcie found Annabel sitting on the garden swing, pale and subdued. The chestnut tree above her cast her friend's face into shadow but Dulcie noticed her hair. Instead of the smooth chignon her dark curls had been allowed to cluster untidily around her face. A small nerve pulsed in her neck and her hands gripped the ropes of the swing but she made no effort to set the swing in motion. Dulcie drew closer, uttering a quiet greeting, remembering younger, happier times when the four of them played here. Nathan, the gardener, had complained bitterly about the marks made on the lawn by their boisterous games of cricket and the less exuberant sessions with the croquet mallets. Even then Annabel had favoured Teddy. Teddy must push her swing. Teddy must be in her team. Later, Teddy must partner her at tennis. Their future together had been taken for granted. Her sudden change of heart in favour of Clive had astonished everyone.

Annabel watched Dulcie's approach without comment and with no change of expression. Suddenly, instinctively, Dulcie knew that coming here today had been a mistake. Mrs Roper had been so grateful to see her and so sure that Annabel would appreciate her visit. She had been wrong, thought Dulcie, but it was too late now to retreat.

She kissed Annabel briefly and said, 'I'm so sorry, Annabel.'

Annabel's mouth tightened. 'No you're not. I know you, Dulcie Moore. You're glad. You think it serves me right. Well, that's because you don't understand.'

Chastened, Dulcie sat down on the grass. She couldn't deny it. She was truly saddened by Clive's death but deep down she did feel that Annabel had been paid back for her cavalier treatment of Teddy. Since she could hardly bear to admit this meanness of spirit even to herself she was not about to admit it to Annabel. 'So why don't you explain?' she asked, plucking a daisy and twirling it carelessly between thumb and forefinger. 'I'm not a mind reader.'

Slowly Annabel turned her head towards her visitor. 'Explain why I didn't become engaged to your brother? Does it matter after all this time?'

'It matters to me.' From the corner of her eye Dulcie saw Annabel press the toe of her shoe into the lawn to set herself swinging. As she watched her friend swing to and fro, Dulcie was suddenly transported back through the years. She saw them at the mid-summer picnic that Mrs Roper always gave them, here on the lawn — when the strawberries were at their best. She saw Teddy, sixteen years old, feeding Annabel with a strawberry dipped in cream and sugar. She heard Clive say, 'Two can play at that game!' and then he was trying to force a strawberry into Dulcie's mouth. Finally she had accepted the fruit and the kiss that Clive planted on her cheek. He had done it to make Annabel jealous. Even then Dulcie had understood the rivalry between the two boys.

Annabel said, 'You're still a child, Dulcie. I envy you that.'

'A child?' Dulcie glared. 'I'm twenty, for heaven's sake! You're only twenty-one. And I'm the one that left home, remember. I'm the one who found a job. That's independence. I'm certainly not a child!'

'You mean your uncle *gave* you a job. It was all so easy, wasn't it? You may be twenty but you know nothing about — about the things that matter. It's not your fault.'

Dulcie swallowed hard and counted to ten. There were plenty of things she could say by way of retaliation — stinging comments she would enjoy making — but then they would quarrel. Then she would never be told anything. Also she must not forget that Annabel's fiancé had just been murdered.

Quickly she changed the subject. 'Is there *anything* I can do?'

Annabel shook her head.

Dulcie wrapped her arms around her knees. 'None of it makes any sense. Why would anyone kill Clive? I don't suppose he had an enemy in the world.'

'Except Teddy, maybe.'

Dulcie refused to bite. 'Teddy wasn't Clive's enemy. A rival, maybe, but not an enemy.'

'Father thinks it may have been a drunk. It wasn't theft. What I can't understand is what Clive was doing there. He should have been with his friends, celebrating. *If* that's where he was killed. They may have just taken him into the church to hide him.'

'They? Do the police think —'

'Might have been more than one.' She sighed. 'Poor Clive. I still can't believe it. The police think he went there to meet someone — but why? And who, for heaven's sake?'

'So you didn't see him at all that evening?'

'Clive? No, of course not. It's bad luck to meet the night before the wedding.'

Dulcie said nothing.

Annabel said, 'It's so damned unfair. Poor Clive did nothing wrong, whatever you and Teddy may have thought at the time. He asked me to marry him and I said, "Yes". I was just as much to blame.' Her voice cracked. 'So why is he dead? He didn't deserve it.'

Tears were close, thought Dulcie and guilt plagued her. She shouldn't have come. Quickly she searched for a change of subject.

'We've got a dog,' she said. 'We've had him a few weeks now.'

'I know. Mother saw your aunt with it down by the river.' She smiled faintly. 'A wild, shaggy-looking thing, she said. All legs.'

'We call him Max. Harriet says it's short for maximum nuisance! He's a mongrel, of course, but that's fine with me. He's got these lovely brown eyes — when you can see them! I didn't expect Harriet to agree to keep him but she's fallen for him, hook, line and sinker! She keeps saying we've got to get rid of him but actually she's as daft as I am about him.'

Annabel tossed her head. 'He was behaving very badly according to Mother. Pulling on his lead. Trying to strangle himself.'

'He'll calm down.' Dulcie hoped that if she said this often enough it would happen. At least the subject of the dog had eased the tension between them and they were no longer sniping at each other. She picked a few more daisies and began to make a chain, not looking at Annabel, saying nothing.

After a long silence, Annabel slid from the swing and sat beside her on the grass. 'I can't tell you everything,' she said. 'I wish I could. But I can tell you why I didn't agree to marry Teddy.'

Dulcie looked at her. Her pale face had flushed.

'Because?' she prompted.

'Because he didn't ask me. Simple, isn't it. I waited and waited and he —'

'But didn't you *know* how he felt about you?' She was appalled.

'I thought I knew. I thought he would propose. And then Clive asked me and I said "No" because I didn't love him as much as I loved Teddy. And he said Teddy obviously didn't love me as much as he did and we quarrelled. And I went on waiting for Teddy and —' Her voice shook. 'And he didn't say a damned thing! I felt such a fool. Whenever I raised the subject he made a joke out of it. Mother kept asking me and I didn't know what to say. Father said he'd ask Teddy his intentions — prod him, if you like, but I begged him not to. Then Clive went to Austria on that skiing trip — to try to forget me.'

'I remember. He was away for ages.'

'Yes. I missed him more than I expected to and then he came back and asked me again.' She drew in her breath sharply. 'Nearly a year had gone past since his first proposal — the longest year of my life — and I suddenly thought "To hell with Teddy!" '

In spite of herself, Dulcie felt the beginnings of sympathy. 'Did you love Clive at all?'

'Of course I did. I loved them both but —' She sighed heavily. 'If you think I behaved badly — maybe I did but I've been well and truly punished for it. I can't explain that to you. You'll just have to take my word for it. It's all gone wrong. Dreadfully wrong. And the worst of it is —' She began to cry softly but almost at once drew out a handkerchief and wiped her eyes fiercely. 'No I won't!' she said. 'I've shed enough tears over them. *Bloody* men!' She met Dulcie's startled look with one of defiance. 'Between them they've broken my heart and now — this. Poor Clive!'

Dulcie put her arms round her and hugged her. Her own eyes were full of unshed tears — for Annabel, for Teddy and for Clive. 'Do you think Teddy still loves you?' she asked cautiously.

To Dulcie's surprise, Annabel drew back sharply.

She said, 'My God, Dulcie!' and crossed her arms tightly across her chest. 'Teddy has been — has behaved abominably. I can't tell you but —' She looked at Dulcie, her eyes narrowed. 'Did he give you any message for me? Is that why you've come? Because if so I don't want to hear it!'

'No. He's very sorry about Clive but there's no message. He's going away this evening but he'll have to come back for Mother and Father's anniversary dinner — they've been married thirty years. I'm sure he'll stay on for Clive's funeral if he can.'

Annabel's expression hardened. 'Tell him not to bother! We don't want him there.'

'But why?' Dulcie, hurt, stared at her.

'Just tell him. He'll know.' She shook her head slowly. 'Anyway, they can't bury Clive yet. They have to keep the body — for their beastly enquiries. They'll release it as soon as they can.'

Dulcie was stricken, thinking of the Braynes' anguish. First they lose their son in tragic circumstances and are told he must suffer the indignity of a post mortem. Finally they are denied the chance to lay the boy to rest. Words of sympathy sprang to her lips but were never uttered. Annabel had relinquished her claim to sympathy by her spiteful words about Teddy.

Dulcie protested, 'It's not Teddy's fault that someone killed Clive!' Her kindly intentions had all but evaporated. She scrambled to her feet, looking down angrily on Annabel's dark head. 'If my brother wants to attend the funeral he will. Anyone can attend a funeral. He doesn't need your permission.' She hesitated. This argument wasn't what she had come for. She wanted to walk away before she said something worse. 'Annabel, I'm sorry. I don't want us to quarrel.'

'I don't care if we do or not! You and your precious brother! You could never see him for what he is. He's not a god, you know. He's as human and as fallible as the rest of us.'

'I've never said he wasn't. I —'

Annabel looked up. 'Oh yes you did. Or you thought it. Still do.' She struggled to her knees and stood up. 'You wouldn't accept that it was Teddy who broke the window in the greenhouse.'

'It wasn't him. He denied it on the bible.'

Annabel tossed her head. 'Well then, he lied. He told me he had broken it.'

'I don't believe you!'

'Ask him!'

Dulcie felt sick. Something in Annabel's voice convinced her that she was telling the truth. She said, 'He was only about twelve! Just a boy.' But her mind raced. So Teddy had *lied.* Her parents had been right to accuse him and she, Dulcie, had hated them for their lack of trust. The eight-year-old Dulcie had flown into a passionate temper in an effort to defend her brother's honour. She had screamed abuse at her mother and had been sent to bed by her father. Her disgrace had been total — *and Teddy had allowed it to happen.* The disillusionment was like a physical pain.

Annabel said, 'You have to love people for what they are, Dulcie. Not for what you want them to be. I love him in spite of his faults.'

Dulcie struggled for breath. She had to get away before she heard more. Quickly she turned on her heel and began to walk swiftly in the direction of the house.

As she did Annabel called after her. 'Your wonderful, darling Teddy! If only you knew!'

Dulcie began to run.

Chapter 4

Jack went back into the room. It was large and airy with sizeable windows of frosted glass. The walls gleamed with white gloss paint. Along the wall, glass-fronted cupboards jutted above a selection of metal tables and glass shelves. Dishes, phials, a roller towel beside each sink. Glass jars of every size, bottles of chemicals and trays of surgical instruments. Four white covered tables stood along the centre of the room and several trolleys waited alongside the far wall. A pile of newly laundered green aprons and a stainless steel container for the used ones. It could have been an operating theatre. It was in a way. Two of the windows were wide open but the smell remained. Jack Spencer repressed a shudder. Chemicals, cold bodies, congealed blood, rubber aprons and gloves. The unmistakable smell of a mortuary. Today a fourth smell lingered. He had already attributed this to the new perfumed grease with which the pathologist tried unsuccessfully to control his frizzy hair.

'Sorry about that,' said Jack, referring to the telephone call which had called him away from the post mortem.

Dr Jeffries, the pathologist, nodded by way of acceptance and continued stitching up the incisions he had made in the corpse. Jack glanced at Blake who earlier had looked distinctly queasy.

'You OK?' he asked.

'Yes sir. Thank you, sir.'

From her stool a little distance away the secretary laughed lightly. 'He hasn't fainted yet.'

Blake's smile was a trifle lopsided but it was a smile.

Jack said, 'Don't put the idea into his head, for Pete's sake!'

He resumed his position beside the body that rested on the second table, trying to maintain an impression of professional detachment. The damage that had been inflicted upon the victim was glaringly obvious. Huge purple bruises, missing teeth, grazes on the right hand and blood in the matted hair. Jack kept his eyes on the dead man, aware that the pathologist was watching him from the other side of the table. Nearly ten years in the force yet still Jack was not entirely comfortable in the presence of death. Maybe that was a good sign, he thought hopefully. Maybe it was healthy to regard the body as a man instead of a numbered tile. He wrenched his gaze from the man's face and flicked open his notebook. Later there would be a written report from the mortuary but the pathologist might have a few ideas too insubstantial to be committed to official paper.

Jack said, 'Mind if we recap?'

'Not at all.' The doctor laid down the needle, surveying his handiwork with a critical eye. 'Time of death approximately ten o'clock. Maybe a little earlier.'

'Could we say between nine and eleven?' He was already writing.

'Why not.' He glanced at the secretary who handed him the notes he had dictated throughout. 'Post-mortem lividity . . . what you might expect.'

Jack said, 'He was found under the altar in St Alphege's church. Could hardly have fallen there so he must have been dragged or carried.' He hoped he'd been carried. That way there would be blood-stains on the murderer's clothes.

'Probably dragged. The heels of the shoe might show something. All the clothes are over there — ready bagged.'

Jack nodded. 'So we can assume the murder took place in the church and not elsewhere. Good. Blood spatters on one of the columns support that theory.'

Jeffries shrugged. 'Sounds about right . . . Let's see . . . Rigor mortis — no surprises there. Dropped jaw, open eyes. When we got the body at twelve-twenty the rigor mortis was still present. As you know, it usually takes up to twelve hours to complete and between a day or two to fade.'

Jack nodded. He should have known but in fact he'd forgotten. He sighed. A young man with all his life ahead of him — and a woman who loved him. He thought guiltily about the letter to Judith which had still not been written. With an effort he returned his attention to the body. Clive Brayne. A young life snuffed out. At least putting a name to him should give them a lead and help them to catch the bastard. He realised suddenly that the doctor was looking at him expectantly.

Jeffries said, 'Am I boring you?'

'Sorry!'

'I said, "Any questions so far?" '

'Sorry. I was thinking. No questions — at least —' He thought quickly. Maybe he should have some questions. 'What about body temperature? Does that tell us anything?'

Did he imagine a small twitch at the corner of Jeffries' mouth?

'Not a great deal, no. The body was lying in a cold place all night on stone and although the following day was sunny, under the altar would still be in shadow.'

'And the weapon? Hazard a guess, maybe.' He tried not to sound too eager.

'Fists, I should say, and a boot. Contusions here, here and here.' He indicated them with a few stabs of his finger. 'A massive beating. Plus a blow on the head but the victim could have hit something on the way down. Or maybe he fell awkwardly and split his head open when he hit the ground. There's crushing of the skull at the back of the head. That's what killed him.'

'Poor devil!' He was disappointed that there

was no weapon. He had imagined a row of dedicated men searching the church.

Jeffries went on. 'There are what look like thumb marks here. The assailant probably grabbed his shoulders, forcing him back — or down,' He looked up at Jack. 'I'd say he was a heavy man, the assailant. You're not looking for a lightweight.'

'D'you reckon the victim put up a fight?'

'Oh yes. There's a torn fingernail as well as a small fracture in the index finger of the right hand. He fought for his life, poor devil. Oh yes. The stomach contents. Our man hadn't eaten or drunk much prior to his death. Any questions? Comments?'

'I don't think so.' He glanced at Blake, wondering whether the man had learned anything. 'Have I forgotten anything, Constable?'

Blake said promptly, 'No scars or tattoos. No other distinguishing marks.'

'Good man!' Jeffries grinned, pleased.

Encouraged, Blake said, 'Blood type?'

The doctor said, 'Type "O".' Glancing at Jack, he raised his eyes.

Jack said, 'Well done!' and tried to hide his surprise. Maybe Blake wasn't quite so useless as he appeared.

The pathologist laid down the clipboard on an adjacent worktop and began to peel off his gloves. 'I'll let you have the full report as soon as it's typed up. I hope you get him. The man's dangerous.'

'I will,' said Jack and at that moment he had no doubts at all.

Not a hundred miles away, in an upstairs room in a house in Folkestone, Reginald Foote leaned back in his leather chair and stared out of the window. He smoothed his thinning hair and grinned at the thought of his visitor who waited in the ante room and was no doubt fuming with impatience.

'Let the stupid bugger wait!' he muttered.

The window looked out on to The Leas, a grassy area to the west of the town which ran between a row of large hotels and the edge of the cliff. Here and there a lone seagull paraded across well-cut lawn. One drummed on the grass with its feet, hoping to fool the worms into thinking it was rain. Cunning that. He liked seagulls. Sparrows fluttered round an elderly lady in a wheel chair who watched intently as they fought over the scraps thrown to them by her young nurse.

He consulted his watch. 'Nearly lunchtime!'

Reginald Foote was hungry. He always was. He blew a ring of cigar smoke and watched it rise to the white ceiling of his office. The room was expensively furnished as befitted a man who might well become the next mayor of Folkestone. The thick, cream-coloured carpet was new. So were the long, draped curtains striped in blue and white. Everything smelled of money. No detail had been overlooked in his attempt to impress.

Harris Enterprises. Not that Harris had been at all enterprising. Quite the reverse. He had vetoed all Reggie's best ideas.

'You were a miserable sod, Harris!'

He had been a skinflint, too. The offices had been shabby and dull. The business had been mediocre. No flair. No ambition. TB had taken him and not a moment too soon. Now Reggie was in sole charge — if you didn't count the sleeping partners who didn't appear on the letterhead for sound reasons of their own. Reggie didn't want to know. They had money to invest and that was all that mattered. He didn't need partners who could kill off his initiatives with lack of enthusiasm, who would never take a risk.

He swivelled his chair so that he once more faced his large, leather-topped desk. If the running-track idea went ahead he'd be made. Mayor and public benefactor. Only one man stood in his way. Arnie Burnett. But something unfortunate was going to happen to Burnett. He had worked out a foolproof plan and by getting Parker out he had already set the wheels in motion.

He brought his fist down on the small bell to summon his secretary. A small, middle-aged woman appeared at the door.

She smiled nervously. 'Yes, Mr Foote?'

'Send Mr Parker in!'

'Yes, Mr Foote.'

He eyed her retreating figure with distaste. For the moment, Mrs Craddock was the cross he had to bear. Fussy Mrs Craddock. No dress sense at all. He had inherited her eight months ago when he became managing director of the firm. He hated the sight of her skinny little legs and pale protruding eyes. With her thick lensed spectacles she looked like a fish. Sometimes in the early days, he'd called her Mrs Haddock, pretending he'd made a mistake. She'd blushed, not daring to correct him. He'd criticised her work and had made her stay late. He'd hoped that he would drive her to resign but apparently she had a husband with a dodgy heart and she needed the job.

The trouble was she was, undeniably, an excellent secretary with good typing and shorthand speeds. She was also efficient, filing anything and everything as though her life depended on it and always able to produce a letter or invoice when it was required. She was also Harris's cousin and had been with the firm for over twenty years. Unfortunately this was not the time to be *seen* to be cruel or unreasonable. He could not afford any bad publicity until his elevation to mayor was in the bag. A disgruntled employee moaning to the press would be embarrassing. The papers would be on to it like leeches. They'd love to nail him but he was too smart by far. They would never get the slightest whiff of anything unsavoury. But Craddock had to go. He needed a new secretary, someone young and beautiful to enhance his image. Mayor of Folkestone! It had a wonderful ring to it.

He glared at the man who entered.

The man stared at him sullenly. He was tall and broad. If he carried excess weight it hardly showed on his large frame. 'That pathetic creature told me you were busy! Like hell you are. Think I'm going to hang around while —'

'Shut up, Parker, and stop whining. You always were a whinger, even at school.' He stared him into submission and watched with satisfaction as the man sat down. 'Now, you bloody fool, tell me what went wrong.'

Albert Parker began a stumbling account but half way through Reggie interrupted him with a furious jab of his cigar.

'I don't want any excuses. You killed him, you idiot! I told you to frighten him. I can't believe I went to all that trouble to spring you just so you could mess up something as small as this. Brayne was a sideline. I thought you could manage him standing on your head! But no! You get carried away. We've got a bloody murder hunt on our hands now. You do realise that, I suppose. You do *read* the papers. You can *read,* I take it. Fellstowe taught you that much, I hope, if nothing else.'

'I learned as much as you did.' Parker began to unbutton his waistcoat.

'Oi!' He pointed to the waistcoat. 'Don't make yourself at home. You're not stopping here for long. Bloody liability, you are. I wish I'd left you to rot in jail.' Getting no reaction he went on. 'So how the hell d'you come to find yourself in this mess?' Parker still didn't answer. 'You know something. Parker? Jail's the best place for people like you.'

'You said you wanted to frighten him.'

'I didn't say *kill* him. I want the cash he owes me. How do I get it if he's dead? Christ Almighty, you're thick, Albert Parker. Thick as two planks!'

'How did I know he'd fall and —'

'You must have hit him too hard.'

'I *didn't!* He must have a thin skull or something. Or had a weak heart. How was I to know? I just punched him around a bit and when he fell over I kicked him. You said he'd be a soft touch. He got up again and went for me so I had to get a bit nasty with him. He tried to run, tripped, sort of spun round and —' He shrugged. 'Down he went. Don't blame me.'

Reggie groaned. 'Oh but I do blame you. I bloody well do! You bungled it. And now you have the gall to show up here wanting your money. Well, there it is. Count it!' He drew a wad of money from the top right-hand drawer of his desk and tossed it into Parker's lap. With distaste he watched the huge fingers thumbing through the notes.

At last Parker's face reddened angrily. 'What's your game, Foote? This is only £100! You said £200 and you only gave me fifty up front. You owe me —'

'I owe you nothing, you idiot. You're lucky to get that.'

'But he's never going to split on you now, is he, if that's what you're worried about. At least I've silenced him for you.'

'You've *killed* him. Don't you see what that means? If it's ever traced to you and back to me — Christ Almighty, Parker! Watch yourself. The tenders are in and the *real* job could be any day now. So stay in the area and keep in touch — but *not* in Folkestone. I don't want to catch even a whiff of you. Because if I *do* I just might drop a hint in the right quarter. Get you banged up again.' He drew on his cigar and blew expensive smoke in Parker's direction. 'You'll get the rest of what I owe you after you do the real job. *If* you get it right. It's got to look like an accident but he's got to die.'

'Who is he?'

'You'll know when I say so and not before. I know you. You're an impatient sod. You'd jump the bloody gun and there's a lot riding on it. If this deal comes off I stand a good chance of becoming mayor. Yes, you heard! *Mayor!*' He was pleased to see the fool's jaw drop. 'So get lost, Parker. When it's over and you've got all your money you disappear. Go to South America. You're always talking about it.'

'I'll want all the money on the dot and untraceable notes. You doublecross me, Foote, and I'll —'

'Don't threaten me, Parker. I got you out of jail, remember. And from now on your name's Stowe. Fellstowe. Got it?' He laughed, enjoying his little joke. 'Now hop it before I change my mind.'

He sat back. He enjoyed bullying people and Parker was getting no more than he deserved. Stupid bastard might have ruined everything.

'Get out!' he snapped. 'And stay away from that girlfriend. The police aren't fools.'

'I have to go somewhere.'

Reggie rolled his eyes. 'You're breaking my heart, you know that?'

Slowly Parker stood up. The sullen expression had never left his face. 'You'll never make mayor,' he said. 'They'll rumble you. You'll see.'

Foote allowed himself an expansive smile. 'I'll make it. You won't. You're a nobody, Parker, and that's all you'll ever be. A *wanted* nobody. There's no way you can hurt me so don't even think it. One step out of line and I'll see that you go down for Brayne. An anonymous phone call. That's all it'll take. Easy as selling candy to a baby!'

To his surprise Parker appeared unimpressed. Placing both hands on the desk he leaned across it. 'You try it and I'll drop you in it face down!'

Reggie met stare with stare. Then suddenly he pressed the burning end of his cigar on to Parker's right hand. With a shriek of pain and then an oath, Parker sprang back from the table, sucking the burn.

'You bastard!' he cried.

Reggie laughed but Parker suddenly snatched

the cigar from his fingers and dropped it on to the new carpet. Before Reggie could stop him, he ground it in with the heel of his shoe, releasing the smell of burning wool. Reggie gave a roar of rage and lunged forward. Parker was heavy but fast. He ran out of the door, through the office and down the stairs. By the time Reggie reached the landing he was already out of sight. Rushing back to the window Reggie saw him running across the grass in the direction of the port.

'Whatever's happened?' cried Mrs Craddock. 'Mr Parker went rushing past me —' He looked at her with loathing. Her fish eyes were almost popping out of her head.

Reggie breathed rapidly. 'He's a bloody peasant! Forget it. And from now on his name's Stowe. Make a note to change his file.'

'Stowe? Oh but —'

'That's what I said. Business reasons. Just do it.'

She nodded then sniffed. 'Is something burning, Mr Foote?' Her gaze fell on the broken cigar. 'Oh dear!' Her face crumpled in dismay. 'Your lovely new carpet!'

He closed his eyes, longing to slap her. Fortunately she had no idea how close she came on occasions to provoking physical violence. He didn't think much of women at the best of times and Mrs Craddock's fussy ways tested his patience.

'For Christ's sake!' he snapped. 'Just clean it up and be quick about it.'

One way or another she would have to go.

Dulcie leaned across the desk and smiled winningly at Gus. 'So do I get to read it?' she asked.

Gus grinned. 'So you can pretend you could do better? No fear!' He pulled the final sheet from his typewriter and reread it with nods of his head and occasional grunts of approval.

She said, 'What's the matter? Frightened I could?' In fact she was desperate to know exactly how much Gus had discovered about the murder. If it turned out that she knew more, she intended to ask Cobsey to let her share the job. If he refused she would go ahead in her own time, amassing whatever information she could until she had enough extra material to convince him. She might even put it together in an article and threaten to offer it to one of the nationals. Well, maybe not threaten. She wasn't a fool and Cobsey would never allow himself to be manipulated that way but she would hint that what she had was too valuable to be wasted.

Gus held the typewritten sheets up to his face and peered humorously over the top edge. 'What's it worth?' he asked.

'Not much.'

He lowered his voice. 'A kiss from those ruby-red lips?' He rolled his eyes.

She clutched her stomach. 'Ugh!'

'Don't be like that, Miss Moore. We're all adults here.'

'You surprise me!'

He lowered the papers and studied them again.

He's dying for me to read it, she thought. Don't rush your fences, Dulcie.

'One little kiss?' he wheedled.

Oh, why not? 'One,' she agreed.

He leaned forward, grabbed her by the arm, pulled her towards him. Taken by surprise she had no time to turn her head and he kissed her full on the mouth. She was astonished by how pleasant it was. For a moment she was unable to say anything. If a kiss from Gus could excite her, how would it be to be kissed by someone who mattered? She made up her mind to think about it and held out her hand for the copy.

Gus grinned. 'I meant one kiss per page —' he began.

Dulcie snatched the sheets from him and, ignoring his protest, ran with them into the lavatory. Averting her eyes from the urinal as she always did, she went into the cubicle, locked the door and sat on the lavatory seat.

> . . . Police are still baffled by the murder on Friday last of a young man whose body was discovered beneath the altar in St Alphege's church. He has been identified as a local man — twenty-six-year-old Clive Andrew Brayne.
>
> Early this morning his parents were too shocked to talk to us but close friends say the family are devastated by the tragedy . . .

Dulcie snorted. 'Close friends! How would he know? He made that bit up. It doesn't take a degree to know they would be devastated!' She read on.

> . . . Mr Brayne was due to be married at the church the day after his murder. Annabel Mary Roper, his fiancée, lives on the Whitstable Road. She is suffering from shock and grief and is currently under sedation. Rigorous investigations are being put in place by the police . . .

'That means they are asking a lot of silly questions and getting nowhere!' she muttered, certain that she could have done a much better job than Gus.

> . . . The team is led by Detective Sergeant Jack Spencer who spoke briefly to reporters earlier today. He said they are following up several leads but at this time they have no clue as to the identity of the killer. 'There seems to be no motive,' Spencer told reporters. He has appealed to members of the public to come forward with information which might lead to an arrest . . .

Detective Sergeant Jack Spencer. She wondered if this was his first murder investigation and decided it probably was. So what would it be like to be kissed by a detective sergeant? She grinned. OK! So she rather liked him. There was no law against that. 'Dulcie!' she muttered. 'This is important. Keep your mind on the copy!'

> . . . Mr Brayne, like his father before him, was a valued member of the church choir and popular with his fellow choristers. One of these. Mark Haverson, said, 'He didn't have an enemy in the world. He was a very decent sort of chap. Maybe they mistook him for someone else.'
>
> On the night he met his death he had intended to celebrate with friends. An incident room has been set up at the Police Station . . .

Dulcie slid from the seat and let herself out of the lavatory. She went back to Gus and returned his copy.

'Very good,' she said. It was good, she thought exultantly — from her point of view. Gus had not been able to talk to the families concerned. He had learned nothing that she did not know.

Gus smiled. 'That's how it's done,' he said. 'It's called journalism!'

Dulcie returned his smile. 'I was interviewed by the police,' she said. 'He's a nice chap, Jack Spencer. We had quite a chat.'

As she had hoped his face fell but he rallied quickly. 'You're a suspect then, are you?'

'A witness. I was there when they found the body, remember.'

He hesitated and in his expression she saw the struggle that was taking place in his mind. Would he, *could* he, admit that she might be able to help him?

Waving the article he said, 'Anything you want to add to this?' He tried to sound disinterested.

'Nothing I want to add, no.'

'Meaning?'

'Meaning I don't want to add stuff to your copy so that you get all the credit.' She leaned forward. 'I know the families, Gus. My brother and Clive and Annabel and I grew up together.' She drew in a long breath. Gus wouldn't like what she was going to say. 'I think Cobsey should let me in on this one. I'm going to ask him. I'm just letting you know so you won't accuse me of being sly.'

'Crestfallen' was the word, she decided, looking at his face. For a moment he stared at her. Then he said, 'It won't wash, Dulcie. Cobsey is dead against you because of your uncle.'

She shrugged. 'I'm going to try anyway. What have I got to lose?'

'Not a lot! Go ahead!' He gave a dismissive wave.

Dulcie hesitated. She suspected that Gus was right. Cobsey still hated having a female in the newsroom. But he *had* agreed, she told herself, that she should be given a probationary period. Dulcie was under no illusions. Cobsey hoped that she would eventually see the error of her ways. Dulcie was equally determined not to.

Taking a deep breath, she walked purposefully towards the office and knocked on the door.

'Come in.'

She went in. George Cobbs lowered *The Times*, slipped a peppermint into his mouth and regarded her from beneath bushy eyebrows. 'Well?'

'Mr Cobbs, I wondered if you would consider allowing me to —'

The eyebrows drew together in a frown. 'Most unlikely!' he said.

'I don't suppose you realise that I actually *know* the dead man's family and I —'

'Gus is covering the murder.'

His expression was fierce but otherwise unreadable.

She pressed on. 'I know but since I also know —'

'Where's the piece on the cathedral? The repairs to the stonework?'

She stared at him blankly. Stonework? Oh Lord! She suddenly remembered. It was one of a list of tinpot assignments intended to bore her into resignation. She said, 'I haven't had a chance to —' and stopped again. She was getting flustered.

He rustled the newspaper. 'I want it on my desk within the hour.'

'But Mr Cobbs, what I wanted to suggest is that I might *help* Gus with the murder story —'

'He doesn't need your help, Miss Moore.'

'— Because I have such good contacts, Mr

Cobbs, and I know I could —'

With a savage movement he screwed up *The Times* and hurled it to the floor. 'Miss Moore,' he said, his face reddening. 'You know nothing. Nothing at all. I think you are forgetting who runs this office.' A large vein pulsed in his forehead, momentarily distracting her. 'You might have a doting uncle who owns the *Standard* but until it is decided otherwise, I run this newspaper. *I* decide who does what and your job — *one* of your jobs — is the restoration work on the cathedral. Now get on with it!'

He snatched up his paper and began to smooth it out, muttering to himself about uppity women. Unwisely Dulcie stood her ground.

She made one last attempt. 'Mr Cobbs, I —'

'Get out!' he yelled, leaping to his feet. 'Are you deaf, dumb and blind, girl? GET OUT!'

Resisting the urge to run, Dulcie walked out. She was smarting under the injustice and her face burned with humiliation. She guessed that Gus had heard Cobsey's side of the exchange and she was aware that he now watched her ignominious retreat with delight. Rather than give him the satisfaction of saying so to her face, she walked right past him, pausing only to snatch up her notebook and a pencil. She went out of the office and down the steps. Once in the street she drew in gulps of fresh air and tried to think calmly and rationally. As she walked towards the cathedral she was seething. They might think they had won that round, she told herself, but the game wasn't over yet. She had a couple of aces up her sleeve and she was playing to win.

Entering the precincts of Canterbury cathedral through the Christ Church gate, Dulcie walked slowly round the outside, shielding her eyes from the sun as she stared upwards. Restoration of the stonework was going on somewhere but she saw no sign of it. She could, however, hear small chipping sounds which seemed to be coming from the roof. High in the sky, the midday sun shone down on to the the towering stone walls, softening the angular contours, casting insignificant shadows. From outside, the glory of the windows was lost and Dulcie spared them little attention as she moved round the familiar building. Moving closer to the walls she laid a hand on the nearest buttress. It was warm to the touch. How many times had she, Annabel and the boys wandered these same precincts, she wondered with a rush of nostalgia. Together they had searched out every nook and cranny of the cathedral's exterior and they were equally at home inside. Nave, choir, presbytery. Unhesitatingly, she could lead a visitor to the archbishop's throne, Becket's shrine, Lanfranc's burial place. She had done so many times.

As she passed the southeast transept the sounds grew louder and she suddenly came across a tower of wooden scaffolding which clung, fungus like, to Trinity Chapel. From somewhere above her a man shouted 'Oi! Mind yourself!' She realised suddenly that something was being lowered to the ground and she jumped back, out of the way.

'You could have been raspberry jam, miss!'

A workman had come down from somewhere above her, clinging to a large open-sided crate. Tied securely to this was what seemed to be a curving section of worn stonework. Dulcie realised that she had stumbled on the restoration work.

'I'm from the *Canterbury Standard*,' she told him and, as always, the words gave her a thrill.

'Oh yes?'

'I'm writing about the restoration.' She waved the notebook by way of proof.

'You'd best talk to the dean,' he said. 'He's in charge of all that.'

'The Dean? Oh, well I will then. But I'd like to talk to you first, if you don't mind.' He looked dubious so she rushed on. Pointing to the stonework that had been lowered she said, 'It's all crumbling away. How can you possibly repair it?'

'We don't. We replace it. Carve out another piece just like this and put it back in place of the worn section.'

'That can't be easy.' She wrote rapidly.

He shrugged. 'It's a matter of tracing round it to reproduce the shape and then carving out a copy. Then up it goes and is popped back into place.' He smiled, apparently warming to the idea of being interviewed. 'Did you know that the original stone comes all the way from Caen in France. Don't ask me how to spell it. Now they match it exactly. That way it blends in nicely and when you look up at it you won't notice the repairs.'

She searched her mind for suitable questions. 'How long have you been a stonemason and what made you take up this line of work?'

His father had been in the trade, he told her, also his uncle and grandfather on his father's side. He'd never thought of doing anything else. Of course he'd had to start small. 'Did a stint on gravestones. You know — "Here lies Ernest Bloggs". I put a couple up in the garden but my Mum hated them. Very superstitious, my old Mum. Said it was bad luck. Reckoned that somewhere an Ernest Bloggs could snuff it because of me. So I done one that said. "Here lies Rinso". but she wasn't amused.' He grinned. 'Then I done a year or two on general building but I didn't go much on that. Out in all weathers. But I was waiting my chance, see. Miss. As soon as there was a vacancy here I applied. Been here ever since. Probably drop dead on the job like my uncle.'

'He dropped dead?'

'Literally.' He laughed. 'Hot summer's day it was, like today. Drank a couple of beers with his sandwiches, like, and, what with the hot sun, it went to his head. Fell off the scaffolding!'

A yell from above reminded him that there was work to do and after thanking him Dulcie left him to it. Talking to the dean sounded interesting but where would she find him? She decided to try inside the cathedral. The interior was warmed by the coloured sunlight that angled through the mote-laden emptiness. As always, the vastness took her breath away and its beauty assaulted her senses. She stood in the doorway, waiting for her eyes to accustom themselves to the diminished light. A quick glance revealed no sign of anyone who might be the dean. Two men stood together at the back, pointing out the architectural features and conversing in hushed tones. An organist was practising. A woman knelt alone in one of the front pews, her head bowed in prayer.

Dulcie spoke to the two men but neither of them knew where she might find the dean. She decided to ask whoever was playing the organ and was halfway down the aisle when she glanced again at the kneeling woman. There was something familiar about the dark hair and slim shoulders. A few seconds later she stopped abruptly.

It was Annabel.

Dulcie's first instinct was to withdraw quickly before she was recognised. Annabel had behaved very spitefully towards her earlier and Dulcie had no wish to provoke further hostility. She told herself that by leaving her to her prayers she was simply respecting Annabel's desire for privacy. But before she could come to a decision, Annabel turned tear-stained eyes towards her.

'Annabel! Oh my dear!' Immediately forgiving the harsh words with which they had so recently parted, Dulcie moved quickly forward. Annabel struggled to her feet. 'Don't talk!' Dulcie whispered, putting her arms round the trembling shoulders. 'Just cry if you want to. I know how you must feel.'

Annabel swayed and almost fell forward, so that Dulcie found herself supporting her. After a few moments she coaxed her down on to the seat and sat beside her, murmuring any words of comfort that felt appropriate. Eventually the tears subsided but Dulcie could see that Annabel was far from recovered. Her breathing was ragged and she shook uncontrollaby.

'Annabel, are you ill?'

A shake of the head was her only answer.

'Are you sure? You look so pale.'

Annabel gave her a strange look. 'I'm not ill. I'm sick,' she said and her mouth twisted into an anguished smile.

'Sick?' Dulcie stared at her. Not ill but sick? Was she confused? 'Does anyone know that you're here?' She suddenly recalled the article Gus had written. 'Shouldn't you be resting in bed?'

'No. No one. I mean yes — I should. But I had to come. Oh Lord, Dulcie, I'm in such trouble. Such terrible trouble — and I can't tell anyone. You've no idea!'

Dulcie forgot that she was a reporter for the *Canterbury Standard.* She remembered only that they had once been so close and, even now, had been drawn together by Clive's death. 'You can talk to me,' she assured her. 'Whatever it is I swear I won't tell a soul. If it helps to tell someone —'

'Oh God! I want to but I can't! And if I told you, you'd despise me. I know you would.'

'I would never despise you,' Dulcie protested, guiltily trying to forget all the unkind things she had said about her at different times.

A cold fear clutched suddenly at Dulcie's heart. Had this anything to do with Clive's murder? If so she, Dulcie, had no right to offer confidentiality. Could Annabel have had anything to do with the death? The suspicion grew in her mind . . . But no. It was ridiculous. Unthinkable. And why should she want Clive dead? Angry with herself she tried to shut out the unwelcome thought.

Annabel wiped her eyes, sighing convulsively. 'It's all so terrible,' she murmured. 'Everyone I loved . . . It can never turn out right.'

'What do you mean by "everyone"?'

'Poor Clive and Mother and Father, Teddy —'

'Teddy? What's Teddy got to do with this?' As her fear grew, her voice sharpened. 'Don't try to tell me that Teddy is involved because that can't be true. I know him better than anyone.'

Annabel shook her head. 'You think you do. I thought I did. But we were wrong. Not that I blame him. It was all my fault.'

Dulcie stood up. 'Tell me!' she said. 'I want to know. All these hints about Teddy.'

'I can't tell you. I promised him and I can't break my word. Don't you see? That's what's so awful. I can't confide in anyone. God help me! What am I to do?' She began to cry again.

With Annabel's words, Dulcie felt a shiver of apprehension and knew suddenly that she didn't *want* to hear any more. What she wanted was to put a great distance between herself and Annabel's secret. She needed to hurry away but couldn't bring herself to leave Annabel in this hysterical state. She might try to kill herself. Dulcie knew that she mustn't allow Clive's tragedy to be followed by another.

She said, 'You are to wait here, d'you hear me? I'm going to find a taxi and you're going straight home. Whatever it is, you should tell your parents. No matter how upset they are, they'll help you.' She stared down at her friend's bent head and her voice hardened. 'But don't, I beg you, drag my brother into this mess. Teddy would never hurt a fly and you know it.'

She almost ran out of the cathedral and into the sunlight, reflecting bitterly on the fact that her kind deed had rebounded. In retrospect, comforting Annabel had been a mistake. The suspicion that Teddy might somehow be involved in Clive's death had shattered her own peace of mind.

Later, while she walked Max, she thought

hard about the events of the day. She had taken Annabel home to her parents who were becoming worried by her unexpected absence. Offered a cup of tea, Dulcie had stayed on for half an hour, while Annabel was persuaded by her mother to go back to bed. Mr Roper, taking advantage of their absence, had confided that between his daughter and his wife he was having 'quite a time of it'. The doctor seemed to think that Annabel was suffering some kind of emotional breakdown that was affecting her physically. She couldn't eat, he told Dulcie, and, if they did persuade her to accept a few mouthfuls of something light, she couldn't keep the food down. She muttered to herself for long periods — they could hear her in the bedroom. She was also difficult to talk to — flying into rages, bursting into tears or refusing to speak at all.

Dulcie's thoughts were interrupted by the arrival of a small poodle in the charge of an elderly man approaching from the opposite direction. Both dogs strained at their leads but, while the poodle simply wagged its tail cautiously. Max threw himself into a frenzy of affectionate greeting — a tangle of legs and tail, leaping about and barking furiously.

'Max! Stop that!' She smiled apologetically at the man. 'He's not usually so silly,' she lied, tugging ineffectively at Max's lead. 'Sit, Max! Sit!'

The man snatched up his poodle and clutched him protectively. He muttered something which sounded remarkably like 'vicious animal' and edged round the frantic dog who was now tripping over his own lead.

'Max isn't vicious,' said Dulcie, offended. 'He's just playful. He makes a lot of noise. He doesn't mean —' She broke off because the man and the poodle had hurried away. Max's wagging tail faltered and his enthusiasm collapsed under this disappointment. Gently Dulcie untangled his legs.

'Now see what you've done!' she grumbled. 'You scared them. You'll be getting a bad reputation if you don't learn to behave yourself.' She remembered something her mother had once said to her. Staring into his brown eyes she added, 'You'll never have any friends!'

Max stared miserably after the retreating poodle, whining softly in his throat. Dulcie leaned down to give him a hug. 'Of course you will! I didn't mean it. I'm not cross with you.' She fished a biscuit from her pocket and he gulped it noisily, spattering crumbs on to the pavement. For a moment she stood watching him as he sniffed eagerly for the last one. Was he ever going to improve? Aunt Harriet thought there was little hope for him and maybe she was right. Possible he was older than they thought, already too old to learn.

With a sigh she turned from Dover Street into Oaten Hill and paused to stare at a black Rolls Royce, one of the fleet of Scam's Taxis. Seeing Max take a suspicious interest in one of the gleaming wheels, Dulcie tugged him away and walked on. Inevitably her thoughts returned to Annabel. What on earth had she meant by all those hints about Teddy? Dulcie took a deep breath and tried to face up to the idea that was beginning to demoralise her. Could Teddy possibly have had anything to do anything to do with Clive's death? On the night before the wedding, had he perhaps asked to meet Clive to beg him not to marry Annabel? If so, perhaps they had argued. An argument might have developed into a fight. *Had Teddy accidentally killed his erstwhile friend?*

She said 'Please God, no!'

She paused while Max inspected a lamp-post and found it suitable. They turned right again into Old Dover Road and were half way along it when she saw the detective waiting for her. At once her throat dried and her heart raced. Was this bad news? He whistled at the dog and as Max leaped forward, the lead slipped from her hand.

'Must you?' she shouted.

He said, 'Sorry!'

Max reached him and began to jump up and down, his tail wagging furiously.

'He was being good,' she told the policeman accusingly. 'Now look what you've done.'

'Don't blame me,' he protested. 'He's your dog. Tell him to sit.'

Struggling to hold the dog back Dulcie said sternly, 'Max, *sit!*' Nothing happened. She hadn't really expected any reaction but repeated the command anyway. Ignoring her completely, the dog hurled himself at the policeman who held up a warning forefinger and said, 'Sit!'

Max immediately sat down, staring up at him as though he were some kind of god.

Hiding her astonishment, Dulcie said, 'Good boy!' Mortified, she threw the dog a reproachful look. What was it about men and dogs, she wondered irritably. To the policeman she said, 'Why are you lying in wait for me?'

'Lying in wait?' He raised his eyebrows humorously and picked up the dog's lead.

Dulcie was not amused. 'Aren't you?'

'No. Your aunt said I'd meet you if I walked in this direction.'

'And now you have?' She held out her hand for the lead and began to walk back towards the house with Jack beside her.

'I want to talk to you about your brother, Miss Moore.'

The words echoed in her mind. 'He's away,' she said. 'Didn't they tell you? I presume you've been out to Grange Park in search of him.'

'I understand he's away. In Cornwall. I suppose.'

She thought rapidly. 'He manages the estate there. He might be in London on estate business.'

'Have you seen him lately? How does he seem?'

She stopped abruptly. 'He seemed perfectly normal. Why shouldn't he?'

'Not upset about anything?'

'No. I mean "yes". He was upset about Clive's death. Of course he was. We all were.'

'Your parents claim that they think he was at home the evening before the murder. They know he was there most of the time but they're not sure about all the time.'

Cold fear clutched her, paralysing her thoughts. 'So — so why — I mean what are you asking me? He wasn't with me.' Aware that she was stammering, she could do nothing to control it. 'If they said he was there then he was. But even if he — if he wasn't at Grange Park, what does it matter where he was?'

'The Ropers seem to think that he and Clive were not on friendly terms — because of Annabel.'

Max was winding his lead around her legs and she stepped out of it, thinking desperately. Her nightmare was becoming a reality. They suspected Teddy. But he couldn't have done anything so dreadful. 'Max! Keep still!'

'Shall I hold him?'

Dulcie gave him a look. 'You won't be able to manage him,' she said. 'He's rather lively.' As she said this her voice shook a little. Panic edged nearer. Blast! He would have registered the tremor and would know that she was upset.

'Let me try,' he said and held out his hand.

His eyes met hers and she suddenly wished that they had met under different circumstances. After a long moment she surrendered the lead. Perversely, she still hoped that Max would prove her right. Instead he trotted obediently along beside the detective, glancing up at him from time to time as though craving his approval. In the circumstances, the small betrayal hurt more than it should have done.

They walked on, waited for a break in the traffic then crossed the road together. Dulcie concentrated on behaving normally. She mustn't let him see just how shaken she was by his questions. Nor must he suspect that Teddy still loved Annabel.

She said, 'Naturally Teddy was upset when Annabel got engaged to Clive but that was ages ago. Probably a year or so. He's — I think he's come to terms with it.' Trying to add weight to this suggestion she added, 'Actually we're all rather pleased. She's very highly strung. Rather serious. Not at all the right person for Teddy.'

'So your brother wasn't with you late on Friday night?'

'I've already said so.' Immediately she wished she had been less dogmatic. It might have helped Teddy if she had pretended not to remember anything too precisely.

'So nobody knows exactly where he was.'

'He knows.'

His smile was thin. 'But he's left Canterbury.'

'That's not a crime. He doesn't have to stay here. Nor does he have to account for every minute of his time!'

He didn't answer.

So what did that mean, she wondered nervously. That Teddy *did* have to account for his whereabouts? She glanced at his face but his expression was unreadable. Presumably they had to learn how to do that. She wished she didn't find him quite so attractive. It would be so much easier to dislike him, so much easier to lie if it became necessary.

Outside her aunt's house he stopped. 'I won't come in.'

She almost pointed out that he hadn't been invited in but thought better of it. She had the feeling that Detective Sergeant Spencer was not a man to cross.

'Goodbye then,' she said, illogically wishing that he *had* wanted to spend a little more time with them.

He said, 'I shall be hoping to talk to your brother. Naturally we have to follow every lead, however slight. It's simply a matter of excluding people from our enquiries. It helps narrow the field. I'm sure your brother will be able to reassure me.'

Her panic increased. Was he trying to let her down lightly? Was that pity she saw in his eyes? For a moment she envied Annabel, tucked up in her warm bed, protected and cossetted. She, Dulcie, was out in the real world suffering the 'slings and arrows'. Still, she had no one to blame but herself. And she could cope for herself. It was Teddy who was her Achilles' heel. Dearest Teddy!, she entreated him silently.

Don't be mixed up in this. Please!

She said, 'Give him my love!'

'I will.' He smiled. 'Thank you for your time.' He nodded towards the dog and said, 'Goodbye, Max.'

Max was watching his every move with his head on one side, the picture of doggy devotion. Dulcie longed to shake him.

She watched the detective walk away and was overwhelmed by a feeling of helplessness. Perhaps she should warn Teddy. But that would suggest that she thought he had something to hide.

'Oh Teddy!' she whispered. 'Maybe I do!'

Chapter 5

Sylvie Hunt was curled up on the worn sofa with *Woman's Pictorial.* She was reading an article about how to give a room a 'face lift' without spending too much money. Maybe checked curtains would brighten up her gloomy little kitchen. Yellow and white would he nice . . . She had just finished the last square of a bar of milk chocolate when Bert arrived. He let himself in with the key she had given him and stood in the doorway, unsmiling. The short beard suited him. So did the wide-brimmed hat. He looked like a gangster out of a movie and he was carrying the carpet bag he'd collected on his last brief visit.

He said, 'Hi, Sylve.'

Hiding her surprise she said, 'Well, look what the cat's brought in!'

'It's good to see you, too! Got a newspaper?'

'You know I never read the papers. Always bad news. My Mum used to say —'

'Your Mum! God, you do go on!'

He looked round the room as though he'd never seen it before and she felt the usual prickle of resentment. So it wasn't the Ritz! Threadbare carpet and cheap pictures on the wall but what did he expect on her wages. She was a waitress, for heaven's sake, at the County Hotel and they paid her a pittance! At least she didn't owe the rent and had nearly paid off what she owed the Gas Board. He'd always been a stuck-up so-and-so.

'You could've knocked, Bert!' She remembered her curlers but it was too late now. He'd seen them. 'Want a cup of tea?'

'Wouldn't say "No".'

'Put the kettle on, then,' she suggested, turning the page and staring at a recipe for apricot jam. She wasn't going to wait on him hand and foot. She had enough of that at work. Bowing and scraping just to get a mingy tip. Smile at the customers, the manager said. Act friendly. All for sixpence. Threepence sometimes. Mind you, once it had been a shilling but he was an American so it didn't count.

Bert threw himself into an armchair, dropped the bag beside him and tossed the hat on to the table. It slid along the polished surface and fell on to the floor. 'Put the kettle on? What's up then, girlie? Lost the use of your legs?'

He looked a bit odd, she thought curiously. Like a cat about to spring. Something's upset you! she thought. Maybe she'd better put the kettle on. He could turn nasty when he was in one of his moods. With an exaggerated sigh she closed the magazine and dropped it on to the floor. 'I thought you'd be in South America by now,' she said. Two days ago he had said 'Goodbye' and now he was back without so much as a by-your-leave. She went into the kitchen, filled the kettle and lit the gas. From the doorway she asked, 'Didn't you like it? Too many gorgeous señoritas?'

'Very funny!'

'What then?' she pressed. 'You said the police'd be looking for you. Said you just wanted your stuff and it was "Goodbye forever". Now you're back. You just stroll in as though —'

'I didn't go.' He spat the words. 'Obviously. I didn't damn well go because I've got one more job to do.'

'So you knew that, didn't you?'

'I meant to hang about in Folkestone but bloody Foote says to keep well away. So here I am. *And* he's mucking me about. Cheating bastard!'

Sylvie murmured something noncommittal. So that was it. Money. She should have guessed. She said, 'You was right. They did come looking for you, the police. "Haven't set eyes on him", I said, looking all innocent. "Gone to Timbuctoo for a holiday." You know something? They've got no sense of humour.' She frowned. 'They might come back though. They might be watching the house.'

'No. They'll think I'm long gone. And you don't know anything. Simple as that. I shan't be here long anyway so don't start moaning.'

'Who is this Foote character when he's at home?'

'Never you mind. The less you know about anything the better.'

She glared at him. 'I might have had someone here. A gentleman friend. D'you ever think about that? That you're not the only man that fancies me?' He was silent and she frowned. 'What d'you mean, he's cheated you. How?'

'He hasn't given me all the money he owes me. I did a little job for him and he —'

She brightened. They'd had some good fun once upon a time. A bit of cash would be nice.

'He thinks he can push me around. Sitting there in his fancy office smoking his fancy cigars with that stupid smirk on his face! Well, he can't. He'll be smirking out of the other side of his face when I'm through with him.'

She liked being seen with Bert. Not that they could be seen in Canterbury since he'd legged it from the prison. They'd have to go somewhere else. She'd chance it if he would. He wasn't bad looking as blokes go and he could be a natty dresser when he was in funds. No cheap suits for Bert. He could be good company when he was in the right mood — but a spiteful sod when he wasn't. 'What little job?' she asked.

'I've told you to mind your own business.'

He was in a bad one now, obviously. She tried to concentrate. 'You mean that chap in Folkestone — the big cheese. The one you went to school with that had the rich Daddy?'

He gave her a sharp look. 'You talk too much.'

Actually he was the one who talked too much,

she thought. Get Bert drunk and he'd tell you his life story. All about the wife who ran off and left him two years after they were married. Not surprising, really, the way he behaved at times. If it wasn't the wife it was the orphanage or the swanky school and the lousy teachers. If it wasn't that it was the rough deal he'd had and the rotten tricks life had played on him. Poor old Bert. It was always someone else's fault. Never his. He'd got a chip on his shoulder as big as a rock. Still, he did look a bit down and, reluctantly, she found herself feeling sorry for him. Plus it sounded as though he had a bit of cash in his pocket.

She said, 'So d'you want to stay with me for a bit?' She wasn't going to let him think he could come and go as he pleased. Wouldn't hurt him to *ask*.

'I don't know. Maybe.'

She took down two mugs and added milk and sugar. Maybe she should tart herself up a bit. If he was staying she might make a few bob out of him. Especially if he'd just been paid for his 'little job' — whatever it was. Robbed a bank, maybe. She tried to imagine him with a gun and a scarf tied over his mouth and nose like they did in the pictures. She frowned. It was coming back now. He'd said something about 'sorting someone out'! Given someone a good hiding, probably. Still, he was right. What she didn't know wouldn't hurt her. She spooned tea into the pot and added boiling water.

'Got to spend a penny!' she said and went instead to the bedroom. She took out the offending curlers. As she did so she remembered the name of the school. Fell-something. No, Folliwell. No . . . Some kid had been killed, larking about. And he'd got the blame. Well, probably was his fault. He didn't know his own strength. Still, if she played her cards right . . .

She smiled at her reflection in what remained of the ancient mirror, fluffing out the blonde curls with her fingers. She dabbed on some powder and slid the lipstick round her mouth. Not bad for the wrong side of forty. It was her eyes. A kind of golden brown. Men loved them. She pushed the curlers into the pocket of her apron, took the apron off and threw it on the bed. She could still turn a man's head. She went back upstairs humming cheerfully. She'd jolly him along a bit. Perhaps he'd get a taxi and take her for a drink in Maidstone . . .

Clarice and James had been happily married for thirty years. The marriage had originally been a love match and, in the years that followed, neither had been tempted to stray. In the first few carefree years there had been no particular worries and the arrival of the two children had created the family. The children's childhood years had been reasonably trouble free. Their son had been an average scholar once he had adapted to life in Fellstowe. He had run away once but the headmaster had assured them that such escapes were fairly common — a normal part of the boarding school experience for some boys. Teddy had failed to get into Oxford. Dulcie had attended the Simon Langton School where she had proved herself an extremely clever pupil.

Only in the last few years had the occasional shadow disturbed the Moores' serenity. Annabel's betrothal to Clive had caused a disturbance and Dulcie's insistence on getting a job had upset them. In all other respects they were a contented couple and the wedding anniversary had prompted a celebration with friends.

Two other friends, the Hattons, had been invited to the dinner. Avril was tall and rather thin; her husband was distinctly portly. They lived at Dover and the two couples exchanged occasional visits. Wilfred had also been included. Teddy had returned and was doing his best to be sociable. Dulcie, watching him from the corner of her eye, was longing to talk to him privately but so far it had not been possible. She had, however, telephoned him at the estate office, to warn him that Spencer was on his way down to interview him. She had also suggested, somewhat deviously, that Teddy might time his journey home, so that they passed each other *en route*. The detective would then have had a wasted journey and Teddy would have gained another day. This way, she could talk seriously to Teddy before the detective did. She intended to make him explain Annabel's unkind remarks and to satisfy herself that he did have an alibi for the night of Clive's death.

Seated at the table Dulcie found herself opposite her uncle. Wilfred, the son of an earlier marriage, was only nine years older than her father, although he looked much older. Tall and stooped with an untidy beard, there was no family resemblance that Dulcie had ever been able to see. He had inherited an ailing family-run newspaper and had coaxed it back into the black by force of character. Later, after a bout of ill health he had handed over the running of the paper to his editor.

Now he smiled at Dulcie. 'So how are you and Cobbs getting along, eh? I thought you'd be a bit of a shock for his system!' he laughed wheezily. 'Pep the old boy up!'

She smiled. 'We don't see eye to eye, if that's what you mean, but I didn't think we would. He'll never forgive me for being foisted on him. You can't blame him really although I'd like a chance to prove myself.'

'Serve him right!' said Wilfred. 'He's had an easy time of it all these years. It was time to rock his boat!' He turned to the lady on his right and said, 'My niece works for the *Standard.* What d'you think of that, eh? A lady journalist!'

Avril Hatton looked at Dulcie. 'A journalist? Good heavens! Clarice didn't mention it.'

Dulcie's smile was brittle. 'Mother wasn't too pleased. But it's such interesting work. You've no idea. Recently I was talking to the men who are restoring the cathedral stonework. The stone comes all the way from Caen, you know.'

Avril's smile showed signs of strain. 'How fascinating. And how — how enterprising of you to take up such employment. I don't think our Felicity would ever be persuaded into — well, commerce. But then we wouldn't allow it anyway. And her fiancé would be very upset if she even suggested such a thing. Gordon appreciates a woman with all the conventional virtues. Some men are like that, aren't they.'

A look passed between her and her husband and Dulcie counted to ten. This was her parents' evening and she didn't want to risk spoiling it.

Teddy, however, had no such reservations. He said, 'Dulcie is anything but conventional, thank goodness. She's an original. Her mind is as sharp as any man's.'

Dulcie flashed him a look of gratitude. A shadow of the old Teddy, riding to the rescue.

Avril stiffened slightly. 'There's nothing wrong with our daughter's mind —' she began.

Her husband said, 'Women can be too clever for their own good!'

Teddy looked at Avril, his eyebrows raised. 'Ignore that unchivalrous remark, Avril. I'm sure Hugh looked for an intelligent partner when *he* went a'wooing!' He smiled. '*And* found one!'

Dulcie almost laughed as, wrong-footed, Hugh opened his mouth and closed it again.

Wilfred did laugh. 'That's put you in your

place, Hugh! You can't get the better of these two, believe me! They hunt in a pack! I always said I'd marry when I met an intelligent woman but I never have. Make what you like of that!'

Hastily Clarice intervened. 'Oh here comes Agnes. I must admit I have quite an appetite tonight. I spent several hours in the garden and that always makes me hungry. I adore the rose garden but taking off the dead heads is such a labour. All that reaching across is hard on the back.'

The prawns in aspic were served and the conversation veered towards safer subjects. A toast was drunk to thirty years of marriage and everyone settled down to serious eating and drinking. A goose with all the trimmings. Covertly Dulcie watched her brother, unhappily aware that he was drinking too much. Trying to blot out — what?

Avril was confiding that they had been forced to dismiss their daily woman. 'Her young man was round at the back door every day!' she grumbled. 'Nice looking, I'll admit, but we had told Mary right from the start. Don't go too far. He was just getting too persistent. She's a silly little thing at the best of times and he was turning her head. She was warned but she took no notice and now she has to go.

Her husband drained his glass. 'You haven't told it all, Avril.'

She blushed. 'Oh well! I wasn't going to but —' She glanced round surreptitiously. 'The silly girl was being sick every morning and you know what that means!'

'No?' said Dulcie who didn't know anything about the facts of life. Her mother had promised to instruct her 'before your wedding night' — which could mean a long wait.

Wilfred, flushed, said loudly, 'What did it mean, Avril?' and roared with laughter.

Agnes refilled his glass and made the rounds of the table, her expression impassive.

Dulcie glanced enquiringly at her mother. Clarice, too, had drunk a little too much. Flustered and rather bright eyed, she whispered, 'She was in the family way, dear.'

Dulcie blinked. 'You mean — ?'

Her mother mouthed the words. 'Going to have a baby!'

Avril said, 'She's been a naughty girl!'

Teddy said rather too quickly, 'Isn't that a rather old-fashioned attitude these days?'

There was an awkward silence. Dulcie glanced at his face and was shocked by his expression.

He said, 'Who knows the circumstances? Perhaps she wasn't naughty. Perhaps she was forced to do something — against her will. It does happen, you know. Why does everyone assume that the woman's always to blame?'

His voice had risen and his eyes were dark with emotion. Dulcie heard the suppressed anger in his voice but her mind was on something else. What had Annabel said — that she was not ill but sick. *Sick.* Oh no! That was impossible! She busied herself with a forkful of potato, pushing it aimlessly round the plate. Could Annabel and Clive — ? She frowned. Was that what Annabel had been trying to say — that she was going to have Clive's child? That meant that Clive must have done something — that they must have been *intimate.* But surely Annabel would never have allowed it. She would have struggled: fought him off. Ugly images presented themselves and she felt a sudden loathing for Clive. The word 'ravished' floated into her mind. Was that what it meant? How could Clive have done such a despicable thing? And now he had got himself killed and there would be no wedding!

Wilfred said, 'What — rape?'

Avril coloured and James said, 'Steady on, Wilfred!'

Wilfred tutted. 'It's only a word. And that's what Teddy's talking about, isn't it?'

Dulcie kept her gaze on her plate. Rape. She knew that rape was sex without the woman's consent. But was that really what Teddy meant? He would surely never speak of Annabel in that dreadful way. He had said he still loved her.

Clarice glanced appealingly at her husband and James said, 'I was reading about poor old Lawrence yesterday. Sad, the way he died. A new novel about to come out and he won't be here to read the reviews. Damned bad luck, whichever way you look at it.'

'All I'm saying,' said Wilfred, ignoring him, 'is that if the girl was raped then she wasn't a silly girl or a naughty girl. She was the unfortunate victim of an attack.'

No one spoke.

Dulcie allowed herself a quick look round the table. Avril was dabbing her mouth with a table napkin. Hugh was concentrating on his food. Her parents were exchanging mortified glances and Wilfred was grinning with delight. She looked at Teddy. He was staring fixedly at his plate. So *that* was it, she thought. Teddy must have found out about Annabel's predicament. But how had he found out — unless either Annabel or Clive had told him? She felt suddenly cold. If Clive had confided in Teddy — or more likely still, if *Annabel* had confided in him — Teddy may have given Clive a hiding that had turned into something worse? Her appetite had disappeared. Slowly she laid down her knife and fork. It was all falling into place so neatly. She *must* talk to Teddy alone.

Teddy said, 'For once Uncle Wilfred and I see eye to eye on something.'

Clarice said hastily, 'Would anyone like any more goose? Or vegetables?'

Both Hugh and Wilfred said 'Yes' and Agnes was summoned.

Avril wagged a finger at her husband. 'Remember what the doctor said!' She turned to Clarice. 'The doctor's worried about his blood pressure and wants him to lose a little weight. Sadly, Hugh has never understood the word "moderation"!'

Wilfred said, 'Nonsense. A man's got to eat!'

Clarice smiled. 'I know it's terribly unpatriotic of me but I'm so glad the Silver Jubilee celebrations are over. All that fuss and those frightful street parties!'

Dulcie, recognising yet another change of subject, agreed a little too heartily. Agnes came in and plates were replenished.

Clarice looked at Dulcie's plate. 'Why Dulcie, you've hardly touched your food.'

Seizing the opportunity, Dulcie said, 'I'm feeling a little faint from the heat.' She looked at Teddy. 'Would you take me into the garden for a moment or two?'

Without waiting for an answer she stood up but at that moment the front doorbell rang and they all waited.

Agnes came into the room and whispered something to James. He frowned. 'Can't hear a word you say, woman. Speak up.'

After a small hesitation Agnes said, 'There's a detective to see Teddy, sir.'

Dulcie, shocked, sat down heavily.

There was a short silence and then Teddy stood up. 'Please carry on without me,' he said with a stiff smile. 'I'm sure this won't take long.'

Dulcie watched him go with a sense of impending disaster.

After a long and awkward silence, Wilfred said, 'They've never caught that Parker blighter — the one who escaped from the prison. They reckon he's miles away by now. He certainly will be if he's got any sense. They're saying it was an inside job. One of the warders, maybe. Bit of cash changing hands. That sort of thing.'

'Oh that's dreadful!' said Avril. 'Surely the warders are above that sort of thing.'

James said, 'What's that? Warders?'

Dulcie could see the effort he was making and guessed that her mother must also be feeling desperate.

Hugh nodded. 'They think the breakout was planned with help from someone on the inside. I'm afraid it's a sign of the times. Corruption everywhere. Even at government level if you ask me.'

Clarice drank deeply and Dulcie watched with growing alarm. The happy celebration dinner was falling apart.

Dulcie said, 'I should think there have always been people in all walks of life who can be bought.'

Wilfred nodded as he cleared his plate for the second time. 'Always a Judas. Society will never change because people remain the same. Someone will always accept the pieces of silver. But that Parker's a swine from all I've heard. The last person who should be helped over the wall. Not that he was, of course. Smuggled out in the laundry van by all accounts. The question I ask myself is "Who put up the money — and why?" And why the dickens isn't the *Standard* on to it?'

'Gus was following that story,' Dulcie informed him, 'but now he's on the murder.

Maybe Cobsey — I mean Mr Cobbs — will let me ask around.' She looked at him appealingly.

He grinned. 'You want to follow it, you ask Cobbs. I've shot my bolt in that direction. Don't want the fellow to resign. He's too good at his job.'

Clarice said, 'Now Wilfred, don't encourage her, please. I don't want her chasing about after dangerous criminals. She might get herself hurt.'

Dulcie said suddenly, 'Shouldn't Teddy have a lawyer or somebody with him?' All faces turned in her direction. 'I mean, if they are asking him questions —'

James said, 'A lawyer? Teddy doesn't know anything. Why does he want a lawyer?' He looked at her in astonishment.

'I just thought — that is, I wondered . . .'

Hugh smiled at Dulcie. 'It's only suspects who need a lawyer, my dear. Teddy was once a friend of poor Clive. That's all. Nothing to worry about, I'm sure.'

It was the first time anyone had mentioned Clive and Dulcie felt guilty. Her mother had specifically asked her not to talk about it. 'Such a sad subject is bound to spoil things,' she had protested.

Now Avril said, 'That poor boy!'

Wilfred said, 'What his family must be going through.'

Hugh shook his head. 'And they can't even bury him. The police won't release the body. Apparently they might need it to —'

His wife said, 'Please dear! Not in the middle of dinner.' She turned apologetically towards Clarice. 'Men!' she exclaimed. 'They're worse than children!'

The door opened and Teddy came into the room. He was very pale. 'Father, can you spare a minute?' he asked and withdrew immediately.

Dulcie jumped to her feet but her father gave a quick look that stopped her in her tracks. She remained standing, staring after them as the door closed.

Clarice said, 'Oh dear! Now what's happened?' She looked frightened and Dulcie took hold of her hand.

From outside the door the sound of raised voices reached them. The front door opened and closed and they heard footsteps on the gravel outside. No one spoke as a car door was opened and then slammed.

Clarice said, 'I think they've gone. Thank goodness for that!' Her voice shook slightly.

Dulcie felt intuitively, that everything was far from 'all right'. She sat down slowly, sick at heart.

Her father came back into the room alone. All eyes were on him as he tried to speak. He cleared his throat and tried again.

'I'm sorry, Clarice,' he stammered. 'They've taken Teddy away — for questioning!'

Jack took the stairs two at a time and rapped on the door of Detective Inspector Berridge's office. Once inside he said breathlessly, 'I've got

Edward Moore downstairs, sir. I'm about to question him about the murder.'

'What's the connection?'

'He doesn't have an alibi, sir, and one of Brayne's drinking companions seems to think he had a grudge. Rivalry over a girlfriend. The woman Brayne was meant to marry.'

'Sounds promising. Keep me in touch.'

'Yes sir!'

'And if you have to lean on him go carefully. The Moores are not nobodies in this town. I don't want complaints or writs confusing the issue. Has he sent for a lawyer or his solicitor?'

'No sir. He refuses to get one. Says he had nothing to do with Brayne's death and doesn't need a solicitor.'

'But you don't think so?'

'I don't know, sir. He's the first one with a motive and no alibi.'

'Fair enough. Run with it but be careful . . . And good luck!'

'Thank you, sir.'

Outside the door of the interview room Jack smoothed his hair and straightened his tie. He took a deep breath, squared his shoulders and crossed his fingers. Uncrossing them he pushed open the door and went in. Blake was standing with his arms folded, trying to look threatening. Edward Moore was sitting at the small table, picking at a hole in the American cloth that covered it. Briefly Jack thought, This is Dulcie Moore's brother. She would probably never forgive him. For a moment he was disconcerted by just how much it mattered to him. Then he pushed the thought aside. He thought, This might be the man who killed Clive Brayne, and he settled for that.

He said, 'Cup of tea?'

Moore shook his head.

Jack glanced at his constable and indicated the chair next to the door. Blake sat down.

To Moore, Jack said, 'You've come here voluntarily to make a statement.'

'You could put it like that.'

'You're sure you don't want a solicitor or a lawyer?'

'I'm not the man you're looking for. I just want to answer your questions and then get home. You interrupted a dinner party. My parents thirtieth wedding anniversary.'

Jack thought, Bully for you, mate! He picked up a pencil and rolled it as though he were making a cigarette. 'Mr Moore, I'd like you to tell me exactly where you were on the evening of the seventh. From, say, six until the following morning.'

'I can't tell you. I've explained that already.'

'Why can't you?'

'It involves someone else. I'm sorry.'

'That's the oldest excuse in the book, Mr Moore.'

'It happens to be the truth.'

'Then let's establish where you *weren't* that evening. You weren't at home?'

'I was at home some of the time. Then I went out. I had to meet someone.'

'You had to meet Clive Brayne.'

'No.'

Jack thought, You're lying! 'But you did see Clive Brayne?'

'No I didn't.'

There was something in his voice — something intangible. An absence of the ring of truth, perhaps. Jack scribbled something meaningless on the notepad and stared at it thoughtfully. Let him wonder, he thought. Let him worry that he had said something significant. He leaned back, steepling his fingers, looking at his suspect thoughtfully, without real hostility. 'You did know the deceased, didn't you?'

'Of course. We grew up together and went to school together. But we weren't together the night he was killed.'

'Were you still friends, Mr Moore?'

'No. Hardly . . . But not exactly enemies either. I wanted to marry Annabel Roper and she chose him instead. Not quite earth shattering, Inspector. Let's say the friendship cooled. But there is no way I would have killed Clive. I'm not a violent man.'

Jack shrugged. 'People who are not violent sometimes act out of character. Under intense provocation or for some —'

'I did not kill Clive. You are wasting your time and mine. You could be letting the real killer escape.'

Jack glanced at Blake who shook his head in exasperation. 'Mr Moore, you had a motive and you will not tell us where you were at the time of the murder. What would you think in my shoes?'

'I might *think* I was guilty.'

'And are you?'

'No. I've told you. I had nothing to do with the murder.'

'So who else wanted him dead?'

'What d'you mean — "Who else"? *I* didn't want him dead!'

His voice had risen angrily and Jack resisted the urge to cheer. If Moore lost his temper he might well give something away. He had seen it happen. A moment's loss of control could open up the whole case.

He leaned forward. 'Who *would* want him dead?'

'I don't have any idea. Couldn't it have been an accident — or a case of mistaken identity?'

'It seems unlikely. Who were you with, Mr Moore? Was it a woman?'

He saw the tell-tale flicker in the eyes and added another line of scribble.

Moore said, 'I don't have to answer any more questions.' He stood up. 'I'd like to go home now. I've finished "helping you with your enquiries".'

Jack flicked the notebook shut. '*Sit* down, please Mr Moore. You're not going anywhere until you have satisfied me that you were not involved in the death of Clive Brayne. Were you?'

The man hesitated. 'Are you charging me? Am

I a suspect? Is that what you're saying?'

He was not so calm as he pretended, thought Jack triumphantly. It was dawning on Edward Moore that he might spend the night in a police cell.

'If you cannot tell me where you were on the night of the seventh then I cannot rule you out. So "Yes", you are a suspect, Mr Moore. If you are innocent I'd like to rule you out and, as you suggest, get on with the search for the killer. But how can I rule you out?' He drew a long breath. 'So sit down, Mr Moore.'

Reluctantly, Moore complied.

Jack straightened his shoulders and reopened the notepad. 'Would this lady you were with want you to be arrested for murder?'

'I wasn't with a lady.'

'I think you were!' He stabbed his finger in Moore's direction. 'I think you're lying. Lying about the woman or lying about the murder. Was it Annabel Roper, Mr Moore? We shall question her also.' He took a deep breath. 'Most women break down under questioning, you know.'

Moore's face reddened. 'Leave her alone, you bastard! She had nothing at all to do with this.'

'With what, Mr Moore? Nothing to do with what?' He felt a further stirring of excitement. His suspect was getting really rattled. Did that make him guilty? Not necessarily, but his instincts told him to press home the advantage.

'She had nothing to do with the murder and neither did I.'

'How can you be so sure? Have you seen her lately? Have you spoken about it? Have you decided on your story?'

'No! *No,* dammit!'

Moore closed his eyes, his mouth a thin line. Jack waited. He had seen Berridge break a man once. He hardly said a word. Afterwards Berridge had said, 'Never forget the value of a long silence. It unnerves them. Gives their imaginations a chance to work. Lets them ponder on their predicament.' Jack drew a small Christmas tree in the bottom corner of the page and added a star to the topmost branch.

Then he looked up. 'So you can't know for sure where she was on the night of the seventh. Nor can you possibly know that she *isn't* involved. You weren't together so you can't protect her, can you? And she can't protect you. I'll be having a little talk to Miss Roper before too long. I do hope she has an alibi.' He laid down the pencil. 'Do you want to change your mind, Mr Moore? Do you want to cooperate and prove your innocence?' There was no reply.

Moore leaned back and stared at the ceiling.

Jack felt a spurt of irritation. He said, 'Mr Moore, I shall be forced to keep you here until you can be questioned in front of a lawyer. Detective Constable Blake will show you where the telephone is. Probably a lawyer will not be available until tomorrow morning. You had better telephone your family.' To Blake he said, 'Then lock him up!'

He could see defeat in the eyes of his suspect plus fear of the unknown. Could he see guilt also? If it were there it was not glaringly obvious and Moore didn't look the type. But looks could be deceptive. Disappointed, Jack wondered if he had been too kind. 'If you have to, lean on him —' Berridge had said. Had the detective inspector been trying to tell him something? If so he had missed it. Maybe he should have played the hard man. *Frightened* the truth out of him. Because Moore *was* lying.

He watched Blake and Moore leave the room then buried his face in his hands. He would have another chance tomorrow when the man had been locked up for the night — probably for the first time in his life. Hopefully he'd be softened up by the experience. The trouble was that time was running out. Was Moore his man? It didn't feel quite right and yet there was motive and opportunity and the lack of a fireproof alibi. It should be him. But if it was then he had no evidence that wasn't circumstantial. He needed a finger or footprint to place him at the scene of the crime — or a hair on the dead man's jacket. Perhaps the forensic boys would come up with something.

Time was always the enemy. A trail could go cold so easily. Moore had been right about one thing. A few hours concentrating on the wrong man could allow the real perpetrator to slip through the net. And if he didn't make an arrest soon they would have to call in the Yard and his chance would be gone. But arresting the wrong man wouldn't help. It seemed too unlikely that solving the murder would be as easy as this. The odds were against it being the first suspect. He groaned with frustration. But upstairs Detective Inspector Berridge was waiting for his report. He went back upstairs and knocked on the door.

Later that night he arrived back at his lodgings in St Peter's Place and found a letter from Judith waiting for him on the hallstand shelf. Feeling guilty he took it upstairs and pushed it behind the clock. He knew what it would say and felt too tired to cope with her reproaches. He went downstairs and discovered that, as usual, his dinner was on a plate above a saucepan of simmering water in the kitchen. A nearby tray contained a small dish of trifle. From the living room he could hear loud snores and music. Mr and Mrs Smith were listening to the wireless. As he went upstairs the elderly landlady poked her head out of the door. As always, year in, year out, she wore a knitted hat. Jack suspected that perhaps she was going bald.

'I hope that dinner's still hot, Mr Spencer, and not all dried up. You're late tonight.'

'Yes. But I'm sure it'll be fine, thank you.'

'Nice bit of neck of lamb and mashed and peas. Hope the gravy hasn't dried up.'

He smiled down at her. 'It'll be fine.'

'Found the murderer yet?'

'Not yet. But we're questioning somebody.'

'Well, I hope you find him! It was all in the *Standard.* Nasty business. I was saying to Mrs Next-door, "We don't expect murderers in Canterbury. This is a respectable town".' She glanced at the hallstand. 'Oh you've found your letter. Nice surprise for you. From your young lady, isn't it?'

He muttered something appropriate and retreated up the stairs, thus avoiding a long conversation. He liked the Smiths but the wife was a born chatterbox and tonight he was too tired to cope with her ramblings.

He ate the meal which refreshed him and washed it down with a small bottle of beer. He wanted to get a good night's sleep. Must be at his best tomorrow. Reluctantly, he reached up to the mantelpiece for Judith's letter. Opening the envelope he was surprised to see a photograph tucked into the folded sheets. The smiling face was endearingly familiar. Serious eyes, brown hair worn unfashionably long, a serene smile. Judith was four years older than he was, an amateur artist of considerable talent. The sort of woman he had always imagined himself marrying. He stared at the likeness, missing the *frisson* of desire that it sometimes aroused in him. Suddenly, uninvited, another image sprang into his mind. A young, vivacious face framed by neat blonde waves. He saw again the excitable blue eyes and the perfect and so vulnerable mouth.

Heard the stammer in her voice as she defended her brother. He also recalled what he had seen of the slim young legs with the dog's lead twisted around them. To his surprise he felt a rush of tenderness followed by something decidedly more masculine.

'Jack! Jack!' he muttered. What on earth had got into him? He must not even think about Dulcie Moore. She was the sister of a suspect. He opened the letter from Judith and began to read.

My dearest Jack

I simply have to write again even though this correspondence is becoming rather one-sided! Writing to you seems to bring us closer just for a while. It is so long since I heard from you and I wonder if perhaps a letter from you has gone astray in the post. If it has then I forgive you wholeheartedly. But darling Jack, a day without word from you is a week. A *week* is forever! I hope the enclosed snap will remind you of what you are missing!

I read about the dead man found in one of your churches and assume you are involved with that. Of course I do not expect you to put pen to paper at the end of a long, hard day but could you possibly get up ten minutes early one day? Just to drop me a line. I will settle for a postcard of the cathedral as long as you have signed it and added a few kisses!

You know I love you. I cannot wait until we have settled our future together but Mother thinks you want to wait for your promotion before we make it official. Maybe solving this murder will hasten the process. I shall keep my fingers crossed.

She sends you her love. I visited your mother yesterday in case she had heard from you but she hadn't had a letter either. Mavis takes good care of her. The house was like a new pin as always.

She went on, talking about her painting and a forthcoming art exhibition to which she was contributing several water colours. She signed the letter. 'Your devoted Judith'.

There was a PS.

Jack, We *must* be together for your birthday which won't be long now. Please, darling, *do* try and arrange to have a few days' leave.

He sighed heavily. She was, of course, a dear, sweet girl. She loved him and assumed that they were going to be married. He hadn't proposed but he knew that eventually he must. All the parents approved.

He recalled Dulcie Moore's awful dog, leaping up and down. What did she call it? Max! He shook his head and carefully propped the photograph of Judith against the clock. In his mind's eye he saw Dulcie's indignant expression as she protested 'He was being good. Now look what you've done!' He wished suddenly that he had an excuse to see her again.

Confused, he glanced at the clock. Poor Judith. It was too late to answer her letter. Maybe tomorrow, he told himself.

'Wednesday the twelfth, five past ten, in the presence of his legal representative, Mr Dennis Twighton . . .'

Stanley scribbled madly in the notebook. Jack gave his suspect an uncompromising stare. Moore hadn't shaved and there were dark shadows under his eyes. They said he had refused anything to eat or drink. Doubtless he had slept only fitfully, if at all. Being locked up was a demoralising experience for all but the most hardened criminals. For Moore it would have been devastating. But devastating enough to shake the truth out of him? He turned to Twighton, the solictor. A self-important prig, in Jack's opinion. Round-faced with a large mouth.

'Have you and your client had enough time to confer?'

'Yes we have.'

Twighton had made himself a little too comfortable, Jack thought irritably. His arms were crossed over his chest and he had stretched his legs out in front of him. Classic, thought Jack disparagingly. Trying to suggest a disregard for the might of the law: encouraging the suspect to feel less threatened. Despite his efforts, though,

Moore still looked ill at ease but with just a hint of defiance in his eyes. We'll have to get rid of that, Jack thought. The question was — what, if anything, had Moore confessed to Twighton? Twighton was no actor and he looked calm enough. Almost bored. Had Moore confessed that he was with a lady? If so then Twighton knew he *did* have an alibi and couldn't have committed the murder.

'So, Mr Moore, would you please take us through the evening and night of Friday, 7 June,' he began.

'I've nothing to add.' Moore stared past him, arms folded, head erect. If he felt himself at a disadvantage he was not going to admit it. Jack felt a grudging spark of admiration for the man.

'Let's start at six pm,' he suggested briskly. 'Where were you at that time, Mr Moore?'

'At home — Grange Park. I've already —'

'Just answer the questions, please.'

Twighton said, 'My client has nothing to add, Sergeant.'

'Detective Sergeant.' Give them an inch . . .

Twighton pursed his lips. 'My client has nothing to add. He's told you all he is prepared to say.'

Jack sighed. 'And have you advised him on the matter? Have you informed him of the risks he takes if he refuses to cooperate with us?'

'He knows. It's his choice.'

Jack turned back to his suspect. 'Did you see

Clive Brayne on the night he was murdered? Yes or no?'

'No.'

'Were you at any time in the church of St Alphege on the night of 7 June? Yes or no?'

'I was not.'

'Yes or no?'

'What's the difference?'

'I'm asking the questions. Were you at any time —'

'No! Oh, for God's sake!'

He was getting angry again.

Twighton gave an exaggerated sigh. 'You have nothing to connect my client to the crime. Absolutely nothing.'

Stanley looked up desperately. 'Sir, I can't keep up.'

Jack held up a hand. 'There's no rush.' He waited until Stanley finished writing. 'You're right, Mr Twighton. I have nothing that puts Mr Moore at the crime scene — yet. The report from the forensic laboratory is due at any time.' Jack glanced at Moore hoping for signs of alarm but saw nothing. 'You deny being at the scene of the crime and you deny seeing the victim.'

'That's right. I was with somebody else but I —'

'I'm not asking who you were with. Just answer the questions.'

Twighton glanced at his wristwatch and sighed loudly. 'Is this really getting us anywhere?

I'm due in court in less than an hour and —'

'Your client might be charged with murder, Mr Twighton.' Maybe he could shake the suspect's faith in his brief. 'Isn't that important to you, Mr Twighton? We might be locking him up. Taking away his freedom. Don't you think you ought to spare your client a little more of your time?'

Moore glanced at Twighton but said nothing.

Twighton, annoyed, stood up and reached for his briefcase.

Pressing home the point, Jack asked, 'What is it, this important case you *have* to attend? A burglary? A traffic offence? Your unfortunate client *might be* accused of *murder!*'

Twighton's expression was venomous. 'Come off it, Spencer! I know what you're up to. You can't charge my client because he's innocent. You've got no incriminating evidence. He's being cooperative — up to a point.'

Jack seized his chance. As he brought his fist down on the table, he raised his voice. '*Up to a point?* Of course he's not cooperating,' he roared, 'and you damn well know it. He's hiding something and you know that, too! He had motive and opportunity — and he can't or won't give me an alibi! He could have done it!' He switched his attention to Moore. He leaned forward aggressively and shouted, 'You were there and you quarrelled and you killed him!'

Moore didn't even flinch. He said, 'I wasn't. We didn't. I didn't kill him.'

Disappointed, Jack continued to glare at him, allowing the silence to lengthen.

Twighton shrugged, making it clear that the histrionic show of temper didn't disturb him in the least. In a bored tone he said, 'Either charge him or let him go. He knows his rights. I know them. You know them.'

Moore said evenly, 'I didn't kill Clive and that's the truth. Twighton knows it but I can't prove it.' He looked at Jack. 'I'd like you to catch whoever did it but I honestly can't help you. I don't know anyone who would have had a reason to kill Clive. He was a thoroughly decent person. We weren't enemies and I'm sorry he's dead. If it *was* murder, I didn't do it.'

It sounded horribly like the truth. Jack hid his disappointment as well as he could. At last, to Stanley he said, 'Have you got all this?'

Stanley said, 'Just about, sir.' He wrote furiously.

Jack said, 'Interview ends at ten twenty-five.'

A moment later they all watched Stanley close the notebook. Jack got up with as good a grace as he could muster and walked to the door.

Twighton glared. 'Well?'

'Your client can go now.' Jack looked at Moore. 'Where will you be for the next week? Here or in Cornwall?'

'I don't know yet.'

'Please inform us if you intend to leave Canterbury — and don't even *think* of leaving the country!'

He walked out, finally convinced that Moore was not the man they were looking for. A whole day wasted, he thought bitterly.

Back to square bloody one!

Chapter 6

Thursday dawned with a clear sky and rising temperature which was offset by a southerly breeze. As Dulcie cycled towards Annabel's home she caught an occasional hint of what Harriet called 'the Canterbury whiff' — a curiously pungent smell which drifted from the various manufacturers in the city — the tannery, breweries and a jam factory. Today, however, she paid it no attention, having more important things to worry about. She had risen early and now, just after seven, was on her way to 'shake the truth from Annabel'! — a prospect which did not appeal. But one which must be attempted, she reminded herself. Her brother had been taken away the previous night and was being held at the police station where he was 'helping the police with their enquiries' — as they euphemistically put it. He might, at any moment, be formally charged with the murder and Dulcie had committed herself to proving him innocent.

She dared not be late getting to work so her confrontation with Annabel needed to be concluded by twenty to nine to allow her time for the return journey. The question of Annabel's pregnancy would have to be raised and as Dulcie steered her way along Westgate Street and through St Dunstan's Within she wondered just how to go about it. It might pay to come right out with it. Three ducks crossing the road ahead of her caused her to ring her bell loud and long and she watched them scatter in confusion. Minutes later, her bicycle propped nearby, she was ringing the doorbell.

The maid answered. When she saw who it was her eyes widened in dismay. 'Oh no! You can't come here! Not —'

'Why ever not?'

'Why because of —' She stopped and her hand crept to her mouth. 'I can't let you in. They won't see you.'

So the news about Teddy had gone round already. Dulcie felt her cheeks burn. Forcing a smile she said, 'We don't know that, do we? Please tell Annabel I'm here to see her — and that it's important.' For a moment it seemed that the maid would argue.

Dulcie said. 'You'll get into more trouble if you don't!'

At last the maid said. 'I'll tell them you're here,' and closed the door.

Astonished, Dulcie stared at the door. Maids were not usually so aggressive. She sighed. It was obviously going to be more difficult than she'd expected. Presumably Annabel had told her mother about the conversation they had had last time she came to the house. Maybe Mrs Roper had decided that she was no longer welcome: an undesirable, the sister of someone even *more* undesirable. It was hurtful but she would persevere.

Moments later the maid returned. 'Mrs Roper says she doesn't want to see you ever again and you're to go away.'

Dulcie registered the note of triumph. As the door began to close she wedged herself into the gap and resisted. 'I don't want to see Mrs Roper. I want to speak to Annabel and I shall stay here until I do. If it wasn't important I wouldn't *be* here.'

'They won't see you!'

'I want to speak to Annabel.'

'She's not even up.'

'I want to speak to Annabel. Tell her that if she won't see me I shall shout my message up to her bedroom. I don't think she'd like that.'

They glared at each other. At last the maid gave in. Leaving Dulcie in possession of the doorway she retreated into the house.

Finally Mrs Roper herself came to the door. She was wearing her nightdress, dressing gown and slippers and was holding a newspaper. She waved this accusingly at Dulcie.

'So it was Teddy!' She almost spat the words. 'Your own brother! His friend! After all they've been to each other. But I should have known. He was always jealous of poor Clive. Look at it!' She flourished the paper and Dulcie read, 'SUSPECT

HELD!'. Mrs Roper's face coloured furiously. 'It's all over the front page of the *Standard.* Your poor parents. I pity them from the bottom of my heart. I really do.'

Dulcie snatched the paper from her and began to read. Mrs Roper went on. 'How you have the cheek to turn up here at this hour of the morning I don't know. But then you always were an odd child, in my opinion. You and your precious brother make a fine pair.'

Ignoring this tirade, Dulcie read the first paragraph and saw for herself just how damning the report appeared. Edward Moore had been taken in for questioning regarding the murder of Clive Brayne . . . and charges could be expected. And Cobsey and Gus had done this! She wanted to bang their stupid heads together. On a previous occasion, when she had complained about a slanted article, Gus had replied, 'It's what sells the paper. It's called journalistic licence.' She hadn't accepted the concept then and today she was twice as sure that it was unethical. Struggling with her composure she handed back the newspaper with shaking hands.

'It was not Teddy,' she insisted. 'And Annabel knows it. And so should you. You've known him for years and you know he could never hurt anyone, let alone kill them. Annabel knows something she isn't telling and I must speak to her.'

Mrs Roper straightened her back indignantly. 'You'll do no such thing. Annabel is still sleeping. What she'll say when she sees this I shudder to think. You'll stay away from my daughter. That's not a request, it's a —'

'Mother!'

Annabel had appeared in the doorway behind her mother. 'I'm not sleeping, Mother, and you know it. Let Dulcie in. She's right. Whatever the paper says, it wasn't Teddy. I've something to say and you might as well both hear it — before Father comes back.' She gave Dulcie a beseeching look. 'Please stay. He's playing tennis with a friend. Mother talked him into it. She wanted to get rid of him for a while. He's like a bear with a sore head since —' Her voice faltered.

Mrs Roper thrust the newspaper into her daughter's hands. 'Read that!' she said. 'And then tell me you have anything to say to the sister of a murderer.' She looked at Dulcie furiously. 'My husband is taking this very badly. He never was very strong at times of crises. He's terribly depressed. Suicidal, almost. I thought it would do him good to get out of these four walls. Thank God for good friends.' She frowned suddenly and looked at her daughter. 'Something to say? What do you mean?'

Dulcie said gently 'Perhaps we should go in and sit down.'

'But —'

'Please Mother. This will be hard enough and I want Dulcie to hear it.'

Unwillingly Mrs Roper allowed herself to be led towards the drawing room and a few moments later the three of them were seated self-consciously. Dulcie inspected her hands which lay folded in her lap. Mrs Roper was staring in bewilderment at Annabel.

'Mother, something rather awful has happened and I'm deeply sorry but it wasn't all Teddy's fault. I take some of the blame for what happened. Oh no, Mother!' she said quickly, seeing her mother's expression. 'Not the murder. I don't know who killed Clive but I do know that it wasn't Teddy. He was with me at the time — in the summer house.' She glanced towards Dulcie who was now watching her attentively.

'The summerhouse? You and *Teddy?* The night before your wedding? I hardly think — !'

'I know, Mother. I'm not proud of what happened. It's all very dreadful but please hear me out.'

Unable to meet anyone's eyes, Annabel stared at the carpet and Dulcie could imagine what the revelations were costing her.

'Teddy wanted to meet me to persuade me to — to give up Clive and marry *him.*'

Mrs Roper gasped. 'Marry *Teddy!* Good God, the man's out of his mind!'

'Mother, please let me tell it all.'

'You mean there's *more?*'

Dulcie said quietly, 'Go on, Annabel.'

Mrs Roper pulled a handkerchief from her pocket and pressed it to her quivering lips. 'I'll swing for that man one of these days!' she muttered with a wild look in Dulcie's direction.

Annabel took a deep breath. 'He came to see

me because — because he wanted to marry me because —' She swallowed painfully and closed her eyes. 'Because I'm going to have a baby.'

The silence was almost frightening.

Dulcie said, 'Don't worry, Annabel. We'll all help you.'

Mrs Roper swayed. 'A baby? Oh no, dear! No!'

Annabel moved to kneel beside her. 'Mother, please try and forgive me. I can't go through with this if you don't say you forgive me.'

Dulcie said, 'But you were going to be married anyway. Why would you marry Teddy?'

Annabel's expression was unreadable.

Mrs Roper cried, 'When I think how fond I was of Clive! How I trusted him! Oh how could he do this to you? Oh God, your father will go out of his mind. This will *kill* him!'

Searching desperately for something positive to offer Dulcie said, 'But a little grandchild, Mrs Roper! How exciting!'

She regretted the foolish words immediately. 'Exciting' was not the way Mrs Roper would see it. 'Catastrophic,' would be her choice. Her daughter would be talked about throughout the city. A love child. Born out of wedlock because of the murder. They had so nearly got away with it. If only the wedding had gone ahead.

Mrs Roper appeared too stunned to speak. Annabel sat back on her heels and looked at Dulcie.

'You don't understand,' she said. 'It's not

Clive's child. It's Teddy's.'

Teddy's child.

It was Dulcie's turn to stare in shocked dismay. Teddy's child? But that was impossible. Clive, perhaps, could have done it but not Teddy. No, not her beloved brother. He would never . . . She swallowed hard, her mouth dry. It must have been Clive. She would never believe Teddy guilty of such an awful thing. It just wasn't in his nature to be brutish.

Mrs Roper was still coping with the news about the pregnancy. 'You'll have to go away, dear,' she stammered. 'Have the baby adopted. It happens all the time. No one need know if we're careful. Oh Annabel! Your father! How shall we tell him?' Tears welled in her eyes.

Annabel said, 'Mother, did you hear what I said? Teddy is the father. Yes, it's true. Please don't look at me like that. That's why he wanted us to marry but I couldn't bear to tell Clive what we'd done. Or you, Mother, or Father. Or anyone. I thought it would be best to marry and let Clive think it was his child. I made Teddy promise not to tell anyone ever. Poor Teddy!' Her voice cracked as she struggled to remain in control of her feelings.

Mrs Roper whispered, '*Poor* Teddy? How can you talk about *poor* Teddy? How could he — How could you let him — Oh!' She began to cry in earnest, long despairing sobs that tore through her, shaking her whole body.

Dulcie thought, Teddy's child! I'll be an aunt!

and, fleetingly, illogically the idea pleased her. Guilt followed. How could she find comfort in this tragedy?

Annabel said, 'I don't know what to do, Mother. You'll have to help me. Please!'

Mrs Roper sobbed, 'Oh my poor darling girl!'

Dulcie's mind was whirling. No wonder Teddy had spoken so kindly about the Hatton's disgraced maid. Sympathising with her plight . . . She tried to recall the conversation over dinner. 'Maybe she wasn't naughty . . .' 'Maybe she had been forced to do something against her will . . .' Her stomach churned suddenly. Was that what had happened between Teddy and Annabel? Suddenly, with sickening certainty, she knew that it had.

Mrs Roper stood up shakily, clutching her dressing gown round her. 'I can't stay here,' she said distractedly. 'I have to be on my own. I have to think. I'll get dressed and then I'll come back.' Without looking at either Dulcie or Annabel she made her way to the door.

Before she could think it over Dulcie asked, 'Did Teddy — did he force you?'

Annabel hesitated. 'He did, yes — but I blame myself, Dulcie. Partly. I admitted that I loved *him* and that was a big mistake. It was back in April when it happened. I keep wondering if it was all my fault. I should have pretended to be hopelessly in love with Clive. If I'd said it was over between me and Teddy —' She shrugged. 'It's easy to be sensible *now*. I keep asking myself if, because I still loved Teddy, I somehow led him on. Did I let him think it was what I wanted?' She swallowed hard. 'Maybe, *maybe,* deep in my heart I wanted it to happen. Who knows?'

'Because then if you were pregnant you'd *have* to marry Teddy? Is that what you mean?'

Annabel nodded. 'Afterwards Teddy wanted me to tell Clive. He said I had no option. I wouldn't. I was too ashamed of what had happened. Teddy wanted to tell him but I begged him not to. I was so terribly confused. Even before I knew about the baby. But I couldn't put it all into words and I was — I was rather frightened. Teddy had been in a strange mood for ages. He lost his temper — when it happened. What I'm trying to say is that he was angry and passionate at the same time. Perhaps I could have fought him off — but I didn't try.' She hesitated. 'It was awful. I'm sorry, Dulcie, but you will never understand how it was. He wasn't the Teddy you and I know. For a while I hated him. I hated all men. I didn't want to marry either of them.'

Dulcie glanced away, unable to face the pain in Annabel's eyes. She searched for something to say but no words came. There was a dull ache of misery deep inside her and she wanted to cry. Annabel's disillusion was hers, too. But tears would never wash away the dreadful truth about Teddy. How would she face him, knowing all this? How could he ever face her, once he knew that Annabel had confided in her?

Annabel touched her hand. 'I know how you must feel, Dulcie, but you'll come to terms with it. When everything's said and done he's still Teddy. And when it was over and he'd calmed down he was so terribly upset and hating himself. So dreadfully ashamed. Beside himself with grief. Oh Dulcie, I'm sorry.'

Dulcie, hopelessly out of her depth, could only shake her head.

'He was in such a state. So full of rage against himself and what he had done. I thought he might do something — You know.'

'Suicide?' Dulcie looked at her in horror.

Annabel nodded. 'I had to say I forgave him and I did forgive him. I'd said I'd marry Clive when I didn't love him. It was a wicked thing to do and now we're both being punished. And poor Clive who did nothing wrong is dead. The night before the wedding Teddy came to plead with me. I was already in bed and he threw stones up at the window — the way we did that night we had the midnight picnic. Do you remember?' A crooked smile touched her lips.

Dulcie nodded. She and Teddy had stayed overnight with Annabel while the Moores attended a Lady's night at James's old regiment. They had smuggled food out and a bottle of milk and huddled in blankets at the end of the lawn. Annabel had been discovered by ants and that had put an abrupt end to the picnic. Dulcie gave a small shake of the head. Were they still the same people, she wondered. That carefree night seemed a lifetime ago.

Annabel was still talking about the present: '. . . so we went out to the summerhouse to talk.'

'Was that when you told him about the baby?'

A small nod. 'He couldn't have murdered Clive because he — he stayed most of the night. He left about three.'

'What will you do? Have the baby adopted?'

'I don't know. He wants us to go away somewhere, maybe abroad. He wants us to get married and keep the baby.'

After a long silence Dulcie asked. 'Do you still love him?'

'Yes. I've never really stopped loving him. Even though he's — Well, he's not the man I thought he was . . . But I'm not the woman I thought I was all those years ago and I'm not proud of myself.'

Another silence.

With a huge effort Dulcie rallied her senses. 'Then who killed Clive and why?'

'I've no idea.'

'They're blaming Teddy. You'll have to tell them you were together Friday night.'

'I will. I needed to tell my parents first and I couldn't gather my courage. You being here helped me on. I don't know why.'

Dulcie glanced at the clock. 'I'll have to go soon. Will you rack your brains to see if Clive ever told you anything about anybody who might have a grudge against him? Maybe somebody from his past.'

'I've been trying to. He told me a story once — or rather half a story — about something that happened when he was at boarding school. There was an accident and a boy was killed. Some stupid test — an initiation or something. Clive saw it although they didn't know at the time.'

'Who's "they"?'

'The boys who were responsible for it happening. One of them was expelled but Clive said it was the other one. Clive had nightmares for ages afterwards. But it was all years ago. He'd been in touch with one of them, though, and quite recently. He was rather vague about why — something to do with the Old Scholars maybe. He was just amused at how this boy had grown up. Put on a lot of weight and losing his hair. Clive said he never would have recognised him if he'd passed him in the street.'

'And did this boy dislike him for some reason? Enough to *kill* him?'

'I shouldn't think so.'

'Who were the boys?'

'I don't know. They were much older than Clive. In another class. One was called Ronnie, I think. They had to climb out of a window or something. Teddy must have told you.'

'No. It's a bit of a long shot, isn't it?'

'Yes. It was probably nothing to do with it but I can't think of anything else.'

Dulcie stood up. 'I'll have to go.' Impulsively

she put her arms round Annabel and hugged her. 'Please let me help if I can. Moral support and all that.' She attempted a smile. She hesitated. 'And will you tell the police? Give Teddy his alibi. I can't bear to think of him in a police cell no matter how awful he's been. He'll die of misery.'

'Of course. I'll telephone as soon as you've gone.'

'I'll see myself out.'

With a final wave to Annabel who watched her departure from the window, Dulcie cycled down the drive and out on to the road. Her mind was a whirl of unhappy thoughts. Teddy was not guilty of murder but he had behaved abominably. She still found it incredible. But Annabel had forgiven him and that made it just possible for Dulcie to do the same. She was immensely grateful for that. She told herself that she would never say a bad word about her friend as long as she lived . . . Although, of course, Annabel had been partly to blame in the first place. Confusion set in with a vengeance.

'Hells bells!' she muttered.

Unable to cope with her thoughts in that direction, she turned her attention to the murder. It certainly was a long shot but she had no other lead. Teddy would be freed but the damage had already been done. The *Canterbury Standard* had a lot to answer for, she reflected grimly. Until they found the murderer the suspicion would always be there in the minds of the general public.

Dulcie decided that she would do a little detective work of her own.

And since she had no other lead, she would start with Fellstowe School . . .

Ellen Bly opened the door of her house in Orange Street to find a nice-looking young man on the doorstep. She smiled. Living alone since her husband died, she was always pleased to receive visitors. Even the man from the Co-op was someone to talk to and added a little variety to her week. This man, however, was a stranger.

'Yes?'

'Mrs Ellen Bly?'

'Ellen Mary Bly. That's me.'

'I'm Detective Sergeant Spencer.'

He didn't look like a policeman. No uniform. 'You sure?' she asked.

'Quite sure.' He smiled. 'Plain clothes, Mrs Bly. As distinct from the uniform boys. I'm investigating the death of the young man you found in the church. May I come in for a few moments?'

She hesitated. 'I was just getting ready to go shopping.'

'I won't take up too much of your time.'

'Oh all right, then.' She opened the door a little wider and he stepped inside, straight into the small living room. 'You'll have to excuse the dust,' she told him, knowing that there wasn't any. It was something her mother used to say.

He refused a cup of tea and they sat down. Toodles, the cat, padded into the room and immediately hurried to ingratiate herself with the detective. That was a good sign, thought Ellen.

'She likes you,' she told him as the cat sprang into his lap. A detective sergeant must be quite high up, she thought, impressed. She smiled at him, clasping her hands in her lap. It was nice to feel useful to important people. He crossed his legs and she noticed his shoes. Dark brown and well polished. Grey socks.

'Would you mind telling me again what happened on the morning the body was discovered. In as much detail as you can manage.'

Ellen stared at him. 'But you've caught the murderer, haven't you. It was in the paper. Somebody called Moore.'

'I'm afraid the *Standard* rather jumped the gun. We didn't *arrest* him, Mrs Bly. We merely wanted to ask him a few questions. We are now convinced of his innocence.'

'But he was in prison all night and —'

'He was released, Mrs Bly. We have to pursue all leads and eliminate those who have a satisfactory alibi. No one can be in two places at once.' He smiled. 'But rest assured we will catch him. All we need is the right lead. If you could tell me what happened that morning —'

She liked the way he smiled. His whole face softened. He'd got nice teeth, too. She told her story again, carefully searching her memory for anything extra.

He asked, 'Did you see anybody in the church or in the graveyard — apart from the body? A stranger? Someone who looked out of place — or had a guilty look about him?'

'Nobody.'

'Did you hear any suspicious sounds — a scuffle, a muffled cough — anything which could have been someone hiding?'

'What, hiding and watching?' The thought made her nervous. She began to imagine that she may have been in danger herself. But had she heard anything untoward? 'No, nothing,' she told him, wishing she could be more helpful because he was such a pleasant young man. 'I didn't hear anything.' she insisted. Not even a mouse!' She laughed. 'They'd all been sorted out, they had. Gassed. No rats or mice there now, thank goodness. Not that I ever saw a rat but my sister had one once in her bathroom. It used to nibble the soap. Soap! I ask you! What must it have tasted like? Of course she didn't know it was a rat until one day she saw this thing hanging down from the geyser. She thought it was a piece of string and tugged at it. It was its tail! Out it ran and gave her a terrible fright. Nearly —'

He said, 'So apart from the deceased the first person you saw was Miss Moore from the *Standard.*' He consulted his notebook. 'She had come to look over the church for an article she was going to write about the wedding.'

'That's right.' Wanting to help him she added 'I might have heard a fluttering sound. Birds nest in the tower. They sometimes fly about.

The vicar says there're bats too. I might have heard one of those.' Pity he didn't want a cup of tea. She could always shop later on. 'You sure you won't have a cup of tea? It's no trouble.' It would be something to tell her son when she wrote next. Supping tea with detective sergeants!

He shook his head. 'Do people often go into the church late at night?'

'Not that I know of. I'm not often there at that time. Only Fridays when there's a wedding on the Saturday. First thing in the morning. That's when I do my bit of cleaning.' She shivered. 'Bit creepy somehow, churches after dark. Eerie. Of course it's not locked until eleven. Unlike some churches I could mention where they lock up after the evening service. Afraid someone's going to steal the church plate, you see, and some of it's very valuable. But our vicar's very strict about that. He says the church is the Lord's house and people must be able to go in and pray. You know — go there when it isn't a service and ask God to help you with your troubles. He's very good like that. The vicar, I mean, not God.'

He nodded thoughtfully. 'So anyone could just walk in at any time up to eleven.'

'That's right. That poor young man might have gone there to pray. Asking God to bless his marriage or something.' Seeing his doubt she said, 'He *could* have.' She wondered if the detective was married. Surely somebody had snapped him up.

'But the other man — the murderer? Why was he there?'

Mmm? That was a tricky one. She said, 'I've been wondering that myself.'

'Unless it was an opportunist thing . . . If a thief followed him in — or maybe dragged him in — intending to rob him . . .'

She remained silent. So this was how they did it. This is how they solved crimes. Thinking about it. Pondering the pros and cons. Perhaps he had a child. He'd make a good father. He had that look about him.

He said 'No . . . I don't think that's the way it happened. It *must* have been prearranged . . .' He stood up. 'Well, you've been very helpful, Mrs Bly. Thank you for your time.'

She followed him to the door. He looked nice in that dark grey suit. Her husband had had one like that once but his had a faint stripe in it. She did like a man who took trouble with his appearance.

At the door he said, 'Rats and mice? In a church? Whatever do they find to eat?'

'Goodness knows. The communion wafers perhaps.'

That made him laugh. 'Washed down with a sip of wine, no doubt!'

She laughed guiltily, putting a hand to her mouth, feeling a little blasphemous. Hopefully God's attention was elsewhere. 'Not any more, though,' she told him. 'The vicar got a man in to kill them all.'

'Just as well then!'

He thanked her for her help although she hadn't been able to tell him much. She watched him walk away. Detective Sergeant Spencer. She felt proud to know him. He'll catch the murdering so-and-so, she thought. All he needed was the right lead.

From Ellen Bly's house in Orange Street, Jack made his way to the Braynes' house on the London Road. It was a large detached house in a quarter of an acre of land just past Aucher Villas. The driveway sprouted an alarming amount of weeds and the wide steps had not been swept. As he was ushered inside, Jack learned that Mrs Brayne had only just risen from her bed.

'The shock, you see,' said Charles Brayne. 'She hasn't the stomach for this sort of thing. No stamina. Life's unpleasantnesses always knock her for six. This trouble with our son —' He left Jack to draw his own conclusions.

They went into a large sunny room, tastefully furnished if a trifle shabby. Jack noted with surprise that the paintwork was in need of some attention and the floral chaircovers were faded.

He smiled at Nora Brayne and shook her hand. 'Don't get up,' he told her.

She looked painfully thin and pale, her eyes huge in a face that had once been beautiful.

'I know this is a dreadful time for you,' he said gently. 'But I must ask you some questions. I am determined to catch the man who killed your son but at the moment we are at a standstill. The man who was helping us with out enquiries has provided an alibi —'

She said, 'I never thought it was Teddy. Not for a moment. He was such a dear boy. Clive thought the world of him — until that silly business with Annabel. The fact is, Sergeant —'

'Detective Sergeant, madam.'

'Oh. Thank you. As I was saying —'

Her husband interrupted. 'He doesn't need to know all that, Nora.'

Jack said, 'I really need to ask you if your son had any enemies or had quarrelled with anyone recently.'

They exchanged a quick glance but neither spoke. Interesting.

'Maybe in his line of work?' he suggested. 'Rivalries within the firm. Anything like that?'

'He works — worked — in the City,' the husband said. 'He was a patent agent. Inventions. That sort of thing. He was expecting to be made a junior partner — before the end of the year, actually.'

'And no problems there that he told you about?'

Charles Brayne shook his head firmly. 'None.'

'Where were they going to live after the wedding?'

Nora Brayne said, 'They were buying a flat in London. A service flat. You know the sort of thing — the stairs and landings are cleaned by someone and the little garden which they all shared would be maintained. It was a sweet little flat — well, not so little actually. We were rather surprised. I made them some loose covers. Pale blue with cream piping and cushions to match . . .' Her voice faltered and tears began to slide down her face.

Her husband offered a large handkerchief and said gruffly 'Pull yourself together, old thing!'

She did, breathing deeply and dabbing at her eyes.

Jack pressed on. He hated to intrude on their grief but the best thing he could do for them was to find the son's killer. 'He was comfortably off, then, your son?' He pretended to scratch at something on his knee but watched them from the corner of his eye. The wife caught her husband's eye and he shook his head almost imperceptibly.

She said, 'Not exactly. I mean "yes". That is —'

Charles Brayne said, 'She means he had sufficient funds.' He hesitated. 'If he had any problems we would have helped him out.'

She said, 'If the flat had been smaller we could have — but with the wedding and everything . . .'

Jack said nothing, eyeing them each in turn, his expression grave. He was letting them know that he didn't believe them. Hoping to draw something further.

The wife gave in first. 'He did borrow a little money —' She gave her husband a frightened glance. 'Not a great deal, of course. From a —' She stopped, glancing for help towards her husband.

Charles Brayne said, 'From an old school friend.'

She nodded. 'That's right. He would have paid it back quite quickly. It wasn't a problem, Inspector.'

'Do you have the name of this friend?'

They both said, 'No'. A little too readily, thought Jack, his suspicions growing.

'And he definitely paid it all back?'

They both said, 'Yes'.

Jack rubbed his chin. 'Would he tell you if he hadn't?'

Nora Brayne put a hand to her mouth.

Charles Brayne said, 'I told you, he could manage it. Are you doubting my word?'

Feigned anger, thought Jack, and not at all convincing. So there were money problems. He recalled the neglected driveway and added this to the faded covers and dull paintwork. Maybe money was tight and the wedding plus the London flat had triggered financial difficulties.

He said, 'The name of your son's friend would be extremely helpful. I assume he has some paperwork — details of the loan and so on. The name should be somewhere.'

'It isn't!' Charles Brayne glared at him.

'You've looked?'

'I tell you it isn't. There is no paperwork, as you call it. A loan between friends is — Look here, between *gentlemen* a handshake is all that's needed.'

'And you've no idea who this gentleman is?'

'I've told you already. We don't know. Clive wouldn't — That is, he *didn't* tell us.'

Mrs Brayne said, 'Of course we didn't press him. It was his business. We just felt —' She stopped abruptly as her husband coughed a warning.

Ah! thought Jack. Now it was coming out. An unsecured loan that wasn't repaid on time. People had committed murder for less. He said. 'Mr Brayne, do you want me to find the man who killed your son? Because if so, I think you should be prepared to trust us. To cooperate with us fully.'

The man's face was reddening and a small muscle flickered in his right cheek. He moved towards the window and stared out, his back stiff and uncompromising. Jack waited but finally it was his wife who answered.

'We don't know who this man is, Inspector. Clive wouldn't tell us. The truth is that we had a bit of an argument because of this loan. We felt that the flat was much too expensive for them but Annabel had set her heart on it and so of course poor Clive had to buy it.' She regarded Jack earnestly. 'Charles and I could have helped him if he — if *she* — hadn't been so ambitious.'

Without turning towards them, the husband said, 'That's right, Nora. Tell them everything. Show us up. Go on!'

She turned on him tearfully. 'I'm not showing us up, Charles. I'm simply telling Sergeant Spencer the truth. Why poor Clive had to saddle himself with all that debt.' She turned back to Jack. 'We liked Annabel well enough. She's a dear girl but very greedy. She was never satisfied. Clive bought her a beautiful engagement ring and she looked down her nose at it.'

He turned from the window. 'No she didn't, Nora. You thought she did, that's all. You'd made up your mind not to approve.'

'I did nothing of the kind, Charles. The way she showed it to us — waving her hand in that nonchalant way as though it was a piece of glass instead of a diamond!'

He glared at her. 'Rubbish. You just wanted an excuse to carp.'

'That's not true!'

'Because you always wanted Clive to marry Dulcie. You know you did.'

Jack pricked up his ears. 'Dulcie Moore?'

Nora Brayne nodded. 'Yes. They were all friends together. Dulcie would have been right for Clive but for some reason they were never more than friends. She took no interest in men. I suppose you'd call her a tomboy. A bit of a scatterbrain but very sweet. And lately of course she's had this notion about a career.' She shook her head. 'Girls today! I don't know. At least Annabel was willing to settle down. I'll say that for her. If only she'd stayed in love with Teddy and left Clive alone. It's never been the same since. The families, I mean. The Ropers, the Moores and us. We used to visit. Go places together.'

Charles said, 'He doesn't want to hear all this, Nora. Family friendships have got nothing to do with anything.'

Jack said soothingly, 'It all helps to build up a picture, sir.' So, he thought, Dulcie had never been interested in marriage. Interesting. There had obviously been no men in her life and he was pleased about that.

To Charles Brayne he said, 'I'd like to know who lent your son money. If you like *we* could go through his papers but we are rather stretched at the moment. Perhaps you would care to do it for us.'

Shocked, they stared at him, recognising the threat behind the courteous words.

The husband muttered something that sounded like, 'Don't leave us much option, do you!' and Jack decided the moment had come to leave them. With a few well-chosen platitudes he drove away, his spirits higher than he could have expected so soon after losing his prime suspect. The Braynes' financial problems just might be the lead he needed. Following it might bring an arrest that much nearer.

His only regret was that Dulcie seemed to be mixed up in all of it and that worried him. She might well decide to go ferreting around on her own or on behalf of the *Canterbury Standard*. Either way she might find herself biting off more than she could chew. He decided to have a few words with her on the subject. The thought of seeing her again lifted his rising spirits another notch. Perhaps now that her brother was off the hook she would be less prickly to deal with. He made a mental note to say something complimentary about her dog.

Sylvie was not feeling very happy as she listened to the detective's retreating footsteps. He had been polite, she would grant him that but she didn't like visits from the police. Never had. In her experience they always spelled trouble. Not that she had given anything away but she had been tempted. Just a little. Bert had been staying with her on and off since Monday and now it was Thursday. He had been sitting around all day, moping, snapping her head off. Slipping out when it was dark and coming back at all hours. No money had been offered for groceries and he could hardly be bothered to answer a civil question.

'Didn't even take me out for a drink, miserable skinflint!' she muttered.

She didn't expect to go somewhere in Canterbury, she wasn't daft. But they could have gone somewhere on the train. With his hat pulled over his eyes and the new beard he had grown no one would see enough of his face to recognise him. Like a gangster. She giggled. Like Dillinger in America.

Even if he didn't want to go out he could have

given her a few pounds to treat herself. He could have bought her a new dress or a bottle of perfume. Not that he was actually mean. He never had been and she didn't think that of him now. He was just too wrapped up in his own problems to spare a thought for her and her feelings. And she was getting brassed off with it — and with him. If they weren't going to have any fun she might as well be rid of him and cast her net somewhere else.

And another thing. 'Unfinished business.' That was all she could get out of him about his little job for the Folkestone chap. That and 'You talk too much!' and 'You ask too many questions!' How charming! She sighed. He'd obviously been paid for the job he'd done even if he hadn't got all of it so why didn't they just jump in a taxi and go to Whitstable for the day. Have a paddle and a saucer of whelks. It wouldn't break the bank. It would be a laugh. They wouldn't be looking for him in Whitstable.

From the window she watched the detective cross the road and walk briskly along the street. Now where was he off to? Off to upset some other poor soul. Pity. She'd have to tell Bert he'd been nosing around and then the chances were he'd take off and she'd never see him again. He could be a bit of a misery at times but she liked being seen with him. He wasn't bad looking even with the beard. If he got the rest of the money he was owed and he *was* going to South America, maybe she could go with him. For a moment she allowed herself to dream, seeing herself peering provocatively from beneath a large straw hat. Sombreros — that's what they were called. South America sounded like a nice country. Sunshine and dancing and all the men calling all the foreigners 'Gringos'. She sighed. He would never take her. He'd make use of her little flat when he needed a roof over his head but he would never take her away with him. She wasn't stupid. He'd think she was too old for him. Probably planned to marry a young woman who could do the flamenco dancing, clicking castanets and stamping her feet. Or was that Mexico?

A thought came to her suddenly. If he wouldn't *give* her any money . . . She thought 'Why not take some?' but it made her heart thump a little. If Bert had made some money it would be hidden somewhere in the flat. He would never dare to carry it around with him in case he was picked up by the police. So all she had to do was find it. She swallowed hard. Would he notice if she took a few notes? Would he think to count it? Surely she was owed something for her hospitality. It wasn't like stealing because he *owed* it to her. The thing was — could she make him see it like that if he found out? Slowly she sat down on the edge of the bed. While she was wondering if she dared do it her mind was busy — thinking of possible places where he might have hidden it.

She muttered, 'And then what? Think, Sylvie!'

If she found it and helped herself she would then have to hide what she had taken. She would have to hide it and deny all knowledge of it. But where was it *now?* Trembling slightly she began to look in and behind cupboards. Nothing. Under cushions and chairs. Same result. Behind pictures. That didn't take long. She went through into the bedroom and finally spotted it under the bed. His old carpet bag. The one he called 'lucky' although what could be lucky about a bag? Silly sod! He had left it with her years ago 'for a few days' and it had stayed with her while he was in prison . . . It *had* been in the attic but now it was under the bed. Aha! She dragged it out. Unzipped it. A shirt missing two buttons and with a nasty browny red stain near the collar. She stared at it.

'Browny *red?*'

Blood? No. Of course it wasn't! Don't even think it. A pair of socks, pants, a tie and a small box of — ? She opened it. Cufflinks. And something wrapped in a piece of old blanket. Slowly she unwrapped it. The bulky brown paper package was securely tied with string. It was money. She *knew* it. A great deal of money!

'Oh no, Bert!' For a long minute she regarded it nervously.

She was still staring at it when she heard the downstairs front door open and close. Was that Bert coming back? Oh God! He mustn't know that she'd found it. Voices came from downstairs. Thank God! He had been waylaid by the landlord. Nosy old devil. Still, it gave her a chance. She rushed to the door and locked it.

Halfway back to the bag she changed her mind. If he found the door locked he would suspect something. Back to the door. Unlock it.

He was almost at the top of the stairs now.

Back to the bed. There was no time. She stuffed everything back into the bag and shoved it under the bed. Tidy it up later.

He was opening the flat door.

She said, 'Oh God!' and threw herself on to the bed. Pretend to be dozing.

He was in the bedroom.

She opened her eyes sleepily. 'Bert!' Smile, she told herself. Her mouth trembled with the effort.

To her relief he grinned and sat down on the bed. 'Stir yourself, girlie!' he said.

'We're going out for a bit of supper!'

Sylvie drew a long breath and sat up. 'A bit of supper? Oh Bert, you're an angel!'

Later that night, Ellen Bly opened her eyes and stared up at the ceiling where the street light threw the familiar shadow of the window panes. The clock ticked, the cat snored quietly in her basket in the corner and Ellen Bly's heart beat loudly. She was a good sleeper and rarely woke in the night. Her mother used to say that she could sleep through a hurricane so something must have woken her. A glance at her alarm clock showed five minutes to twelve. Reluctantly she sat up, still listening. She got out of bed and padded to the window to look down into the street. Two drunks lurched past on the other side of the road. It was usually a pretty quiet street after the pubs had closed and the drinkers had gone home. Except that once a couple of stray dogs had fought right outside the window until her neighbour sorted them out.

'Funny!' she murmured. The street was now empty. She wavered, wanting to go back to bed but afraid to leave unanswered questions in her mind. She would never sleep unless she was *sure* all was well. The cat woke and mewed sleepily and she bent to stroke her.

'Go back to sleep, Toodles. It's nothing.' She would go down to the kitchen just to be on the safe side and while she was there she'd get herself a biscuit. Night starvation could be nasty. Halfway across the bedroom she hesitated. It *was* nothing, wasn't it? She hesitated. Then froze. Surely that was a creak from the stairs. The third stair up had always creaked. It had been a bit of a joke between her and her husband. Her heart began to race.

'Who's there?' she called and the tremble in her voice frightened her more than the creak. Now she *knew* she was nervous! Too scared to open the bedroom door and look along the landing. Much too frightened to go down to the kitchen.

With a whimper of fear she threw herself back into bed and pulled the bedclothes up over her. She closed her eyes. If she couldn't see it, it wasn't there.

'Our Father, Which art in Heaven,' she whispered.

When she finished the prayer she took a chance and popped her head out of the bedclothes. The cat had left her basket and was crouched in the middle of the floor, staring at the crack under the door. Her tail moved slowly from side to side.

Ellen murmured, 'Oh God! Help me!' No, *no*, she told herself. This wasn't happening. It was a nightmare. Things like this happened to other people, not to her. She waited, heart thudding. At least now she couldn't hear the creaking stair. She retreated under the bedclothes again where the sound of her thumping heart seemed to have doubled. She would count to ten and then pop her head out of the bedclothes and have another listen.

In her imagination footsteps came nearer until they reached the bedroom door . . .

Click!

She heard it. A tiny click and then silence.

Now her heart raced so that she felt faint. That *wasn't* the latch on the bedroom door. It couldn't — *mustn't* — be. Because that would mean someone was opening her door and that would mean —

Oh God! She was being so ridiculous. If she went on like this she would die of a heart attack and all for nothing! There was only one way to find out. She would *look!*

'One . . . two . . . three . . .' Her whispered

numbers faltered. Pull yourself together, Ellen, she scolded silently. There's no one there! She slowly drew back the covers until her head was free. Now all she had to do was open her eyes . . .

A large man was standing beside her, silhouetted against the window. It took a few seconds for her to realise that it was actually happening. Then she realised that he held a cushion in his hands.

He said, 'Sorry, old duck, but you know too much!' and she thought she recognised the voice from somewhere. Before she could scream he leaned over her and pressed the pillow against her face.

CHAPTER 7

Fellstowe School, near Horsted Keynes, stood in its own extensive grounds. It was a large Georgian building which, once 'a rich man's castle', was now a prestigious school. With several cabinet ministers as ex-pupils, the school enjoyed a growing reputation and the waiting list for entry was formidable. The new wing had been added in the late nineteenth century to form an 'L' shaped property. This extension housed the dormitories and staff quarters.

As the station taxi carried Dulcie along the broad curving driveway she remembered the numerous occasions on which the Moores and the Braynes had attended the various Open Days. Teddy had won the occasional prize for effort and Clive had been academically successful in a modest way. Although Teddy was younger than Clive they had somehow maintained the friendship while they were at school. Now, she smiled, remembering Teddy flushed with victory, when he won the long jump for Drake, his house, and again when he received a book as a prize for 'industry'. How was it, she wondered, that he knew nothing about Clive's involvement with the fatal accident all those years ago? Or was he simply keeping quiet about it?

Robert Simms, the current headmaster, was a small, jovial-looking man. He welcomed her cheerfully when she was shown into his study but his warmth cooled as she began to expand on the reason for her visit.

'Miss Moore,' he said, 'there cannot be a need after all these years to rake up an unhappy episode in the school's past. Nothing of that kind goes on here nowadays. I can assure you of that.'

Dulcie leaned forward. 'None of what, Mr Simms? This is the problem, you see. We don't know what happened all those years ago but we do think it might have a bearing on the — on recent events.'

'When you said you wanted to talk to me about something concerning your brother I naturally thought —'

'Mr Simms, this *does* concern Teddy. It also concerns another of your ex-pupils — Clive Brayne. You have probably read of his murder.'

He nodded. 'Poor young man. Such a promising pupil. We were very saddened by his death. Such a tragic waste.' He looked at her, eyes narrowed, suddenly wary. 'In what exact capacity, Miss Moore, are you here?'

'I'm a journalist, Mr Simms, but I am —'

'A journalist!'

He makes it sound like a cockroach, Dulcie thought irritably, but hiding her feelings she produced a polite smile. 'For the *Canterbury Standard.*'

'A *lady* journalist?'

'My uncle owns the paper,' she told him. 'It was once a family affair but my father declined to go into the firm. My brother Teddy is tied up with the running of the family estate in Cornwall so my uncle thought it a good idea that I should learn something about the newspaper.' She was rather pleased with this distortion of the facts. It sounded quite plausible.

'But this — this interview —'

'Oh no! Not an *interview.* Nothing like that,' she said. Reassure him before he clams up, she thought desperately. 'One of your ex-pupils has been murdered and another of your ex-pupils has been, but is no longer, a suspect. Officially, that is, but what of the public? Mud sticks, Mr Simms, even to a school. There must be a great many people out there who still think my brother is guilty and associate him with Fellstowe.' She felt ashamed of this line of argument but had decided that this was the only way to ensure the headmaster's cooperation. He had to feel it necessary for the good name of the school. 'The only way to prove him innocent, Mr Simms, one hundred per cent, is to find the real murderer.'

'Well, of course I see your reasoning but —'

'Please. Let me finish and then you'll see how important it is that you help us.'

Briefly Dulcie sketched in again the details of Clive's death and the fact that Teddy had been suspected. 'Of course he is innocent,' she concluded and saw him breathe a sigh of relief. 'He was really only a suspect because they had no one else and Teddy and Clive had both loved the same girl. There had been some rivalry between them but the police are quite satisfied now. Teddy *might* have had a motive but he didn't commit the crime. We have no idea who killed Clive and we have to look for anyone who might hold a grudge. Now, Clive's fiancée told me yesterday about an occasion when a boy died in some kind of escapade. Clive was somehow involved and she thought the hostility between the boys might have lasted through the years. Might, in fact, have some bearing on Clive's death. I simply wanted to rule out any possible connection. Detective Sergeant Spencer said that ruling out false leads is vitally important.'

The headmaster's expression changed from relief to dismay. 'I can accept that,' he said. 'I am simply unwilling to discuss that unfortunate affair because I was only a junior housemaster at the time and — you must understand this, Miss Moore — because the parents of today's boys know nothing about it. It is my responsibility to see that they never do. It would do the school's reputation —'

Dulcie saw that she had rattled him. She counted to ten. 'If you will not talk to me, Mr Simms, you will almost certainly have Detective Sergeant Spencer here to ask you the same questions. Wouldn't the arrival of the police alarm the parents? Don't you think I am your best bet?'

Blinking, he moved back, marginally increasing the distance between them. 'Are you — are you *blackmailing* me, Miss Moore?'

'Certainly not!' She hoped she looked suitably shocked. 'Mr Simms, I can leave right now, if you wish. But what I want is to give the details to the police in a discreet way. I have no reason to wish to damage the school in any way. My family has great respect for Fellstowe. As far as anyone knows I am merely a sister of an ex-pupil who has called in —'

'All right! All right! I understand you perfectly!' His tone suggested that though he might be forced to understand her, he certainly need not like doing so. 'I will tell you what you need to know and then you will have to excuse me. I always take a bible class Fridays at eleven.'

Dulcie said, 'Do you mind if I make a few notes? These are not for publication, of course, but the police will be grateful for a few names.' He stared at her unhappily as she produced pencil and notebook. She added, 'I'm sure that what we both want more than anything is to help them find the man who killed Clive Brayne.'

He nodded. 'If you'll give me a moment I'll ask my secretary to find the relevant log book. The minutiae of school life is faithfully recorded on a daily basis . . Perhaps you'd like a cup of tea.' It came out reluctantly.

'No thank you.' Dulcie had no desire to prolong the proceedings.

He disappeared into an adjoining room and returned a few moments later with a bulky leatherbound book. 'Let me just refresh my mind,' he said, making it clear that Dulcie was not going to be allowed a look at the entries. 'Ah! . . . Yes. Of course.' He leafed through it to find the required date, skimmed the handwritten page and then closed the book, leaving one finger inside it to keep the place should it be necessary. He cleared his throat and began. 'There was, we later understood, a certain ritual that new boys were expected to undergo — to prove themselves, you see. Quite, I hasten to add, unknown to the authorities who would have stamped it out immediately had they known.' He waited and when Dulcie made no attempt to write said 'Perhaps you should make a note of that. That we had no knowledge of the so-called rites. None at all.'

Dulcie scribbled obligingly.

He pulled anxiously at the end of his nose as he went on. 'Apparently older boys required the younger ones to climb out of a window on the third floor and shin down a rope to an open window on the second floor. Then they climbed in. That was it.'

Dulcie, appalled, said nothing. In her notes she wrote 'Mad! Disgusting!'

'Apparently the two older boys on this occasion were Parker and Foote. They were as thick as thieves — not easy boys to deal with. That I *do* recall.' He shook his head at the memory.

'Parker was a strange lad. No family to speak of. Mother left them and father committed suicide. Very sad. But he was very bright — if he'd wanted to get on which he didn't. Didn't seem to care. Didn't appreciate how lucky he was to have the chance of a decent education.'

'How did he get to this school then?'

'Ah! He was very fortunate. One of the governors at the orphanage was an old Fellstowe boy and he paid for Parker to come here. Thought it was his only chance to make good . . .'

'And Foote?'

'Hmm. Foote was a different kettle of fish. We'd had his family for several generations — father and grandfather. A very well-respected family, on the whole. And the young Reggie always looked so innocent. So open and friendly. A jolly child, you might say. He was chubby and he had a round angelic face and big blue eyes. Mrs Stokes, his house matron, thought the world of him when he was young.'

He fiddled with the log book tugging at a stray thread from the binding. Dulcie stared fixedly at her notepad, afraid to break the flow of reminiscences now that it was underway.

The headmaster's shrug was resigned. 'But, of course, boys grow up and change. Eleven, twelve — roundabout then. Very significant years for boys. It's all a matter of direction, you see. The older Foote tended to rely on his grandfather's name. Natural, I suppose, but irritating. He could be difficult.' He sighed. 'Sly, as I recall . . .'

'Sly?' She glanced up from her writing.

He leaned forward. 'Strictly between you and me, I never quite trusted him. Funny . . . some boys you can take to, others you can't. I could never quite take to Foote. Still, the grandfather was a surgeon. *Sir* Randolph Foote! . . . Eyes. That was it. Marvellous eye surgeon. Very famous in his day — and wealthy. He endowed the school clinic.' He reopened the log book and studied the entries. Closing it again he said 'On this occasion, when the new boy was less than halfway down, one of the others shook the rope to frighten him and he — he fell.'

'To his death.'

'I'm afraid so. He was rushed to hospital with severe head injuries and for a day or two it seemed just possible . . . but it was not to be. It was a black day for the school. A terribly black day.'

A pretty black day for the dead boy and his grieving parents, thought Dulcie. She asked, 'And how was Clive Brayne involved in this — this tragedy?'

'He was in Reggie Foote's "house". In Drake. Your brother's house. You obviously understand the system. Competitive spirit. It inspires loyalty. The four houses are Nelson, Drake —' Seeing her expression Simms abandoned the explanation. 'They let Brayne watch the attempt.'

'Had Clive already done this climb?'

'Oh yes. It became clear, to our horror I may add, that all the boys had done it. And quite safely. That's the point.'

Another idea struck her. 'Even Teddy?'

'One presumes so.'

Dulcie drew a long breath. How dare they, she thought furiously. How dare they pretend to be competent to run a school and yet allow such idiocies to take place? With an effort she bit back a scathing comment. It might have been Teddy who fell to his death, she thought soberly, imagining the last plunge into darkness. Her throat tightened at the thought of Teddy lying on the ground, broken and lifeless. Life without Teddy! She couldn't bear to think about it. Or it might have been Clive. How ironic that he had survived the stupid ritual only to die horribly not so many years later.

'So Teddy knew nothing?' she prompted.

'He would have been allowed to witness one attempt, certainly, but not this one.'

'You mean it was considered a privilege?' she demanded incredulously.

He had the grace to look ashamed. 'Only among the boys, Miss Moore. You must know something about the mentality of young boys. You have a brother. They can be very headstrong, reckless creatures. And do remember — no other boy had died — or even been injured up to that time.'

'So who shook the rope? Parker or Foote?'

He shook his head. 'Ah! There you have me, Miss Moore. We were never one hundred per cent certain,' he admitted. 'They each blamed the other. Finally, quite suddenly really . . . Parker admitted it and was promptly expelled.'

'Suddenly?' She gave him a keen look, sensing something in the slight hesitation.

'He had denied it for days and very convincingly. Young Foote had seemed less sincere but had not wavered in his denials either. The headmaster was on the point of expelling both of them, to be honest. But then abruptly Parker confessed. It was a great relief.'

'I'm sure it was.' Dulcie kept her gaze on the notebook and scribbled furiously. Easier to get rid of Parker and keep Sir Randolph's grandson. Mustn't upset the goose that lays the golden eggs. Might need another clinic sometime! 'And that was the end of it?' she asked.

He shrugged. 'As far as the school, yes.' He frowned. 'I shall never forget the way Parker went off, head up, shoulders back, as though he had done something to be proud of instead of — Well, instead of *killing* someone. He had a strange look on his face as though somehow he had *won!*'

'What happened to him? I mean, where did he go? Back to the orphanage?'

'Initially — he was only fourteen at the time — but we heard not long after that he'd run away. Stolen some money from the office and slipped away in the night. The police kept a lookout but boys absconding from orphanages were fairly common.

He seemed to be thinking and Dulcie waited.

He went on. 'Yes, Parker was a bit of a bully and he had a very hasty temper. What we call a short fuse. I remember once he found a mangy-looking dog. A ghastly animal. Skin and bone with sores round its muzzle. He'd kept it hidden in the coalstore for nearly a week, feeding it on scraps he'd saved from his own meals. Insisted the animal was devoted to him and wanted us to keep it as a school mascot. Naturally the headmaster said "No" and that the dog would have to be put down. The boy went berserk. Used some very abusive language and hurled a small paperweight through the window behind you.' He whistled softly at the memory. 'He earned himself a week's detention and two thousand lines. When we read some years later that he'd killed someone we really weren't too surprised. Saddened, of course,' he added hastily, 'but not entirely surprised.'

'He was sent to Canterbury Prison,' Dulcie reminded him. 'Now he's escaped. He might somehow be involved with Clive's death. You do see, don't you, that we need to understand all this.'

The headmaster nodded. 'We hoped we could *tame* him, if you'll excuse the word. I did think at one time that he might have done well in one of the armed forces. He had that aggressive streak that could have been put to good use.' He glanced pointedly at his watch but Dulcie ignored the hint.

'And Foote?' she asked. 'Do you know where he is now?'

Mr Simms brightened. 'Well, last time I heard he was on the Folkestone Town Council and very highly regarded. We have his nephew in the school so we hear all the news. There's talk of him becoming the next mayor. That would make us all very proud.'

Folkestone? Dulcie kept her face straight. Not a million miles from Canterbury. A bit of a coincidence. Could Parker and Foote have met up again? Simms said they had been 'thick as thieves'. Could they possibly be in cahoots again? She closed her notebook and stood up. 'I'm extremely grateful for your assistance,' she told him. 'I shall pass this information to the police. It may prove invaluable.'

'I do hope so. And you will remember our little . . . I mean, I have told you this in confidence for the good of the school.'

She smiled. 'We'll keep the name of the school out of the paper, never fear,' she told him.

On the train back to London, alone in the first class carriage, she wondered whether in fact she would tell Jack Spencer what she had learned. Part of her wanted to keep the information to herself — to see how far she could go with it. If only she could be instrumental in tracking the real murderer Cobsey would have to take her seriously.

There was another part of her, however, that wanted to share the information with Detective Sergeant Spencer.

And she wasn't at all sure why.

Later that same day, in the Murder Room, Jack sat across the table from Blake and sipped his tea which the latter had just made for him. The room was already becoming depressingly familiar with its motley collection of furniture on loan from other more permanent locations. The battered desks, mismatched chairs and a blackboard which had seen better days. One wall was partly covered by a huge pinboard to which reports and photographs had been pinned. On the opposite wall a large street map of Canterbury hid part of the window. There was one large cupboard. Beside it, on the floor, there was a pile of files.

Earlier Jack had spent a fruitless hour with Sylvie Hunt, a known associate of Albert Parker. She had stuck to her story that she hadn't seen him since he broke out of prison and never wanted to see him again. She insisted that she had no knowledge of his whereabouts, no knowledge of how he was sprung and no knowledge of his future plans. Except to say that once he had talked about going to South America to make a fresh start. She did admit that once they had been more than friends but that she was now older and wiser. She had refused him permission to 'take a look round' without a search warrant.

Jack didn't believe any of it but he had been unable to shake her from the story. He had returned depressed to the police station, aware that Scotland Yard officers were due to arrive on the early afternoon train from Charing Cross.

Blake, reading his thoughts, said, 'It's on the board, sir. Detective Chief Inspector Gough and a DS Allan.'

'He'll be carrying the bag for Gough.'

Blake looked blank.

'A junior chap always accompanies a detective chief inspector. He carries the suitcase.' Seeing that Blake was still mystified Jack said, 'They bring stuff with them that they might need. Magnifying glass, fingerprint kit, notebooks, rubber gloves, plaster of Paris — casts for the making of.' He grinned. 'Get the idea?'

'Oh. Right, sir. Sort of portable forensics.'

'Something like that.' He drew his brows together. 'DS Allan? Don't think I know him.' He didn't add that he would have preferred a detective *constable.* Allan was also a detective sergeant. Same rank.

Blake said, 'And Gough? Any gen on him?'

'Can't remember much about him to be honest. It was probably five or six years since he last came to Canterbury. Maybe more.'

'Still, sir, we've had a few extra days to ourselves, with Gough getting an ulcer.'

The new chief, assigned to the job earlier, had been taken ill with stomach pains, delaying his arrival in Canterbury.

Jack said, 'Fat lot of good it did us! We haven't cracked it. Does he want to see me?'

'Says he does but they've gone to the mortuary. They seemed OK.'

'They all *seem* OK,' said Jack. 'That ruddy Hunt woman. I *know* she's lying. Parker's been there.' He filled his detective constable in on the little that Sylvie Hunt had revealed. 'She didn't seem worried that he might show up while I was there.'

'You mean she knew where he was?'

'Maybe. She made such a thing of him *probably* being miles away. I tried to frighten her. You know the drill, Blake. Threatening to bring her in for questioning. Penalties for withholding information. Nothing worked. She seemed so cocksure, somehow. If she hadn't seen him how could she be sure he wouldn't turn up there?' He sighed deeply. 'Women! What do they see in men like Parker? She knows he can be violent. Damn her! I just wanted something more concrete to take to Gough.'

'Were they an item, sir? It was a bit before my time.'

Jack shook his head. 'Not exactly common-law stuff. But he certainly stayed there from time to time. And he gave her a black eye more than once.'

'You think she'd lie for him?'

'Women are funny creatures, Blake. I wouldn't like to say she wouldn't.'

'Can't we get a search warrant? Go through the place like a whirlwind!'

'Not enough grounds. They'd never wear it.'

There was a knock on the door and a young PC put his head round it. 'Someone to see Detective Sergeant Spencer,' he said. 'Female.'

Jack groaned. 'What's it about? Must it be me?'

'She asked for you by name. Shall I wheel her in?'

'If you must!'

Blake said, 'Sylvie Hunt? Maybe you *did* get through to her, sir.'

Jack shrugged but his hopes rose fractionally. Had she had a change of heart? He crossed his fingers.

A moment later Dulcie Moore came into the room. His disappointment lasted less than a few seconds as he looked at her. She wore a blue flowered dress under a crisp white jacket and looked good enough to eat.

'Miss Moore!' To think he had almost refused to see her! 'What brings you here?'

She looked so earnest, he thought, amused. He wanted to say, 'You've brightened my day!' but with Blake present it was impossible.

She regarded him soberly. 'I have some information which might be of use to you in connection with the murder of Clive Brayne.'

Jack caught sight of Blake's rapt expression and smiled. His own depression had lifted a little at the sight of her. 'In connection with the murder of . . .'! She sounded just like a policeman, he thought. Then he remembered that he was no longer in charge of the case and hesitated. He glanced at Blake and saw that he was thinking along the same lines. She should be talking to

Detective Chief Inspector Gough from the Yard.

Blake looked at him. 'But the Chief's not here, sir.' He raised his eyebrows. 'It's probably *urgent!*'

Dulcie said, 'It's urgent for me because I took the day off work without permission and I have to get home and pretend I was under the weather.'

Jack indicated the third chair at the table and Dulcie sat down.

Blake said, 'Cup of tea, miss?'

'Thank you. Yes. Plenty of milk if possible and one sugar. I can't drink it too hot.' She spoke to Blake but contrived to smile at Jack and he returned the smile, momentarily forgetting the 'urgency' of her communication. How wonderful that she had come to him. He had been trying to find an excuse to call on her.

She said, 'It may be nothing, but I've been to Horsted Keynes to Fellstowe School to talk to the headmaster — a Mr Simms. I had to promise — Well, a sort of half promise — that we'd keep the name of the school out of the newspapers.' She waited, puzzled, and he realised that he was still smiling at her. 'Aren't you going to make notes?' she asked.

'Er — notes! Of course.' While he found paper and a pencil Blake produced a mug of tea for their 'informant'. Dulcie thanked him.

He said, 'Would you like a biscuit?'

Jack said, 'Have we got any?'

Dulcie said, 'No thank you.'

Blake hovered hopefully but Jack said, 'Perhaps you'd make a start on those reports, Blake.'

'Reports?' It was Blake's turn to look puzzled. Then catching the look on Jack's face he said, 'Oh yes. *Reports,*' and wandered away, rolling his eyes expressively.

Jack drew in his chair and looked at Dulcie. For a moment he wondered what it would be like to kiss her but Judith's face floated reproachfully into his mind and he made an effort to return to business.

Dulcie leaned forward, the mug of tea clasped in both hands. She began a story about some schoolboys and Clive Brayne and her brother. A story about some kind of dare that went wrong. When she had finished he wondered what to say. It all seemed a million miles from what had happened a week ago in St Alphege's church.

He sipped his tea thoughtfully, not wanting to disappoint her. 'That's all very interesting, Miss Dul— Miss Moore,' he said. 'What I don't quite see is why either of the boys — or men as they are now — should suddenly decide to kill Brayne who had nothing to do with the accident.'

'He was a witness.'

'But after all these years? I could understand it if, say, Parker had killed the other one —'

'Reginald Foote.'

'Yes. If maybe Foote *had* been to blame and Parker had killed *him* instead of Brayne. But even then, it's years ago. A lot of water under the bridge . . .' He shrugged.

She swallowed and he could see that she was sick with disappointment. 'I just thought —' she stammered, 'that with Parker escaping from the prison and this Foote person living at Folkestone . . . Doesn't it seem a *bit* of a coincidence? I thought there might be a link. After all Clive and Parker and Foote did know each other once. Suppose they'd been in touch recently?'

'About what?'

She hesitated. 'About anything. I don't know.'

Hastily he said, 'It's certainly worth looking into, Miss Moore, but I have to tell you that as of today I am no longer in — in sole charge of the case. A Detective Inspector Gough has been sent down from Scotland Yard.'

She said, 'Oh, that's not fair! You've worked so hard —'

'I'm still on the case, Miss Moore. It's the way we work in the police force. It always happens in a murder investigation that is slow to show results. Canterbury has a small city force. We call in Scotland Yard as extra resources when we're under pressure. Extra manpower. That sort of thing.' He hoped Blake wasn't listening.

'So you do think it was murder.'

'Or manslaughter. Unfortunately we spent vital days suspecting your brother who seemed —'

Her eyes flashed dangerously. 'Don't try to pin the blame on Teddy!' she protested. 'He didn't ask to be a suspect and I did *tell* you he couldn't be guilty. If you wasted time it was your own fault!'

'I know. I know. What I meant was —'

'I know what you meant! That he had wasted valuable police time and — and resources.' She glared at him. 'I bet you didn't even say you were sorry, did you? To Teddy? For putting him through that ordeal and for making everyone think he might be a *killer.*'

Stung by her rebuke he leaped to his own defence. 'You might remember, Miss Moore, that your precious brother didn't help us. He wouldn't give us an alibi. He *made* himself look guilty as hell. Yes. I do mean it. Your brother *made* us lose valuable time! We could have prosecuted him for that. So in a way it's his damned fault they've called in Scotland Yard.' He sat back in his chair, fuming. 'Sorry? He should be apologising to *us!*'

She shrank back, obviously disconcerted by the attack but after a moment she said, 'You're right. He was in the wrong. I'm sorry.'

He suddenly admired her. It was never easy to admit to being wrong. He said gently, 'You are getting too involved, Miss Moore. You should leave this to us. Go back to your newspaper. Do your job.'

'You mean I'm being a nuisance,' she said, subdued.

'You could never be that!' he said earnestly. If *only* they had met under different circumstances . . . and then there was Judith.

She sighed. 'So now I have to tell all this to the Scotland Yard man.'

'No. I'll pass on all the information.'

She drew a deep breath. 'Have you found out *anything* else?' she asked. 'I mean, are you following any other leads?'

He thought of Sylvie Hunt. 'I have been interviewing someone,' he told her. 'A close friend of a man who — Well, actually, she's a friend of Parker. Or was. Claims not to be seeing him now. But we're still keen to find him and trace his movements. It's a long shot, of course, but —'

'It's not quite such a long shot now though, is it?' she said. 'Now that you know that he and Clive *knew* each other.'

'No, it's not.' She was very sharp, he thought. In fact she was right. The tenuous link between Brayne and Parker might alter things. He had to give her full marks for initiative. Feeling generous he added, 'Your information has been a great help, Miss Moore.'

She opened her clutch bag and took out a piece of paper. 'The name, address and telephone number of the school, head-master and everything.' She held it out and he accepted it gravely, resisting the urge to touch her hand.

She said, 'If you have to visit the school you won't send anyone in uniform, will you. I did promise.'

'You have my word.'

She drank a few mouthfuls of the tea and

stood up. 'I must go.'

He walked as far as the door with her and was about to open it when it burst open. Stanley was framed in the doorway, his ruddy face even brighter than usual.

'Sir!' he cried. 'There's been *another* murder!'

Stanley led the way up the stairs and flung open the bedroom door. His boringly routine house-to-house enquiries had suddenly thrown up a second murder and he was thoroughly enjoying the subsequent limelight.

Jack regarded the room soberly. On a chair below the window he saw a pile of neatly folded clothes that would never be worn again. Below the chair, a pair of shoes. On the chest of drawers there was a small swing mirror, a pot of powder and what might be handcream. A woman was dead. Jack experienced a deep sense of failure.

Stanley said, 'The cushion came from the downstairs sofa. He must have —'

'*He?* Who are we talking about, Stanley?'

Stanley paused, immediately wary. 'Well sir, I assumed it was a man. Probably Parker —'

'Don't assume anything. Not ever.'

'Yes sir. I mean, No sir!'

'It could be Parker. It's looking increasingly like that, but we don't know for sure. Mustn't go barking up the wrong tree again.' Jack sighed, 'Lucky old Gough!' The cat he had seen in the house earlier rubbed itself affectionately against his trouser leg.

'Pity the cat can't talk, sir.'

'Yes it is. Toodles.'

'What, sir?'

'It's the cat's name. I was here, talking to Mrs Bly. Better get a neighbour to look after it.' He still hadn't glanced at the bed. He wasn't glad that a woman was dead but the case was developing in an interesting way and he would have liked to handle it himself. He would like to solve it just to prove to himself and everyone else that he was good at his job. That's what he was paid for. Instead Gough and his bag man were going to walk right into it. Two murders! It would make the headlines. He moved reluctantly towards the body.

'Smothered with that cushion, sir.'

'You don't *know* that. The scenario *suggests* that that's what he did. Never jump to conclusions, Stanley. She might have been poisoned and then arranged on the bed and the cushion placed nearby.'

'Sorry, sir.'

'You're probably right but always look for alternatives.' He stared down at Ellen Bly. Her mouth was open in a soundless scream. Her eyes stared sightlessly. Jack *knew* she had been awake and terrified. 'The bastard!' he whispered. 'Poor woman.'

'Let's hope he took her while she was sleeping, sir.'

'I don't think so.' He leaned down, towards her. 'Almost certainly asphyxia,' he said. 'Look at the mouth — cyanosis.'

'Sir?' Stanley leaned forward, peering intently.

'The blue tinge of the lips . . . a closer examination will show tiny spots in the white of the eyes . . . What else might you look for?'

'Um — Fingernails — that is, *under* them — if she fought him off.'

'Good . . . And her hands, Stanley. They're still clenched. She may have been pummelling him. Ah!' Gently opening the cramped fingers of the left hand he discovered a brown button. 'Bingo!'

'Terrific, sir!' Stanley was excited. 'If we get someone and he's a button missing —'

'If . . . Did I send word to the photographer?'

'Yes, sir, you did.'

'He's taking his time!'

The dead woman was wearing a nightdress, sprigged cotton with ribbons at the neck. Jack said 'Who removed the cushion?'

'The neighbour, sir — before I could stop her.'

'And you haven't touched anything?'

'Certainly not, sir!'

Jack registered the unspoken reproach with a faint smile. Beside the bed, on a small table, an empty mug stood beside a brass alarm clock. He took out a handkerchief and gingerly picked up the clock. The alarm hadn't been set.

Replacing it carefully he said, 'Talk me through it, Stanley.'

The young detective drew himself up self-consciously. 'Well sir, I was pursuing my enquiries in Orange Street and knocked at this particular door and there was no answer and the lady next door came out and said *she'd* been knocking earlier and how it was unusual for Mrs Bly to not be about. She wanted to tell her that a man had been hanging around and she thought it might be one of us wanting to ask her some more questions about when she found the body in the church.'

Jack nodded. 'Go on.'

'We went round to the back of the house, sir, to look through the window and see if perhaps she'd had a heart attack or had a fall. She might have been lying on the floor unconscious but there was no sign of her and then I noticed that the kitchen door had been forced.' He stopped to draw breath. 'We gained access to the premises at precisely three-fourteen and —'

'Just the bare bones. You're not on the witness stand.' He ignored Stanley's offended look.

'Well sir, I told the neighbour to wait outside because of footprints and suchlike and I went upstairs. But she followed me up, sir, and ran past me into the bedroom. She started screaming and snatched off the cushion which was still over the victim's face. She got quite hysterical, then and was crying and everything. I got her downstairs and told her to go home and wait for someone to interview her so she's still there. Or should be.'

'You did well.'

'Thank you sir. I found the room exactly as it

is and ran to the end of the road and phoned in. Oh yes, I made the back door secure before I left the premises.'

'*Very* good.'

Stanley blushed. 'Thank you sir.'

They were interrupted at that moment by the arrival of Jeffries, the police doctor.

'Another one, Jack?' he demanded. 'There'll be no one left in Canterbury at this rate.' He looked at the inert figure on the bed and frowned. 'Poor soul!'

Jack said 'Ellen Bly, householder. Cleaner at the church. She found the body in the church.'

Jeffries gave him a startled look. 'So it's connected?'

'Afraid so.'

Stanley coughed pointedly.

Jack grinned. 'Point taken, Stanley! OK. It *looks* that way but it might be pure coincidence. Never assume. Right, Stanley?'

'Right, sir.'

Jeffries opened his bag and withdrew a thermometer. 'Saw Gough earlier. And his sidekick. Left them to it and went for a pint and pie.' Jeffries smiled. 'And no doubt you've sent a car round post haste to break the news of this little problem and deliver them to our door?'

Jack's mouth twisted briefly. 'I sent a chappie on a *bicycle,* actually but they'll be here before long. Gough's got himself a motor. A Jowitt. Nice for some! He's called a briefing — first thing tomorrow morning.'

'That should be interesting.' He pulled on rubber gloves.

Jack said, 'Why her? I keep asking myself. How could she have been any sort of threat? . . . Unless she knew something that she didn't tell us? Didn't I ask the right questions? Dammit! And did Parker — if it *was* him — did he know I would talk to her? How could he know who found the body?'

'It was in the paper, wasn't it?'

'Oh God! Of course it was! What's the matter with me?' Jack slapped his forehead, exasperated with himself. 'So was there something about the way the body was found that was the clue? Parker must have been covering up something. But *what,* for God's sake?' He rubbed his eyes tiredly. 'I must have missed something. If so I'm responsible for —'

'Don't go down that road, Jack,' the doctor said quickly. 'We all make mistakes. Everything's clear with hindsight.'

'But I interviewed her. Took down her statement. I don't understand.'

'Probably knew something she didn't know she knew — if you get my meaning.'

Jack sighed heavily. Thank God for Gough, he thought bitterly. He certainly wasn't making much progress left to his own devices. His confidence was ebbing rapidly. His first murder case and he was beginning to suspect he was not quite up to it. He needed to impress Gough and he had nothing to offer. Please God, he thought, give me a break! He said 'Well, time of death as soon as possible, please.'

Jeffries said, 'That girl's downstairs — Dulcie whatever-her-name-is. The one from the *Standard*.'

'Damn!' He turned to Stanley. 'Get rid of her, will you. I don't want her mixed up in this. If it *is* Parker then he's dangerous. The first death just *might* have been unintentional. This one wasn't.'

Stanley disappeared and Jack heard an argument developing on the pavement outside. He went to the window and watched as Stanley sent a resentful Dulcie on her way. His pleasure at the sight of her was quickly dispelled by the sight of a motor car pulling up outside. His heart sank.

Gough and Allan had arrived.

That evening Harriet and Dulcie relaxed in armchairs either side of the fireplace. Between them Max lay staring into the crumpled red crêpe paper which did duty in the summer when the fire was unlit. Harriet was reading a novel and smoking. Dulcie had long since given up her various attempts with cigarettes. The smoke made her cough. She was staring into space with the day's *Standard* folded in her lap. Max glanced up at Dulcie and whined hopefully.

'He wants his walk,' said Harriet.

'I thought you'd taken him out earlier.'

'He's probably forgotten *that* walk.' She laughed. 'He wants *you* to take him.'

Dulcie leaned forward to pat him and he immediately jumped to his feet and began to bark. Dulcie feigned incomprehension. 'What d'you want then? I can't speak dog language. The sooner you learn to speak English the better for both of us.'

He put his head on one side which meant that one ear stuck out. This made him look comical and appealing and Dulcie was convinced he knew it.

'Oh you love!' she cried. 'I'll take you for a walk later. I promise.'

Recognising the word 'walk', Max renewed his barking.

'Stop it!' cried Dulcie. 'Ssh!' Max began to jump about.

Harriet said, 'Stop him! He'll have that little table over!'

Just as predicted, the dog cannoned into the small table. Somehow Dulcie reached out and caught the vase as it fell.

'He'll have to go,' said Harriet. 'I've told you before. That animal is untrainable.'

Dulcie hugged him. 'Hush!' she ordered. 'Your auntie doesn't like noisy dogs.'

'His "auntie" doesn't like dogs full stop!' said Harriet. 'Never have done. Never will.' She pointed an accusing finger at him. 'You need a smack,' she told him.

'Oh no!' said Dulcie. 'He's just boisterous.'

'They're like children. They need discipline.'

Dulcie was tempted to point out that Harriet had never had any children. How did she know what they needed? A knock at the door sent Max into a further frenzy.

'There!' said Dulcie. 'He's wonderful as a guard dog!'

She held his collar while her aunt opened the door to discover Charles Brayne on the doorstep. Within minutes Max had been banished to the kitchen and Harriet was pouring three sherries.

Charles Brayne seemed to have lost weight, thought Dulcie as she sipped her drink. No doubt he had lost his appetite, poor man. The shock and grief of his son's dreadful death obviously accounted for the dark rings under his eyes and the way he fidgeted with the sherry glass. She recalled a day the two families had spent in London on Clive's twelfth birthday. A visit to Regent's Park zoo followed by a special tea in Claridge's. Then he had been a booming, avuncular figure. Now he was a shadow of his former self.

They all talked politely for a few moments about nothing in particular until finally Charles Brayne brought himself to the purpose of his visit.

'Dulcie, I would like your newspaper — that is my wife and I would like —' He broke off, swallowed hard. Then he took a deep breath and started again. 'We want the *Standard* to advertise the fact that we are offering a reward for any information that leads to the arrest of the man who killed our son. Anyone who can point the police in the right direction. It's what we want to do and we don't want the police or anyone else telling us otherwise.' He looked at them defiantly.

Harriet said, 'Sounds like a good idea to me, Mr Brayne.' She looked at Dulcie.

Dulcie nodded. 'Why should anyone want to dissuade you?' she asked. 'I think it's a very good idea — but you could have gone straight to the paper,' she said. 'You could have approached the editor, Mr Cobbs, directly.'

Charles shook his head. 'I want it done in a certain way,' he explained. 'I want you to persuade your editor to make a — a *tasteful* feature out of it. No bald headlines. No screaming capitals. Nothing blunt or ugly.' He leaned forward eagerly. 'I thought maybe a paragraph or two about Clive's life. His success at school. The respect in which he is — *was* — held by his colleagues in the office. A mention of Annabel and the grief she feels at losing him. That sort of thing. Then come to the reward. You'd be just the person to write it, Dulcie, because you knew him. You were fond of him once — as a friend. I mean.'

Dulcie said, 'I never stopped being fond of him,' and felt hypocritical. 'We were just overtaken by events.'

'I know.'

From the kitchen Max began to scratch at the door. Harriet stood up. 'I'll take that wretched animal for a walk,' she announced. '*After* I've given him a smack. He's being very naughty.' She gave Dulcie a martyred look, stubbed out her cigarette and left the room. Dulcie listened anxiously. Max gave a sharp yelp and then all was silent. The front door opened and closed.

Charles Brayne said, 'We miss our old dog. Knew every word we said. You remember Rollo?'

Dulcie nodded. The cocker spaniel had accompanied them everywhere, impeccably behaved.

'Had to have him put down. Blind as a bat towards the end and then kidneys.'

Dulcie didn't want to think about Max growing old. She said hastily 'I'd like to help you with the reward feature. I'll certainly write some suitable copy and offer it to Mr Cobbs. It would be a privilege.'

'Thank you, Dulcie.' He found a handkerchief and blew his nose loudly.

'But I must impress on you that I can't *make* him print it although I don't see why he shouldn't.'

'It's all we can do for our son. We feel so helpless.'

'You must miss him dreadfully.' She wondered how it would feel to lose someone so close to you; someone you adore. Heartbreak, she thought. A whole world shattered. How could life ever be the same again?

He nodded. 'We thought of taking our offer to the police but then Nora thought they might not like the idea. Suppose another criminal came forward with the information. One criminal deciding to expose another one — just for the money. The police wouldn't want a criminal to benefit from the offer but, quite frankly, Dulcie, we don't care who it is. If he or she goes to the police and helps us find Clive's killer . . .' His eyes filled with sudden tears. 'We have to do something for him, Dulcie. My wife is in such a state . . .' He covered his face with his hands. 'If only we could bury him and know that he was at peace. It's the thought of him lying in that dreadful place, alone. Nobody caring . . .' He gulped air, forcing back a sob. 'And now they're saying there's been another death. Poor woman. This man's beyond the pale. Evil. Wicked. I'd like to get my hands round his neck. Whatever Clive may have done, he didn't deserve to die!'

Dulcie glanced quickly away. 'Whatever Clive may have done'? What on earth did he mean by that? Had Clive *done* something to antagonise his killer? It seemed unlikely — unless the killer *was* Albert Parker and it *did* have something to do with Fellstowe and the fatality all those years ago . . .

In the early hours of the following morning, she was still puzzling over the remark when sleep claimed her.

CHAPTER 8

Mrs Craddock walked briskly westward along The Leas. To a casual observer she was a middle-aged woman in a skirt and hand-knitted twin set, taking some exercise. In fact she was on her way to work, albeit fifteen minutes earlier than usual. Although her face wore a bland expression, her thoughts were dark with the hatred that had been growing within her. The focus of her hostility was her employer whom she loathed. He had made her life a misery and had stolen from her the pride she had always taken in her work.

At night, before she slept, she amused herself by devising ways to kill him. Nothing, she was sure, would give her greater pleasure than to watch his life drain away — except, perhaps, to stand beside his grave and spit upon his tombstone. Mrs Craddock was not a violent woman. She loved her disabled husband and looked after him with unflinching devotion. She also cooked twice a week for her sick neighbour and cleaned her elderly mother's house every Saturday morning before she went shopping. If it wasn't for Mr Foote her life would be reasonably fulfilling.

Collecting a bottle of milk from the step she carried it upstairs and let herself into her office. She unwound the cord to the window blind and rolled it up. Arranging her cardigan on a padded hanger, she hung it behind the door. She went through into her employer's room and pulled back the curtains. She looked out across the grass to the sea, relishing her first sight of it. The blue grey water never failed to thrill her. One day, she would take a trip on the ferry boat that sailed from the harbour to Boulogne in France. The trip would be the one excitement in her life. The big adventure. Each month she saved a shilling from her wages and they were mounting up nicely. Of course, she would have to pay someone to look after her husband while she was away but she had taken that into account when she had done her sums. Another eleven months and she would have enough.

She straightened Mr Foote's desk blotter, lined up pens and sharpened pencils. Her mouth twitched. How wonderful to stab him through the heart with one of his own newly sharpened pencils! She sat down in his chair, twirled right round in it and stood up again. How he would hate it if he knew that miserable little Mrs Craddock had dared to park her miserable little bottom in *his* chair. He would probably want it fumigated.

Opening his cigar box she set it on the desk at an angle to the blotter. Was it possible to inject a cigar with poison, she wondered. Would it alter the taste? She poked her tongue out at the framed photograph of Mr Foote shaking hands with their local MP. The obsequious expression on Mr Foote's face made her almost nauseous.

'If you ever become mayor it'll be a dark day for Folkestone,' she told him then scurried back to her own room.

When Mr Foote arrived she was busily typing but she glanced up with a smile that hurt her pride.

'Good morning, Mr Foote,' she chirruped but received no answer. Not that she wanted one from a man like that. If she met him in heaven she'd have to be rude to him.

He walked past into his own room and she heard the sound of his briefcase being set down on the desk and unlocked. He rang the bell and she went in.

'Get me a cup of tea and then take a couple of letters.'

She fussed over the tray. He didn't mean a cup. He meant a pot of tea which in turn meant sugar bowl, milk jug, strainer. With her previous employers she had always added a small vase with one or two flowers, fresh from her garden. She had prided herself on the discreet, personal touch. Mr Foote had laughed at the idea.

While he sipped his tea he dictated three letters. One was to a fellow councillor suggesting a round of golf. The second was to accompany a cheque. He was donating ten pounds to the Police Benevolent fund.

He began the third, 'Dear Mr Brayne, You will no doubt be aware —'

Mrs Craddock said, 'Excuse me, Mr Foote, but you've forgotten the address.'

'I'll deal with that myself. And don't interrupt.'

'I'm sorry. I just thought —'

'Don't. It doesn't suit you.'

She felt her cheeks flushing.

'. . . You will no doubt be aware that earlier in the year I was foolish enough to lend your son the sum of £400 which he needed for the purchase of a flat. The interest rate was fixed at ten per cent. The repayments were only made for two months and the amount indicated on the enclosed statement is now outstanding . . .'

Mrs Craddock opened her mouth to protest that the unfortunate man's son had just been murdered but she bit back the words. The harsh wording of this type of letter was quite familiar to her. Mr Foote's business practices left much to be desired in her opinion. He was officially a property developer but he also raised money to finance various enterprises and lent money to people like poor Clive Brayne.

'. . . This sum comprises the original capital plus the interest. I would be grateful if you could settle this debt within one calendar month from the above date. If the money is not forthcoming I shall be forced to take action through the courts for settlement . . .'

Mr Foote poured himself a second cup of tea

and said, 'Well, get on with them.'

Mrs Craddock went back to her room and closed the door. Her heart ached for the Braynes. Their son scarcely cold in his grave and this monster was worrying them about what was to him a paltry sum.

She sat down and slid a sheet of paper and a carbon into her typewriter. As she did so her eyes strayed towards the filing cabinet. Vaguely she remembered another letter which concerned this same debt. It had gone to the son. The copy would be under 'B' . . . Frowning she tried to concentrate her thoughts. There was a third letter, surely, concerning this particular debt. But that had been sent to someone else. It would be in the special file she kept at home which contained all the copies he screwed up and threw into the basket. The communications he referred to as 'off the record'. The ones she always thought of as 'shady'. The question was — to whom had he sent *that* letter? And what exactly was it about? For some reason she associated it in her mind with a recent visitor who had referred to her as 'that pathetic creature'. She couldn't remember his name but presumably he would be in Mr Foote's diary.

As she began to type she felt a flicker of hope, a sudden reemergence of self-confidence. Pathetic, was she? She would wait until Mr Foote went out for what he referred to as his 'liquid lunch' — she always hoped it would choke him but it never did — and she would go through the files again. Some day, somehow, she would discover an irregularity which she would exploit. When that day came she would find a way to pay him back for all his petty cruelties. She reminded herself that she was not a downtrodden hack but a woman with a brain and a mind of her own. She smiled briefly.

Even a worm will turn.

The murder room was subdued at eight-thirty the following morning. Jack glanced round him. There were five other people, all holding mugs of tea and discussing the case. The original team were present — Jack himself, Blake and Stanley — with the exception of Berridge. There was also a young constable whose sole job it was to 'man the desk' and answer the telephone while the rest of the team were out and about. It was also unofficially his job to make numerous cups of tea and run out for buns and meat pies whenever anyone was hungry or bored. He went by the name of Bridges and Jack was under no illusions about him. He was not the brightest of the year's intake but he needed to be fully informed about the case. Information coming in while the others were out would need to be accurately assessed and acted upon when necessary.

There was also Detective Chief Inspector Gough and Detective Sergeant Allan, the two-man team from Scotland Yard. Allan, a tall, dapper individual, called for quiet. He was smartly dressed with highly polished shoes. The 'Chief', by way of contrast, was of average height, build and appearance: unimpressive, in fact. But that was deceptive, thought Jack, unwilling to underestimate the man and hoping they could work together without friction. It all depended, he thought, on the man's attitude to the local team.

'I'll get right down to business,' said Gough. He adjusted his steel-rimmed spectacles and stared round the room. 'I've read the files and I've seen both bodies. I'm inclined to think that, with the church as the link, the two crimes might be related. Any comments?'

Jack said, 'I'd say so, Chief. The woman was a cleaner at the church and may have seen something without realising it. The killer must have wanted to ensure her silence.'

'But you interviewed her, didn't you?'

'Yes, sir. But you'll have read my report. She didn't give me anything on him.'

'We're assuming it was a "him"?'

'The pathologist reckoned so because of the weight behind the blows to the first victim.'

Gough twisted his mouth in a way that indicated disatisfaction. 'Two different MOs?'

'Yes sir. If it *is* Parker he doesn't seem to have a regular method. First time, the one he was jailed for, he used a ligature.'

'No joy there, then. This time he seems to use whatever's to hand.'

Gough looked around. 'Anyone else come in on this? Any other ideas?'

No one spoke.

Jack said, 'The first suspect now has an alibi —'

'So I see. So you think we should forget him?'

'I think so, sir.' As soon as the words were out Jack wished them unsaid. He should be less specific. He had left himself no room to manoeuvre.

'Hmm? Well I'm not so sure. It's worth another try. I'll get round to him myself sometime. He'll be thinking he's in the clear.'

Jack struggled to regain some ground. 'I've warned him not to leave the area without notifying us first. He manages an estate in Cornwall and is often down there.'

'So I'll be able to find him when I want him.'

'Yes sir.' He rushed on, grateful that he had got something right. 'I really think it's more likely to be the other suspect. He has a history of violence.'

'But no apparent motive.' Gough patted the pile of reports which sat on the table beside him. 'Anyone chased up this break-out?'

Jack cursed inwardly. 'I did originally — before I was pulled off for this lot.'

'So nobody has been back to check again? Who got Parker out and *why* they did? Could be significant, don't you think?'

Damn. They had let the trail go cold. 'Could be, sir, but we were switched to —'

'Wonderful!' Gough's tone had sharpened. 'No follow-up. Because? You decided against it? You know something we don't know? Or you overlooked it?'

Jack said, 'I'm sorry, sir.' He was aware of the many pairs of eyes upon him. A rollicking from the Yard man at the first briefing. Not a very good start and they'd all know it.

Gough frowned. 'Might be important. Might throw up a link or a motive.'

'Yes, sir.'

Gough said, 'Allan? Anything you want to say?'

Jack stifled a sigh of relief as the attention switched to the 'bag man'.

Allan said, 'The note about the Fellstowe school story's a bit of a long shot, isn't it?'

Jack shrugged. 'Member of the public came in with the idea. It might —'

Allan said, 'Bit more than a member of the public, isn't she? Sister of the first suspect?'

'Well yes. Might be worth a follow-up. I don't think we can discount anything at this stage.'

Gough said, 'Not with two murders in a week, we can't!' He studied his notes. 'Dulcie Moore. Anything else we should know about her? Works as a *journalist?* Bit eccentric, is she?'

'Not really, sir. She works in her uncle's firm and just happens to be connected through her family. Brayne was a close friend etc. She was determined to clear her brother's name — hence her private investigation.'

'We don't want her muddying the water, do we. Try to discourage her.'

'No sir. Will do.'

Jack was trying not to dislike the man from

Scotland Yard. He told himself that the comments were fair. He, Jack had not done a very good job and he blamed himself for the second murder. Ellen Bly had known something and he should have got it out of her. But surely Gough might have thanked them for the efforts they had put in so far even if they hadn't got a result. They'd been making all the right moves.

Gough sighed. 'Well, we seem to be going nowhere fast. There was a girlfriend, wasn't there? I seem to remember.'

Blake spoke up for the first time. 'A Sylvie Hunt, chief. One time associate of Parker. Claims to know nothing.'

'Who interviewed her?'

'I did.' Jack groaned inwardly. Were *all* his failures going to be paraded before the rest of the team? He tried not to catch anyone's eye.

Gough smiled at Allan. 'We'll let you loose on her! Bring her in. Scare the hell out of her. If she's lying frighten the truth out of her!'

Too late Jack wished that *he* had brought Hunt into the station. Maybe she had been too confident in her own home. He wanted to hope that Allan also would be unsuccessful with the woman but from the point of view of the case he knew he mustn't think like that. They were a team whether he liked it or not and the job was to find and nail the killer.

Gough said, 'I'll get over to the prison. Check it out. Push them around a bit. If they've got a bent warder I want to find him.' He looked at

Blake. 'You go back to the boy's parents. See if they know anything they haven't told us about the son. He must have arranged that meeting in the church. So it looks as though he knew his killer. Find out who he mixed with. His colleagues at work. Might be a London connection. Anything and everything. Something might slip out. Don't give up too easily. Wear them down. Every family has skeletons in the cupboard. If they've got one I want to know it.'

'Right, sir.'

Gough looked at Stanley. 'You must be Stanley. Ask around about Parker — in pubs, low-life haunts.' He drummed his fingers on the table. 'And get hold of a mugshot of Parker. Show that around. And we desperately need a motive for the first killing. Think Motive, all of you, with a capital M.' He glanced at Jack. 'Anything I've forgotten? If not maybe you'd like to tag along with me. See what we can get out of the inmates of His Majesty's Prison. Find out who shared a cell with Parker. That sort of thing.'

Jack wanted to throttle him. Gough had deliberately left him nothing of importance to do. Bastard. Well, he wouldn't let him see that he cared but he certainly didn't want to tag along with him to the prison. Any DC could do that. He pursed his lips thoughtfully, praying for inspiration. There must be something else he could follow up.

Inspired he said, 'I was planning another chat with the vicar, sir. He might know something he thinks isn't worth telling.'

Gough looked as though he might say 'No' but he agreed, with just enough reluctance to make it clear he thought it a waste of time. Then he waved his hands in a gesture of dismissal. 'Go to it, then lads!' he said.

Jack, seething, was the first out of the room.

While Jack was setting off towards the vicarage, Dulcie was reading out her copy, ignoring the fact that Gus was trying to appear disinterested.

' "The parents of Clive Brayne, murdered a week ago, have put up a reward for information leading to their son's killer . . ." '

Dulcie glanced up. 'I wanted to mention the reward in the first para to hook the reader but I'm not mentioning the actual sum until right at the end. What d'you think?'

Gus shrugged. 'Sounds OK. Read the rest of it.'

'I meant, d'you think that's the way to do it? Keep back the actual sum?' She felt sure it *was* but she was being generous, giving Gus a chance to be helpful, deferring to his experience.

'It's OK,' he repeated.

She went on. ' ". . . Charles Brayne told our reporter yesterday that the loss of their son had devastated them. Nothing would ever be the same again. Clive had had a wonderful future ahead of him and —" '

'Ahead of him?' Gus protested. 'That phrase is

unnecessary, surely. You can't have a wonderful future behind you!'

Frowning, Dulcie reread the sentence. 'But if I leave out "ahead of him" it will say "Clive had had a wonderful future." That can't be right.'

He shrugged again. 'It's your copy!'

Dulcie hesitated. Was it a fair comment or was he being awkward? 'We-ell — I'll come back to that bit. Now where was I? Oh yes —'

' ". . . his colleagues had been full of praise for his astute handling of the firm's affairs. Nora Brayne told our reporter —" '

Gus stabbed the air with his pencil. 'You've already said "Charles Brayne told our reporter". Now it's "Nora Brayne told our reporter". You're repeating yourself. You could say "Nora Brayne explained" or "Nora Brayne said".'

'Oh! I'll alter that bit then.' She made the correction. Maybe she was misjudging him and he really *was* trying to be helpful.

' ". . . Nora Brayne said that she and her husband had been looking forward to their son's marriage and the prospect of grandchildren at some time." '

Dulcie stopped suddenly, conscience-stricken. The first grandchild they might have had would have been Teddy's child.

Gus said, 'Is that it then?'

She gave him a look that would freeze butter. 'You know it's not it. I haven't come to the interesting bit yet.'

'You're taking your time.'

'You keep interrupting, that's why.' She continued.

' "... As Charles Brayne put a comforting arm around his wife's waist he said that they wouldn't rest until the murderer was brought to book. Anyone giving information to the police that led to his arrest would be richer by five hundred pounds . . ." '

She smiled broadly. 'Not bad, is it?'

Gus screwed up his face. 'Brought to book! Ugh! That's a terrible cliché.'

'Is it? I rather liked that phrase.'

'The trouble is, so did hundreds of other writers! It's been worked to death.'

She pencilled in another note then looked up. 'But on the whole is it good?' She desperately wanted his approval before she took it in to show Mr Cobbs.

'On the whole — it's not too bad!'

'Marks out of ten?'

He considered, grinning. 'Six!'

'Six? Is that all?'

'And a half!'

'Thanks for nothing, Gus. I'll do the same for you one day.'

She sat down at her desk and rewrote it then typed it up again. Then she showed it to Gus who said 'Better.'

With her head erect she marched over to the door of Mr Cobbs's office and knocked twice. Glancing back she saw Gus raise a thumb in a comforting gesture of solidarity.

'Come in.'

Her employer was leaning back in his chair with his feet resting on the table among a jumble of cluttered papers. A half-eaten bun acted as a paperweight.

He said, 'Well?'

She held out her report. 'I wondered if we could use this, Mr Cobbs. It's a — Well, a sort of scoop.'

He glared at her, making no effort to take it from her. 'For your information, Miss Moore, we're a provincial newspaper not one of the nationals. And what would you know about scoops?'

'If you read it, Mr Cobbs, you'll see what I mean.'

'I thought I sent you to talk to the organisers of the Flower Show. A Mr Arthur Pye if I remember rightly.'

'I'm going there as soon as you've read that.'

Snatching the paper from her he said, 'I'll be glad when your six months is up and that's the truth!' With an elaborate sigh he began to read what she had written. Dulcie waited.

He looked up. 'So *you* think we should use this?'

Dulcie struggled with her disappointment. He was going to say 'No'. Blast him. 'Yes, sir, I do.'

'*You* think this is newsworthy.'

'Yes I do. Very newsworthy.' He was going to turn her down. She knew it. 'All that money, sir!

People will be interested. They'll talk about it. The police don't know about it yet. That's why it's a scoop.'

'And you think it's well written, do you?' He waved it in front of her.

She swallowed. 'Yes I do.'

'You do?'

She tried to read his expression and failed.

'So do I,' he said.

She stared at him, startled. Was she hearing things? 'You *do?*'

'I like it. We'll use it. Well done.'

A huge smile lit up her face. 'Oh *thank* you, Mr Cobbs!' She wanted to throw her arms around his neck. Suddenly she hoped he had a kind wife, a nice house and adorable pets.

He didn't return the smile. Instead he glanced at the clock on the wall. 'You're going to be late for the Flower Show interview.'

Beaming, Dulcie backed out of the office, broke the good news to Gus and then raced down the stairs in search of Mr Arthur Pye.

The vicar regarded Jack unhappily. 'I don't think I can add anything to what has already been explained by my curate, Mr Fellowes,' he said. 'As you know I was away at the time of this unfortunate incident — in Mayfield, to be precise, burying a very dear friend. We were at school together. Still, he's in God's hands now. By the time I returned to Canterbury the church had been sealed off. For the first time for twelve years I was not allowed to enter my own church.'

Recognising the reproach in his voice, Jack said, 'I'm sorry about that, reverend, but I'm sure you fully understood the need to preserve the crime scene intact. We have no hope of collecting useful evidence once other people are allowed in. As it is we do have a rather good footprint which may or may not help us. It does not belong to the victim or to Mrs Bly or Miss Moore.'

'Poor Mrs Bly. I find it so hard to believe anyone would kill a defenceless woman — or why they should want to. And what a dreadful way to die. I just pray that she was asleep when it happened and that she knew nothing about it. She was a dear soul. No malice in her at all.'

Jack listened patiently for a few minutes while the vicar extolled the virtues of his church cleaner. Then he said, 'It just might belong to the perpetrator.'

The vicar frowned. 'Might belong — ?'

'The footprint.'

'Oh! Yes. I see.'

He had a deceptively youthful appearance. Jack wondered whether it had anything to do with a clear conscience. A round pink face, dark curls and a boyish way of talking which were slightly at odds with his twelve years' experience. Add to that his years of training and he must be well over thirty.

The vicar tutted. 'And do you have any idea,

Mr Spencer, who this wretched man is? This *perpetrator?*'

'Wretched man'? That description, thought Jack, must be the understatement of the year. Presumably it must be difficult for a man of the cloth to find a suitable way to think of a brutal murderer. Could a man who had killed two innocent people conceivably be 'one of God's creatures'? In Jack's book the murderer must be found and punished for his crimes. An eye for an eye, a tooth for a tooth.

He said, 'We do have a new lead and we're reasonably hopeful. Further than that I'm not allowed to say. We don't want him to know that we're interested in him.'

'Ah!' The vicar's eyebrows rose. 'That sounds promising.' He fumbled in the pocket of his robe and produced a handkerchief. Having blown his nose he said, 'I understand that someone from Scotland Yard has come down to help you. They say two heads are better than one. So that's good, isn't it.'

'Very good.' Jack found himself justifying the situation. 'It's quite normal when there is more than one serious crime to be investigated. The Canterbury force has limited resources and the London team are very experienced. A sort of "murder squad" — and Detective Chief Inspector Gough is very well qualified to help us.' He had made that sound almost heartfelt he thought, amused. 'Coming from London, of course, they are very familiar with this type of crime . . .' He referred to his notebook. 'Just as a matter of interest, vicar — did Mrs Bly always clean the church in the morning when there was a wedding due? According to our reports. Mrs Belling who turned up to do the flowers, seemed rather surprised to find her there.'

The vicar thought about it. 'Actually, I don't think it was. It wasn't her normal practice. She would normally do it the evening before if there was going to be a wedding. She said she felt in the way with Mrs Belling seeing to the flowers and wedding photographers turning up to prepare themselves — the best places to set up the tripod and that sort of thing. And often the *family* chose to do the flowers and *they* would be bustling around. She felt "de trop", Mr Spencer, if you see what I mean.'

Jack nodded. 'I keep thinking that I'm missing something here. It's been bothering me. Something Mrs Bly said . . .' He shook his head. 'It'll come to me, I suppose.'

'Maybe Mrs Belling could enlighten you,' the vicar suggested. 'They must have talked together because Mrs Belling was coming to do the church flowers that morning and she, too, was barred from entering.'

'I'll talk to her — although I'm sure one of our lads will have taken a statement.' Jack stood up and took his leave.

He was on his way out of the door when he remembered the business of the rats and the mice and turned back. 'I understand that you had a bit of a problem with mice,' he said tactfully.

'Mice? Not that I know of.'

Hardly going to want to admit it, thought Jack, but he persevered. 'You had a man in to get rid of them. A rat-catcher, presumably. Mrs Bly said something to Mrs Belling about him using gas. As a humane means of extermination.'

The round face expressed total incomprehension. 'I don't know where she got that idea from,' the vicar told him. 'We do have the odd rat or mouse, most churches do, but as for needing a rat-catcher —' He shrugged. 'You've got me there, I'm afraid.'

'You mean you didn't engage a rat-catcher.'

'Certainly not.'

'What about the rector? Might he have —'

'No, Mr Spencer. It would not be up to Mr Fellowes. It would be *my* decision. We don't have a problem with vermin and I hope no one is suggesting that we do.'

Jack stared at him, suddenly alert, all his senses straining to grasp this unexpected information. A wild idea dawned. If there were no official rat-catcher, then the man Ellen Bly referred to must have been an impostor. Someone who pretended to be gassing rats was a man who had to invent a reason for being in the church. Suppose that had been the night of the murder — then Mrs Bly might easily have stumbled upon him when she turned up to do her cleaning. He might already have killed Brayne . . . And that would explain *her* death! Was it feasible? He felt a sudden sense of triumph as he recognised the potential significance of this lead. With it came a rush of hope. Maybe he could redeem his reputation.

The vicar was watching him closely. 'Are you all right, Mr Spencer?'

With an effort Jack returned to reality and the fact that the vicar was talking to him.

'. . . I was saying, Mr Spencer, that any time you might wish to attend one of our services, you'd be most welcome.'

Jack nodded distractedly. 'Thank you. I'll bear that in mind.'

They shook hands and Jack asked for Mrs Belling's address. He set off at a brisk walk in the direction of her house but by the time he had gone a hundred yards he was running.

Chapter 9

Annabel answered the door and Dulcie was appalled to see the change in her appearance. Her face was pale and her eyes had a haunted look. Hiding her dismay Dulcie began, 'I'm sorry to call on a Sunday but —'

From behind Annabel, Mrs Roper called, 'Who is it? We don't want to see anyone.'

Dulcie said, 'I needn't stay long. It's about the Flower Festival. Arthur Pye sent me to speak to your father.'

Annabel looked startled. 'The Flower Festival? Heavens. We'd forgotten all about that. You'd better come in.' Lowering her voice she said, 'We're in the middle of a family row. A crisis to end all crises. Can you bear it?'

'I expect so.' Dulcie could guess what it was about.

Annabel whispered, 'Whatever I say, back me up!' as she led the way into the drawing room.

The room smelled, as it always did in summer, of beeswax polish. Light from the large windows was reflected in the ornate mirrors. Dulcie had always loved the room's tranquil atmosphere but this was noticeably absent today. Several newspapers in pristine condition were piled on a side table, obviously unread.

Eddie Roper stood by the unlit fire, his face sullen, one elbow resting on the marble mantelpiece. He looked harassed. Maude, his wife, stared up from the sofa, her face pale, her hands nervously stroking an elderly black cat which was sprawled across her lap.

Maude said crossly, 'What on earth do you want, Dulcie? Trust you to pop up at the most inopportune moments.'

Before Dulcie could answer, Annabel said, 'She's come from the *Standard* about the Flower Festival,' and both parents looked at her blankly.

Eddie recovered first. 'Good God! The Festival. When the hell is it?' he said.

Dulcie said, 'According to Mr Pye when I spoke to him yesterday it's in two weeks' time.'

He looked horrified. 'Two weeks? Where are we now? I've lost all sense of time with all this hanging over my head!'

His wife snapped, '*Your* head? What about me? What about Annabel? We're all in this together, Eddie.'

'It's the seventeenth today,' Dulcie told him. 'The Festival is on the twenty-ninth. A Saturday.'

Annabel indicated a well-stuffed armchair. Dulcie sat down and Annabel seated herself on the arm. Dulcie's interest quickened at the prospect of conflict. Her own home had always been a remarkably peaceful place. If there had been quarrels they had been kept from the children. Because of this, Dulcie had always found other people's quarrels rather exciting. She excused her insensitivity by telling herself that every good journalist had this inborn curiosity about other people's lives.

She flipped open her notebook. 'Mr Pye said you had been kind enough to say you would open the Festival and that it could be held in the garden here. Apparently there will only be one large marquee —'

Maude said, 'What's this got to do with you, Dulcie Moore?'

Dulcie's smile was deliberately charming. 'An article in the *Standard* will be a useful piece of advance publicity. The newspaper will be donating a couple of prizes, too — for the best red rose and the best children's posy.'

The Flower Festival was held each year to swell the restoration funds for the cathedral. Dulcie could imagine how much the Ropers had been looking forward to hosting such a prestigious event. Until now, of course, when it was probably the last thing they wanted to think about.

Maude said, 'Oh blow the Festival. All those people tramping over the lawns!'

He glared at her. 'You were keen enough earlier when they asked us. Keen as mustard then.'

'That was then!' she protested.

Annabel gave an exaggerated sigh and met

Dulcie's sympathetic gaze.

Dulcie said, 'Mr Pye wanted to know if you were still willing to hold it here. He's been unwilling to trouble you at such a sad time and was hoping to hear from you.'

'We'll cancel!' said Maude.

Eddie said, 'Cancel? Oh that *is* a clever idea! That *will* set the tongues wagging. That's just like you, Maudie!'

Annabel said, 'There's no need to be sarcastic, Daddy. Mother was only thinking what would —'

'I know what she was thinking. Personally, with only a fortnight to go and all the work that Nathan's put in on the lawn I'd vote we carry on. Show people we can still hold up our heads in spite of everything.' He gave Annabel a nasty look.

Annabel said, 'That's right. Blame me. I suppose it was my fault that Clive was killed.'

'It was your fault you weren't marrying Teddy! None of this would have happened if you —'

Maude said, 'And Teddy's fault we're having this family conference.' She transferred her anger to Dulcie. 'It's thanks to your brother and his *disgusting* behaviour that our daughter has to be sent away in disgrace to —'

Dulcie rose to the bait. 'I don't think it was rape, if that's what you're suggesting.'

The cat, sensing trouble, wriggled from Maude's lap and fled from the room. They all watched her go.

Annabel said, 'It wasn't rape. I never said it was. He didn't *force* me. He just — We seemed to —'

Her mother clasped her hands. 'Don't keep using that awful word! I can't bear it.'

Annabel looked at Dulcie. 'I keep telling them. Teddy and I have talked it over. We want to get married and we want to keep the baby.' She looked from her mother to her father. 'You won't listen, will you. You won't even *try* to understand.'

Neither of them answered her.

Dulcie said, 'It sounds like a sensible idea to me. Getting married, I mean. The sooner the better, probably.'

Annabel gave her shoulder a grateful squeeze but her parents immediately closed ranks.

Her father said. 'You are hardly the best judge, Dulcie, of what is best for Annabel. I'm sure Annabel doesn't want us to become social outcasts. If she and Teddy marry before poor Clive is cold in his grave there will be unpleasant gossip. The child must be adopted. It's the normal procedure in these matters. Best for everyone. Somewhere there's a childless couple who desperately want a baby.'

Maude said. 'You part with the baby as soon as it's born so you don't have time to grow attached to it. It's all very civilised. A holiday with my sister Evelyn in Switzerland. We'll tell people Evelyn's been ill and needs Annabel as a companion while she's convalescing.'

Annabel said, 'How many more times? I don't want to part with the baby.' She looked towards Dulcie who took her cue promptly.

'Neither would I,' she said. 'Plenty of children born out of wedlock bring great joy to their parents. And an eight months' convalescence? Is that quite believable?'

Maude said, 'It won't be so long as that. Annabel won't look — won't *show* — until about five months. Six if she's lucky. She can wear a strong support corset and —'

'Mother! Stop it! I tell you I won't do it! I'm over twenty-one and, whatever you say, I don't have to do it.'

Maude went on as though she hadn't spoken. 'There's sure to be a decent clinic in Berne and the child can be adopted from there. Nobody in England need ever know.'

'I tell you I *won't* agree to it, Mother. You can't drag me to Switzerland by force.'

Eddie waved a clenched fist. 'You stubborn little fool! You're lucky we haven't turned you out on to the *street!* My God, you're an ungrateful girl!' His face had reddened. 'Some fathers would have done that, you know. Some fathers would cut the daughter off without a penny. It may sound harsh but, frankly, I'm beginning to sympathise with them.'

Maude said, 'Eddie! Don't talk such nonsense. Whatever will Dulcie think.'

What she meant, thought Dulcie, was 'What will people think if Dulcie repeats this conversation'! She was beginning to feel sorry for Maude Roper. She said, 'I'm sure Teddy isn't after your money, if that's what you're implying.'

Annabel, wearying, said, 'Must we all quarrel? Dulcie's a friend of the family.'

Eddie snorted. 'Some friend! It's her bloody brother that's —'

Dulcie said, 'But it will be your *grandchild.* You'll be handing it over to complete strangers who might not take good care of it. How ever could you bear it? And suppose — just suppose — that Annabel never has another child. You'd always be thinking and wondering —'

Eddie, furious, wagged a threatening finger. 'That's quite enough from you, Dulcie. You always were a meddling child. This is nothing to do with you.' He glanced at his wife who was visibly shaken by Dulcie's words about the grandchild. 'And you've upset Maudie. That's so like you, Dulcie Moore. You must put in your two penn'orth! Just like the way you interfered over Annabel's confirmation dress. It was a perfectly acceptable dress and Annabel would have seen reason. But no! You took her side and we ended up paying for another dress.'

Annabel said, 'That was years ago, Father. For heaven's sake! And it was only a matter of pounds. The first dress was too babyish. Mother agreed afterwards, didn't you, Mother?'

Maude looked flustered. 'It wasn't about the money. Not really. It was because Evelyn was so proud of having made it for you. She made your christening gown and she'd always said she'd make your confirmation dress. So naturally —'

Annabel cried, 'Forget the damned dress! What on earth does it matter *now?*'

Eddie glared at Dulcie, 'If Dulcie had kept her nose out of things we'd have talked you round.'

Annabel said, 'Arguing about that stupid dress after all these years! It's bloody ridiculous!'

'Annabel!' Maude shook her head despairingly.

Eddie said, 'So this is what it's come to, after all our efforts to raise you well. You sound like a fishwife!'

'I learnt it from you!' Annabel's voice shook.

The ensuing silence lengthened.

Dulcie intervened. 'Perhaps we should get back to the Flower Festival.'

Eddie was not to be sidetracked. 'It's a pity Dulcie doesn't spend more time thinking about her own life instead of interfering in ours. She ought to be married by now but oh no! She has to upset her parents by becoming a journalist!'

Annabel said, 'Perhaps she doesn't want to marry. Not every woman does.'

Maude said, 'Of course she does,' and they all looked at Dulcie.

'I do want to marry but not yet. I want to live a little first. I want —' Dulcie stopped. Why did she feel the need to justify her decision? She said firmly. 'I came here to talk about the Festival. May I please have an answer for Arthur Pye.'

'Bugger Arthur Pye!' Eddie fumed. 'I'd like to

tell him what he can do with his Festival!'

Maude screamed, 'Edward Roper! No one is allowed to talk like that in this house What are you thinking of?' She took a long breath and turned to Dulcie. 'We'll have the Festival here as arranged.'

He stared at her. 'But five minutes ago you said cancel it. All those people tramping over the lawns. That's what you said. Now I'm saying we call it off and you're arguing with me. Sometimes I wonder about you, Maude.'

Maude said, 'Well, it's mutual, I can assure you!'

'God! Women!'

Annabel groaned. 'Father, *please!* Now who's being uncivilised!'

Maude stiffened. 'Don't you dare speak to your father like that!' She waved her hands in a gesture of despair. 'Why should we cancel it? We've waited years for the chance to host it. We might never get another chance.'

Annabel said, 'Say yes then! What does it matter? It's only one day.'

Dulcie said, 'If you *are* willing to host the Festival there are a couple of queries.' She took out a pencil.

Eddie, struggling with his temper, hesitated. 'Hang on now. What d'you really feel, Maudie?'

After a moment's thought she said, 'Suppose Clive's funeral is on the same day?'

Dulcie glanced at Annabel in surprise. 'Have they said they're ready to release his body?'

Her friend nodded. 'It's possible. Apparently they've done all their hateful tests.'

Maude drooped, suddenly exhausted. 'I suppose we could always slip away from the Festival — or ask the Braynes to choose another day for the funeral.' She drew a long breath. 'That poor boy. I still can't quite believe it. I can see him now, Dulcie, sailing that toy boat on your pond. He was only about eleven then and so proud of himself.'

'Until he overbalanced and fell in!' Annabel smiled faintly at the memory and another silence fell.

It was broken by her father. He thrust his hands into his pockets and said, 'Right then. Tell Pye we'll go ahead exactly as planned. We might as well salvage something from this God-awful mess.' His shoulders sagged. 'So what are these couple of queries, Dulcie? I don't mean to be rude but we've got more important things to talk about.'

One query was the choice of caterers for the cream teas. Did Eddie want to choose them? No, he didn't. He didn't give a damn who they were. The second was about lavatories. Were there any in the house that were conveniently placed or should they arrange one of those canvas affairs with a bucket?

Maude said, 'Oh no! They smell so terrible. The women can use the lavatory off the boot room and there's another which Nathan uses. It's down by the old greenhouse and not exactly glamorous but the men won't mind. We can put up a sign with an arrow.' She put a hand to her head. 'I shall have to lie down shortly,' she told them. 'My head is simply banging away.'

The last query was on the subject of the raffle. Maude had volunteered to collect suitable prizes. Was she still willing to do this? No, she wasn't. Couldn't face her friends at a time like this. She was sorry but there you are.

Dulcie stood up, stowing her notebook and pencil in her jacket pocket. 'In my article I'll be saying how brave it is of you both to carry on,' she told them. 'And how, in spite of the tragedy, you don't want to let people down. Oh, and that you know the cathedral restoration fund is a worthy cause. That sort of thing. Is that OK? I'll only refer to Clive's death. Nothing else.'

She had half hoped for gratitude but none was forthcoming. She made her 'Goodbyes' and left, but she felt their hostility following her as Annabel saw her to the door.

'I'm sorry they're so awful,' said Annabel, 'but I know they're going through a terrible time. And you were wonderful. Thanks.'

Dulcie kissed her. 'I hope you and Teddy get married,' she said. 'And keep the baby. I'm wholly in favour.'

Annabel's laugh was shaky. 'Apart from me and Teddy, you're in a minority of one,' she said.

That evening Jack arrived at the police station just before five for the session that Gough called debriefing. As soon as he pushed open the door he saw a rear view of Bridges, bending forward to pat a shaggy white dog.

'Good boy then? Eat up your nice dindins!'

Jack laughed. 'Dindins! Now I've heard everything!' he told the young constable.

Bridges straightened up hurriedly. 'Someone brought it in, sir. Causing a disturbance in the Buttermarket. Fighting with another dog and then rushing through Christchurch Gate and running amok in the cathedral precincts. Nipped someone on the ankle.'

'Anyone important?' Jack found himself hoping Max had gone for the Archbishop. That would give Dulcie a scoop for her newspaper.

'No sir. One of the men working on the stonework. Not a bad nip.'

Jack said, 'I know that dog. It's called Max. It belongs to Dulcie Moore.'

Bridges looked disappointed. 'Are you sure, sir? It's not wearing a collar and nobody's been in to claim it. I thought I'd take it home with me — until it's claimed, that is. My Mum's mad on dogs. We used to have three but they all died of old age and —'

'I'll take it back to its owner. I know where she lives.' His spirits had risen considerably at the prospect of a few words with Max's owner.

'Will you have time, sir?' The constable glanced at the clock. 'The Chief's ready and waiting. There was only you and Allan to come. I'll be going off duty soon and —'

Jack grinned. 'Bridges, are you listening to me? I said *I'll* take it to its owner. Got it?'

'Yes, sir.'

Belatedly recognising Jack, Max began to bark ecstatically and managed to step on his dinner, sending half a round of cheese sandwich skittering across the floor. Allan, stepping through the doorway put his foot on it and cursed.

'What the devil — ?' he grumbled.

Jack patted Max on the head and whispered, 'Good boy!'

Bridges, hiding a grin, muttered excuses and found a cloth with which to remove the mess from Allan's shoe.

To Allan, Jack said briskly. 'Now you're here we can make a start. We're all waiting,' and moved smartly out of the room.

They made their way along the passage. A notice had now been stuck on to the door with the words MURDER ROOM on it. Jack went in. He was incredibly cheered by the thought that he now had an excuse to see Dulcie and he was revising his opinion of her dog. She would be so frantic about it, she would surely be grateful for the animal's safe return. He wondered whether he would suggest that, as Max had been tied up for several hours at the station, they should take him for a quick walk round the block for a bit of exercise. As though tuned in to Jack's thoughts Max began to bark.

Allan said, 'That bloody dog!' and sat down.

Gough said, 'Can't someone shut it up?'

'I'm returning it to the owner,' said Jack. He got up and closed the door which Allan had left ajar. This muffled the sound and Gough muttered, 'Thanks.'

Gough asked for the various reports and one by one the men concerned reported on their progress. Jack was mortified to realise that they had covered quite a lot of ground. Sylvie Hunt had now admitted that she *had* seen Parker and more than once. Jack wondered how much pressure Allan had used to get that much information from her. Perhaps he himself had been too easy on her. He tried to imagine Allan roughing her up but failed.

Gough revealed that the laundry man who had driven the van in which Parker had escaped was not the regular driver. The regular man had been paid £50 to lend the van. Fifty pounds and no questions asked. He was being held in a cell overnight while they investigated his claims. One of the warders on duty on the morning of the escape had been away sick ever since. Name of Marshall. A visit to his home suggested that he had scarpered with whatever they had paid him. His wife had gone too and his elderly mother who lived in the next street claimed to be worried about him. Quote — It's not like him not to say if he was going away on holiday — Unquote.

They had a couple of good prints from the church pews.

Blake had some interesting information about

the Braynes. It appeared that the son had borrowed a lot of money which he failed to pay back. His parents had now received a threatening letter from someone in Folkestone who said he wanted the money repaid within a week.

Gough drew a long breath. 'You saw the letter?'

'Yes sir. Signed by a Reginald Foote.' He referred to his notebook. 'The Leas, Folkestone. Firm called "Harris Enterprises". They seem to be connected with another firm called "RF Finance". Probably a moneylender. Could be a subsidiary. *Could* be shady.'

'I reckon the Braynes are way out of their depth,' said Blake. 'They're obviously worried to death about all this on top of losing their son.'

Gough frowned. 'How much are we talking about?'

'Nearly £500, sir.'

Gough whistled. 'On top of all the wedding expenses and everything. That's tough.'

Stanley said, 'I expect they could cancel some of them — like the church choir and the bell ringers. But not the caterers. They'd have prepared everything.'

Jack said, 'But how can they put up this reward if they're short of cash?'

Allan shrugged. 'Search me. Perhaps they've got stuff they can sell — jewellery, pictures. That sort of thing.'

Jack said slowly, 'I wonder if this is the tie-up we've been waiting for, sir. Suppose young

Brayne borrows some money without telling his parents and then can't pay it back . . . The lender might have leaned on him — literally. Tried to frighten the money out of him —'

Gough said, '— and went too far!' He scratched his head. 'Which would make the moneylender in Folkestone our man. And not Parker.' He pursed his lips. 'Is it making any sense?'

Jack said, 'I'm not sure yet . . . Could someone have borrowed money from the Folkestone moneylender to spring Parker? But if so, why?'

Everyone fell silent, all hoping to come up with the answer and earn a smile of approval from their 'Chief'.

Jack said, 'Someone needed Parker out. So someone wanted a job done.'

Blake grinned. 'Anyone robbed a bank lately?'

Allan said, 'Not Parker's style, from what I've read.'

Jack leaned forward eagerly. 'Maybe the man with the money is the lender in Folkestone. Maybe he wanted Parker to be his muscle. Maybe he wasn't meant to kill Brayne but he went too far and then . . .'

Allan shook his head. 'You don't spring someone just to act as a debt collector. Perhaps he's got another job planned for Parker.'

Gough said, 'Why kill Mrs Bly?'

Jack's moment had arrived. He said, 'Because she must have seen him at the church the evening before and could identify him. I believe she stumbled on to the murder scene and the killer pretended to be a rat-catcher. She told Mrs Belling she'd seen such a man but I've spoken with the vicar who vehemently denies engaging the services of a rat-catcher.' He had all their attention and it felt good. 'Now let's assume the killer only beat up the first victim but it went too far and he killed him. Now he has a charge of murder or manslaughter to face if he's caught. So why not get rid of Mrs Bly? What's he got to lose? They can't hang him twice! He only beat up the first one — it wasn't meant to be murder. Once he'd accidentally killed Brayne he'd be looking at murder or manslaughter. What did he have to lose? No reason not to get rid of the cleaner. The vicar says he knows nothing about this so-called rat-catcher. But Mrs Bly goes back next morning to do her cleaning and finds the body. The rest we know.'

Heads swivelled from Jack to Gough. He took his time. Jack noticed. Or wasn't he convinced?

At last Gough said, 'So the so-called rat-catcher was in the church and had just murdered Clive Brayne. Cleaner turned up unexpectedly . . . Mmm? He may not have known his victim was dead then. If he had known he might have killed her. If she'd seen anything but we know she didn't. She was very lucky.'

She's dead, thought Jack. How lucky can you get? He said nothing.

Gough frowned with concentration. 'When he heard later that Brayne was dead, he knew Mrs Bly might give a description of him, so he got rid of her . . . My God, Jack, this could be it!'

Jack, thrilled, heard the excitement in the detective inspectors voice. His spirits soared.

Allan, grudging him his moment of triumph, said, 'But we still don't know why Brayne came to meet Parker?'

You mean sod, Jack thought. You don't want the local boys to succeed. He said 'Maybe he thought he was meeting Foote, the moneylender, to discuss ways of paying off the debt. So much a month plus so much off the arrears. That sort of thing.'

Stanley was trying to keep up. 'Funny place to meet anyone that time of night.'

'Granted,' said Jack, 'but I don't suppose Brayne had much choice. I dare say our man thought a church would be empty at that time. And he was right. The moneylender might have threatened to disclose the debt. On the eve of his wedding that would have been disastrous.'

'Poor bastard!' said Gough, surprising Jack to the realisation that he *did* have a heart.

Stanley tried again. 'Maybe he used to go to that church once upon a time and knew there would be nobody there.'

Gough looked at him. 'A Christian churchgoing murderer! Wonderful!'

Jack watched Stanley shrivel under the sarcasm and knew how bad it felt. He said, 'But Stanley might have a point. Chief Parker spent some of his early years here in Canterbury. He went to the council school in Northgate for a few years. He was orphaned quite young and stayed with his grandparents for about a year but he was such a handful they sent him away to an orphanage. While he was there they realised he was very intelligent and one of the wealthy patrons took pity on him and paid for him to go to a decent school. Not that it did any good. Parker must have been *born* a villain.'

Gough, surprised, said, 'You've done your homework.'

'I was on the escape before I was switched to the first murder, sir.'

'Ah! . . . So where are we exactly?'

Jack said, 'So our best bet is to find the Folkestone moneylender and lean on him. See what happens.'

Gough nodded. 'You get down there first thing tomorrow. Talk to Foote and check him out with the Folkestone police. Anything a bit "iffy" — we need to know. And watch yourselves. These men could be heavy. After a few years in the murder squad you get a nose for it. I've got a very bad feeling about this one . . . Meanwhile I'll get on to the bent warder's —' He stopped and rolled his eyes. '— *Alleged* bent warder's mother and any nosy neighbours she might have. Now. Stanley . . .'

He began to allot jobs to the rest of the team and Jack allowed himself to think about Dulcie. He was longing to share his success with her although he knew he couldn't be too specific. He would simply drop a few hints that he had impressed the man from The Yard. Maybe if they took the dog for a walk she'd ask him back for a cup of tea. Or something to eat. He could always tell his landlady he'd been working late. She was used to that. He paid for all the meals even if he didn't eat them.

'Right,' said Gough. 'We'll call it a day, lads!'

When Jack returned to the front desk, Max was no longer barking. He was lying down with his head on his paws, looking soulful. When he saw Jack he leaped to his feet but before he could open his mouth Jack pointed a stern finger and said, 'You dare!'

Max looked puzzled. He barked once but stopped abruptly as Jack's threatening finger moved nearer.

'One more sound and you'll be cat's meat!' Jack told him.

He signed the dog out. 'I can't take him like this,' he protested. 'No collar or lead.'

The desk sergeant raised his eyebrows. 'What's wrong with a bit of string?'

'It'll cut into his neck if he pulls — and he will!'

He rummaged around and found a spare belt which he made into a collar. The string would do for a lead. He set off for St George's Terrace in high spirits, rehearsing what Dulcie might say and how he would reply.

The house was one of a short row of attractive stuccoed buildings which faced outward from the city. In front of them was the road and beyond that railings. From here, on market days, bystanders could look down on to the cattle and sheep moving fretfully in their pens. The views were attractive but Jack wondered how smelly it was on market days in midsummer.

Harriet opened the door and said, 'Oh Max! There you are!' To tone down her delight she added, 'Blasted dog! Turning up like a bad penny.' But she leaned over to ruffle his fur and her tone was full of affection.

'I'm afraid, Miss Moore, that —'

'Call me Harriet. I hate formality.'

'Harriet? Right I'm afraid the dog was causing a disturbance in the Buttermarket area. Fighting with another dog. And then he ran into the cathedral grounds and took a bite out of somebody's ankle.'

She laughed. 'Max! You have had fun.' She opened the door wider. 'Come in,' she told Jack. 'I've been looking everywhere for him. I was just going to pour myself a brandy. Maybe you'll join me. Not much fun drinking alone.'

'Thank you,' he said, relinquishing the improvised lead and hiding his disappointment. So Dulcie was out. Maybe he could stay on until she came back.

Harriet said, 'I came back from the shops and found him gone. I thought I'd checked the back door but I must have forgotten. It's never fitted properly. On a windy day it's a nuisance and sometimes Max can rattle it loose. He's a clever dog when he wants to be. Dulcie would be broken-hearted if anything happens to him. She's hopelessly smitten with the animal. Can't think why.'

'He wouldn't eat,' Jack told her, settling into the armchair she had suggested for him. 'Mind you, cheese sandwiches aren't ideal. I expect he's used to better things.' He unfastened his jacket and loosened his tie a little when she wasn't looking. He was longing to say. 'Where is she?' but knew he must be patient. Eventually Harriet would mention her niece's whereabouts if he steered the conversation in the right direction.

'Drink this.' Harriet handed him a generous brandy. 'I'll just give this wretched animal something to eat.'

He examined the room with interest. Comfortable, unfussy furniture. A good carpet. One or two nicely framed pictures that looked as though they might be worth a bob or two. He was not very knowledgeable about art. On the mantelpiece there was a solitary photograph in a bright silver frame. Recently, maybe lovingly polished, he thought. A young man in army uniform stared nervously into the camera.

Coming back into the room Harriet saw that he was studying it. 'That's Lionel. I should have married him but I was too pigheaded. I was a Suffragette and didn't want to know about weddings and babies. I wanted to march and wave banners and get myself chained to railings.' She raised her glass in a toast. 'It was heady stuff, at the beginning. Dulcie would have loved it. She's so disappointed that she missed it. Mind you, it got very nasty towards the end.'

She could have been pretty in her younger days, thought Jack. He tried to imagine Dulcie as a Suffragette — marching down the Mall or throwing herself under a racehorse. He didn't like it. Thank God they were done with all that nonsense.

Harriet said, 'Bit before your time, I suppose — Votes For Women. Nearly twenty years ago.'

'I know about it, of course.'

'Do you smoke?' She reached for a silver cigarette case and snapped it open.

'Thank you.' He took out the silver lighter Judith had given him and lit Harriet's cigarette and then his own.

Harriet drew on hers and sighed with satisfaction. 'I worshipped Emmeline Pankhurst. We all did. When she was sent to prison I felt quite murderous. I was frightened by how passionate I felt — and how helpless.'

'But didn't she throw bombs or something?'

'She blew up Lloyd George's villa and quite right too. It was worth thousands of pounds so they put her away for four years.'

Jack said, 'And quite right too! You can't go round blowing things up! A man would have gone to prison. Why not a woman? Sauce for the goose, Miss — I mean Harriet!'

Jack thought about the imprisoned women.

They had gone on hunger strikes and been force fed. The thought of anyone forcing a tube down Dulcie's throat sickened him. To change the subject he said, 'What happened to Lionel?'

'He was killed in 1917. I blamed myself in the way people do. I should have married him. I could have made him happy for a few years before the Germans killed him.'

He said, 'I suppose your niece has a — I mean, she'll be getting married one of these days.' He regretted the unsubtle remark as soon as he had uttered it.

She smiled. 'For the record there was a young hopeful named Gerald but he got what you young people call "the brush off". Tactfully, of course. Dulcie is very soft-hearted. At the moment she's fancy-free, thank goodness.' Her expression changed slightly. 'Is there a Mrs Spencer?'

He hadn't expected such a direct question and was unprepared for it. 'No!' He was immediately ashamed of his betrayal of Judith but there was no way he could let them know the truth.

She raised her eyebrows. 'No wedding bells on the horizon? Now that does surprise me.'

She meant it as a compliment but Jack had the uneasy feeling that she had seen through the lie.

'There was somebody —' he began, almost stammering in his haste to convince her. 'We thought it might work out but — Well, it didn't.'

'She didn't break your heart, I hope. Or don't policemen have hearts?'

'They do,' he said, 'but no.'

'You broke hers.'

She was a little too perceptive, thought Jack. If she'd been a man she'd have made a good detective. Her words had disturbed him. Would Judith be broken-hearted if he ended the relationship? It was a terrible thing to do to a woman. How on earth would he find the words to tell her? He could imagine how she would react — He stopped suddenly. What on earth was he thinking of? Breaking up the long relationship with Judith? For Dulcie Moore — a young woman he hardly knew. A woman who didn't even like him very much and whose brother had been a suspect in a murder case. Was he mad?

Harriet said, 'Dulcie is breathtakingly pretty but she also has a good brain and she values her independence.' She smiled to soften the words. 'Not an easy fish to land! Let poor Gerald be a warning to you!'

He was beginning to suspect that she was clairvoyant and could see into his confusion. Abruptly he decided that it would be better not to see Dulcie tonight. No doubt Harriet would tell her of their conversation and Dulcie would suppose him to be free of any romantic ties. The lie bothered him. His mother always said, 'Be sure your sins will find you out.'

After a decent interval, when he had finished his drink, he said, 'Well, I'd better be on my way. Tell your niece not to worry about Max. No one is pressing charges. He did no real damage.' End the visit on an official footing, he told himself. And *don't* mention Dulcie again. 'I should keep an eye on him on market days. Wednesday and Saturday mornings, as I'm sure you know. He could cause plenty of havoc there. We don't want cattle stampeding up Bridge Street and into the town.' He grinned, bending to fondle the dog. 'Might have to arrest you, eh Max!'

Pausing on the doorstep his good intentions suddenly deserted him. He heard himself say, 'Where *is* Dulcie, by the way?'

Harriet put a restraining hand on Max's collar. 'She's gone to Folkestone. There's someone she wants to talk to. Something to do with an interview. She was being all mysterious and playing it close to her chest.'

'Folkestone?' Alarm bells rang in Jack's brain. He felt suddenly cold. 'Did she say who it was?'

She looked at him in surprise. 'A Mr Foote. I think it was . . . Mr Reginald Foote.'

CHAPTER 10

Dulcie arrived early. A middle-aged lady was already on the steps, a milkbottle in one hand, her handbag in the other.

'Good morning,' said Dulcie, smiling. 'I'm a bit of an early bird, I'm afraid. It was the train times.' A lie, in fact. She had travelled down the night before.

'Are you Miss Moore?'

'Yes.'

'I'm Mrs Craddock, Mr Foote's secretary. It was me you spoke to on the phone yesterday.' Opening the front door, she gathered up a handful of mail. 'You're very early but you can come up if you like — unless you fancy a walk. The Leas are lovely at this time of day.'

'No thank you. I'm not dressed for walking.' Dulcie held up her right foot, displaying a slim, buttoned shoe. She had deliberately arrived early in the hope that she might talk to the secretary before Reginald Foote arrived.

'We're upstairs,' the woman told her, leading the way. 'Such a glorious view across the Channel.'

Once in the office, Dulcie duly admired the view and then sat down. She watched as Mrs Craddock took off her jacket, draped it carefully over a coat hanger and hung it up behind the door.

Dulcie had spent the night in Lee Court, a small hotel in one of the nearby roads. Her room, the cheapest, had been at the top of the building and the sound of seagulls pattering across the roof tiles had woken her just after five o'clock. The early start had given her time to perfect her none too plausible reason for being here.

There was a kitchenette leading off the room and Dulcie watched Mrs Craddock stand the bottle of milk in a terracotta cooler and top it up with water from a small glass jug.

The door bearing Mr Foote's nameplate was on the other side of the room.

'So you're writing an article for a magazine?' Mrs Craddock smiled polite encouragement.

'Yes.'

'Mr Foote was very pleased that you were coming.'

'Good. Is he a nice man to work for?'

'Oh yes! Very nice. He's probably going to be mayor, you know, and the publicity from your article will be very welcome. Important people need publicity, don't they.'

'Mayor? My goodness!' Dulcie smiled. 'So then you'll be the mayor's secretary. A big step up for you, too. It must be very exciting.'

Mrs Craddock said, 'Very exciting at times,' and then 'Excuse me' and went into her employer's room. Dulcie took the opportunity to try, unsuccessfully, to read the postmarks on the envelopes which lay across the desk. She glanced in at the secretary who was busy with an orange duster and quickly crossed to the filing cabinet which stood behind Mrs Craddock's desk. A — L and M — Z. Stifling her qualms, she pulled open the second drawer and began to look for the name Parker . . . Nash, Ogden, Pratt, Prestwick, Riggs, Robbins, Salter, Stowe . . . No Parker!

'Blast!'

She went to the door of Mr Foote's office and glanced around. 'I was lucky Mr Foote could spare me half an hour at such short notice,' Dulcie remarked. 'I'm sure he's terribly busy most days.'

'Oh he is. Busy busy, as they say.' The secretary came back into the outer office, glanced at the clock and hurried to remove the typewriter cover. She inserted paper and carbons. 'He's hoping to get the go-ahead to start work on a running track. For athletics, I think. Running, high jump, that sort of thing. Then he *will* be busy. They've all tendered for the work.'

'And will he get it?'

Mrs Craddock shrugged. 'That's the big question at the moment — although he sounds very confident. Almost too confident. He'll be so disappointed if he doesn't. There are two other firms — Locke and Co and Robbins Burnett. Not that Locke and Co stand much chance. Mr Foote says they're too small.' She smiled. 'Well, actually he calls them amateurs! Robbins Burnett might get it but we hope not. They're very reliable but Mr Foote can't stand poor Mr Burnett. Calls him a boring old "f" word!' She blushed. 'I won't say it but you know what I mean. Says he's got no imagination.'

'Oh dear!' Dulcie laughed lightly. 'So it's a fight to the death between Robbins Burnett and Harris Enterprises. Pistols at dawn!'

Dulcie fancied Mrs Craddock's smile was a little strained.

She pressed on. 'You must enjoy the work — such a pleasant office and working for such an important man.'

Mrs Craddock was extracting a clean handkerchief from her jacket pocket and transferring it to her sleeve. 'I consider myself very fortunate.'

Dulcie hid her disappointment. She had been hoping for a few womanly confidences — maybe even a few grumbles about the boss. A disenchanted secretary might have been usefully indiscreet. Never mind.

The sound of the front door and heavy footsteps on the stairs sent Mrs Craddock hurrying to her desk. She sat down and her hands were poised over the typewriter by the time Reginald Foote came into the room.

'Miss Moore!' A beaming smile. 'How nice to

meet you.' He held her hand a little too long and Dulcie recognised the appreciative expression on his face.

He was a large jovial looking man with blue eyes. It was easy to imagine the chubby, angelic boy Simms had described.

'Good of you to see me at such short notice, Mr Foote. You said nine-thirty but I'm a bit early.'

'Doesn't matter, dear lady. I hope my secretary has been looking after you.'

'She has.'

His expansive smile now embraced his secretary. 'Tea for two, please, Mrs Craddock.' He smiled at Dulcie. 'Mrs Craddock is without equal. She looks after me splendidly. Now, come along into the inner sanctum and we'll talk.' To his secretary he said, 'Mr Stowe is popping in this morning, some time. Let me know if he arrives while Miss Moore is still with me. Ask him to wait.'

A flicker of apprehension appeared on Mrs Craddock's face but she nodded without comment.

Following Mr Foote into his office, Dulcie was disconcerted. He appeared to be a very charming man and not at all what she had expected. It was difficult to imagine this man mixed up in anything unpleasant, unethical or illegal. He looked like everybody's favourite uncle. When Dulcie was seated, he settled himself comfortably behind his desk and lit a cigar and for a moment Dulcie enjoyed the smell of it. Cigar smoke reminded her of her maternal grandfather.

'So, Miss Moore, what is it exactly you want to talk about? I'm all yours for twenty minutes or so.'

He smiled again — or was it a leer? She hoped it was because she didn't want to like this man.

He went on. 'In my line of business I don't often get the chance to talk to pretty women!'

Thankfully, Dulcie adjusted her opinion of him, downward.

Before she could answer he went on. 'Which magazine is this article intended for?'

'*Women's Pictorial.*' Another lie.

'You work for them?'

'Freelance. I'm actually employed by the *Canterbury Standard* but my editor thought this particular idea was more suited to the magazine market. Women want to know about their children's schooling. I'm only talking to people who are going somewhere. Successful people like yourself. And I'm examining the role their schooling played in their development.' She was surprised how convincing it sounded. 'There's been some talk lately — a small controversy I suppose you'd call it — about the benefits of a boarding school education as opposed to day schools. Good boarding schools, I mean.'

'Ah!' he looked pleased. 'You mean Fellstowe. Wonderful place. Fine traditions. I was fortunate as a boy to be a part of that tradition.' He waved his arms to encompass the room. 'It didn't do me any harm, as you can see. I work hard — and I play hard.'

'Some people feel that segregation from the opposite sex and separation from the parents are not necessarily in a boy's best interest. I want to put both sides of the argument, Mr Foote.'

The secretary came in with a tray and poured two cups of tea. She didn't speak and Foote watched her with a certain amount of impatience. Something in the wordless encounter made Dulcie think that maybe their relationship was not so happy as Mrs Craddock had suggested. When she had gone Dulcie repeated her earlier comment.

'Some people talk through their hats, Miss Moore.' He laughed, coughed and recovered. 'Ten to one they didn't have the benefits of a decent education. There'll always be "haves" and "have-nots", Miss Moore. You can quote me on that.'

She smiled as she made another note.

He said, 'You do shorthand?'

'Yes. Shorthand and typing. My parents wanted me to go to a finishing school in Switzerland but I wanted to do something useful. My aunt helped persuade them to let me go to Miss Marks Commercial College. Now, of course, I can type but I can't cook!'

He was looking at her with undisguised admiration tinged with something that might have been lust. Dulcie found it easy to ignore.

'So you weren't miserably homesick,' she suggested.

'Homesick? Certainly not. I revelled in being away from home. That's part of the value of boarding school, Miss Moore. Makes you stand on your own two feet. You learn to stick up for yourself.' He leaned forward suddenly. 'What is your Christian name, Miss Moore?'

'Dulcie.'

He sat back. 'Dulcie! What a pretty name. A pretty name for a pretty woman.'

Somehow she managed to look pleased. She felt she ought to simper but didn't know how.

Lowering his voice he said, 'Miss Moore, how would you like to give up your job and work for me? I shall probably be mayor before the year's out.'

'Oh! But what about Mrs Craddock —' She was genuinely shocked.

He leaned forward. 'What about her? She's past it, between you, me and the gatepost! Finds it a struggle. I'm keeping her on while I can. But she won't be able to cope, you see. Not fair to humiliate her. Much *kinder*, I think, to let her go. But a bright girl like you — you could have a good career. You could go places with me. Meet important people. I shan't stop at being mayor, you know. I've set my sights higher still.' He leaned forward, waving cigar smoke away with a pudgy hand. 'For your ears only, Miss Moore — Member of Parliament!' He tapped the side of his nose.

'Mr Foote! My goodness! I won't tell anyone!' She looked at him, wide eyed. Convince him.

'So you'll think about it?'

'Of course I will.'

He leaned back, satisfied. Dulcie's hands trembled slightly as she busied herself with a handkerchief. She had finally glimpsed the real Reginald Foote. Vain, ambitious, *ruthless.* Poor Mrs Craddock. Quickly she changed the subject. 'I was talking to Mr Simms, the present headmaster of Fellstowe, a few days ago. He was telling me about the things the boys did to prove their "manhood". Before his time, of course, but I was very impressed.'

She had expected him to become cautious when this subject was raised but he appeared to be quite at ease. He drew deeply on his cigar and studied the glowing tip.

'The ritual, you mean.' He swivelled his chair to and fro, considering. 'That was certainly a test of character. Oh yes! When you'd done that you felt twice the man you were before. It gave you that certain confidence. Great pity when they stopped it. It was tough, I won't deny that, but so good for morale.'

If you lived, thought Dulcie, writing again. 'You had to climb down a rope, isn't that it?'

He shrugged. 'Sometimes a rope. Sometimes knotted sheets.' He hesitated. 'Of course there were occasional accidents. One boy broke his leg.'

She looked up innocently. 'And they still allowed the ritual to continue?'

'Well, they didn't know, of course. The boy said he'd been trying to run away. You didn't split. Oh no! That would have meant Coventry. A wall of silence. You've heard of it surely.'

She nodded.

'You would never betray the ritual. That was understood. Loyalty. Brotherhood. They are Fellstowe virtues that are sadly lacking in this country today.'

'So how on earth did the teachers find out about it?'

For the first time she detected a wary look as he thought about his answer.

'There was a tragedy. A fatal accident. I was involved in it myself, actually. A boy was going down the rope and — and someone shook the rope. Stupid thing to do. I shouted to him to stop but it was too late. The boy fell and — and died later. Head injuries. Poor lad. He'd been so looking forward to it. It was a matter of pride, you see.' He shrugged. 'There was an enquiry. Par— That is, the other boy was expelled, naturally.' He rearranged his features to suggest regret. 'I've lived with the memory all these years, Miss Moore. It left a lasting impression on me. A *burden.* It might have crushed another boy but I was able to rise above it. That's what Fellstowe did for me.'

'And the boy who was expelled?' Dulcie kept her gaze firmly fixed on the notebook.

'He —' There was a pause. 'I don't know what

happened to him. Hardly the sort of person you'd want to keep in touch with.'

She glanced up. 'So Fellstowe had its failures as well as its successes.'

He hesitated. 'A very few failures. Parker wasn't really Fellstowe material.'

Parker! The name had finally slipped out. Dulcie kept her face straight.

'The boy came from a very odd background. Some sort of institution.' He shrugged. 'Even a school like Fellstowe can't perform miracles, Miss Moore. It can only —'

At that moment they became aware of raised voices from the outer office. A man's voice was raised in anger and Mrs Craddock was trying to quieten him. Dulcie and Foote stared at the door.

He said, 'That bloody man!' and jumped to his feet. Before he could move further however, the door burst open and a tall, heavily built man stood in the doorway. The craggy face might have been handsome but now it was distorted with anger. The large meaty hands were clenched and he was breathing heavily. The sort of man, thought Dulcie, that she wouldn't like to meet in a dark alley.

Totally ignoring Dulcie's presence, he shouted, 'Where's the rest of it, you bastard? You're not going to short-change me!'

Behind him Mrs Craddock was wringing her hands. 'Oh Mr Foote, I'm so sorry —' she gasped. 'He wouldn't listen to me. He pushed past me —'

Dulcie saw that she was close to tears. So who was this, she wondered excitedly.

To the man, Foote said, 'Get out! You can see I have someone with me —'

'You can have the Pope with you for all I care!' the man shouted. 'I'm not waiting on you. Not ever. You think you can push me around —' He suddenly noticed Dulcie. 'You, girlie! Hop it. Come back later.'

Incensed, Dulcie slowly stood up.

Mrs Craddock still hovered in the doorway, her shoulders hunched defensively. She said, 'Mr Stowe, *please!*' and her voice shook.

Before Dulcie could decide what to do Foote had come round the desk and now grabbed the man by the arm.

'I said, "Get out" and I meant it. You learn to wait like everyone else. You —'

The man shook his arm off. 'But I'm not everyone else, am I, old chum?'

He gave Foote a hefty push which sent him staggering back but the desk saved him from falling.

'I'm your whipping boy. The boy Daddy bought off! The one who does your dirty work!' He waved a fist in front of his face. 'So I deserve some respect. You —'

Dulcie's eyes narrowed. Whipping boy? The boy Daddy bought off? Her mind raced back to her conversation with Simms at Fellstowe. Stowe, *Fellstowe?* Was 'Mr Stowe' really Parker — the man who had most probably killed Ellen

Bly and Clive Brayne? He certainly appeared to have a violent nature. For a moment she was frightened but common sense told her that, even if it *were* him, he would hardly commit murder in broad daylight and with two witnesses. It seemed that Foote owed him some money . . . Simms' words came back to her again. He'd said that Parker suddenly changed his plea from 'Not guilty' to 'Guilty' — and then left looking *as though he had won.* So had Foote's ultra-respectable father *paid* Parker to take the blame for what had happened?

Mrs Craddock said, 'Gentlemen! Stop this!' Her hands were clasped in front of her chin. 'All these squabbles —'

So, thought Dulcie, the men had met before — and *fought* before.

Foote had suddenly rallied. He had taken hold of the lapels of the intruder's jacket and, with a huge effort, was propelling his unwanted guest backward against the wall. Stowe's head struck a framed photograph and dislodged it. It fell, cracking the glass and Foote swore. 'You come here, throwing your weight around! I could put you away for the rest of your life and I'm bloody tempted to! I could —'

'You owe me, you swine!'

Dulcie decided she had been ignored long enough. She said, 'This is ridiculous! Two grown men —'

Stowe threw her a look of deep loathing. 'I told you, girlie, to get out of here!'

'I don't take orders from people like you!' Dulcie snapped. 'And don't call me "girlie".'

Mrs Craddock's eyes widened and she gasped with horror. Reaching into the room she plucked at Dulcie's sleeve. *'Please!'* she begged. 'He'll *hurt* you. Come out while you can.'

As the two men wrestled clumsily, Dulcie backed away a little but continued to watch, fascinated. Violence was new to her and her pulse was speeding. Were Stowe and Parker one and the same? Jack would be very interested.

Mrs Craddock had withdrawn into the other room. White-faced, she cried, 'You're making things worse, Miss Moore. Come out of there, for heaven's sake!'

Dulcie, wildly curious, stood her ground. She must know what the fight was about and if it had any bearing on the murders.

'You're going to regret this, Foote!' Stowe lunged forward pushing Foote violently in the chest — a push which sent him staggering backward. As he went down he clutched at the desk and, instead, caught the flex of the table lamp. As it fell it dislodged various other items. Ink spattered from a toppled inkwell and a pile of files slid off on to the carpet. Foote, flat on his back, brought his feet up and kicked out wildly. Stowe dodged and in doing so collided with Dulcie, knocking her off balance.

'You — you clumsy brute!' she yelled, frantically trying to steady herself. Mrs Craddock screamed as Dulcie, staggering, hit her head on the edge of the door and she fell to her knees. More surprised than hurt, Dulcie found Stowe looming over her.

'Are you deaf, you meddling little bitch?' he demanded. He grabbed her by both arms, jerked her to her feet and thrust his furious face into hers. 'Get out and stay out before I do something I might regret!'

Dulcie struggled. 'Let go of me, you thug!'

With a shout of rage, he shook her violently as though she were a rag doll. 'I said "Out" and I meant it.' He hurled her backwards through the door and into the arms of Mrs Craddock who somehow managed to steady her. The door slammed with great violence and Dulcie, humiliated and furious, muttered her thanks.

Mrs Craddock fussed over her. 'Oh I do *wish* you hadn't aggravated him!' she insisted. 'I did warn you. I know what he's like.'

'I'm fine!' Dulcie insisted although she was seething inside. She was insulted by his attitude and mortified to have been bundled out of the room so unceremoniously. Struggling to regain her poise, she heard the fight continuing. Mrs Craddock glanced anxiously towards the door.

'You should have come out,' she told Dulcie. 'He told you to get out. Anything might have happened.'

Dulcie straightened her clothes and smoothed her hair. 'Don't blame me! They're grown men, for heaven's sake! What a way to behave!' She drew a long, ragged breath and then another.

There was a muffled crash and then silence. The two women looked at each other warily.

Dulcie said, 'Hopefully they've killed each other!'

'Oh don't say that!' Mrs Craddock looked positively stricken.

'Hadn't you better call the police?' Dulcie allowed herself to be guided to a chair and sat down gratefully. Her back ached suddenly and she touched the back of her head gingerly, exploring for a swelling. Now that it was over, she discovered that she was more shaken than she cared to admit. Mrs Craddock was right — she had been told to get out of the room and she should have done so. Her own behaviour had been less than intelligent but wild horses would never drag such an admission from her.

Mrs Craddock stood uncertainly, her hands fluttering over the telephone. 'The police? Oh no, I'd better not. Mr Foote hates the police. He pretends not to because a possible future mayor shouldn't think like that but sometimes he calls them bullyboys. Are you sure you're all right? We have got a first-aid box but there isn't much in it, to be honest.'

Dulcie ignored the question. 'Do you know Mr Stowe well?'

'Mr — ? Oh, Mr Stowe! Yes. He's been before but —'

She broke off, cringeing, as there was another shouted exchange from the adjoining room. Dulcie caught the words 'Sit down and shut up!'

There was an abrupt silence.

Dulcie said, 'Why don't *you* sit down, Mrs Craddock. You're very pale. It's all a bit upsetting. What a dreadful man, that Mr Stowe. I wouldn't like to be alone with him.'

After a moment, the secretary sank on to her chair and leaned her elbows on the desk as the shock took effect. With her face in her hands she said, 'I'm so glad you're here.'

Dulcie said, 'Take deep breaths, Mrs Craddock. You'll feel better in a moment.'

The secretary gulped air into her lungs. 'Mr Foote always makes him wait. I don't know why. He knows how angry he gets. It's as though he does it on purpose.' She pressed a hand to her throat, struggling to control her breathing. 'He's been coming here for years. He does some work for Mr Foote —'

'Work?' Dulcie forgot her aches and pains. 'What kind of work?'

'I don't know too much about it, actually. They have some kind of private arrangement.'

An evasive answer, thought Dulcie, intrigued.

Mrs Craddock went on. 'Mr Stowe went abroad or something. We didn't see him for years and now he's turned up again. Apparently they were at school together. A sort of love-hate arrangement. Once they were both in a good mood and laughing and joking. Mr Stowe gave me a five pound note. It was my birthday and I'd made some little iced cakes.' She smiled. 'I used to make them when I worked for Mr Harris. He loved them.'

Her sigh was a giveaway, thought Dulcie.

'Anyway Mr Stowe said "Happy birthday, girlie!" and thrust the note into my hand. I was astonished!' She smiled faintly. 'He said, "You deserve a medal, working for this 'b' word!" ' She bit her lip. 'I won't say it but you know the one I mean.'

Dulcie nodded. 'A fiver! Good heavens!'

'Yes. It was wonderful. I put it straight into my savings.'

Dulcie said, 'Stowe? That's an unusual name.'

Mrs Craddock glanced guiltily towards the connecting door and said '*Isn't* it!'

Dulcie wanted to cheer. She said, 'He reminds me of someone whose face I've seen recently. Same heavy build and the same shaped face.' Mrs Craddock glanced away. Dulcie laughed. 'Maybe he has a double.'

Mrs Craddock looked back at her and seemed about to say something. Then she swallowed hard and contented herself with a little shrug.

Dulcie whispered, 'Perhaps he's leading a double life!' She grinned. 'Dr Jekyll and Mr Hyde!'

Mrs Craddock said, 'Except he's almost never nice Dr Jekyll! Lately he seems to turn up out of the blue — hardly ever has a proper appointment — and always puts Mr Foote in a bad mood.'

Dulcie nodded. 'He scared me dreadfully.'

'How's your head?'

Dulcie felt the beginnings of a bump. 'I'll live! It serves me right for lingering. I should have listened to you.' She frowned. '*Girlie!* I've never been called that before! But then I've never been thrown out of a room before. I suppose there's always a first time . . . D'you think he's been drinking?'

'No. We'd have smelled it on his breath. He's just got a nasty temper — and he doesn't know his own strength. Once he broke a cup. Just slammed it down on to the saucer and snapped off the handle. I couldn't match it up so I had to buy a different design. A whole set, mind you. Mr Foote was not best pleased.'

'Poor Mr Foote. He won't want that sort of man calling in when he's the mayor.'

'If Mr Foote ever —' Mrs Craddock stopped again. Abruptly she stood up, smoothing her dress. 'Well, I don't know what to say now,' she said. 'Do you want to stay on and finish the interview when he's free?'

Dulcie didn't want to miss anything but nor did she want to twiddle her thumbs while they condescended to remember her existence. If she was honest she was also nervous. Stowe, or whoever he was, was a powerful man and he might not take kindly to finding her still waiting around. Her head was beginning to ache and suddenly she wanted to get home. She had found out what she wanted to know without being rumbled so perhaps discretion would prove the best part of valour.

'Perhaps you could find out how long he'll be,' she suggested, not wanting to give in too easily.

Mrs Craddock looked dubious. 'I don't really fancy going in there to interrupt them. They seem to have calmed down and Mr Foote won't want to be disturbed,' she said.

'Then I'll be on my way. Will you thank him for his time and say if I need any more information or further clarification I'll telephone.' She paused at the door. 'Will you be all right alone? I'll stay if you like.'

Mrs Craddock shook her head. 'I'll be fine, thank you. I'm used to these — er — these little bust ups.' She hesitated. 'And please don't tell the police. Mr Stowe might — Well, he's a man to bear a grudge. You really shouldn't get on the wrong side of him.'

Dulcie felt a shiver of apprehension. 'It's a bit late to worry about that now! I hardly think he'll be sending me a Christmas card!'

She said 'Goodbye' and went downstairs, making plenty of noise. She was conscious of unfinished business and half hoped that Foote would call her back. Outside, she paused on the pavement and glanced up, identifying the window of Foote's office. It gave her an uncomfortable jolt to see two intent faces behind the net curtain.

Apparently temporarily reconciled, both men were watching her leave. As she walked hurriedly away, she was under no delusions. Stowe-cum-Parker would not forget her. Nor would he forgive. Too late she regretted her ill-judged defiance.

She had made a dangerous enemy.

Detective Sergeant Jack Spencer sat in the outer office listening to the rattle of the typewriter. 'Mr Foote won't keep you long,' she had told him brightly. He'd better not. Jack was not in a good mood. It appeared that Dulcie had been here. They had missed each other by half an hour. Damn.

The secretary glanced up shyly. 'Mr Foote seems to be very busy this morning. Very popular. First the young lady then Mr Stowe and now you.'

'Stowe?' He frowned. Wasn't that the name of the school Parker and Foote had attended? 'Are you sure that was his name?'

Mrs Craddock avoided his eyes. 'I think I'm sure,' she said. 'Funny thing, but the young lady seemed to think he reminded her of someone else.' She gave Jack a strange look. 'Maybe he's got a double.'

Jack groaned inwardly. Could it have been Parker? If it *was* then he'd been within an ace of making the arrest of the year. He drew a photograph from his pocket. 'Was this the man called Stowe?'

She took it unwillingly. 'Mr Stowe has a beard,' she said. 'This could be him but on the other hand . . . beards hide so much of a face, don't they? I mean, there's something similar about the eyes but — Mr Stowe looks older.'

Jack hadn't expected anything more. The photograph had been taken when Parker was committed to prison nearly eight years ago. His hair was receding and he had put on weight. Even without a beard he had changed. Why weren't villains photographed again when they left prison? It would be more use than these. He tapped his foot, listening to the cries of the seagulls, thinking about Dulcie.

The clock on the wall showed ten o'clock. 'Please tell your Mr Foote that I'm still waiting,' he said sharply.

She rose obediently. 'Detective Spencer, was it?'

'Detective *Sergeant* Spencer. And I haven't got all day!' He'd like a pound for every time someone got his rank wrong!

She stood up quickly and her gaze went to Mr Foote's office and then back to Jack's face. 'This doesn't mean that —' She whispered, 'Not Mr Foote?'

She didn't seem particularly startled by the idea. Jack noted. Nor unduly upset. He said. 'Just routine enquiries. We're currently investigating two murders in the Canterbury area.'

'Canterbury?' Now she was startled. 'What a coincidence. That young lady was from Canterbury. But she was interviewing Mr Foote for a magazine.'

Jack was growing impatient. If it *was* Parker he might still be in the Folkestone area. Unless he had legged it to the railway station or jumped on a bus. *If* it was Parker he must have nerves of steel — or a low opinion of the law. He had nothing definite to go on. He said, 'Has Mr Foote got someone with him?'

'No, he hasn't.'

'Then why the hell is he keeping me waiting?' He stood up. Too late he suspected delaying tactics. 'Tell Mr Foote that I want to see him — *now!*'

As soon as Dulcie set foot in the office of the *Standard* she knew something was wrong. More wrong than usual. Bob, listening to someone at the other end of a telephone, rolled his eyes expressively. He jerked his head towards Mr Cobbs's room and put an imaginary gun to his head.

Dulcie saw with relief that her employer's office door was shut which gave her a moment to compose herself. Surely when she told Cobsey what she had learned in Folkestone about Parker alias Stowe he would change his tune. Adopting a confident smile she said, 'I have an ace up my sleeve, Bob!' but her colleague was still talking to his invisible contact.

She sat down at her desk and wondered where Gus had gone. Maybe he was covering the council meeting which should have been her assignment. In which case he would *not* be pleased and would, with good reason, blame her. She was just debating whether or not to slip out and relieve him when the door to her editor's office opened.

He saw her and his face reddened. Not a good sign.

'You!' he shouted. 'Get yourself in here pronto.'

At least he hadn't addressed her as 'Girlie'! She followed him in, heart thumping. The room smelled of peppermints.

'Mr Cobbs —' she began, 'I have some dramatic news. When you hear it you'll —'

As she stammered through an account of her morning's activities, he sat down and put his feet up on the desk. Then he put his hands behind his head. She could see that he was enjoying himself. Why did men in power become so unreasonable?

He allowed her to finish the story. When she faltered to a stop he thrust a finger in her direction. 'You're finished! Fired. Sacked. Unemployed.' He took out his watch. 'As from now.'

Dulcie stared at him. 'You don't mean that,' she said faintly. 'I only went because I wanted to find out — because I thought —'

'You know what thought did!' The triumph was evident in his voice and his expression.

Had he been patiently waiting for this chance, she wondered, shocked. Worse, had he *known* that eventually she would overstep the mark? Or was he bluffing? She felt a moment of hope.

She said, 'I promise I won't do —'

'No you won't, Miss Moore, because you won't be here.' He raised his eyebrows. One point to Cobsey.

'Mr Cobbs, you should at least listen to what I have to say.'

'Gus is wasting his valuable time at the Town Hall when he should have been talking to the City

Fire Brigade chief. He should have been discussing the risks of a serious fire in Canterbury. Another Abbot's Mill disaster, maybe. It was to be the first of an important series about —'

'I could do it instead,' she offered rashly.

The bushy eyebrows drew together into a frown. 'How can you, Miss Moore? You are no longer a member of my staff and I shall have *great* pleasure in explaining to your uncle exactly why we have sacked you. It will take some time. For your information the following are a few of the points I shall make. You are unreliable, inexperienced, headstrong. You take time off without permission, you fail to turn up to assignments, you are an embarrassment to this firm.' He took a breath. 'You do not know the meaning of the word "teamwork" and you tell lies.'

'Lies? I do *not* tell lies!' Crushed, she struggled to retain her composure.

'No? A little bird told me that when you were supposed to be ill in bed you were, in fact, at a certain school in Horsted Keynes. Unless the headmaster of Fellstowe is lying. He seemed to think you had been commissioned to write an article for a magazine.'

Dulcie closed her eyes. Yes, she *had* lied. 'I'm sorry. If you will only give me one more chance I swear I'll *never* let you down again. Not in any way.' Cornered she resorted to using her charms, opening her blue eyes, parting her lips in what she hoped was an appealing way and arranging her features into a look of suffering entreaty. Once her father had said, 'Who could deny that child anything?' Her mother had answered, 'Don't encourage her to rely on her looks, dear. They don't last.'

Mr Cobbs appeared well able to resist her charms. 'Clear your desk and go!' he said.

Dulcie felt tears pressing at her eyelids. She was genuinely hurt; totally shamed. Her uncle would be so disappointed. Her mother and father would gloat. Only Teddy and Harriet would be kind. What made it worse was the knowledge that she had no one to blame but herself. It was a dark moment.

Three minutes later, blinking back tears, she scribbled a message to Gus, said 'Goodbye' to Bob and crept away from the *Canterbury Standard.* Now that it was over, she realised just how much she had enjoyed it.

Harriet listened in silence as, twenty minutes later, Dulcie recounted the story of her dismissal. Curled up on the sofa with Max sprawled across her lap, Dulcie's hands were clasped around a mug of liberally sweetened cocoa. Harriet, convinced of its curative powers at times of great stress, had insisted.

'The man's a pig!' said Harriet. 'A real chauvinist. I can't think why Wilfred keeps him on.'

'He's a very good editor.'

'But not a very nice human being. I bet he's not married.'

'He isn't.'

'I thought as much. Hates women. Or else he's afraid of them. Probably had a domineering mother. I know the sort!' She snorted her disgust. 'Still, you've no need to go home. You can stay on here, with or without a job.'

Dulcie hadn't given that aspect of her situation any thought. 'Oh but I've no wages. I mean, the rent for my room . . .' It was getting worse, she thought miserably. Her parents would now insist that she return home. The disgrace was unbearable. So much for her bid for independence. Her mouth trembled and she hastily hid behind the rim of her mug, drinking too large a mouthful and spilling some down her chin.

Harriet leaned across and dabbed with a handkerchief. 'Look, Dulcie, I don't need rent,' she told her. 'If necessary we'll tell your parents that you're going to be my companion. Accommodation in exchange for services. So stop feeling so damned sorry for yourself. It's not the end of the world.'

'Oh Harriet! Would you?'

'I've just said so. And I'm taking you out to dinner tonight. It will cheer you up. We'll go to the County Hotel and we'll eat too much and drink too much and thoroughly enjoy ourselves. Let the Cobseys of this world go hang!' Brushing aside Dulcie's protests she stood up. 'We'll push the boat out, as they say. I'll treat myself to some oysters to start with. I know you don't like them. I'll go round now and book a table. Max could do with a walk.'

Hearing the word 'walk', Max hurled himself from Dulcie's lap.

'Traitor!' muttered Dulcie, abandoned in favour of greater pleasures. In her present state of mind even this small betrayal undermined her. As she heard the door close behind her aunt and the dog, Dulcie's waning self-respect took a final plunge. She gave way to bitter tears of frustration and self-recrimination.

She was splashing cold water over her ravaged face when the doorbell rang and she hurried to answer it. Assuming that her aunt had forgotten her key, she was taken aback to find Detective Sergeant Spencer on the doorstep. His immediate look of kindly concern reminded her just how swollen and discoloured her face was and a fresh surge of tears coursed down her cheeks. He followed her into the house and before she knew what was happening he had put his arms around her. Sobbing against his chest she was aware that he patted her back and murmured words of consolation. It was very pleasant and entirely novel and she allowed it to continue as long as she dared. Eventually, however, she straightened up, sniffing loudly and gratefully accepted his offer of a handkerchief.

'I'm sorry,' she said, dabbing at her eyes.

He said, 'So am I. It was not my place to — to —'

She smiled. 'It was kind of you. No need to apologise. I'm not usually so stupid.' She indicated a chair and he sat down. 'I've had a terrible day,' she told him and, resuming her place on the sofa, explained what had happened.

He listened without interruption until she had finished. 'He might reconsider,' he suggested. 'Mr Cobbs. You know how it is. Heat of the moment, sort of thing.'

Dulcie shrugged. 'I don't think so. He *wanted* to sack me. He's been longing to prove to my uncle that employing me was a mistake. He gave me enough rope and I hanged myself.'

'I came to see you because I understand you were at Harris Enterprises this morning.'

Startled, she said, 'How did you know? You went there? Ah!' In her present mood it seemed unwise to keep anything back. 'I think I saw Parker,' she told him. Seeing his look of alarm she added, 'Only briefly. They said his name was Stowe but the secretary seemed to be hinting —'

He leaned forward. 'Does that mean that he saw you? *Parker* saw you?'

'If it was him.'

'We've just received a new likeness of him — an artist's impression as he probably is now. It was waiting for me when I got back to the station. I'd like you to take a look at it. We've also got a couple of fingerprints from the church. It's a case of matching them. It takes time.' He took a folded likeness from his pocket and Dulcie studied it.

'That could be him,' she said. She went on to

describe what had happened during her visit including the fight in Foote's office. She was suddenly disconcerted by the expression on the detective's face. 'What's the matter?'

He sat back with a long sigh. 'We think it was Parker who killed Brayne. We think he killed Mrs Bly because we're almost certain she saw him at the church the night of the murder. Now you've seen him with Foote. If they're in cahoots, and it certainly looks that way, Parker might now consider *you* a threat.'

The words and the look on his face sent a shiver down Dulcie's spine. Resolutely, she thrust the fear away. 'But what could they be in cahoots about?'

'That's the question!' He shook his head unhappily. 'It's possible that Parker is Foote's "heavy", if you know what I mean. He does the dirty work. He could have been sent to deal with Brayne who owed money to Foote. Too many coincidences, Miss Moore. Coincidences but no *proof.* Mrs Bly would have nailed him so she had to go.' He relapsed into silence, thinking.

Dulcie said, 'But why should he still be in this area? Why doesn't he skip the country if he knows he could be re-arrested at any moment?'

'Exactly! He's a cocky bastard — er — so-and-so. Must think he's smarter than us. Or that he's invisible.'

He was tracing the piping on the arm of the chair with a slim, well-kept hand which Dulcie found immensely attractive. Not unlike

Teddy's. Then she remembered how his arms had felt around her. Not at all like Teddy's arms! And Harriet had said there was no 'Mrs Spencer'.

He went on, half to himself. 'He's waiting for something — probably another job. Maybe something for Foote. Something big. Foote might be able to pay good money — enough to facilitate Parker's escape abroad. Spain. Mexico . . .' He looked up suddenly. 'But it's you I'm worried about. That's really why I'm here. I don't want you to be his next victim.'

Dulcie shivered.

He went on earnestly. 'I'd like you to be *very* careful where you go and what you do. When you're alone, I mean. Don't walk the dog in lonely places. Keep the doors locked if you're alone in the house. That sort of thing. Sensible precautions. Please, Miss Moore. I don't want to frighten you but I —'

'You *are* frightening me!' She tried to make light of it.

'I'm sorry.' His tone softened. 'I can't seriously imagine him trying anything if you are out with your aunt or your brother but alone you might be vulnerable.' His expression changed again. 'Talking of your brother, the Chief wants to talk to him but it's only a formality. He is still around, I hope, and not in Cornwall.'

Dulcie thought he was and said so.

He said, 'The victim's body has been released. I think the Braynes have arranged the funeral for tomorrow. Poor souls. It's hard to come to terms with a death but a little easier after the funeral.' He reached out and took her hand in his. 'Please be careful. For my sake if not for your own.'

'For your sake?'

He looked at her and the moment lengthened. 'I'd really hate to lose you, Miss Moore.'

Her pulse rate was rising. 'Could you possibly call me Dulcie — or is it against the rules?'

His smile was wonderful. 'Off duty I could.' He released her hand with apparent reluctance. 'Maybe we could — What I mean is, perhaps I could take you out. One day.'

She nodded.

He swallowed. 'Tonight maybe? If I'm free.'

If only she could say 'Yes'. 'Not tonight, I'm afraid. I'm going out with my aunt.'

'I see.'

'Tomorrow night? Oh no! Forget I said that!' She had seen the surprise on his face and bit her lip. What her mother would call a forward hussy.

He smiled, 'Whenever we can manage it. With this job it's always a gamble.'

A key in the front door signalled the return of Harriet and the dog and with it the end of a promising exchange. Dulcie had to be content with what had already passed between them.

But as she said 'Goodbye' a few moments later and watched him walk up the street, her spirits had almost recovered from the day's disappointments. She liked the way he walked with a slight roll of his shoulders and a long firm stride.

She whispered, 'Detective Sergeant Spencer, I rather *like* you!' Smiling, she closed the door.

Suddenly, the warning about Parker was the last thing on her mind.

Chapter 11

It was just before seven when Jack let himself in and he was halfway up the stairs when his landlady called to him. Her knitted hat bulged with hidden curlers but her smile was ecstatic. He looked at her with surprise. Had she come into a fortune or won some money on the races?

'Mr Spencer, I've got a surprise for you!' she announced and there was a distinct twinkle in her eye. It occurred to Jack that perhaps her usual teatime bottle of stout had been replaced by something stronger.

'A surprise? How lovely.' He hoped that whatever it was would not take long. Her surprises were usually his favourite pudding or a letter from home. Today, he desperately wanted to be on his own to think seriously about Dulcie Moore. The few moments that he had held her in his arms had convinced him that a friendship would be possible between them. More than a friendship if he was lucky. He would think of somewhere he could take her where he was not likely to be seen by his colleagues. Striking up any kind of relationship with the sister of a one-time suspect would be considered neither prudent nor suitable and he was sure Gough would disapprove if he found out.

'It's not treacle tart,' his landlady told him and Jack heard a chuckle from her husband. 'Much nicer than that! Now close your eyes!'

Jack groaned inwardly but he was intrigued. Whatever had she concocted that warranted all this fuss?

'Now open them!'

Judith stood in the doorway, smiling at him. *Judith!* For a moment he was breathless with dismay. She had appeared once before out of the blue but then he had been overjoyed to see her. Today her unexpected visit was an unpleasant shock. Thank God Dulcie had been unable to accept his invitation.

He stammered, 'What on earth — ?'

She stepped forward and kissed him lightly. 'Happy birthday, Jack!' she said.

He had forgotten how attractive she was with the smooth dark hair and calm, wise face. She was immaculate in a slim-fitting dress, white linen jacket and lace gloves. Her long hair was wound smoothly around her head.

'My birthday? Good heavens! Is it? I've been so busy . . .'

Mrs Smith said, 'Lucky for you your young lady didn't forget. *She's* got a surprise for you, too.'

Judith slipped her arms through his. 'I'm staying in Canterbury overnight and I've booked a table for two for dinner. A celebration. It's all arranged for seven-thirty although I did tell them we might be late. I explained that policemen are rarely on time!' She laughed.

Mrs Smith gave Jack a playful push. 'So off you go and get ready. And don't worry about your bit of dinner, Mr Spencer. I'd made enough for three but then your young lady turned up. Mr and Mr Smith will have extra big helpings tonight. So we're not complaining.'

Jack led the way upstairs, his hand in Judith's, his panic growing with every step. Judith knew him very well and would certainly have registered his less than enthusiastic welcome. Serve you right, he told himself. You should have written. Now he would have to tell her face to face that he couldn't marry her.

When they reached the privacy of his room Judith closed the door behind them and immediately turned to him. Her sweet face was anxious.

'What is it, Jack?'

'What d'you mean?' He forced a smile, playing for time, praying for inspiration.

'You seem so distant. Your expression — is this surprise of mine a mistake?'

'Of course not. I was surprised, that's all. Couldn't think straight. I'm so damned tired and worried by this case. Not really in a birthday mood.'

'Is that all?' She kissed the tip of his nose. 'They're working you too hard. All the more reason then why I should take you out and cheer you up!' She stepped back, pulling off her gloves, unbuttoning her jacket. 'I've missed you, darling! You'll never know how much.'

'I've missed you.' To his guilty ears the words rang false but her expression did not change. She kissed him again and said, 'Shall I run you a bath? We haven't got a lot of time.'

To gain time he said, 'A bath? Oh, the hotel! I suppose so.' The thought of an evening of feigned togetherness appalled him. Hell and damnation! Lack of time plus a disinclination to see the unkind words on paper had delayed the letter and now it was too late. He sighed, rubbing his face tiredly.

Last time she visited she had run his bath and he had enjoyed the hint of domesticity. Now he felt trapped by her proprietory manner.

'I think we should talk —' he began.

'We can talk over dinner,' she told him.

Her tone was just a little too brisk, he thought warily. Did she suspect something?

As soon as she left the room he covered his face with his hands. The evening stretched ahead interminably. Perhaps he should tell her now. Yes, that would be best. There was no way he could sit through the meal, pretending to enjoy the occasion and then tell her the truth. Whatever his faults, he was not a hypocrite. He *must* tell her now. The sooner he explained the sooner she would recover from the rejection. He quailed at the prospect of hurting her but *not* telling her would be worse. He took a deep breath as her footsteps returned.

She put her head round the door, winked and said, 'Bath's ready, sir!'

'But Judith, I —'

'No "buts". I'm just popping downstairs. Mrs Smith is copying out a recipe for me. Won't be long, darling.'

'Judith, wait a minute. I — !'

She had gone. Damn! Now what was he to do? Reluctantly Jack made his way along the landing to the bathroom where the frosted-glass window was already steaming up. Closing the door he turned the key in the lock and drew a long breath. How was he going to break the news without breaking her heart? His reflection stared back from the misty mirror. There was panic in his eyes.

'Oh Judith!' he groaned.

He had lost the initiative, he told himself grimly.

As any good policeman knew, that was a bad mistake.

The dining room at the County Hotel was elegant with basket chairs, spotless white linen and sparkling glasses. A small vase of flowers graced the centre of each table. Feeling a little happier, Dulcie had chosen soup as her first course and was finishing a bowl of beef consomme.

'How were the oysters?' she enquired.

'Middling to good. You should persevere with them. They're good for you.'

Dulcie grimaced. 'My soup was wonderfully comforting. It is, at this very moment, warming the cockles of my heart!'

They were looking forward to rack of lamb.

The waitress appeared at the table. 'Was everything to your liking?'

They told her that it was and she whisked away the plates, returning a moment later to brush the few crumbs into a small pan.

Dulcie watched the small ritual with growing impatience. She was longing to tell her aunt about Jack and was trying to pick the right moment. It was at times like this that she missed Annabel who had been her confidante for so many years. Annabel would have understood her excitement whereas Harriet, being scornful of men in general, might scoff. At last the meal arrived. Covers were removed to reveal the lamb, the vegetables and a gravy boat.

Harriet said, 'Looks delicious!'

The waitress smiled at Dulcie and said, 'Enjoy your meal.'

Dulcie nodded, wondering how best to broach the subject of Jack, considered various options but when they were finally alone all good intentions were swept away in her eagerness to talk about him.

'You remember the detective?' she began, a forkful of potato poised midway to her mouth. 'Detective Sergeant Spencer. He's asked me out.'

Please, Harriet, she thought desperately, say

something approving. Don't spoil it for me.

'He has, has he?' Harriet gave her a quick glance and chewed thoughtfully. 'What did you say?'

'I said "yes".'

Harriet gave a little shrug that spoke more clearly than words. She attended to her lamb, apparently intent only on her food.

Dulcie couldn't bear it. 'Don't you like him?' She laid down her knife and fork. 'What's wrong with him?'

Harriet glanced up. 'Did I say I didn't like him?'

'You didn't say you did.'

'I'm not going out with him, am I?'

Dulcie regarded her aunt with dismay. 'But you disapprove.'

Harriet did not argue with this statement.

Dulcie picked at the food on her plate, her appetite dwindling. It wasn't only that she wanted Harriet's approval. She also wanted to continue living with her aunt in the comfortable harmony they had enjoyed to date. Was her friendship with Jack going to spoil that?

She said, 'You said he was fancy free. It's not as though he's a married man. He's polite. Well-mannered. Nice-looking.'

Harriet gave her a long look. 'I'm surprised at you, that's all. I thought you were going to concentrate on your career and leave men until later. That's what you told me and I believed you. I thought you had your head screwed on the right way.'

'Harriet! He hasn't *proposed!* He's only asked if he can take me out. Anyway, I've been sacked. I haven't *got* a career, thanks to Cobsey!'

Another shrug greeted this small outburst.

Bitterly disappointed, Dulcie put her knife and fork together and pushed the plate away. Serve Harriet right if she had paid for a nice meal and it was wasted. All she had to do was be nice about Jack. It wasn't too much to ask. She waited in vain for her aunt to comment on the wasted food.

After a moment or two Dulcie said firmly, 'Look. Forgetting my career for the moment, what exactly have you got against Jack?' Even to herself she sounded belligerent.

'Against Jack? Nothing. Since you obviously think highly of him I can't see why my opinion matters to you.'

She continued to eat, ignoring Dulcie's lack of appetite. Dulcie watched her unhappily. This was worse than she had expected. Was Harriet hurt, she wondered uneasily. Had she perhaps enjoyed the fact that they had both excluded men from their lives? Had that been an important factor in their friendship?

Eventually she asked soberly, 'Is it just that you don't like men, Harriet?'

Harriet laid down her own cutlery. 'I didn't say I didn't like them. A few are bearable. Others are obnoxious. The nice ones . . .' She sighed deeply. 'They can break your heart,' she said. 'You have no idea.'

'But the man you loved was killed. He didn't desert you *willingly*. You can't think that, surely. It's so — so *illogical!*'

After a long silence Harriet said quietly. 'There was another man, Dulcie. Much later. A lawyer.' Her eyes were dark as she remembered him and her voice shook slightly. 'Nobody else in the family knows anything about him. We met in Switzerland while I was on holiday with Elsa, my girlfriend. He was there alone on business. I fell in love with him. Love at first sight. So foolish . . .'

Their waitress returned and stared with surprise at Dulcie's plate. 'Have you *finished?*' she asked.

Harriet nodded and the plates were removed without further comment. They decided against dessert and asked for coffees.

'I wouldn't spend time alone with him because of Elsa but we arranged to see each other again when we were both back in England. We met in London. I was so sure he loved me.' Her mouth tightened. 'I didn't know then that he was an accomplished liar.'

Dulcie said, 'Oh Harriet!' knowing that this story would have an unhappy ending.

'His name was Alec Dart. He was ten years younger than me and very attractive. We met half a dozen times and then without any warning or explanation, he said it was all over. Said he couldn't explain. I must accept it . . . We quarrelled. I thought I deserved an explanation. I certainly deserved better than that. I tried to get the truth out of him. He told me that he was being sent abroad again by his firm. In desperation I tried to find him through his firm but what d'you know?'

'He didn't work there?'

'Oh he worked there. The secretary said, "Is that Mrs Dart?" ' She looked at Dulcie and her bitterness was obvious. 'He had a wife. I saw it at once. Either he had tired of me or his wife was getting suspicious. I shall never know. Unfinished business. I hate that.'

Her aunt's face wore a haunted look and Dulcie knew that she was seeing him again in her mind's eye. Seeing him, wanting him and hurting again after all these years.

'I'm so sorry!' she said, all her resentment gone.

Harriet swallowed. 'I would have preferred the truth, however hurtful. I wasn't a silly young thing . . . I wouldn't mind so much if I could forget him. Instead I have to face the unpalatable truth. I still think about him and it still hurts like hell! So much for maturity and common sense.' She nodded as the coffee tray was placed on the table and muttered, 'Thank you.' The waitress turned away. 'So — I do know what I'm talking about, Dulcie. I'm trying to save you from a similar hurt. You don't know much about this Jack Spencer.'

Dulcie sighed. 'Didn't you ever see Alec again?'

'Yes. Two years later. On a train going to London. With a younger woman and a boy. She was expecting another child.'

'Did he see you?'

'Yes. He pretended not to. I looked out of the window but I saw him reflected in the glass. He must have been panic-stricken. There was plenty of room in my carriage but he hustled them past. I heard the boy say, "But why, Daddy? There's plenty of room." '

Dulcie's heart ached for her. She searched for something to say that would soften the unhappy memories. 'It doesn't mean he didn't love you.'

Harriet's eyes hardened. 'Don't make excuses for him, Dulcie. He'd lied to me all the way along. He was already married. I could tell by the boy's age.'

'Harriet, it doesn't mean he didn't love you. Just that circumstances —'

Harriet's smile was bleak. 'I've tried that argument, Dulcie. There's no excuse for him. He knew there was no future for us and he knew he would break my heart. He would still have a loving wife and child. I would be all alone. It happens all the time, Dulcie, so you listen to me. Never take a man at face value. I'm not saying it will happen to you but it *could*.'

In silence, Dulcie poured the coffee.

At last she said, 'Jack's not married. I'm sure he's not. At least I'm almost sure.'

Harriet said, 'Maybe not. He seems genuine enough. I'm not trying to upset you. But you're young and trusting. I was neither but I still got my fingers burned.'

Dulcie was abruptly overwhelmed by her own good fortune. Jack Spencer was *not* married. She *knew* it. She forgave her aunt totally for her unwelcome advice. Maybe over the years Harriet had convinced herself that a woman could be happy alone; had decided to make a virtue of necessity. Dulcie was still free to choose. She could look forward to some kind of career and a single existence or she could marry. The latter idea had never appealed — until now and she had to admit that Jack Spencer was responsible for her change of heart.

She said, 'But, assuming that Jack *isn't* married and ignoring the fact that he's a policeman — he can't help that — do you like him? Please Harriet. Be honest.'

To Dulcie's relief, her aunt smiled. 'Assuming all that —' She pretended to think deeply about it. 'I don't *dislike* him.'

'Harriet! That's not good enough!'

Harriet laughed. 'Then I like him, Dulcie. He seems very likeable. Not necessarily *loveable* but nice enough to take you out one evening. Will that do?'

Dulcie drew a deep breath of relief. Smiling, she reached out her hand and Harriet took it in her own.

And then, glancing past her aunt in the direction of the door, Dulcie froze. Her smile faded.

Harriet, puzzled, asked, 'What is it?' and

twisted in her chair.

In shocked silence they both watched Jack Spencer walk into the restaurant with an attractive dark-haired woman clinging to his arm.

Almost at once Jack saw them.

Harriet said, 'Oh my Godfathers!'

Dulcie was speechless. With dismay she saw the guilt writ large in Jack's eyes. The waitress was leading Jack and his companion straight towards them, indicating an empty table behind them. For a moment Dulcie thought that Jack was going to ignore them.

'Miss Moore!' He paused beside their table. 'And the other Miss Moore!'

Dulcie could not smile at this pathetic attempt at a joke. His forehead had broken out in a fine sheen of perspiration she noted. Serve him right, she thought furiously. She was choked with anger and the irony of her aunt's recent comments was not lost on her. Jack's timing had been impeccable.

Harriet recovered first. She forced a smile and said, 'Let me guess, Mr Spencer. This is your sister.' She smiled at his companion. 'I think I see a likeness.'

There was no likeness at all.

Jack hesitated fatally.

The woman said, 'Hardly. I'm Jack's fiancée. This is a surprise visit because it's his birthday and what do you know? He'd forgotten.' She smiled at Harriet but her eyes quickly moved to

Dulcie. 'Since Jack's forgotten to introduce us, I'm Judith.'

Harriet said, 'Pleased to meet you. I'm Harriet and this is my niece Dulcie.'

As Jack stammered his apologies, he avoided her eyes and Dulcie almost pitied him. So there was no Mrs Spencer. At least that had been true up to a point but there was *a fiancée.* There was a knot of anger forming inside her and she could guess what Harriet was thinking. She was inclined to agree. It seemed that nice Mr Spencer was no better than any other man. Another accomplished liar. She stared hard at Jack and was glad to see that he looked almost as bad as she felt. But he was to blame so he deserved to feel terrible. Harriet was trying to save the situation but why should they help Jack?

'Jack, how *could* you?' Dulcie said.

Judith gave her a sharp, questioning glance and looked at Jack.

Harriet said quickly, 'How *could* you forget a birthday?' and laughed a little too loudly.

Jack reached for the straw. 'I've been so busy. The murders. Everything.'

Harriet looked at Judith. 'Canterbury is not a very safe place. I expect Jack told you we have an escaped murderer on the run in the area.'

Judith's smile had faltered. 'He hasn't written for ages but I read something in the newspaper. Is this man still around?'

She looked at Jack who said, 'We think so.'

Dulcie, given time by Harriet's intervention,

resisted the urge to make a scene. Illogically she wanted to punish Judith but she was uncomfortably aware that the other woman, too, must be shocked and afraid. And Judith was his fiancée. No doubt she loved and trusted him. Poor Judith. What kind of man was he to doublecross the woman he was going to marry?

The waitress, tired of waiting, coughed and indicated a table a few yards away.

'Sorry,' Jack told her. To Harriet and Dulcie he said, 'Excuse us, won't you' and the two of them moved on. Dulcie was glad that their table was behind her. At least she need not look at them.

For a moment Dulcie stared at the tablecloth, wishing herself anywhere else in the world. Slowly she raised her head and looked at Harriet.

'Smile!' Her aunt mouthed the word.

'I can't,' said Dulcie through stiff lips. 'I think I'm dying!'

'No you're not!' Harriet raised her glass and said, 'Smile, damn you! Don't allow him to hurt you.'

Dulcie picked up her glass and forced her lips into a lopsided grin. 'I'm going to be sick!'

'You can't be sick here.'

'I will!'

Harriet laughed, as though amused by something Dulcie had said. 'You can be sick at home!' she muttered.

Dulcie swallowed, her throat dry. 'I have to get out of here.'

Harriet raised a hand for their waitress and asked for the bill. Dulcie waited in agony for the settlement which seemed to take forever. The desire to look over her shoulder almost hurt. As though reading her mind Harriet said in a low voice, 'They're not looking too happy. There's a distinct chill in the air. Hardly speaking and pretending to study the menu.'

As they stood up to leave, Harriet whispered, 'Must we say "Goodnight" to them?'

Dulcie hesitated. She didn't want them to have a good night. She didn't think she could bear to speak to either of them again. Nor could she bear to look at Jack. Her mouth twisted unhappily.

'Definitely not!' she said and, stiffnecked, she followed her aunt from the restaurant without a backward glance.

Jack busied himself with the wine list until he heard the chairs move and knew Dulcie and her aunt were leaving. The waitress said 'Goodnight'.

Jack said, 'Red or white wine?'

Judith was watching them go. 'How odd!' she said. 'They didn't say "Goodbye" to us. I thought they were friends of yours.'

He could not meet her eyes. 'Not exactly. The brother was a suspect in the case. I had to interview Dulcie but fortunately her brother was cleared. Red or white wine?'

He knew it was a mistake as soon as the words were out.

'Jack! When have I ever drunk red?'

'White then. Sorry.'

She was fiddling with the table napkin, folding it into its original fan shape. 'But Harriet called you Jack.'

'Er — Did she? I didn't notice. She's a bit odd, actually . . . Or we could have champagne instead?' What on earth was he talking about? Neither of them cared for champagne and Judith had once described it as 'horribly over-rated.' Pull yourself together, Jack!

'Are you all right, Jack? You sound a bit — well, I don't know. Have they upset you?'

'Of course not. It's always awkward with the relatives of suspects. You have to be friendly to encourage them to drop their guard.' He plunged on. Anything to change the subject. 'Actually we're going to bring the brother in again. They've found a fingerprint at the church. On one of the pews. It's definitely his.' He brushed sweat from his forehead. Shut up, Jack. That's classified information at the moment. He felt as though he was losing his mind.

She ignored the distraction and said coolly, 'But just walking out on us like that. Rather rude, I thought. Didn't you?'

He shrugged. This persistence was something about her that he had never liked. Sometimes she was like a dog worrying a bone. 'Perhaps they're offended about something,' he suggested.

'You mean — because we met them in here? They might think you're following them — or shadowing them or whatever you call it?'

Jack bit back a sharp reply. She knew it wasn't that and she knew *he* knew it wasn't. Judith wasn't stupid. Quite the opposite. A little too perceptive. She had sensed that there was something between him and Dulcie. So perhaps he should tell her now. This was the ideal opportunity to make a clean break with her. If only he could find the necessary courage. He said suddenly, 'Actually she's a very nice person.'

'You mean the young one, I presume.'

He looked at her and saw that she had paled. She was suffering. Poor Judith.

'Yes. Dulcie.'

'A very nice person.' She dwelt on each word. 'So why did she walk out on you like that, without a word? Nice people have better manners.' Getting no reply she went on. 'I thought her rather silly actually — and slightly overdressed. Not your type at all.'

The waitress came for the order but Jack waved her away. Words came in a rush, without forethought. 'Look here, the truth is that I was going to write to you, Judith. I'm terribly sorry.' The silence lengthened. 'I didn't know how to tell you —' He was floundering miserably and he knew it and hated himself. He was making it all worse. Breaking it to her in the middle of a restaurant. What a fool! 'Judith, I didn't mean this to happen . . .' He lapsed into silence again. Where were the words to do this gently?

She swallowed, pressing the napkin to her

mouth. Her eyes never left his face. He saw disbelief, anger, grief and humiliation.

'Judith, I can't tell you how difficult this is — to say what I have to say . . .'

'About Dulcie? About you and that mannerless girl?' Her eyes widened. 'Oh I see. *That's* why she went out in a huff. She didn't know about *me!* Jack Spencer, you are the — the worst kind of — you are utterly —' Tears sprang into her eyes. 'How could you?'

They both registered the fact that those same three words had been spoken earlier. And by Dulcie.

Jack mumbled, 'She didn't know. I was going to tell you first and then her —' Oh God! Why was he making such a mess of everything?

She was suddenly very white and agitated. 'You were going to tell me what exactly?'

He closed his eyes. 'That I can't marry you.' He almost flinched as though she might retaliate physically.

'You don't mean that!'

He shrugged.

'You can't mean it, Jack?'

She didn't believe him. How could he convince her? 'I never stop thinking about her!' He blurted out the words and then realised the truth of them.

She said 'That's infatuation, Jack. Or obsession.'

She was struggling to stay calm and his heart ached for her. She was hoping against hope, he thought. Better to put her out of her misery. 'I'm in love with her.'

At last she was frightened, no longer able to hide it. His guilt increased. She had done nothing to deserve this.

'I was going to talk to you — to explain.'

'Because of her?'

He nodded.

Various expressions flitted across her face and her lips trembled. 'I can't believe you would do this to me,' she said in a low voice. 'After all these years when you know how much I love you. How much we mean to each other. The plans we made.'

Jack wanted to say, '*You* made them!' but didn't. The middle-aged couple at the next table were listening unashamedly to their conversation and Jack rounded on them fiercely. 'Are we speaking loudly enough for you?' he demanded, relieved to find someone who was also behaving badly. 'Have you missed anything?'

Judith cried, 'Jack, *please!*'

She hated scenes. Well, too bad, he thought desperately. This was now a scene. The situation was already out of control and things could only get worse.

The man glared. 'We're simply trying to enjoy our meal,' he said. 'For your information, you and your petty squabbles are of no interest to us whatsoever!'

His wife, embarrassed, muttered, 'Ignore them, dear, *please.*'

Jack said, 'Well, it didn't look that way to me!'

The wife rallied to the defence of her husband. 'Murray's right. We couldn't care less about you.' To Judith she added, 'But the sooner you are through with *him* the better, I should think!' and cast a disgusted glance in Jack's direction.

Judith said, 'What I do is no concern of yours' and covered her face with her hands as other diners turned in their direction.

The man said, 'Disgraceful way to behave!' and he and his wife turned back to their meal, flushed with righteous indignation.

Jack stared at the tablecloth, ashamed and desperate for a way to escape. Judith, standing abruptly, provided it for him. 'I shan't be dining with you after all, Jack. I hardly think now that a celebration is in order.' She picked her room key from the table. 'I've changed my mind — about *everything.*'

Stammering, Jack made a final effort to undo the damage. 'Judith, please. Don't go like this. I truly didn't want to hurt you.'

Murray muttered, 'Damned funny way of showing it!'

Judith leaned forward and her expression had hardened. 'I think I understand, Jack. I'll leave on the first train in the morning.' Making no attempt to lower her voice she said, 'But don't think you'll get away with this. There's such a thing as "breach of promise", remember. I'll be talking things over with Mummy and Daddy and our solicitor.'

To the couple at the next table she said, 'I do apologise for my companion's behaviour. I hope we haven't spoiled your evening.'

The man said, '*You* haven't, my dear,' and his wife said, 'I'm sure you're doing the *right* thing!' but before she had finished speaking Judith had turned away and was halfway across the room. The waitress, helping her on with her stole, cast curious glances in Jack's direction.

Well done Judith, thought Jack, staring shamefaced at his cutlery. A great exit. He felt unwilling admiration for her and immense regret about his own performance. He was a real swine.

The waitress hovered uncertainly and Jack looked up wearily. 'A double whisky, please.' He considered the ruins of the evening with a sense of growing helplessness. Judith had gone, vowing vengeance. He had upset Dulcie and probably ruined his chances there. He could see no way to put any of it right just at the moment so he might as well drown his sorrows in drink.

The next day was fine. Too good for a funeral, thought Gough. A clear sky with wispy clouds and a warm sun. No breeze. He and Spencer stood discreetly to one side of the mourners who, sombre in deepest black, had now gathered at the graveside.

Gough sighed. 'They always look so sinister, don't they. Mourners, I mean. There's something ominous about people in black.'

Spencer shrugged. 'They wear it all the time

on the continent. The women, that is. The older they are, the more black they seem to wear. I can never understand it. It gets so hot, you'd think they'd wear white to reflect the sun. They paint the houses white.'

Gough listened in silence. Trust Spencer to bring up 'the continent'. Apparently he'd once spent three days in Spain unsuccessfully pursuing a villain. Ever since he talked like a seasoned traveller. Gough had very little time for foreigners. They could paint their houses sky-blue pink for all he cared. 'The continent!' Insufferable prig.

Gough was feeling distinctly uncharitable ever since the funeral had sprung an unwelcome surprise. There was no sign of Teddy Moore, the man they wanted to interview. In a way, hardly surprising since Brayne had pinched his girl and yet he might have shown his face if only to show there was no lingering ill will. Unless there *was*. And that was what they wanted to talk to Moore about. What was even more surprising, there was no sign of Annabel Roper either. Surely common decency required that the erstwhile fiancée of the dead man would appear at his funeral to pay her last respects.

To Spencer he said, 'This Roper woman — she can't *still* be confined to bed with a broken heart. I'm getting a nasty feeling that the two of them are in cahoots. What do you think?'

'God knows!'

Gough said, 'Leave God out of it. I'm asking

for your opinion.' He had heard rumours that Spencer had got himself drunk last night. If so he probably had a nasty hangover. Serve him right. The man was too big for his boots.

'Sorry, Chief. The pair of them? Yes, I think you could be right. Shall I have a word with the Ropers? Dig a bit.'

'Do that. I'll talk to the Moores.' Spencer didn't react although gossip about him and Dulcie Moore had been circulating in the murder room for a few days. A quick glance at the lady in question revealed that she was keeping her gaze firmly on the coffin. Not so much as a glance in Spencer's direction. Not that he could blame Spencer. She was a stunning young woman. Today, in a neat black skirt and jacket, she peered out at the world from beneath the brim of a black straw cloche. Most men would fall beneath the spell of those blue eyes. Except her boss, of course. It was rumoured that she no longer worked for the *Canterbury Standard* although no one seemed to know why.

The vicar was reading the familiar words in that certain voice. Why did they do that, Gough wondered irritably. Singing the words without music. They must teach it at theological colleges. He let his gaze move over the mourners. Harriet Moore, in her way, was also a striking woman but it was difficult to guess her exact age . . . Mr and Mrs Brayne clutched each other. Poor souls. It must be hell on earth to lose a son like that. To know that his last moments were full of fear and pain. The killer had a lot to answer for but they'd get him. He'd be behind bars before he could say 'knife'! They'd got posters up now of Parker, an artist's likeness. Might jog a few memories. The public were so damned *slow* to react. 'Didn't want to get involved' or 'Didn't think it was important'. You'd almost think they *liked* having a killer on the loose. He shifted his weight from one foot to the other, squinting against the sun . . . The Ropers looked pale and agitated. Perhaps the daughter really *was* ill . . . There were a few other faces. Quite a crowd, in fact. Either the Braynes had a lot of friends or curiosity had brought in a few odd bods.

There was an elderly man standing beside James Moore. Very frail looking.

Gough nudged Spencer. 'Who's the old boy?'

'That's Wilfred Moore. Bit of a recluse but not short of the odd bob or two. Owns the *Standard.*'

'Ah!' He frowned. 'What's the connection?'

'The Moores and the Braynes have been friends for ages. The Ropers, too. Goes back a generation at least.'

'But not so friendly now, I take it.'

'You could say that!'

At a word from the vicar, the father of the victim stepped forward and, taking the spade from the gravedigger, sent the first scattering of earth down on to the coffin. Gough sighed. 'Ashes to ashes etc!' he muttered. 'Another poor bastard gone to an early grave.' He looked at Spencer.

'That fingerprint bothers me. Could it possibly have been Moore who killed Brayne and not Parker?'

'Parker definitely did the Bly woman.'

'Answer the question, dammit!'

'I don't think so but anything's possible.'

Gough wanted to shake him. So he had a hangover. No excuse to fall down on the job. 'Don't think so' and 'Anything's possible'. Dammit, he was being *paid* to have an opinion.

Gough said, 'Right! The party's as good as over. Let's go get 'em!' Leaving his detective sergeant to tackle the Ropers he made his way between the gravestones towards James and Clarice Moore.

Dulcie saw him coming and changed direction to avoid him. Funny, he thought.

'Mr Moore, could I have a word?'

James Moore looked thunderous. 'At a time like this?'

His wife looked close to tears. Interesting.

'It's about your son. We expected him to be here and —'

'So did we!' Moore answered. 'Don't ask me where he is because my guess is as good as yours, Inspector.'

The wife said, 'He might have gone back to Cornwall.'

Gough raised his eyebrows. 'Back to Cornwall? Now that would be very naughty of him. We asked him to stay in Canterbury or to —'.

His wife said, 'Well, maybe not, then. At least we don't think so.'

'Don't talk to him!' Moore told her sharply. To Gough he said, 'This is a private function. A funeral is no place for the police to come snooping.'

She said, 'But James, they're only doing their duty and they have to be told. If they were looking for Dulcie's killer or Teddy's you'd want other people to cooperate.' Ignoring his obvious anger she turned back to Gough. 'We think he and Annabel have gone away together. It's all rather complicated. They were so much in love once and then — Well, these things happen.'

Her husband growled, 'You're babbling, woman!'

She went on as though she hadn't heard. 'The truth is, Inspector, that we don't know and I — I really can't bear all this terrible secrecy. So much deceit. It's so terribly thoughtless of them — and to choose today of all days! Poor Clive dead and they can't even —'

Moore broke in. 'Have you got children, Inspector?'

'Yes I have.'

'Then you know what it's like. Nothing but damned heartache and worry and more heartache. Happy families! My God! Whoever coined that phrase wanted his head examined!' He shook his own despairingly.

Gough's eyes narrowed. 'Gone away *together?* You mean they've *eloped?*' This is all I need, he thought furiously. We get a fingerprint that places Teddy Moore in the church on the night of the murder and he's *eloped!* Wonderful! 'Have you any idea where they might go, if not to Cornwall? Any far-flung relatives maybe?'

They shook their heads. Gough felt vaguely sorry for them. One of his own two boys had been a constant source of trouble until he met a young nurse who reformed him. She had been the making of him. Oh yes. He knew all about being a parent. He glanced up as Spencer strode across the churchyard towards him.

'They've both gone missing,' he told Spencer, neatly preempting the news that they had lost their quarry.

Mrs Moore said, 'Is it anything important, Inspector? I mean, do you *have* to talk to him?'

Gough looked at her. Yes I damn well do, he thought. Because I might want to arrest your son for withholding evidence or accuse him of manslaughter. I might even charge him with murder. Yes, madam, you *could* say it was important. He said, 'Don't worry, Mrs Moore. We'll catch up with him later.'

Gough watched them walk away. They were victims, too. Their world was falling apart. Debris. The world was littered with people like them. He sighed. Spencer was watching Dulcie Moore who was deliberately avoiding him. He wanted to say, 'Stay single, Spencer. It's a lot easier on the nerves.' They watched the Moores rejoin their party.

Spencer said, 'The Ropers think they're together. What d'you think, Chief? Gretna Green?'

'We'll put a few calls through.' He pursed his lips thoughtfully. 'But what's their hurry? You'd think they'd let this lot blow over first. Bun in the oven? If so that might explain a lot.'

The congregation was drifting away. Black rats leaving a sinking ship, he thought obscurely. They regrouped outside on the pavement, muttering in small groups, getting into motor cars, slamming doors. Abruptly his mind was made up. He turned to his detective sergeant. 'We've got to get this sorted and soon. If Teddy Moore shows up in Gretna Green I want him to find us waiting for him!'

CHAPTER 12

At the Braynes' home, the mourners mingled self-consciously, talking in voices as subdued as their clothes. The two detectives were not present, a fact which everyone appreciated. The only splash of white was the crisp white apron which belonged to the maid, especially hired for the occasion to serve a selection of small sandwiches, vol-au-vents, tea and cakes. Dulcie spotted Harriet talking earnestly to Uncle Wilfred — no doubt discussing the fact that Dulcie had been sacked, she thought ruefully, keeping her distance. Looking for some way to make herself useful, she found Mrs Brayne and offered to help carry round the refreshments. She was given a firm 'No' with not even a 'Thank you for offering'. It was obvious the Moores were being held responsible for Teddy and Annabel's absence. In her heart Dulcie couldn't blame them for their hostility. She, too, thought the timing unforgivable although she suspected the reason for her brother's flight. Presumably they had decided to marry and keep the child and a quiet wedding as far away as possible seemed a good solution to an increasingly difficult situation.

She was also aware that the police now wanted to talk to Teddy again and this knowledge terrified her. Prior to last night's fiasco at the County, it would have been so easy to ask Jack what was happening but now that possibility was denied her. Aware of his gaze during the funeral service, she had refused to meet his eyes and had totally ignored the presence of the two detectives. She had agreed loudly with Harriet that a police presence at the funeral showed a sad lack of discretion on their part. It seemed that intruding on to private grief did not trouble them. That was the police for you!

Holding a cup of tea. Dulcie nibbled her sandwich unhappily, aware that the presence of the Moore family at such a gathering was hardly suitable, either, and yet conscious that to stay away would have been worse. She looked up as Mrs Roper approached and felt an immediate rush of compassion. Annabel's mother's face was chalk white, her eyes red-rimmed, her hair carelessly arranged. She had aged about ten years, thought Dulcie.

'Mrs Roper, I'm so dreadfully sorry —' she began but to her surprise Annabel's mother did not immediately snap her head off. Instead she took her by the elbow and led her out into a deserted corner of the hall.

'I must talk to you,' she whispered. Her fingers clutched at Dulcie's sleeve with such agitation that Dulcie had to set down her cup and saucer on a nearby window sill.

'My dear, I must tell you something and ask your help.' Her voice was so low that Dulcie had to lean towards her. 'My husband is determined — Well, you know what men are like. They don't understand these things the way we do although he is her father and should at least try.'

Dulcie nodded, waiting for comprehension.

'He told Annabel that if she married Teddy it would be without his blessing and they would never be welcome again. In our home, I mean.' Tears ran suddenly from her eyes and Dulcie put an arm round her. 'I think that's what they mean to do — to get married and I think they've gone to Gretna Green. I haven't dared suggest this to my husband because he'll never forgive them. He'll be beside himself with rage. He's a man who can't bear to be thwarted and he's always adored Annabel. All this has quite destroyed him, you know. How he's coping inwardly I'll never know. I thought this morning when we found her gone that he'd have a fit! Quite literally.' She pulled out a handkerchief and dabbed at her eyes. 'I want you to promise that you'll let me know if you hear anything. Anything at all. Not that I ever wanted anything for Annabel but happiness but I don't want her to marry Teddy. It's all been so terribly sordid and horrible and I wanted her to make a fresh start with another man. Someone we could all be proud of.'

These last wistful words went straight to Dulcie's heart and her own eyes filled with unshed tears. She, too, wanted to be proud of Teddy but it was becoming impossible to defend him. 'I think he meant well towards her —' she began.

Mrs Roper drew back sharply and stared up into her face. 'Oh no! He's not the man you think he is, Dulcie.' She blew her nose and put away the handkerchief. 'If you only knew!'

A tight knot of fear developed somewhere inside Dulcie and she felt cold with sudden apprehension. 'What?' she demanded. 'Tell me!'

She saw Mrs Roper's indecision and gave her arm a shake. 'You want my help, don't you? Then tell me what you know or I won't give it.'

Mrs Roper cowered back as though she had been struck and Dulcie felt ashamed of her bullying tactics. And yet she must know what was happening. What had Teddy *done?*

'*Tell* me!' she insisted. 'Right now!'

Mrs Roper opened her mouth to speak but at that moment Harriet appeared in the hall.

'Oh there you are, Dulcie,' she said. 'I was thinking of going home. That dog of yours will be wrecking the place but . . .' Seeing Dulcie's expression she added, 'Still, another few minutes won't make much difference. If he tears up the kitchen it won't be the first time!' and she withdrew.

Dulcie looked at Mrs Roper. 'Tell me!'

'Only if you swear to tell no one that I've told you.'

'Of course I do!'

Mrs Roper drew a long breath. 'Annabel told me in strictest confidence and my husband knows nothing about it.'

Dulcie wanted to scream, 'Get on with it!'

'Your brother *was there,* Dulcie. At the church — the night Clive was killed. But he swears he didn't kill him.'

Dulcie sat down suddenly on the hallstand seat and took a deep breath. Teddy was *there?* But that meant Teddy had lied and that was impossible.

Mrs Roper went on. 'He says Clive sent him a note asking him to meet him in the church. Apparently he —' Her voice trailed off and she looked past Dulcie who turned her head to see Mr Roper watching them from the doorway.

He looked at his wife grimly. 'We're going, Maude,' he told her. 'We're not staying where we're not wanted. Come along.'

Dulcie said, 'Oh but we're talking, Mr Roper. About —' Searching her mind for a topic that would *not* arouse his suspicions was not easy. Clive, Annabel, Teddy. They would all inspire his wrath. '— about the flowers,' she improvised. 'Such beautiful tributes. So many people thought very highly of Clive. I'm sure —'

He looked through her. 'I said we're going,' he repeated stonily.

To Dulcie's dismay, Mrs Roper stood up. She threw Dulcie an agonised glance and Dulcie suspected that she had desperately wanted to share the burden of whatever it was she knew.

'Please!' hissed Dulcie.

Mrs Roper hesitated. 'I'd better go,' she said. 'I'm sorry.'

Her husband said, 'What are you two whispering about?'

'We're not whispering,' said Dulcie untruthfully.

Mrs Roper walked slowly towards her husband. He took her arm possessively but Dulcie read the signs of repressed anger.

Dulcie called out, 'May I visit one day soon?' She was speaking to Mrs Roper but he answered for her.

'No you may not!' he said loudly. 'Your brother's done us enough harm already and I'll thank you, Dulcie Moore, to stay away from us.' He took his wife's arm none too gently and hurried her to the front door. A moment later, without a word to anyone they were gone.

That same evening a note was delivered by hand to a house in Wear Bay Crescent, high on the east side of Folkestone. There was no envelope. The paper was unlined, the writing neat, the spelling accurate. It said — 'Come to the beach to the east of the harbour if you want to hear something to your advantage. Ten o'clock.' Arnold Burnett, who lived at the house with his mother, stared at her.

'Who brought this, dear?' He was middle-aged, bespectacled and had a scholarly air about him. He might have been a teacher but was instead a partner in Robbins Burnett. The only *working* partner, in fact. Stanley Robbins had put up most of the money twenty years ago but now he was past it. Never had dealt with the day-to-day stuff. Arnold carried the firm, they both knew that. He had the flair for business; the eye for opportunities. He talked with clients and architects and hired the contractors. Without Arnold Burnett the firm would fall apart.

His mother smoothed down her apron. 'I don't know, dear. I found it on the mat.' She was a tiny woman nearing seventy. They had been close since his mother was widowed when he was eleven. 'I can't make head or tale of it, Arnold. Is it a *joke?*'

'How on earth should I know?'

'It came while I was taking my nap. Mrs Kemp next door said a boy on a bicycle brought it. A delivery boy. "Something to your advantage?" I wonder what that means?'

He reread it. 'It means someone is playing silly beggars!'

'Isn't that what solicitors say when you've come into a lot of money?'

'They do, dear, but solicitors don't send delivery boys to poke messages through letterboxes. Anyway, who do we know who's rich and about to peg out?

He took off his jacket and his mother hung it on the hall-stand while Arnold tugged his waistcoat down over an ample stomach. He screwed up the note and pushed it into his trouser pocket. It intrigued and excited him.

For a delicious moment he wondered if it could be from Miss Garland, his secretary. Poor woman was rather smitten and had once invited him and his mother to Sunday lunch. He had recognised the ploy for what it was and had declined without telling his mother. He allowed himself a secret smile. Miss Garland always sent him a Valentine. She disguised the writing and he always pretended not to know who had sent it.

'Will you go, Arnie, to the beach? It says "to your advantage".' His mother followed him along the passage. 'You could stroll down there after you've had your dinner. I've done us a rabbit pie with bacon and onions.'

He washed his hands in the kitchen and said, 'Smells good!' but his mind was still on the mysterious note. 'Ten o'clock? It'll be dark by then. I don't fancy hanging around the beach in the dark, especially there. Not particularly salubrious.'

'Don't go then, dear.' She handed him the towel and he dried his hands.

'I don't think I will.' He felt a pang of regret as he said this. He was always complaining that his life was too predictable.

Something to my advantage, he thought curiously as he went up the stairs to the bedroom. Changing into his casual clothes he thought, It can't be money. That would come in a proper way through a solicitor. So why the secrecy? Unless . . . Could it be something to do with the tender they had put in for the town's new racing track? He felt a *frisson* of excitement. Was somebody in the know going to tell him that they'd won it? That would put Foote's nose out of joint and no mistake. Oh! How he would *love* that! But he would know in two days' time anyway. So why the cloak and dagger stuff?

His mother's voice floated up the stairs. 'It's on the table, Arnie!'

'Coming, dear.' He smiled at his podgy reflection. His mother loved to cook for him. And pies were her favourite. She *did* have a light hand with pastry. Rabbit. Mutton. Beef with a drop of ale in the gravy.

He sat across the table in the cosy kitchen. That was another habit they had fallen into. The dining room was only for Sundays and what his mother called high days and holidays.

He enjoyed the pie and the sherry trifle but the invitation to the beach rendezvous continued to jostle at the back of his mind. Suppose it *was* Miss Garland. He could always slip away again before she saw him. And never, *never* let her know that he knew . . . But no, it couldn't be her, could it? It would be so out of character unless there was more to Miss Garland than anyone suspected. He had once seen her coming out of a public house with a man but the next day, when he teased her about her 'fancy man', she had insisted it was her brother. He tried to imagine Miss Garland loitering on the beach in the dark.

It wasn't easy. It would have to be something important. Good God! He drew a sharp breath. Was it a *leap* year? Was she going to propose?

At last he said, 'I suppose it won't do any harm, just to go along and see what's what.'

His mother smiled. 'Just as you like, dear. It's a bit of excitement, I suppose. Will the tide be in or out?'

'The tide? Oh I see . . . In, I think. Yes, in.'

'Don't go getting your feet wet!' she laughed. 'It'll be a bit of fun.'

He laughed and glanced at his watch. 'Might as well stroll down. The walk'll do me good. Bit of exercise.'

Albert Parker was leaning against the side of the fishing boat. The moon was occasionally obscured by cloud but there was still enough light to see by. The sound of the sea filled his ears and he was vaguely aware of the smell of cold seaweed and rotting driftwood. The wooden boat struck chill against his back and the temperature had dropped considerably since the sun went down. His feet were uncomfortable in borrowed wellington boots. He had tucked his trousers into them, hoping to pass for a fisherman if he was unlucky enough to be noticed coming or going. Only the cigarette comforted him. The deserted beach was uninspiring and he wanted to get the business over and done with.

'Come on!' he muttered. 'We haven't got all night!'

Thankfully there was no one else on that particular stretch of beach and best of all no inquisitive dogs.

'Where the hell *are* you?' he demanded. Gone ten already. Maybe he wasn't coming. That would stymie the exercise. He'd have to think up something else and that meant hanging around in Kent. Not a very wise thing to do. Only a matter of time. That damned artist's impression was *good!* He'd had a nasty shock. Still the hat helped and the police would no doubt be sifting through dozens of alleged sightings of him. Getting closer all the time, though. Thank God for his time in the nick. Frankie had taught him a lot while he'd been in there. Parker blew out a cloud of smoke and inhaled deeply. Godawful place. He would never go back there. He'd die first, if he had to, but he'd take as many with him as he could. They wouldn't get rid of Albert Parker without a struggle.

Ah! He straightened up, peering through the gloom. That could be him! Arnold Burnett, the Mummy's boy. Foote had promised he would be easy meat. He sighed. It would be a lot easier if he could strangle the silly sod but, no, it had to look like an accident. Don't tell me the sordid details, Foote had insisted. Just do it. I want to open the paper and read about his accidental death.

He coughed and saw the man's head turn sharply in his direction.

'Come *on!*' he muttered. 'Over here!'

The man hovered on the edge of the pavement as though poised for flight. He stared up and down then took a few hesitant steps on to the beach. Parker gave him a minute or two to get nearer, then stepped out of the boat's shadow. Enjoying the sense of power he told himself, 'Go carefully, Parker. Don't panic him.'

'Who's there?' The voice shook a little.

Parker grinned. He whispered, 'It's Nemesis!' Raising his voice he said, 'Evening!'

Again the man glanced around the deserted beach. 'Good evening.'

Suspicion was there and doubt and fear. Years in prison had finely tuned Parker's hearing. He waited. If the fool stayed where he was he'd live to tell the tale. For a few more days, anyway. 'Mr Burnett, is it?' Better not kill the wrong one.

'Yes it is. Actually I'm expecting someone —' He looked round. Sounded disappointed. Who had he expected? Born fools, some people. They deserved all they had coming to them.

'It's me,' Parker told him.

'You? But how — that is, have we met?' Burnett came towards him but stopped when there were still a few yards between them.

Ask me no question, I'll tell you no lie! Parker grinned. 'That's right. Let's walk.' Taking a chance he sauntered towards the shoreline, willing Burnett to follow. If the man lost his nerve he'd lose him but he couldn't risk frightening him.

After a few seconds he heard Burnett hurrying

to catch up with him.

'But what's it *about?*' he demanded breathlessly. 'And why the mystery? I almost didn't come.'

You'll wish you hadn't, old chum! Parker almost smiled as his victim trotted along beside him. He said 'It's about the tender —'

'Oh it *is!* I did wonder. Look here, who *are* you?'

Parker stopped, pretending to scratch his ankle, and glanced back the way they had come. There was no one. He strode on, away from the streetlights.

Burnett stumbled after him, muttering irritably under his breath. 'Look, stand still a minute, can't you. What's it all about?'

He sounded anxious as well he might.

Parker improvised. 'Mr Foote is wondering about a merger.' Like hell he was!

'A *merger!* Good God!' Burnett stopped, astonished.

Now! thought Parker. He turned and punched Burnett hard in the middle of his flabby stomach.

'Agh!' Burnett doubled up with a grunt of pain. While he staggered, gasping for breath, Parker grabbed his arm and swung him round so that he lost his balance and fell into the shallow water. The fall had winded him and before he could draw breath to cry out for help, Parker knelt beside him and put his left hand over his mouth. He knew he must be careful. Not too much pressure or it would show up at the post mortem. It had to look like an accidental drowning. He rolled the terrified man over, pressing him face down into the water. He began to wade backwards through the shallow waves, dragging Burnett with him into deeper water.

God, he was heavy! Hell and damnation! Must keep his face under water. That way he couldn't scream. After what seemed an eternity the water deepened and flowed suddenly into Parker's boots. It was colder than he had expected but he had little time to consider such small inconveniences. His victim, contrary to expectations, was beginning to fight back. Somehow he twisted his head and bit Parker's wrist.

'You bastard!' Parker grunted and instinctively he snatched his hand away. As he did so a wave caught him unexpectedly. He flailed backwards and went under. When he came up Burnett had lifted his head free of the waves and was desperately sucking air into his lungs. His eyes were wide and terrified. Then he tried a scream. 'Help!'

The word was an apology for a scream. A hoarse, garbled sound. Probably didn't carry far but Parker was taking no chances. He clapped his hand back over Burnett's mouth. 'Shut up, you fool!' Let's hope he doesn't have rabies, he thought and was glad he was going to kill him. Glad it was now that little bit more *personal.* A touch of revenge sweetened the deed.

Burnett was twisting and plunging, turning,

waving his arms and kicking out wildly with his legs. Foote had insisted that Burnett would offer little or no resistance. Bloody typical. Overweight and unfit, Foote had said. 'You could have fooled me!' Parker muttered, tightening his grip around his victim's throat. He squeezed, glancing shorewards for any sign that the one cry for help had alerted someone.

Nothing.

Burnett was weakening although he had somehow managed to hook an arm around Parker's right leg. They were in water now that reached to Parker's waist and he continued to hold Burnett's head under the water. Which meant he had to bend down to maintain his grip around his throat. A wave slapped him in the face, making him gasp and swear. An unwelcome thought struck him. How the hell was he going to walk back through the town dripping wet? Have to pretend he was drunk if anyone challenged him. They'd assume he had fallen in.

'Die, can't you!' he muttered as Burnett continued to thrash weakly beneath the water. 'You're not going to make it!'

Changing his tactics, he lifted Burnett's head clear of the water and brought a heavy fist down on top of his head with a satisfying thud. Useful little trick. He smiled. Thanks, Frankie!

Burnett vanished below the water. Parker waited, cold and exhausted. He shivered, his chest heaving with effort but pleased with his achievement. He had done it. Now he could collect his money and get out of the country for good. That damned poster worried him and there was still that damned girl. He considered her fleetingly. Smart little bitch! He hated women like her. They thought that because they were pretty they could have it all their own way. Stuck-up little piece. They were all the same. Give him an honest whore any day.

But was she any kind of threat? She *had* seen him with Foote. Parker wasn't happy about it. Foote should never have agreed to give her an interview. That was his stupid vanity. She had seen him as Mr Stowe so shouldn't have made the connection. Foote had insisted she wouldn't make one but then he had also insisted that 'Mummy's boy Burnett' would be a pushover. And he hadn't.

Cutting short his reflections on the girl he watched the drowned man float in the water beside him then drew a small flask of whisky from his pocket. This was his own idea and he was rather pleased with it. He unscrewed the lid and drank a large mouthful, relishing the small warmth it gave him. Then he grabbed Burnett by the hair and forced the neck of the flask into his mouth. When it was empty he tossed it into the water. Timing the waves, he gave the body a push away from the beach. With any luck the tide would take it out when it turned. Certainly no one would find it tonight.

With a mock salute he said, 'Bye, old chum,' and began to wade back to the shore.

As he splashed through the waves the whisky gave him false courage and he smiled broadly.

'Nothing to it!' He staggered up on to the shingle, collapsed into a sitting position and breathed deeply. He looked at his hand where Burnett had bitten it.

'Bloody savage!' he muttered. He rubbed it briskly then felt for his cigarettes. 'Damn it!' They would be soaked. He struggled to his feet and set off across the beach, weaving unevenly for the benefit of any passers by. Heading for the cheap attic room he had rented above the music shop he thought only of dry clothes and more whisky.

Nearly an hour later Dulcie sat up in bed. Something had woken her and her heart was racing as she listened. Her first thought was that Max was whining but she could hear nothing from the direction of the kitchen. Her conscience smote her at the thought of him. He had chewed through another lead and she had been forced to smack him. Harriet had insisted that if Dulcie didn't do it, she would. Dulcie had tried to make a small smack look like a big one and when it was over she had whispered 'Sorry' with her face close to his ear. She recalled his funny, reproachful face and cocked ear. Harriet had insisted that he spend the evening in the kitchen in deep disgrace. They had argued. Harriet had won and Dulcie had sulked, ensuring that they both had a miserable evening. Her aunt could be very hard, she reflected.

'He'll never learn,' Harriet had told Dulcie severely, 'unless you're firm with him. Some things are allowed and some things aren't. Chewing his lead is one of the latter.' Throwing back the covers Dulcie now pulled on her dressing gown and went out on to the landing. She listened and heard a slight sound — almost like a groan. It came from the bathroom.

She tapped on the door. 'Harriet? Are you all right?'

Receiving no answer she opened the door. Her aunt lay on the floor, groaning. Switching on the light Dulcie saw that her face was flushed unhealthily.

'Harriet!' She knelt beside her aunt. 'You're ill! What's happened?'

Her aunt's lips moved but the jumbled words made no sense. Dulcie snatched a large towel from the edge of the bath and folded it into a pillow which she placed under her aunt's head. What else should she do, she wondered frantically.

'Come on!' she urged herself. 'Think!' What was she supposed to do with a person who was barely conscious? Gently she coaxed Harriet on to her side so that if she was sick she wouldn't run the risk of choking. 'I'll call Doctor Madden,' she said. 'I promise I won't be long.'

Without waiting to dress or find a key she pulled on a dressing gown and ran downstairs. Max began to bark furiously.

'Stop it, you idiot! I'm not an intruder!'

Outside, thankful for the moonlight, she paused to wedge the doormat across the sill and then ran to the telephone box on the corner of the road. With her finger poised over the dial she swore under her breath. She had forgotten to bring the doctor's number. Back home again, ignoring the renewed barking, she snatched the address book from the hallstand and ran back. By the time she was connected she was quite breathless and her fingers trembled. The doctor's wife was rather cross at being woken from a deep sleep but she could hardly refuse to waken her husband. House calls were part of his duty and this, Dulcie told her, was certainly an emergency.

'My aunt is almost unconscious!' she insisted. 'Of course it can't wait until the morning. She might be *dead* by then!'

Without arguing further, she hung up and ran back to the house, leaving the door propped open for the doctor. Upstairs her fear grew. Her aunt was now very still and couldn't be roused. Dulcie ran some water and bathed her face then sat with Harriet propped in her arms. Harriet was *never* ill. She prided herself on her strong constitution, declaring that no germs would dare try to attack her. Indestructible, she had insisted with a laugh.

'Oh Harriet! Please be all right!' she begged.

After what seemed an interminable wait the doctor's motor car could be heard pulling up outside the house and within minutes Dulcie was surrendering her responsibility. She could see, however, by the doctor's expression, that he was thoroughly alarmed by Harriet's condition. He began by peering into her eyes and feeling around her neck for glands. He took out a thermometer then shook his head.

'I don't need a thermometer to know she's running a high fever. You did well to call me.' Loosening the neck of her nightdress he placed the end of his stethoscope on her chest and listened intently. 'Hmm!' He sat back thoughtfully. 'She didn't fall, I take it. I don't see any bruises. Would you have heard if she had?'

'I don't think so. I was asleep — although obviously something woke me but she may have called out for me. It's possible. Maybe she felt ill or sick and staggered along to the bathroom — or crawled along —' She fell silent.

'Mm?'

Dulcie waited impatiently for the verdict. Doctor Madden had been the Moores' doctor for years. He must have *some* idea, she thought despairingly.

He sighed deeply. 'Has she shown any signs, Dulcie, that this may have been coming? That *something* might have been developing? Any unusual symptoms?'

'Not that I know of. She was fine when we went to bed. Oh —' Her eyes narrowed. 'She did eat oysters — they're her favourite shellfood — but that was a day or two back. We went to the

County. She *was* sick later that evening but nothing much and the next day she seemed to be fine . . . Except that today she did complain about her feet before she went to bed. Said they felt puffy and a bit painful. I didn't think anything about it really.' She looked at him anxiously. 'Why? Do you think —'

He straightened up, shrugging his shoulders. 'Food poisoning might have triggered something else. It can happen occasionally. Difficult to say at this stage.' He was patting Harriet's face and shaking her in an attempt to bring her round. Without success.

'Not diabetic. Can't be that . . .'

Alarmed, Dulcie picked up on the doctor's comment. 'What do you mean? She's not in a *coma* is she?' The thought terrified her.

He began restoring things to his bag. 'To be honest, Dulcie, I'm puzzled. She'll have to be admitted to hospital. We'll need to keep an eye on her and run some tests.'

Dulcie tried to stay calm but it was difficult. She always hated to hear a doctor admit that he was unsure. How could they treat Harriet if they didn't know what was wrong? She said, 'Shall I call an ambulance?'

He stood up, his face grave. 'If we could manage to get her down the stairs I'll take her in my motor. It'll be quicker. Your aunt is very ill.'

Dulcie fought down her fear and somehow, between them, they hoisted Harriet to her feet and with difficulty carried her down the stairs and out to the waiting car. They propped her on the back seat and Dulcie prepared to step in with her.

The doctor looked at her dressing gown and slippers. 'You're not coming dressed like that, are you?'

'Are you going to wait while I change?'

'Of course not but —'

Her glance was withering. 'Then I'm coming like this!'

Dulcie put Max in the kitchen, filled his water bowl and gave him a bone. Then she hurried outside and climbed into the car beside her aunt. As they drove through the deserted streets, she supported Harriet who seemed to be burning up with fever. Once her aunt groaned. Twice she opened her eyes but at no time did she seem aware of her surroundings. Nor did she recognise Dulcie and each time she quickly lapsed once more into insensibility.

Holding Harriet's hand in hers, Dulcie prayed. 'Please God take care of her. Don't let her die.' She remembered the way her aunt had tackled Jack Spencer head on. 'This is your sister, I suppose. I can see a likeness . . .' Loyal, no-nonsense Harriet.

She remembered her aunt saying that Max must be punished. Well, probably she was right, Dulcie conceded, regretting the sharp words they had exchanged earlier. If anything happened to Harriet . . . Max *was* a very unmanageable dog and she, Dulcie, *was* too lenient. She had simply been unable to concede her weakness where the dog was concerned. Why was it always so hard to admit to a mistake? Now, with hindsight, she felt horribly guilty.

Oh Harriet! She tried to imagine the house without her aunt's cheerfully loud presence and tears filled her eyes.

'Oh *please* God!' she whispered. 'Let her be indestructible!'

Two days later Mrs Craddock reread the account of Arnold Burnett's death. She felt very sick and she was cold with fright. An angler had discovered his body washed up on the beach a few miles further along the coast at Dover. At first the police had treated the death as an accident. Arnold Burnett appeared to have been drinking and was presumed to have fallen into the water. Later, in view of what the police called 'extenuating circumstances', the police decided to treat the death as suspicious. According to his mother, it appeared that he had gone to meet a mysterious 'someone' who had sent him a note. This had been found in the victim's pocket although the police were not revealing the exact wording. His mother told a reporter only that it promised 'something to his advantage'.

'Poor, *poor* woman!' whispered Mrs Craddock. 'And poor Mr Burnett.' She had met him once or twice when he came to the office, once when he had accused Mr Foote of sharp practice. In the ensuing argument Mr Foote had called him evil-minded fool' and Mr Burnett had called him 'an out-and-out crook'. She had also seen him a few times in her church with his mother.

She folded the newspaper and hid it in the bottom drawer of her desk. If Mr Foote mentioned the death she would pretend to know nothing about it. She busied herself with her usual duties and after a while the trembling eased. She sucked a sugar lump and gradually the nausea faded. She wanted to forget about Arnold Burnett but she kept thinking about his poor mother and what a shock it must have been for her. Knowing your only son was dead was bad enough but to know his death was 'suspicious' was awful. The article said she was 'distraught' and 'being comforted by relatives'.

And now, of course, Mr Foote would almost certainly be awarded the lucrative contract he was hoping for. Wasn't it *too* much of a coincidence, she asked herself.

The front door opened and closed and Mr Foote bustled into the office.

'Good morning, Mrs Craddock!' He was smiling broadly.

'Good morning Mr Foote.' She was astonished. Didn't he know about Arnold Burnett?

He tossed his hat on to the hatstand and unbuttoned his jacket. She followed him dutifully into his office where he threw himself into his seat and revolved to and fro.

He smiled. 'I want you to pop along to the nearest bakers and buy two large chocolate éclairs!' The smile broadened. 'We've got something to celebrate.' He snapped open his briefcase and withdrew a bulky envelope. 'And while you're out go to the bandstand and give this to Mr Stowe. He'll meet you there.'

The nausea and the shaking returned. 'Yes Mr Foote.' She looked at the package. It could be money, she thought, suddenly fearful.

'Yes, today's a big day for Harris Enterprises. A very big day.'

He seemed suddenly to sense her reluctance. 'What? What's the matter? Cat got your tongue?'

She shook her head. 'What are we celebrating, Mr Foote?'

He eyed her suspiciously. 'Are you *shaking,* Mrs Craddock?'

'I — Yes, I — I think I have a slight chill.'

'Well, you can't have time off, if that's what you're hoping, because we are about to become very, *very* busy.' He positively beamed. 'Harris Enterprises have won and we'll be choosing contractors for the work. A big feather in the old hat, that! *That's* what we're celebrating, Mrs Craddock.' He rubbed finger and thumb together. 'A lucrative contract that takes "yours truly" one step nearer to being Folkestone's next mayor!'

He must be *very* happy, she thought. He wasn't even being sarcastic and that made a nice change.

He was wrapping the package in more brown paper and she watched as he tied it securely with string. He glanced up and his expression had changed. 'I want you to walk up to Mr Stowe and place this in his hands *without a word!* Do you understand that, Mrs Craddock? *Without a single word.* Your job is to hand it to him, not to talk to him.'

Her heartbeat quickened. 'I understand but — supposing *he* says something — *asks* me something?'

'You just walk away. You know how to walk, don't you — one foot in front of the other.' He walked two fingers across his desk. 'Walk away, Mrs Craddock. I'm finished with the man. There's nothing for either of you to say.'

'But he can be violent —' she began.

His eyes narrowed. 'What d'you mean violent? What d'you know?'

She flinched at the chill in his voice. 'I mean, a few days ago when Miss Moore was here — you said yourself he's a bit too handy with his fists.'

He looked relieved. 'Oh that! That was nothing. Don't forget we were at school together. That was just a rough and tumble. Kid's stuff. He's not *violent.*' He gave a small, private smile. 'Wouldn't hurt a fly.'

What about *people,* she thought.

'Just give him the package — and don't forget the eclairs.'

'And if he says anything?'

'I've told you. Walk away.'

She fetched her jacket and put it on. 'What about your tea?'

'Later. We'll have it with the éclairs.'

She picked up the package, wondering if she dare push him just a little. It was the not knowing that was so hard on her nerves. 'Did you see in the paper, Mr Foote, about poor Mr Burnett?'

'What? Oh, the accident, you mean?' He busied himself with a few papers, pushing them around for no reason, not meeting her eye. 'Yes. Poor chap. Seems he might have been drinking. Some people have no head for drink.'

'Drinking? Oh surely not.' She watched his expression. 'Mr Burnett was a very decent man.' She saw no regret in his face — and no surprise either. Her suspicions increased.

'Arnie Burnett was a fool, Mrs Craddock.'

She said, 'I keep thinking about his poor mother.'

'You're not paid to think, Mrs Craddock. You're paid to get on with your work. So run your little errand.' He indicated the package.

'Yes, Mr Foote.'

She picked it up and tucked it under her arm.

'And if you lose the package you're *sacked,*' he called after her. 'I mean that.'

She left the building and began to walk along The Leas in the direction of the bandstand. Terrifying suspicions filled her mind. She was *sure* that her employer and so-called Mr Stowe knew something about Mr Burnett's death. It was almost too frightening to be true but if she was right she was not going to let them get away with it. As she walked she had an idea. A dangerous idea that made her suck in her breath, astonished by her own temerity. No. She must leave it to the police. Except that they didn't know what *she* knew. They had no evidence . . . Was there any way that she could ensure her own safety and that of her husband? It would need careful thought — and then *more* careful thought. She shivered with apprehension. It was a mad idea. Mr Foote and Mr Parker were in another league. She must stay out of it for her husband's sake if not for her own. If anything happened to her . . .

She drew a long breath. So why did it seem so *right?* If she could summon the courage to put the idea into practice it would be the perfect revenge. She would repay Mr Foote for all the small cruelties he had inflicted on her over the past months.

As she reached the bandstand, still undecided, she saw Mr Stowe sprawled in a deck chair, long legs crossed at the ankles. He was leaning back, arms crossed, a hat tilted over his face as though to protect him from the sun's rays. At *this* time of the morning? Incongruously a small child played nearby under the watchful eye of its mother. The large coloured ball bounced against Mr Stowe's legs and he patted it back with a smile. The mother smiled at him. Mrs Craddock wanted to shout *'Don't!* He's not what he seems. He's a wicked, monstrous *bastard!'* The word shocked her.

She walked across the grass and threw the package into his lap. His eyes met hers. Cold, uncaring eyes. Yes, she thought with a jolt of fear. He could have killed Arnold Burnett. She turned quickly away on legs that shook.

'Hey! Girlie!'

She quickened her pace. Thank goodness for the presence of mother and child. He could hardly do her any harm here.

'Mrs Craddock! Get back here!'

In her haste to be gone she tripped and almost fell. She imagined him getting up from his deck chair and running after her. He would run faster than she could. Swallowing, her mouth dry, she stopped in her tracks but did not turn round. Sure enough she heard him pounding towards her. He grabbed her arm and swung her round. He can't kill me, she told herself again as she looked up into his face but his fingers round her arm were painfully tight. Deliberately so.

He said, 'A little something for the messenger!' and thrust something into the pocket of her jacket. It crackled softly. Money, she thought with a shudder.

'No!' she stammered.

'A little something for your piggy bank.' His fingers tightened. 'So say "Thank you" to the kind gentleman.'

Her throat constricted. She tried to speak — anything to get away from him — but nothing came out. Could he have killed a man? Was she standing inches away from a murderer? She recalled Miss Moore's visit. 'He reminds me of someone called Parker . . .' She fought the urge to run. If he knew she had guessed he would kill her, too.

'Say "Thank you, Mr Stowe!" ' He thrust his face close to hers. 'What's the matter? Not used to men giving you money?' He laughed. 'No, your type wouldn't be. Wouldn't know how to earn it, girlie, would you!' He laughed, releasing her arm.

She wanted to spit in his horrible face; to throw the money on to the ground; to accuse him of killing poor Arnold Burnett. But the brute strength of him terrified her.

He said 'Well?'

If she didn't say it he would never let her go. She knew that. 'Thank you,' she said, her voice an anxious, ridiculous squeak. It seemed to satisfy him. Or perhaps he had lost interest in her and wanted to count his ill-gotten gains.

'Well off you go then!'

She took her chance thankfully and hurried away, stumbling across the grass to the path, breathing heavily, feeling unclean. She didn't once look back and when she was sure he wasn't following her she snatched the note from her pocket. A pound. How *dare* he! Anger flared within her. And how dare he call her 'Girlie' in that hateful way. Miss Moore had objected and so did she. She looked around for a waste bin but, like policemen, they were never there when you wanted them. An old man shuffled towards her, unwashed, unshaven.

'Here,' she said. 'Buy yourself some breakfast.' She thrust the note into his hand and walked on. She felt better. More in control.

'Laugh while you can, Mr *Stowe!*' she muttered. 'You'll be laughing on the other side of your hateful face before I'm through with you!'

She had taken the decision without even realising it.

Chapter 13

At the hospital that afternoon Dulcie arrived with a bunch of carnations to find the ward sister barring her way with a smile of recognition. Carrot-red hair peeped from below the white head-dress, her starched apron was immaculate. Pencils and the finger-holds of a pair of scissors protruded from her top pocket and a watch was pinned to the bib so that it hung upside down.

'Only two visitors at a time,' she said. 'Miss Moore already has her brother and sister-in-law.'

So her parents were here. Dulcie felt a rush of guilt because she still hadn't been home to see them. 'Have they been here long? I could wait.' I've no work to go to, she thought bitterly. I've got all the time in the world.

Sister said, 'I'll tell them you're here and I expect one of them will swap places with you.'

Chairs lined the corridor and Dulcie sat down. Further along a middle-aged man sat silently weeping. Her instinct was to rush along and offer comfort but she hesitated. Maybe it would be an intrusion. Maybe he needed to shed the tears. Grief must out. That's what they said. She was thankful she needn't shed tears for Harriet.

She stared around at the pale green walls above the darker tiles, hating the smell. Disinfectant, rubber-soled shoes and cheap floor polish. A young mother passed, her expression tight with anxiety. She was trailing a child, their shoes squeaking across the linoleum. A few moments later Dulcie's mother came out of the swing doors, her face lighting up with pleasure at the sight of her daughter.

'Dulcie, darling!' They hugged briefly. 'Why haven't you been to see us? Is it too much to ask for a daughter to visit her parents?'

Dulcie said quickly, 'How's Aunt Harriet? Yesterday she wasn't so good. She seemed very weak and a bit vague.'

'They say she's improved a little. Stable is the word. They do love it, don't they. Poor Harriet. She was never a good patient. Like your father in that respect. I'm sure they're finding her difficult. At least she can't smoke in here.' She made no attempt to hide her satisfaction. 'Still, you go on in, dear. She's looking forward to seeing you.'

She sank on to the nearest chair as Dulcie made her way along the corridor and into the ward which held about twenty female patients and their visitors. Next to Harriet the curtains were pulled around the bed's occupant. A nurse hurried out, briskly efficient.

Dulcie went forward smiling. At least Harriet looked a little better. There was a domed cage of some kind beneath the bedclothes to keep the blankets from her feet but apart from that she didn't appear uncomfortable.

'Porridge!' she was saying loudly. 'I said I suppose you charge extra for the lumps. The nurse gave me a funny look. No sense of humour, some people. And it's so noisy at night. Feet pattering up and down and people snoring.' She caught sight of Dulcie and brightened. 'Dulcie! How on earth are you managing without me?' she demanded. 'Eating, I hope, although I can't imagine what.'

'Of course I'm eating!' Dulcie leaned over to kiss her and presented the flowers. 'I can do scrambled eggs now.'

'Oh what lovely flowers!' A passing nurse whisked them away, promising to find a suitable vase.

Harriet smiled. 'Flowers and grapes. I'm doing rather well. Scrambled eggs? Good Lord!'

Dulcie was delighted to see that her aunt's colour had improved. The previous day had been fraught with worries as the doctors struggled to keep her conscious and to discover the cause of the symptoms.

James said, 'They're waiting for the results of tests but it might be some form of arthritis — rheumatoid arthritis, perhaps. As soon as I heard the name it rang a bell. Uncle John had it. It was rather nasty, I'm afraid.'

Harriet rolled her eyes. 'He's a great comfort, your father.'

He said hastily, 'But that was *then*, this is *now*. They know more about it.'

Harriet said, 'Well my blasted feet ache like mad so they don't know that much about it.'

'They have to be sure before they start the treatment. Give them time. You always were terribly impatient.'

'Look who's talking!' She raised her eyebrows. 'Your father, Dulcie, is the world's worst. We both had chicken pox and I just got on with it. Calamine lotion, the lot. James here was an absolute pest. Talk about cry-baby. Whining, fidgeting, scratching. Wouldn't take his medicine. Mother was in despair with him. I was back at school a week or more before he was.' She shot him a triumphant look. 'So don't start telling *me* how to behave, James.' She gave Dulcie a wink. 'Actually I'll be fine as soon as they let me come home.'

James frowned. 'Don't be so hasty. Let them do their job. You'll get home all in good time.'

Harriet said, 'Wilfred called in earlier. Stayed about two minutes!' She grinned at Dulcie. 'He hates hospitals. He wanted to know why Cobbs sacked you. Wasn't really interested in me.'

Dulcie groaned. Her failure was being trumpeted far and wide. The higher you climb, the further you fall. She could imagine all the tongues wagging. Well, what did she expect? She was a mere woman and journalism was *men's* work.

'I suppose I ought to go and see him.' She said it reluctantly. Wilfred's house was the gloomiest she had ever been in. Why he persisted in living in such depressing style was a mystery they had all long since decided was unsolvable.

Harriet said, 'Your father has had a letter.' She looked at James.

'Teddy and Annabel are in Gretna Green — or rather they *were*. Silly little fools. Teddy ought to have more sense. They thought they could simply roll up there and get married but it's not quite that easy apparently. Either the bride or groom has to have been in residence there for three weeks prior to the so-called wedding.' He tutted disapprovingly. 'Pledging your troth "over the anvil" in a gloomy little smithy! How crass! I can't see why he has to marry the wretched girl.'

Dulcie wondered how much he knew. She said, 'Probably because he loves her. If the Ropers had been more understanding they would probably never have run away in the first place! Her parents didn't even try to understand how they felt.'

He glared at her. 'Well, listen to Miss Know-it-all! Since when have you been the fount of all wisdom?'

Harriet said sharply, 'Do you mind, James! I'm an invalid, remember. If you two want to quarrel go and do it somewhere else.'

Dulcie said, 'Sorry!' To her father she said, 'So what are they doing now? Coming home or staying on?

He rolled his eyes. 'They've gone to ground seemingly. Waiting out the three weeks, I suppose. It seems the police were up there but they'd already slipped away. Gough descended on us when he got back to Canterbury as though we were to blame for the fiasco. Can't help you, I told him and it was the truth. I said, "Parents are usually the last to know what's going on!" They seem to think Teddy *was* in the church that night. Said they had a fingerprint that proved it. Well, why bother us, I said.' He sighed. 'God knows what Teddy was up to if he was in the church! I'd like to wring his neck and that's the truth. Your mother is worrying herself sick about him.'

Dulcie felt a prickle of unease. Mrs Roper had said something similar about Teddy being at the church. Surely it was impossible? She sighed heavily. The comfortable world in which she had grown up seemed to be crumbling around her. No one was what he or she seemed. She felt dislocated, adrift.

To change the subject, Harriet said, 'How's Max?'

'He's fine.' She wouldn't mention that he had chewed up one end of the kitchen rug. That could wait.

A nurse came up to them. 'Your wife wants to be off,' she told James.

He rose obediently to his feet. 'Well then, old thing!' He smiled at Harriet. 'See you soon. Keep your pecker up!'

They watched him go.

Dulcie said, 'Poor Father! He's not used to all these shocks.'

Harriet snorted. 'He's had it too easy,' she

said. 'Now he's getting a taste of what it's like for the rest of us. It won't hurt him to suffer for a bit. Good for the soul!'

Dulcie said, 'I haven't heard a word from he-who-shall-be-nameless. Not that I expected to.'

'You're better off without Jack Spencer.'

'Am I?'

'Believe me!'

The carnations reappeared in a glass vase.

'Lovely,' said Harriet. 'Thank you.'

The bell rang to announce the end of visiting hour. Dulcie prepared to troop out with the rest of the visitors.

Harriet said, 'Are you all right in the house alone?'

'Right as rain. Don't worry about me. I've got Max!'

'Don't remind me! But I mean it, Dulcie. Lock up at night.'

'I will.'

Walking back along the corridor Dulcie admitted to herself that she had lied. Alone in the house at night she was not at all confident and took Max up to bed with her. Officially he slept on the floor but each morning found him asleep at the bottom of the bed. Harriet would have a fit if she knew but she never would. For the time being, the dark silent house seemed just a little less empty — a little less *threatening* — with the dog in the bedroom.

She reached the reception area and saw Detective Inspector Gough waiting for her. He rose to his feet and moved towards her. The expression on his face made her heart miss a beat.

He had bad news for her and she knew it was about Teddy.

They had found him and he was under arrest. 'I'm sorry, Miss Moore —' he began.

She stared at him. As he held out his hands in a gesture of helplessness she was aware of a feeling of unreality.

'It's Teddy, isn't it?' Her voice sounded higher, unfamiliar.

'He — I'm afraid he's —'

She said, 'He didn't do it!' Awful pictures formed inside her head. Teddy in prison. Teddy *hanged.* For a moment she couldn't hear what the detective was saying. She watched his lips move soundlessly as he framed the dreadful truth. Then the sound returned and she caught one or two phrases.

'. . . under a train . . . nothing anyone could do . . . quite deliberate.'

She said, 'Teddy's *dead?* Under a train? I don't believe it. No!'

'I'm afraid so.'

Teddy had *killed* himself. Now she knew there was some mistake.

'That's not possible!' The words came out through stiff jaws as her whole body tensed in an effort *not* to believe. Teddy would *never* take his own life. He would never do that to her. She *knew* it. There was a strange roaring noise inside her head as though grief were rushing in.

'I'm sorry.' Gough shifted uncomfortably.

It was true. Dulcie stared at him dully. Awful to be the bearer of such bad news, she thought, without feeling the slightest pity for him.

He went on. 'He left a letter —'

'For *me!*' A small sob of gratitude escaped her. He had not abandoned her. She had been in his thoughts to the end.

'For Miss Roper. He said —'

'For Annabel? I don't want to hear it!' Her voice had risen as she fought a growing hysteria. She glanced around. 'My parents — Oh God!'

'I've broken the news to your parents. They've gone home in a taxi. Your mother was in a state of collapse and I thought it best . . .'

'Harriet!'

'I shall tell her now.'

She nodded distractedly, feeling a violent shiver run through her. Teddy was *dead!* He had deserted her. How could he do that to her? Tears streamed down her face. Turn the clock back, please God, and undo this terrible thing.

The policeman was guiding her to a chair.

'No!' she cried. Ignoring his objections, she dodged away from his outstretched arms and ran along the corridor. She flung open the doors and rushed out into the sunlight. Colliding with an elderly man, she cried, 'Sorry. *Sorry!*' through blinding tears.

Sorry! It echoed in her head. A terrible, heartless word.

She was going to be sorry for the rest of her life.

The carriage was almost empty for which Jack was thankful. This must, he thought, be the worst day of his life. He settled himself against the seat back and stared at a view of Blackpool on the partition opposite. Below it a small, plump man was opening up a copy of the *Evening Sandard* which he had found in the rack above his head. Day-old news. Anything to fill the time and make the journey pass more quickly. Jack wished there was something, *anything* which could take *his* mind off the journey — and what lay ahead. Especially that.

The man looked up from his paper. 'Never any good news, is there? I don't know why they go to all the bother of printing it all. Why not just one page that says. "Everything's as bad as it was yesterday." ' He chuckled.

Jack gave him a thin smile that was meant to discourage further conversation. The other occupant was a woman in her thirties. She ignored them, staring fixedly at her fingers which were busy with a piece of knitting. Beside her, in a small basket, she had what looked like lunch — a package wrapped in a serviette, a banana and a small thermos flask. Jack wished he had thought to bring something to eat but there had been no time. Gough had been emphatic that he catch the next train. Not that there was any hurry. Dulcie's brother was dead.

He glanced at his watch as the train lurched forward and gathered speed, leaving the station behind. Ten twenty-one exactly. Teddy Moore was dead. Guilty conscience? So had he killed Clive Brayne? 'Talk to the Roper woman and the porter'. Gough had told him, his face set in furious lines. If they had lost their murderer, Gough would be leaned on heavily from above and, not for the first time, Jack was glad that he was no longer leading the investigation. Nothing was working out and the papers were having a field day. First the Burnett death had been tentatively linked to Parker by way of Foote and now Moore had topped himself. He glanced at his watch. Gough would be breaking the news about now, he reflected. He could imagine the Moores' faces — the colour draining away, the horror as they listened to the awful facts, their features crumpling as the truth dawned. Thank God that task had fallen to Gough. Poor Dulcie would be told. He tried to ease his shoulders which were tense and uncomfortable. Her big brother had thrown himself in front of a train. That's how desperate he was. She would never forget that.

The woman said, 'Could we have the window up a bit. There's a bit of a draught.'

Jack feigned deafness but the plump man sprang up gallantly and closed it. 'How's that, madam?'

She smiled her thanks.

He said, 'Would you like the paper?' and waved it enticingly.

'No thank you. Reading in a train makes my

eyes ache.' She smiled. 'I can knit, though. Funny, isn't it.'

Very funny. Jack thought he would probably never see the funny side of any thing again. Ten twenty-five. He glanced out of the window. London at its dreary worst, he thought dispassionately. Rows and rows of tawdry houses darkened by the smoke from passing trains. Their meagre gardens full of rabbit hutches, sheds and assorted rubbish. Briefly, his heart ached for the inhabitants. Ached, in fact, for the whole world which today appeared particularly dreary. His own part in the production was worse than most and he was deeply depressed.

Dulcie would be torn apart by the news of Teddy's terrible death. She would never again be the innocent, carefree young woman that she had once been. Had her wretched brother known that? Had he understood what he was doing to those who loved him? The tragedy would change Dulcie's life. Jack's tragedy was that he would be unable to offer the smallest words of comfort because Dulcie would never speak to him again. He was astonished at how quickly his own life had fallen apart. Not forgetting Judith. Her latest letter was in his pocket and he knew the brief wording by heart.

'Jack, You will be pleased to hear that I can no longer care for you the way I did nor do I want to share my life with a man I cannot trust. Your behaviour was abominable — I cannot tell you how shocked I was to realise your true nature. Daddy wants me to pursue this through the courts but I am trying to dissuade him. Less said, soonest mended. Try as I may, I cannot find it in my heart to wish you well. Judith.'

Short and to the point, he thought bitterly. No doubt 'Daddy' wanted to tear him limb from limb and 'Mummy' was shedding copious tears on her daughter's behalf. Not that he blamed them. Any parents would feel that way if their beloved daughter had been humiliated. And he liked them all. And they had liked *him*. Not many people wanted their daughter to marry a policeman.

'Stop it, Jack,' he told himself with a sigh. Concentrate on the job in hand. This is a murder investigation. Think about the coming interview with the porter who had been the last person to speak to Moore. Why had he done it? Remorse? Guilt? Despair — or all three? Had he said anything about Clive Brayne? Was Teddy the man who had killed Brayne? Jack tried to concentrate. The train clattered through the leafy suburbs, left the town behind and finally ran through fields.

At ten past eleven the knitting woman ate her sandwiches, scrupulously careful with the crumbs. She drank from the flask but ignored the banana. Jack stretched his arms above his head. He must change at Carlisle. If he forgot he would end up in Dumfries and Gough would not be impressed.

The train slowed and stopped. The woman

gathered her possessions and the plump man leaped up once more to help her. A young woman got in with a baby in her arms, seen off by a tearful mother. Everyone had their own griefs, thought Jack wearily. Whoever said that life was a vale of tears certainly knew what he was saying.

The baby started to cry and Jack felt like joining in.

Resolutely he turned away, staring out at the landscape. Make the most of it, Jack. For a few hours there would be no demands on him. The train ride was a gift. He closed his eyes and tried to sleep.

Kenneth Mackay the porter was fifty-two but the dark uniform did wonders for him. Or so Sheelagh kept telling him. The young laddie's death was, undoubtedly, the most exciting event in his life but the interview with a senior detective came a close second. Not that he looked the part. Detective Spencer was very young and a little unsure of himself. He was a dour man with a strange accent but his suit was smart enough and his shoes shone.

'Tell it in your own words,' the policeman had told him and Kenneth was trying to do just that. They were seated in the office, drinking tea while station master Briggs fussed at his desk with this and that, not wanting to miss anything.

The detective asked a lot of questions and wrote most of the answers down. Where would they all be without their notebooks?

'Said he wanted to catch the early train, sir. I told him, the first train now is an express. It won't stop. They just toss out the newspapers and carry straight on.' He paused to crunch a piece of shortbread. At least old Briggs had had the decency to part with a couple of biscuits. Usually kept them to himself in a tin in the bottom drawer of his desk and thought no one knew.

Kenneth marshalled his thoughts and continued. 'You wanted the milk train, I told him, but you've missed it by a mile! He said he'd catch the first one *after* the express. I said I'd best have a wee look at his ticket. He looked kind of surprised. Said he'd forgotten. Where to, I said, and he gave a bit of a shrug. Good question, he said. Then he said Carlisle would be fine so he paid me and I got him a ticket. Not a fare dodger, sir. Not the type at all. You get a nose for these things. Being on this particular station you get a feel for people. Green especially. So young and excited. They think Gretna is going to solve all their problems.' He shook his head. 'It rarely does, if you want my opinion.'

'How did he seem? Nervous? Worried?'

'Not particularly.' He thought about it. 'Weary, I think that's the word. A wee bit weary. Of course now I can see why but then —' He shrugged. 'I took no notice. I sat down next to him for a couple of minutes. Just by way of being friendly. As I said to my wife after, I sensed he was wanting a bit of company.'

Was that really true, he wondered suddenly, or had it been the other way round. Had Kenneth Mackay wanted someone to talk to . . . ? Och, what did it matter who wanted what. 'Poor Sheelagh had a bit of a fright — that's the Scots spelling, sir. Two e's and then a — g — h. Me going home in the middle of the morning. White as a sheet and shivering. Proper shock it was because you don't *expect* it, sir.'

No answer. Just scribble, scribble. Not exactly chatty but then he was from the south. Canterbury in Kent. You couldn't get much further south. He'd looked it up on the map.

'I made a comment or two about the weather. At first he seemed a wee bit quiet but once he started talking he was away. Had I ever done anything frightful, he asked.'

The detective looked up sharply. 'Frightful? Meaning what exactly?'

Kenneth shrugged. 'So frightful, he said, that you never could undo the trouble you'd caused. I thought, now what sort of question is that?'

'He didn't tell you that *he'd* done anything particularly frightful?'

'No. Asked did I have a wife? Any bairns? Three. I told him and all doing well. My eldest lass is bright as a pin. That's Elspeth, sir. E — l — s —'

'I know how to spell it. Just get on with it, will you.'

A miserable devil, this one, thought Kenneth.

He caught Briggs's eye and saw his raised eyebrows. Thinking the same thing, no doubt. Sassenachs. 'Well sir, he started saying things about Fate. About it being against him. Conspiring. That was the exact word. Everything was going wrong . . . No. Tell a lie, sir. Everything was turning sour. One minute you've got it all, he said, and the next it's turning sour . . .'

He waited. That's right. Write it down. Much good it'll do anyone. Quite a smart-looking man, really. Detective Sergeant Spencer. Pity that detectives didn't wear uniforms. There's something about a uniform that steadies other people in an emergency. People know where they are with it. He had done his own bit of steadying yesterday — calming down the train driver who looked fit to have a heart attack. Mind, he'd gone to pieces himself when he got home to Sheelagh. Then he'd needed a wee bit of steadying!

'Did he mention a man called Clive Brayne?'

'Clive? Oh aye! He did. "Poor Clive!" He said that several times. And "Poor sod!" If you'll pardon my French.'

'Did he say why? Did he elaborate at all?'

'Not a thing, sir. It was all rambling, if you see what I mean. Thinking aloud. Bits of stuff that made no sense — except to him I dare say. And I wasn't taking that much notice at the time, not knowing then. He mentioned an Annabel. I remember that distinctly. Unrequited love, I said to myself. Afterwards, of course. Very hard to bear. My uncle shot himself because the woman he loved had run off with another. Shot himself through the mouth with his army pistol. Robbie Mackay, same name as mine. Small c, small k.'

Did they teach policemen shorthand, Kenneth wondered, watching the pencil move across the page.

'Mr Mackay, are you quite sure Moore didn't say anything else about Clive Brayne? That he'd hit him, maybe, or they'd had a fight? Or an argument that got out of hand?'

'Oh aye. He said he should have lent him the money. He could have afforded it. Kept saying he was sorry. "I'm sorry!". "Oh God, I'm so sorry!" It was about not lending the laddie some money. Aye. That's what was eating him up. But I told our local chap all this when I made my statement.'

The detective gave a half smile. Probably the best he could manage in the circumstances.

'I just need to hear it from you, Mr Mackay. You might remember something that escaped you earlier. Don't worry. I'll read your statement before I go back.'

And why should I worry? My conscience is clear. No one's going to put the blame on me. 'There was not a thing I could have done to save him, sir. It was all over in a flash. I keep asking myself what I could have done but there was not a thing. Sheelagh said, "Couldn't you have grabbed him?" The answer's "No". One minute he's sitting next to me on the seat and then the train comes and he's up in a flash and he's running forward, arms outstretched as if he was a bird and going to take off. I opened my mouth to shout but by then he'd jumped.' Just thinking about it dried his mouth. 'Makes me shiver just to talk about it. He gave this one wee grunt as the engine hit him. And the driver! Poor man. He jammed on the brakes and the wheels were screeching like all the banshees in hell.' He took out a handkerchief and dabbed his face. Strange how fear makes a man sweat.

'It must have been terrible for you.'

'Oh aye. Terrible's the word.'

The detective seemed to be thinking, reading back through his notes. Then he said, 'Did he mention a man called Parker?'

'Parker?' This was new. 'Not a word.'

'A moneylender by the name of Foote?'

'Foote? No, sir.' If the laddie had mentioned a Foote or a Parker it would be in his statement.

Kenneth was aware of Briggs, all ears. Wishing that it had been him, no doubt, being interviewed and chased by the newspaper men. If he hadn't been tucked away in his office with his cups of tea and his precious shortbreads he might have been the one. No one to blame but himself.

The detective sighed. 'So you don't recall anyone else mentioned? His mother or his father maybe?'

'Not that I recall. It was all Clive and Annabel. And what a selfish brute he was. His words, not mine.'

'Mr Mackay, did he mention Dulcie? Give you any message for her?'

Now what? 'First I've heard of a Dulcie.' The man was beginning to irritate him.

'Never mind. It was nothing.' Tapping his pencil on the edge of the notebook. 'And afterwards — when the train stopped?'

'Well now, it was a good way up the track. An express train takes a lot of stopping. I was puffing by the time I got there. I expected a mangled mess and that's the truth but not at all. The body was way back, where the engine had tossed him. He's just lying there, very still. Peaceful. Not much blood. Just a sort of a dent across the side of his head. Where the engine caught him. Crushed the bone, sir, and a bit of blood oozing. His hair was a bit matted.'

Briggs couldn't wait any longer. He said, 'It was me rang for the police and the ambulance.'

Trust him!

The detective glanced at him. 'I see, sir. Killed outright, was he?'

Briggs nodded. 'That's right. All over in a flash the doctor said. That'll be some comfort to his family.'

Poor old Briggs. Can't abide playing second fiddle. 'That's right, sir,' said Kenneth. 'Station master took charge of it all.' Give him some of the credit. They had to work together when this was all done. He sighed. Yesterday, after it happened, Sheelagh had made him a mug of hot tea with a tot of whisky in it. He would need another one soon if this policeman didn't get to the end of his questions. He said, 'Is that about all, sir?'

The policeman had stopped scribbling and was staring into space. After a long pause he looked at Kenneth. 'And he said nothing about Dulcie. She's his sister.'

'His sister? Oh the poor wee thing! No sir, he didn't.'

Dulcie sat in the middle of Teddy's bed, her knees drawn up, her head bent. Beside her, eye-ing her doubtfully, Max allowed his tail an occa-sional thump. He gave a little bark and, blindly, she put out a hand and patted him. Tears flowed on to Teddy's school cap which she held pressed close to her face in an attempt to draw to her any slightest whisper of Teddy that remained within the soft grey folds. She wanted to remember the schoolboy Teddy, uncluttered by recent events. The handsome boy who had shown her his room at Fellstowe, his desk in the schoolroom which bore his newly carved initials and the gloomy dining room where ninety boys shared their meals.

She wanted to remember the Teddy who had run behind her, clutching the seat of her first bi-cycle. 'Don't look back!' he had shouted as she finally rode unaided but she had wanted to see the approval on his face and, turning, had wob-bled into a clump of nettles. . . .

Teddy had taught her to sing 'Frére Jacques', standing her on the table to perform the song to her suitably astonished parents. He had trusted her to feed his rabbit when she was four years old. She could still remember the rabbit's soft nose and the thrill as the lettuce leaf was jerked, nibble by nibble, through the mesh of the hutch. When Teddy went away to boarding school she was bereft — as she was now.

Teddy had taken her to Sparks barn, explaining in gruesome detail about a ghost that haunted it on moonlit nights. She had run screaming with excitement and had tripped over an old wheel. Teddy had carried her most of the way home . . .

Dulcie drew in a long, raking sob and the sound of it reminded her that downstairs her parents and Wilfred also grieved. She had come here to seek and to offer consolation but as soon as she entered the house her feet had carried her up the stairs to her brother's room. Here, if anywhere, she would find some trace of him. Something to cling to, something to help fill the space that had once been his.

'He's gone, you see,' she told the dog. Hearing her voice, he edged closer and gave her outstretched hand a comforting lick. 'For ever!' she added and began to cry again. She sobbed for a long time and when he whined she said, 'Silly old thing!' and cried her heart out in earnest.

'Why? *Why?*' she whispered. Could *anything* have been that bad? The detective had said that Teddy arranged to meet Clive at the church but then refused to lend him the money he needed.

Well, that was mean. There was no denying that. Mean, rotten and not like Teddy at all. But it was also understandable. Teddy wanted Annabel. He *deserved* her. So why should he help Clive out of a mess? She sighed deeply. The Teddy she knew and loved didn't do things like that. He was — he had been — kind, generous, forgiving. Hadn't he? A small doubt flickered but she stamped it out. Of course he was kind. He was the best person she had ever known in her life. So why had he refused to help Clive? Human frailty, perhaps. An error of judgement made in the heat of an argument on the eve of Annabel's wedding. And how could Teddy have known the way it would end? He hadn't murdered Clive. He'd behaved badly and had made some mistakes but nothing to *die* for!

'How *could* you?' she demanded, overcome by a wave of anger. How had dying made anything better? It had made everything worse. 'I'll never understand!' she told him. 'And I'll never forgive you!' Teddy had taken the easy way out and had ruined her life. She could never forgive him even if she wanted to. 'Never!' she cried, her voice cracking with anger as fresh tears welled in her eyes.

With her anger, however, came the abrupt realisation that she could not go on if his memory was tarnished by bitterness. Reproaching Teddy was not going to save her. Intuitively she now recognised, somewhere deep within her, that her beloved brother had not been as wonderful as she had believed nor as saintlike as she had always pretended. The dark truth was that he was flawed like everyone else. She stopped crying to consider this heresy. The idea was unbearable but perhaps she could accept it and still love him. She frowned. 'Love is not love Which alters when it alteration finds . . .' Shakespeare had said that all those years ago and now she clutched the thought to her.

Perhaps she could still love her brother.

Sliding from the bed she crossed to his chest of drawers and found herself a large handkerchief. Wiping her eyes and blowing her nose, she wondered if she was sufficiently in control to go downstairs to her parents. They needed her.

'And poor Harriet, stuck there in the hospital!' she groaned. Her aunt had loved Teddy dearly and the loss would hurt her immeasurably. She pressed a hand to her heart which felt painfully small and hard within her chest. Frozen. Never to beat softly again. Never to recover from the anguish of Teddy's death.

'Oh God!' she whispered tremulously. 'How could you let this happen? How could you let him do such a thing? Where *were* you?' Someone must be to blame for what had happened, she reasoned bitterly. God was supposed to watch over his sheep. Maybe He was to blame. She wondered if she would ever be able to enter a church again or press her hands together in prayer.

Leaning against the chest of drawers, she tried

to see some reason for what had happened. There must surely be some logic to the tragedy. If it was just a whim, an aberration of some kind, then she could not bear it. Teddy's life was too precious to be squandered for no good reason.

'So *why?*' she demanded again. Max, pressed against her legs, whined softly. She patted his rough coat. 'You're a darling, Max! You want to comfort me, don't you!'

She found another of Teddy's handkerchiefs, saw his initial in the corner and felt fresh tears forming. No, she was not ready to go downstairs. She was in no fit state to comfort anybody. She moved to the window and looked out at the view that had been *his* view for so many years. Blurred by tears it was still recognisable. It was the best view, out across the lawn to the rhododendrons which now were past their best. A faint smile touched her lips as she remembered the big scene when she was nine. She had demanded the best view, bewailing the unfairness of life; the injustice of being punished for being born later than Teddy. Why should *he* have the best bedroom. Wasn't it *her* turn? A real tantrum with stamping feet and shrill accusations of injustice.

'I'm truly glad it was your room,' she told him now. 'Truly glad.'

She stared out, trying to give him a last glimpse of the view through her eyes. To the left was the old summer house. He had once promised that when he was married she could move into his room. Now he would never be married; would never be *anything.*

'Oh *Teddy!*'

Another funeral. Another wasted life. Unseeing, she stared across the lawn, trying to find a way to come to terms with the disasters. She thought of Clive Brayne's body huddled beneath the altar. She thought of Teddy sitting huddled on the station bench, screwing up the courage to kill himself. If only she could make some sense of it all she might see a way to live the rest of her life. She needed a way to deal with it. Something to *do.*

Standing at the window, she lost track of time. Eventually, slowly, painfully her thoughts began to organise themselves, falling piece by piece into some kind of pattern. At last one idea dominated the others. Whoever killed Clive was also to blame for Teddy's death. If Clive hadn't died, Teddy would never have had to bear so much guilt. He would have hated himself, of course, for his treatment of Annabel and the small-minded revenge he had taken on Clive. But the total burden of guilt would never have been heavy enough to die for.

If Albert Parker had robbed her of her brother she would somehow ensure that he was punished. The thought of retribution gave her a sense of purpose and she straightened imperceptibly. Now there was something she could do. Action she could take. She would dedicate herself to avenging Teddy's death.

'I'll get you, Albert Parker!' she told him. 'With or without God's help I'll get you.'

Max put his paws up on the window sill and rested his nose on his paws. He cocked his ears but for once Dulcie ignored him.

'Albert Parker!' she repeated.

The dog ran to the bed and scrabbled beneath it. He came back with a slipper in his mouth. Teddy's slipper. He dropped it at Dulcie's feet and sprang back barking encouragement. He barked again, looking comical and endearing.

She stared at him without seeing him, aware of a kind of peace growing within her. There was something she could still do for her brother. Picking up the slipper, she went out into the passage and threw it. Max raced after it, head down, tail outstretched. Over running, he crashed into the far wall.

She said, 'Max! You idiot!'

From below her father's footsteps sounded in the hallway. 'What's going on up there? Are you all right, Dulcie?'

No, she thought. I am not all right and I never will be all right again. 'I'm just coming,' she told him.

She looked at the dog who held the slipper in his mouth. 'Keep it!' said Dulcie. 'He would like you to have it.' She was halfway to the top of the stairs when she had a sudden thought. She went back to Teddy's room, took down great-grandfather's picture. For a moment she studied the picture Teddy had hated.

She took a deep breath and said, '*Bloody* Grandfather's *bloody* picture!'

Then she placed it on the floor and stamped on it. As the glass cracked she felt a small spurt of triumph.

She walked slowly downstairs, exhausted by her grief but buoyed up by her newfound purpose. First, her parents needed her.

Then she had things to do.

Chapter 14

Less than an hour later Agnes, red eyed and still trembling from the shock, came into the sitting room to tell them that a young man from the *Canterbury Standard* wanted to see Dulcie.

Wilfred bridled. 'The *Standard*? Good God! Send him away, Agnes, for heaven's sake! We don't want to be badgered at a time like this.' Grief had sharpened his voice.

'But he says he has —'

Dulcie said, 'Is it Gus?'

'I don't know his name. Ginger hair. He just said he must speak to you personally.'

Clarice made as though to rise but Dulcie forestalled her. 'I know him, Mother. I'll deal with it.' Anything to distract her, she thought. Anything to help her think about something else; to ease momentarily the sorrow which lay across her like a heavy shroud.

Downstairs, Gus waited on the front step.

He said, 'I'm sorry, Dulcie, about everything.' He glanced at her face and looked away, embarrassed by the tell-tale signs of grief. 'Your brother, I mean.'

'Thank you.' She held the door open. 'I'll be all right if you don't talk about him. Just at the moment I'm . . .' She let the sentence die and he nodded.

She led him through into the dining room and they sat down at one end of the table. He said, 'This arrived for you this morning,' and drew a slim package from the inside pocket of his jacket and handed it to her. 'It came by hand. A woman brought it in.'

'A woman? Who was it?'

'She refused to say. Cobsey got rather cross but she refused pointblank. A mousy-looking woman.'

Dulcie frowned. 'What on earth — ?'

'She said she couldn't come to your house because —' He shrugged. 'Because it was too dangerous.' He bent to ruffle the fur on Max's neck. 'She seemed very nervous.'

'Dangerous?' Dulcie turned the package over in her hands. Her name was written in ink in large red capitals. MISS D. MOORE. She stared at it for a long time, her mind dulled by misery. A package.

Gus said; 'Aren't you going to open it?'

Good question. Was she? 'I suppose so.' She slipped off the string and unwrapped it carefully.

Gus said; 'Too thin to be a bomb!'

'A *bomb?* Why should anyone want to blow me up?' As the contents slid out they saw a small assortment of letters and postcards. 'What on earth — ?' she repeated.

'All your old love letters!' Gus suggested.

Dulcie picked up one of the cards. It had been posted in Canterbury and the message was terse. 'Mission accomplished'. She frowned then handed it to Gus who also stared at it without comprehension. A second card had been torn in half and pasted back together. It was unfranked and had presumably been sent through the post inside an envelope. It said 'You owe me, you bastard!' There was no signature.

Gus, shown it, said 'Language!' and raised his eyes. 'Does this lot mean anything to you?'

She shook her head and picked up a note which had been scribbled in pencil on a sheet torn from a memo pad.

'Tell him St Alphege's at nine . . .'

She blinked. St Alphege's? The church where Clive was killed. Her stomach churned. A note telling someone to tell someone else to be at the church. Was all this connected to the murders?

'Can you describe the woman?' she asked, trying to reject what she knew in her heart. The woman had refused to give her name *because it was too dangerous.* Because it concerned *murder.* Excitement mingled with fear but she struggled to stay calm.

Gus frowned. 'Ordinary. Jacket and skirt. Glasses. Mousy hair. I didn't take much notice, to tell you the truth.'

'And what exactly did she say?' Dulcie smoothed out the carbon copy of a letter which had obviously been screwed up. It began 'Dear Mr Brayne . . .'

'Gus!' she cried. 'Listen to this! "Dear Mr *Brayne* —" '

'Brayne?' His eyes narrowed. 'Our Mr Brayne? As in *Clive* Brayne?'

She nodded. 'You will no doubt be aware that earlier this year I was foolish enough to lend your son the sum of £400 —'

'Four hundred quid? Jesus Christ!'

She said, 'Language!' but her mind was racing ahead.

Gus stared at her, serious at last. 'It's from that moneylender.'

'Reginald Foote. Harris Enterprises.'

'So this Mr Moneybags is probably part of it — of the murders!' His eves shone.

Suddenly Dulcie's mind whirled. She knew exactly what Gus was thinking. Quickly she gathered up all the letters. 'You don't get to see another one until you swear that this is *my* story.'

'What? Dulcie, for heaven's sake!' He looked horrified.

'You've only seen a part of this and it was sent to me — all of it. I shall probably take it straight to the police or I might — I don't know *what* I'll do with. But if you want to be in on it you have to promise. Otherwise you won't see another thing.'

He glared at her. Weighing his options, she thought.

She said, 'My uncle, Wilfred Moore, is in the

other room. I can take it all to him and cut you out entirely. I mean it, Gus! You go along with me or not at all. It's up to you.'

He made a last attempt. 'We didn't have to pass it on to you. It came to the *Standard.*'

'That doesn't make it yours. It had my name on it. See!' She snatched up the brown wrapper and waved the red letters in front of him. Max leaped for it, sensing a game. 'Get *down!*' she told him. He began to bark.

'That dog needs training!' said Gus.

'Who asked your opinion?'

Quick to realise his error he bent to pat Max. 'Sorry. But he is a bit boisterous. My sister took her dog to obedience classes and —' He looked at her, suddenly alerted by her silence. 'What, Dulcie? What is it?'

She said, 'Hang on . . .' and looked at him thoughtfully. 'Yes . . . Of course!'

'What?'

She stared at him, wide eyed. 'I think I know who delivered these letters!' She gave him a triumphant look. 'I shall telephone this person — in just two minutes. You have to promise or leave now.'

He said, 'I never thought you could be so selfish, Dulcie Moore. I mean, this could mean a lot to me. Do a lot for my career.'

'What about *my* career?'

'You got the sack, remember?'

'Well, I could *un*-get it! Cobsey will have to eat humble pie and take me back!'

The silence hung between them. At last he said, 'Oh all right. You've got it. I promise.'

'On your honour?'

He raised a hand, making a mock oath.

She beckoned him and, wonderingly, he followed her into the hallway. From the telephone book she extracted Reginald Foote's number and dialled. She put a finger to her lips as Gus opened his mouth to speak.

An unfamiliar woman's voice answered. 'Harris Enterprises. How can I help you?'

Dulcie said, 'It's Dulcie Moore. May I speak to Mrs Craddock, please.'

'I'm afraid she doesn't work here any more. She left yesterday. Rather suddenly, actually. Her husband was taken ill. I think that was it.'

'I see. *She's* not ill, is she?'

'I don't think so. I'm just filling in, actually, until Mr Foote finds somebody to take her place. He's just popped out but I could take a message.'

A horrible suspicion had entered Dulcie's mind. 'She is all right, isn't she? Mrs Craddock. Have you spoken to her at all? Today, I mean.'

'Well, just for a moment. She rang to say was I managing OK and not to mind if Mr Foote was a bit bad tempered. He had a lot on his mind.'

'Such as?'

'Such as? Oh I see. I don't know actually.'

'Has a Mr Stowe called in?'

'Stowe? Not that I've noticed.'

'You'd have noticed!' Dulcie assured her. 'Could you give me Mrs Craddock's home address, please?' She waited then scribbled it down. 'You've been very kind. Thank you — oh, by the way, I shouldn't consider making that a permanent position. Mr Foote's not an awfully nice man.'

'He's *what?* Not awfully nice? How d'you mean, not — Oh! Here *is* Mr Foote!' Dulcie heard a door open and the temporary secretary said, 'Actually, it's someone for Mrs Craddock. She — oh!'

Foote bellowed 'Who is this?' He had obviously snatched the receiver from the woman's hand.

Dulcie hesitated. The threat in his voice was obvious.

'Who the hell is this and what d'you want with Mrs Craddock?'

As Dulcie replaced the receiver her hand was trembling. This was a man who had been involved with Clive Brayne's death. And indirectly with Teddy's. She was aware of a cold chill which slowly enveloped her. Foote had written those letters. Probably to Parker. Foote might or might not know that copies of his incriminating letters had been sent to her. Or sent to someone . . .

She looked at Gus, suddenly terrified. 'Did I give the girl my name?'

He frowned. 'I don't know.' Seeing her look of exasperation he added, 'Don't ask me. I don't remember everything you said.'

Dulcie closed her eyes, clasping her hands in

front of her mouth. 'Please, *please* say I didn't!'

Later the same day. The murder room. Gough glanced at the clock. Six-thirty on the dot. He cleared his throat, glancing down at the papers he held and at once the buzz of conversation died. He checked his team — Allan, a tower of strength as always, Spencer back from the wilds of Scotland — a bit unreliable, woman trouble, for God's sake! Blake, promising young man, Stanley, OK, two newcomers on loan from Folkestone. Untested.

He introduced the latter and said, 'As you all know we're liaising on this one. Less than an hour ago Reginald Foote was arrested at his business premises, Harris Enterprises, on The Leas in Folkestone. On suspicion of conspiracy to murder one, Arnold Burnett also from Folkestone.'

Blake raised his hand. 'Arrested, sir, or taken for questioning?'

One of the Folkestone chaps said, 'Taken for —'

'*Thank* you!' Gough's tone was icy. 'He addressed his question to me, I believe.'

The man coloured. 'Sorry, sir!'

Gough addressed Blake. 'He was taken in for questioning —'

Allan said, 'Helping the police with their enquiries!' and they all laughed.

Gough allowed himself a smile. 'He's fingered Parker but he's guilty as hell himself. He'll be charged with conspiracy.'

There was a ragged cheer and a 'thumbs up' from Blake.

Gough went on. 'He's blaming it all on to Parker, of course, but he was the instigator. He used Parker first as heavy-duty debt collector and paid him well to ensure his silence. Brayne was an accident. Claims he knows nothing about Ellen Bly but admits Burnett was a business rival. Foote wanted to be mayor and Burnett was in his way. Foote says Parker offered to get rid of him. Chances are he paid Parker to do the honours.'

'Some mayor!' muttered Allan and there were murmurs of agreement. Gough nodded. 'Foote's falling over himself to cooperate. Wants to turn King's evidence and do a deal. He's also suggesting — and it *is* only a suggestion, mind — that our Miss Moore might be vulnerable. He's —'

Spencer's head snapped up. 'Dulcie Moore? How vulnerable?'

'It seems she and Parker have already had a run-in in Foote's office. She gave him a piece of her mind which wasn't too clever of her and Parker practically knocked her down. Hates her guts. Never has had much time for women and Miss Moore's definitely not in favour. Our job is to get Parker before he gets to Miss Moore or anybody else.'

Spencer said, 'Why should he hang around any longer? If he was paid to kill Burnett, he's presumably got all the money he's going to get.'

Gough nodded. 'Point taken, Spencer, but you went along that road a while back, assuming Parker was well gone. He was here all the time. Let's not make the same mistake twice.' He glanced round. 'Any more questions? Right. We'll let the press know that we've got Foote. Give Parker something to sweat about. If he's here and if he's worried enough he might make a mistake! I'd like to get the bastard. We've got Foote and we'll be hanging on to him. Let's try for a double whammy!' He glanced at Spencer. 'Let's have a recap on that correspondence. Not everyone knows the details.'

The detective sergeant stood up. He explained how the letters and postcards had come into the hands of Dulcie Moore and had been handed over to him.

Gough said pointedly, 'Spencer, you notice, and not me!'

Spencer looked uncomfortable as well he might. 'I — we know each other, sir.'

Gough's expression dared anyone to make further comment. He picked up the story from Spencer. 'Naturally we're keeping the news of the documents to ourselves for the moment. If Parker found out he might skip. If he's still around we stand a chance.' He turned to Spencer. 'What was all that about Miss Moore acting as bait?'

Spencer hesitated. 'Miss Moore feels very strongly that her brother's suicide could be traced indirectly to whoever killed Brayne and she's made up her mind it was Parker. She was in a bit of a state, actually. Shell shocked, I suppose you'd call it. She insisted she wanted to act as bait.'

'Bait?'

'To try and catch him.'

Allan's eyes narrowed. 'Doing what exactly?'

'A secret meeting between her and him. She wanted to get something in the *Standard* to the effect that she has information but hasn't yet handed it to the police. Hoping he'd try and get to her first and when he did we'd catch him. I told her it was out of the question. She wouldn't take "No" for an answer. We had a bit of a — well, a row, I suppose.'

Excited murmuring broke out as the men considered the implications of the offer.

Spencer said firmly, 'Can't use a member of the public like that. Much too dangerous.'

You would say that, thought Gough. But it was fair comment. 'Of course we can't,' he said.

Allan said, 'It was a very plucky offer, though. Not many women would be willing to risk their necks. She's got guts.'

Spencer sighed. 'She's making it a personal crusade, I'm afraid. Didn't take kindly to my refusal. I have to say, sir, she's rather unpredictable. I'm afraid she might do something reckless and we don't want her hurt. I wondered if we could post a uniformed chap outside the house for a day or two. To scare Parker off if he does try something.'

Gough frowned. 'Protection, you mean. You really think it's necessary?'

'I don't trust her, sir. She stormed out muttering under her breath. She might do it anyway. She's back on the staff of the *Standard* now — or so she says.'

Gough groaned inwardly. Women! 'Just for a day or two, then — to be there from time to time. Can't tie someone up all day.'

Stanley raised his hand. 'What about a decoy, sir? She arranges to meet Parker but when he shows up it's one of us dressed like her?'

Blake grinned. 'You volunteering?'

Cornered, Stanley said, 'Do I *look* like a woman?'

Blake said, 'I'm a bit worried about you, Stanners!' and they all laughed.

Gough watched Spencer who was still playing it very cool. Dulcie Moore was more than just a member of the public to him so he wouldn't find this easy. Maybe he was not such a bad chap. Nothing a bit of experience wouldn't put right. He said, 'So do we know who sent her the letters?'

Spencer went on, "The contact is thought to be a Mrs Craddock who was Foote's secretary until yesterday.' He looked enquiringly at one of the Folkestone men and sat down.

The man stood up nervously, a little intimidated by finding himself the focus of attention. Gough watched him fumbling with his notebook. Probably his first murder case, he thought. Rare chance to shine.

The man cleared his throat, flicking through the pages. 'I made my way to the house of the aforesaid Mrs Craddock —'

Gough said, 'Save the big words for when you're in court!'

'Yes sir!' He blushed.

Gough shook his head. A policeman who blushed! Wonderful!

'I — er — received no answer to my knock. A neighbour told me they had gone away suddenly to her sister's place in Devon. She said she didn't know where.'

Gough said, 'If she said she was going to Devon it's probably Yorkshire! She's hardly likely to leave a trail. Any reason given for the sudden departure?'

'Sister taken ill, sir.'

'Right.'

'But when I checked with the landlady *she* said they'd paid up the rent on the flat to the end of the month and would be sending for the furniture later. She didn't know where they'd gone.'

Gough said, 'Obviously the sender of the correspondence now fears her brave gesture might rebound. To avoid retaliation she is getting out. Wise woman . . .' He nodded at the other Folkestone man. 'Let's hear yours.'

The man stood up abruptly. 'Interviewed Foote's temporary secretary who said she was warned not to stay there by an unidentified woman whom we've now identified as — Dulcie

Moore!' There were a few grins. 'Harris Enterprises is now closed for business.' His sitting down was equally abrupt.

'Is that it?'

'Yes sir. I was then sent straight here and told to wait further orders.'

'Right . . . So-o,' Gough looked round. 'Where does all this get us? We now know that probably Foote wanted various people bumped off and used Parker, paying him handsomely for doing it. Wonderful! A charming couple. Our job is to nail both bastards and see that they hang! If we can get them a fair trial along the way so much the better. If not, let's hang 'em anyway!' He flexed his shoulders wearily and said, 'Someone put the kettle on, will you. I need a "cuppa".'

It wasn't a question and after a moment's hesitation Bridges rose to do the honours. Gough looked at Stanley. 'Remind us about the prison breakout.'

Stanley talked about the van driver who had given a statement about a nameless man from Folkestone who had arranged for Parker to be 'sprung'. Marshall, the conveniently sick warder, had now been traced to Malaga where the Spanish law protected him. A letter to his mother, intercepted by the police, hinted at sudden wealth. This was greeted by groans and muttered oaths.

Allan's 'We're on the wrong ruddy side!' earned an appreciative laugh.

Gough said, 'Any questions, gentlemen? Comments? Pearls of wisdom?'

Spencer said suddenly, 'Any update on the Hunt woman?'

'She's the nearest thing we've got for an address for Parker. I know we've been there a couple of times but are we getting a bit too casual there?'

Gough looked at Stanley.

He said defensively, 'We wanted a search warrant but it was denied. We kept a bit of an eye on the house but didn't see sight nor sound of him. Honestly, sir —' He appealed to Gough, 'He'd have to be cracked to use the Hunt woman's place.'

Gough said irritably, 'You kept "a bit of an eye"? Is that really good enough?'

Allan intervened. 'Stanley did the best he could. We still haven't got the resources we need for this case. Upstairs are so bloody tight with their money. We have to ask for every damn paperclip. You know how it is.' He broke off as Bridges walked round with a tray full of mugs of tea.

Spooning three spoonfuls of sugar into his mug, Gough blew on the tea to cool it. He looked at Spencer. 'You're right, though, Spencer. We mustn't let anything slide. Keep the pressure on the bastard. Get round to the Hunt woman when this meeting ends. Give Hunt the third degree if you have to. If she knows *anything* I want it.'

'Right, sir.'

There were a few more questions and new assignments were handed out. At seven thirty-five Gough had had enough. He had had very little sleep in the last forty-eight hours and he was half dead on his feet.

'Right lads! That's it for now!' He swallowed the last of his tea as one by one the men in his team drank up and left the room. Let them all get on with it. He needed his bed.

As soon as Dulcie woke the next morning, the blackness settled around her like a fog. Monday 23 June. Teddy's funeral. Her brother's *funeral.* Little had she guessed when she attended Clive's funeral that Teddy would be next. Max pushed his way into the bedroom and she patted him absentmindedly. Other thoughts flooded into her mind and with these came a rush of energy. It was the day of the funeral but there was also the *Standard* to look forward to. It would be here soon. Adrenaline began to pump through her. She rushed from the bed to peer from the window into the street. The paper boy was further along the road so their copy had already arrived. Presumably it was the sound of the paper through the letter box that had roused her. Rushing downstairs she snatched it from the mat and stared at the front page.

'Done it!' she muttered. So much for Jack Spencer's caution! She had beaten him. Cobsey had come up trumps. She smiled faintly. The headline was 'NEW DISCLOSURES'. Clever, Cobsey! she thought. She read the article aloud.

> Dramatic new developments have taken place in the hunt for the killer of Clive Brayne, found dead recently in St Alphege's Church. Secret documents of an incriminating nature have been sent to a member of the *Canterbury Standard*'s staff. After examining these, she intends to hand the collection of letters and notes to the police. The sender of the documents is not known at this stage. The information contained in the letters seems to link the escaped convict Albert Parker with the murder. The death of Arnold Burnett in Folkestone is also featured in the information. Miss Moore, a friend of Clive Brayne, said yesterday, 'I hope they catch him. He is a wicked man — a danger to innocent people . . .'

No mention of Teddy. Dulcie had insisted on that. The clue — 'she' — was to alert Parker to her identity. The quote was intended to make him angry and vindictive. The laughter died from her face as she reread the brief article. It was no joking matter. She knew that well enough. Jack would be livid. He had been so determined to keep her out of harm's way. Her parents, too, would have a fit when they saw the article and Uncle Wilfred would fall on Cobsey from a great height. But nothing mattered, she reminded herself. You had to crack eggs to make an omelette. What mattered was that Parker would read it and, hopefully, would come after her. Now the police would be forced to go along with her plan. She drew a long satisfied breath.

Poor Jack. She felt a moment's compassion. When he saw the paper he would be furious. She had made a fool of him and he would probably never forgive her but who cared. He was nothing to her now. The police would have to act. Undercover — plain clothed — whatever they called it. They would have to conceal a policeman in her house and maybe a non-uniformed officer outside. The doors would all be unlocked, the windows enticingly open. If Parker approached he would be caught. If by some miracle, he managed to elude the watchers and break in, he would still be caught. Nothing could go wrong.

She let Max out for a few moments then made a dish of bread and milk for his breakfast. Upstairs, while washing and dressing, she tried to concentrate on Parker, refusing to let thoughts of Teddy intrude. This was no time for weakness. She had taken matters into her own hands and must be strong enough to see them through. As she brushed her hair she wondered fleetingly how she would feel if she ever found herself face to face with Parker. Could she spit in his face? There was little else she could do to show her disgust. She remembered how she had last seen him, watching her from Foote's window as she left the office. He had huge strength, a nasty temper and brutish ways. She shuddered at the recollection of his voice. 'Get out, girlie. Hop it!'

Well, she had hopped it on that occasion but not now. Now she had a score to settle with him.

'I'll get you, Parker!' she muttered.

Glancing at the clock she saw that it was nearly eight-thirty. She had promised to go home and help her parents prepare for the meal that would follow the funeral. Then the family would travel to the church together. She swallowed hard, biting her lip to keep back the tears. But at least she had done what she could.

'Darling Teddy, *help me!*' she whispered shakily. Without her actions, Parker might well slip away to a foreign country and enjoy the proceeds of his crimes. She was going to stop him. Fuelled by her anger and grief, she felt strong enough to go through with it.

Downstairs again she called Max. There was no sign of him.

'Damn!' she muttered. If she went in search of him now she would be late arriving at Grange Park. On the other hand, she could not leave him to wander the town all day. There was no knowing what he might get up to. She would fetch a jacket and have a quick hunt round in the immediate vicinity. She ran upstairs, pulled on her jacket and crossed to the window. She peered hopefully up and down the street — and then froze, sick with shock and disbelief.

'Oh *no!*' she cried. 'No! The hateful, rotten *buggers!*' The unfamiliar obscenity hung in the air as she stared down into the street. On the far side of the road was a uniformed policeman. He was leaning over the railings, looking down on to the cattle market, large and entirely unmissable. She felt a huge rush of dismay followed by one of utter helplessness.

She said, 'Jack *bloody* Spencer! You've done this!'

He must have seen the paper before she did. Had he guessed that she might try something? If so he was brighter than she thought. And this was his answer. The disappointment crushed her. With a uniformed policeman virtually on her doorstep, there was no way Parker was going to walk into her trap.

Constable Bridges was already fed up and it was only ten past nine. Monday mornings were always a bore. The others had all gone off to their various assignments leaving him alone. Wonderful! — as Gough would say. Waiting for the kettle to boil, he leaned on the desk and re-read the article headlined 'NEW DISCLOSURES.' He grinned. Poor old Spencer. His face when he saw the headlines! He'd gone red and then white. Almost *green.* Blooming technicolour! What a treat.

'Naughty, *naughty,* Miss Moore!'

He wouldn't like to be in her shoes when Spencer caught up with her. Not that she'd got away with it but she might have done. Spencer had been clever there. Pulled the rug from under her and no mistake.

Still, poor kid. Her brother was being buried

later today and by all accounts the two of them had been close. It was natural she'd want to get even with Parker but he was a mean devil and she was better off out of it.

'Leave it to the professionals, dear!' he muttered. 'We'll get him.'

That is, they *might* get him. Parker was a crafty whotsit. On the run for weeks now. God knows how he did it, with every copper on the beat looking for him and his mugshot on every other lamp-post.

He glanced up as a woman entered.

'Can I help you?' His smile was perfunctory. Lost her cat, probably, or left her umbrella on a bus. Life was a thrill a minute in the police force. He should have joined the Boy Scouts.

She hesitated then approached the desk. 'I want to speak to someone. Someone in charge.'

There was something vaguely familiar about her. 'I'm in charge,' he told her loftily.

'It's about —' She lowered her voice nervously. '— about Albert Parker.'

Bridges stifled a yawn. 'Seen him, have you?' They'd had all the nutters in here since the reward was mentioned. All claiming they'd seen him.

'Not exactly.'

She glanced over her shoulder as though expecting him to walk in the door behind her. Fat chance! He gave an elaborate smile and drew a pad towards him. Taking a pencil from behind his ear he asked, 'Name and address?'

She gave it and suddenly he was interested. Sylvie Hunt! Parker's fancy woman. His pencil hovered. This might be interesting.

She leaned on the counter of the desk and took a deep breath. 'The grocery boy came to my door this morning. The thing was I hadn't ordered anything for this morning . . .'

His heart slowed. The grocery boy. He wrote down 'G. boy' and waited.

'He gave me this note and I don't know what to do. I don't want to go with him, you see, not after what he's done. But I know him — he won't take no for an answer.'

Bridges stared at her. She didn't want to go with the grocery boy because of what he'd done to her. What on earth was she talking about?

'You know him?' he asked. It was her turn to look blank. He said, 'What's he done exactly, this grocery boy?'

She rolled her eyes in exasperation. 'Not the boy. *Bert.* Here. Read it for yourself.'

The note was written on the back of a paper bag. '. . . S — Be packed and ready. S A. Remember? They'll be looking for one. B . . .'

'B?'

'I call him Bert. Albert. I'm "S".'

'Ah!' His interest quickened once more. A note from Parker had to be important. But what exactly did it mean? 'One what?' he asked at last.

'One person. One person travelling. He means if there's two of us they won't be suspicious.' Her fingers drummed anxiously on the desk top.

'Isn't there anyone else I could talk to?'

' 'Fraid not, madam.' Blinking cheek! What was wrong with *him?* 'And what is SA? Salvation Army?'

She gave him a sharp look. 'This isn't funny. I'm scared.'

'Sorry, I'm sure, but what does the note mean?'

'SA is South America. It was always a bit of a joke between us. When he got enough cash together we were going to disappear. Make a fresh start in South America. That kind of thing.'

'And now he's got the money?'

'Oodles of it.'

He wrote 'oodles' and added an exclamation mark.

She went on earnestly. 'Anyway, it's not on now — after what it says in the papers about him. There's no way I want to be carted off by the likes of him. Not anywhere. I mean, do I look like a gangster's moll to you?'

Bridges bit back a 'Yes' although she had nice eyes. A sort of golden brown like a lion's eyes. And pretty hair. Must have been a bit of a looker once upon a time. Still was, if you liked older women.

She leaned closer, lowering her voice. 'If he thinks he's dragging me round the world and him a blasted *murderer!* I mean, Jesus Christ! What does he take me for? Specially since he's only doing it to get past you lot. He'll dump me the minute we get there and do a bunk with the money. Where will that leave me? I don't speak whatever they speak there. I'll be in a right mess.'

'Spanish,' said Bridges. He'd spotted that in *National Geographic* last time he was at the dentist. He nodded sagely. Let her see who she was dealing with. 'They speak Spanish in South America.'

'Well, I don't!'

He wrote down 'S America — Spanish' and said, 'So don't go with him. Say no.'

'Say no?' She tossed her head scornfully. 'You don't know Bert. He's a mean sod. I want protection, like the other one. Miss Moore. I went round there but she was out. She's got a bobby outside her door and I want one outside mine.'

'You went to see Miss Moore?' he asked. 'D'you two know each other?'

'Know each other? Course we don't. Well, not exactly *know* each other. She wouldn't remember me. I was just going to warn her, that's all. I reckon I owe her that much. Tell her Bert's got it in for her. He called her a meddling little cow and maybe she is but that doesn't mean he has to do her in.'

'Do her in?' Alarm bells rang. 'What, kill her?'

She shrugged. 'Maybe not *kill*. How do I know. But he'll want to pay her back. I know the way his mind works — and he's been spying on her. He told me. Saw her out walking the dog one night and followed her home. She's got this dog —'

'You mean Max. I know him.' He smiled. 'We

had him in here one day. Nice little thing really. Took quite a shine to me. Dogs are like that. They like men. He'd got out somehow and run away. Bit someone, if I remember rightly.' He drew a deep breath and glanced at his notes. 'Look, are you sure about all this? About him going after her? If I was in his shoes I'd be legging it by now. Over the hills and far away. Bit of a risk, isn't it?'

'Try telling him that. He's as stubborn as a mule. Bert is. But he knows Canterbury like the back of his hand. He was born here, remember?'

'So was I.' Not that it was any great shakes, he reflected. Dead in winter and crowded with sightseers in summer. Famous cathedral but not much else.

'Well, you'll know Sparks barn then. He's been hiding out there. On and off. She glanced nervously over her shoulder, adding 'Oh Lord! I never said that. If you tell Bert I'll deny it.' She watched him writing with growing impatience.

'Didn't stay with you then?' He tried to imagine the pair of them having a cosy cup of cocoa together. Then he transferred to their bedroom and enjoyed that little fantasy for a moment. What on earth did she see in a bloke like Parker?

She hesitated. 'Ask no questions, hear no lies. Kipped down with a couple of mates, too. Money talks. You'd be surprised how many mates you find when you've got a wallet full of notes!' She sighed. 'He used to be fun, once upon a time. Always good for a laugh. Now he's got a chip on his shoulder like a blooming log!' She gave a little shrug. 'Prison did that.'

Bridges snorted. 'My heart bleeds for him!'

She regarded him earnestly. 'He never meant to kill that bloke. The first one, I mean. It was just a scrap outside a pub. Went a bit wrong, that's all. They wouldn't listen to him. Got it all wrong.'

'A bit wrong?' Bridges snorted. 'Come off it! He went home, got a piece of cord, went round to the bloke's house and strangled him! *Went a bit wrong?* You must be joking, lady!'

'That's not how I heard it.' She looked shocked. 'He said the bloke wrestled him and was going to kill him. Had to strangle him. Self defence. They wouldn't believe him. Your lot framed him, he said.'

'Framed him? Talk about gullible!' That told her straight. He watched her expression change. He wondered what she was like in bed and how many times Parker had had his way with her. A gangster's moll! Yes, he could see her in the part. He tried to remember what she'd come in for. 'So why are you so keen to help Miss Moore? What's she to you?'

She shrugged. 'She stuck up for me once. They'd have sacked me for sure but she made out it was her own fault.'

Now what was she on about? 'They? Who's they?'

'The County Hotel. I work there. Waitress. I spilt this soup over her new blouse. I'd been there a few weeks and I knew her aunt by sight.

Always gives me sixpence. Anyway the young one said she'd stuck her elbow out and caught the edge of the soup dish. Said it would wash out and gave me a wink. You know.'

Bridges didn't know. She'd lost him but it didn't matter. Finally he wrote, 'wants bobby' and pursed his lips regretfully. 'About the protection. We don't really have anyone to spare. I'll see what I can do for you. See if I can work a miracle.' He pushed the pad towards her and offered the pencil. 'If you'd just like to check through these notes.'

She read it aloud. ' "G. boy. oodles! S America — Spanish. Sparks barn. Wants bobby." Is this it?'

Bridges said, 'I shall fill the details in later — unless, of course, you want to write it all out yourself?'

'Hoity-toity!' She signed it and pushed the pad back to him. 'And you won't tell Bert it was me told you?'

'We always protect our sources, madam.' . . . Well, usually! . . . 'My advice is stay indoors and keep the doors and windows locked.'

Reluctantly she turned to go, looking totally unconvinced. Bridges watched her. Dregs of the earth, he reflected. Hate the boys in blue until they're in trouble then it's 'I want protection!'

'I should start learning Spanish!' he told her retreating back and grinned.

Chapter 15

By the time Dulcie returned to the house she was more worried than cross. Max had disappeared into thin air and the large policeman was still stationed on the other side of the road. Not that he would see much, she reflected irritably. He was leaning on the railings, staring down on to the deserted cattle market. As she approached the house he turned hastily, touched his helmet respectfully and said, 'Morning, miss. Constable Crampton. I'm to keep an eye on things here.'

She gave him a slight nod, not trusting herself to speak. She was halfway up the steps when a delivery boy on a bicycle drew up alongside. She recognised the red-headed lad from Burgess's in Mercery Lane.

'Miss Moore?' he asked, taking a folded paper from his pocket.

'Yes — but I haven't ordered anything —'

He glanced nervously towards the policeman. 'A man said to give you this.' He pressed the paper into her hand.

'Which man?'

But he was already riding away, standing on

the pedals for extra speed. The note was short and to the point.

'YOUR DOG'S DEAD. IF YOU WANT THE BODY IT'S IN SPARKS BARN'

She longed for disbelief but the message was precise. Her hand shook and her mouth went dry. 'Your dog's dead!' Parker had killed Max!

'Oh no! *No!*' she whispered.

Dazed by the suddenness of the tragedy, she stared blindly at the note. Parker had brought about her brother's death and now he had killed an innocent dog. Unwanted, the thought entered her head that this was his revenge for the article in the *Standard*. This was her punishment. Guilt swamped her. *She* was responsible for this final act of barbarism. She gave a little moan and covered her face with her hands. First Teddy and now Max. In her mind's eye she saw the dog, lifeless and silent. No more naughty tricks, no more endearing ways, no more doggy devotion. It was utterly unbearable.

'You all right, miss?'

The policeman had crossed the road to stand beside her. She nodded then shook her head. Without a word she handed him the note.

As he read it his mouth tightened with disapproval. 'Now that is nasty,' he said. 'That is *disgusting!* Who'd do a thing like that?'

'It's from him. Parker. I know it is.' Her lips trembled. 'He's killed Max to punish me for — for . . .' Choked, she let the sentence falter to a stop.

He shook his head, frowning. 'Shows you the sort of man he is.'

Dulcie struggled to control herself. 'I must go and get him,' she said. 'Max, I mean. There's plenty of time before the funeral.'

'Funeral? Ah yes! Your brother.'

She couldn't bear the look of pity on his round face. 'I'll go now.' She still hesitated.

'Should I tell the Chief?' he asked. 'I'm supposed to be keeping an eye on you. He'll have my guts for garters if —'

'No need to bother him.' On an impulse she added, 'But you can tell Detective Sergeant Spencer if you see him. If not I'll tell him myself. I expect he'll come to the funeral.'

Still she stood irresolute, drained of energy, reluctant to take the first step towards the sight of her dead pet. She remembered Parker's large hands and imagined them round the dog's neck. And Max would be so trusting. Or perhaps Parker had hit him over the head with something. She hoped it had been quick. If only she hadn't let him out. If only she had kept an eye on him. Or *trained* him better. Everyone had said he was unmanageable but she hadn't tried hard enough with him. It was all her fault. She took a deep breath and then another. Don't cry, she told herself. It won't bring him back. You failed him and you must live with that. She would ask Harriet if they could bury him in the garden.

'Oh God, Parker!' she whispered. 'How could you? My poor, darling dog!'

Seconds passed but she remained immobilised by a dark and deep misery. Finally she became aware that the policeman was watching her uneasily. If she didn't go soon he might try to talk her out of it. She screwed up the note and pushed it into her pocket. Then she collected her bicycle.

The constable said, 'You sure you're OK, miss?'

Dulcie forced a smile to her frozen lips. 'Fine, thank you.'

Back in the murder room Jack found Bridges tapping away at a typewriter.

'Anything new?' Jack asked. The question was perfunctory.

'The Hunt woman came in, sir.' Bridges grinned. 'Wants some protection. Says Parker wants to take her to South America. Learn Spanish, I told her. That's what they talk there. She didn't know. Says he's got his hands on some cash and is going to split.'

'She's seen him? *Recently?*'

'Apparently. Well, not exactly *seen* him but got a note from him. Get your stuff packed. That sort of thing.'

'Damn! I hoped the bastard had moved on. Can't think why he's hanging around Canterbury.' Jack picked up Bridges' notebook. 'Oodles?'

'Of money, sir.'

'Sparks barn?'

'Somewhere he's been hiding out. The derelict barn, sir. They say it's been haunted since someone was killed there years ago. We used to dare each other to go in. There was a loft with all this rotting hay. Rickety old ladder going up. Used to scare me half to death but I never let on!' He grinned at the memory. 'Then some kids set up a swing and cracked one of the beams. Mind you they were rotten any way. The parents reckoned it was dangerous. After that we weren't allowed to go there. Before the beam broke we went there once for Hallowe'en —' Bridges smiled at the memory. 'It was pitch black that night. No moon at all. My brother Tim had a bit of a turn. He was always highly strung. A sort of fit, it was.' He frowned. 'A *hysterical* fit. That's what the doctor called it. Course my Dad blamed me for taking him. I got a right walloping.'

Jack said, 'Shut up, Bridges!' His uneasiness was crystallising into a certainty. Something was wrong but *what?*

'Sorry, sir.' Obviously offended, Bridges bent over the typewriter.

Jack studied Bridges' notes. 'What's this G. boy?'

'Grocer's boy. A boy delivered the note to her. The note from Parker.'

Jack hesitated. Was this important? He wanted an excuse to go round to see Dulcie. 'Explain the rest of these hieroglyphics.' He listened carefully. 'So Miss Hunt thinks he may be after Miss Moore.'

'Yes sir.'

'Well, we've got her under observation but I'll get round there just in case. She ought to be on her guard — though how Parker's going to get to her at a funeral is anybody's guess.'

A brief conversation with PC Crampton did nothing to reassure him.

'Killed her dog? Christ Almighty!' Jack stared at him, appalled. 'She'll break her heart!'

'She *was* upset, sir. Like chalk. Poor girl.'

'She adored that animal. Idolised the silly thing.' Jack could imagine Dulcie's grief, so soon after losing her brother. 'And she's gone to fetch it, you say?'

'Yes sir. Said there was plenty of time before the funeral.'

Jack leaned over the railings and stared down at a stack of wooden fencing that was used to make pens for the cattle and sheep. 'I wonder if that's it,' he reflected. 'If that's what he was hanging on for. The chance to even the score with her. To kill her dog. Maybe he *has* decided to get out while he still can. Perhaps that was his parting shot.'

'Pretty mean thing to do — taking it out on the dog. I mean, sir, it's not the dog's fault.'

Jack shrugged. 'But that's the type he is. An unscrupulous, cold-hearted —' He broke off with a start. 'Unless — God Almighty!'

'What, sir?'

Agitated, Jack straightened up. 'Unless we've underestimated him and he's turning the tables.

Playing Miss Moore at her own game.' He ran his fingers through his hair. Was his imagination working overtime, he wondered. Doubts crowded in. For a moment he was almost convinced that he was wrong. Parker had done his worst and had slipped through the net. He was on his way to South America! Or was he? Was that what they were *supposed* to think? Inspiration struck suddenly. 'Bait!' he cried. His intuition hadn't failed him. 'That's *it!* The dog's body is bait and now *he* intends to catch *her!*'

They stared at each other — Jack with growing alarm, the constable with incredulity.

'Bait, sir? You mean he knows she'd go looking for it. Because of this morning's paper? And I let her go!' He was a picture of dismay.

'You couldn't have known.' Jack's mind raced. 'How long ago did she set off?'

'About ten minutes, sir. Maybe fifteen. On her bike.'

Jack swore. 'I'm going after her. I'll grab a taxi from Scam's.' He saw his constable's eyebrows lift. 'You come with me. We'll telephone the station from Scam's and ask for reinforcements — also an ambulance and —'

'But are you *sure,* sir. I mean the Chief —'

Jack's eyes flashed dangerously. 'No I'm not sure but I'm taking no chances.' Panic-stricken, he began to run, his mind in a turmoil. If he was right, Dulcie, totally unprepared, would come face to face with Parker. Sickened, he visualised himself discovering Dulcie's body and fought to keep the terrible image at bay. He must get there before she did if it was humanly possible.

Forcing a way through the crowded pavements he muttered, 'Sorry, madam! Excuse me! *Excuse* me, sir!' as his elbows dug into resentful flesh. He glanced back at the constable lumbering behind him, redfaced with the effort. 'Come *on*, damn you! We haven't got all day!'

He began to pray. Scam's, in Oaten Hill, was southeast of the town. The Military Road was northeast. He was going to need a miracle.

Parker sat in the hay loft, binoculars to his eyes, watching through a hole in the rotting wall of the wooden barn. A hole he had punched through some time ago; a hole which gave him a commanding view of the Military Road and anyone who travelled along it. Westward he could see past the military cemetery and St Gregory's vicarage. In the other direction he could see the Infantry Barracks of the East Kent Regiment and beyond them the Artillery Barracks. He was waiting for a single cyclist — a young female cyclist. If the boy had delivered the message, she would come. He was sure of it. And then he would put his hands around that slim little throat and squeeze until her face turned blue. But first he'd knock her about a bit. Wipe that supercilious smile off her face. At the thought of her he felt a spurt of rage. Towards her and that stupid old bat in Reggie's office. Oh yes! He knew who'd sent those letters but she had been too smart. She'd upped and left. Lucky for her. It was probably her who'd shopped Foote who was no doubt wetting his pants and spilling everything he knew.

At the thought of Foote his expression hardened. The fool would do anything to save his own skin. Blame someone else — just like he had done at school. But that was what money could do for you. It bought favours and all those years ago it had bought Albert Parker. Twenty pounds had seemed like a fortune. It *was* a fortune to the young Parker. It had seemed a good idea at the time. He was going to be expelled anyway, along with Foote so why not be paid handsomely for going. It had done him a favour really, because it had shown him a way to get rich. Do other people's dirty work and take their money for doing it. But now it was *his* turn to have the money and Foote's turn to rot in jail! He grinned. As soon as the girl was dead he would be on his way, with Sylvie.

The dog, tied to the wall behind him, whined and tugged on the string.

'What's up?' he said without taking his eyes off the road. The dog barked.

He thought about Sylvie. He needed her. Also he didn't want her blabbing to the police. She'd come. She'd be a fool to say 'No' to a chance of the good life in Mexico. Not that he was going to keep her once they'd left England. He'd get rid of her at the first opportunity. She wasn't the brightest and it would be easy enough to ditch her when they got to Mexico. He'd simply pop into a men's lavatory and climb out of the back window. She'd just sit there watching the door marked GENTS. Or was it HOMBRES? He grinned. Poor old Sylve. If she'd been ten years younger, perhaps . . . And he'd soon pick up a bit of Spanish. He knew some already. Gringo . . . amigo . . .

He glanced round. The money was in a brown leather suitcase. Not a new one that might look suspicious. He'd bought it in a junk shop and polished it up a bit. Mustn't look too affluent. The sight of it reassured him. This time he had got it right. This time there was no one to grass on him. He would never see the inside of a prison cell again. From now on it would be señoritas, rum, sunshine and the life of a gentleman.

The dog whined again.

'What's up then, eh?' It was a nice little thing, really. He liked dogs. Had always wanted one. The dog seemed to like him. 'Poor old lad.' Leaning backwards, he just managed to reach it and patted its nose. Impulsively he put down the binoculars and moved back to untie the string. Once free the dog leaped joyfully towards him, frantically trying to lick his face. He moved back to his position by the hole in the wall and the dog stayed close, tail wagging, giving little yelps of excitement. He patted the straw beside him. 'Sit, boy!' At once the dog obeyed, looking adoringly into his face. 'Life's tough, isn't it. You'll be an orphan soon, like me. No mistress! See?'

He wouldn't kill it. Couldn't. He'd like to take it with him but it would be a dead giveaway. He'd get one, though, as soon as he got himself settled. Dogs were loyal, they adored their masters and they didn't get huffy or smart. Not like women. Not like that stuck-up little piece who called herself a journalist. Not like that cow he'd married all those years ago. Or crafty old Craddock. It was a bit of luck, finding the dog. He'd recognised it straight away and it seemed as though someone up there loved him after all. He'd known at once how to use it to get at the girl. Dulcie bloody Moore. Never trust a woman.

He picked up the binoculars again and studied the road. For the first time it crossed his mind that she might not come. Had the boy delivered the note?

'Come *on,* girlie!' he muttered. 'I want to be away from here.'

Free time always used to be his enemy. He hated having time on his hands but he'd got the money to think about now and how to spend it.

'Are you coming, Miss Moore?'

He thought about Arnold Burnett and smiled slowly. Why did people make such a fuss about killing? It was always so *easy.* Like taking sweets from a baby. It was the shock that did it every time. As soon as they realised they were being done they gave up the ghost. Hardly ever fought back. Like the old busybody from the church.

Hardly even wriggled. Some people were *asking* for it.

And Dulcie Moore was one of them.

Dulcie caught sight of the familiar barn and her heart pounded painfully. For a moment she wobbled but then straightened the bike. She mustn't stop pedalling, she told herself. She had to face whatever dreadful sight awaited her. Even in death, she still adored him. She would carry him home in the bicycle basket, brush him gently then she'd wrap him in a clean towel. While she was at the church he would lie in his own basket in the kitchen. As though he were sleeping, she thought, and again the tears came unbidden to her eyes. This evening, after the funeral, she would visit Harriet in the hospital and ask for permission to bury him in the garden.

Dismounting at the gate to the field, she stared at the old barn. The wooden shingles of the roof had curled with age and the heat of many summers. The door hung open, crooked as always on its one remaining hinge. The planking of the walls had blackened over the years and it seemed smaller than she remembered. Slowly she made her way across the grass, steeling herself for the ordeal ahead. Being told that Max was dead was one thing, seeing him was another. She reached the door of the barn and stepped inside, resisting the urge to call him by name. The barn smelled the way she remembered it. Decaying hay, damp soil and a hint of corn dust. For a moment she closed her eyes, trying to will herself back to her childhood when murder and mayhem were not part of her everyday life. For the first time she realised just how sheltered her childhood had been. A united family, caring parents, the best that life could offer. Maybe there is a price for everything, she thought dully, and this is the price *I* have to pay.

Silence hung in the shadows. As her eyes became accustomed to the gloom she moved forward, searching for a glimpse of the dog. She swallowed hard, willing herself to go further into the dank recesses of the building. A few thin slivers of light pierced the darkness where the sun entered through cracks in the wall and in these beams dust swirled. It took less than a minute to discover that the lower part of the barn contained only clutter — old sacks, and a collection of rusting machinery and the ancient, rusting tractor.

'Oh Max. My lovely dog. Where are you?' she whispered as she moved towards the loft ladder. It was stronger than it looked and bore her weight without giving way. She was halfway up when a sound from the hayloft startled her. A slight scuffle. Probably a bird. She climbed on until she could see the entire loft which was still piled with rotting hay. Climbing out, she was immediately transported back many years to her notorious leap from the glassless window. A faint smile touched her lips. How surprised

Teddy had been! And how proud *she* had been when he reluctantly applauded her daring.

'Now where —' She stepped carefully, testing the beams as she went.

Suddenly Dulcie heard what sounded like a muffled whine. Puzzled, she went to investigate — and almost stumbled over a man who was crouching behind the hay. She gave a choked cry and stumbled back.

It was Parker and he was holding Max! Not a lifeless Max but one that wriggled, trying to dislodge a handkerchief that had been tied round his muzzle. Adrenaline rushed through her as shocked relief mingled with a terrible fear. Her first thought was that was her dog was still alive. The second was that Parker meant to kill them both.

'So, girlie, you came!'

'Don't hurt him!' she cried. 'Please don't. He's only a dog. He's never done you any harm.'

Max finally wriggled free of the offending handkerchief and gave a tentative bark of welcome. He did not, however, struggle towards her but leaned back affectionately against Parker's chest. Dulcie sensed betrayal. A *man's* dog! Harriet had been right.

She said, 'Max! Come on!' and patted her thigh.

Parker's meaty hand went at once to the dog's collar, restraining him. He said, 'You and that cow Craddock! Interfering bitches, the pair of you.'

'There are worse things to be!'

'Such as?'

She longed to say 'murderers' but the word sent a shiver through her and she said weakly, 'You know what I mean.' Was there any way, she wondered, that she could get down the ladder with Max under one arm? Hardly, she conceded. 'Why did you say he was dead?' she demanded, playing for time. They were alone here. He could easily wring the dog's neck and then turn his attention to her. Presumably he wanted her to see Max die. A great surge of loathing swept her and she lowered her eyes hastily.

'Why? To get you here, of course.'

'I might not have come.'

'I like a gamble.'

Frantically she considered her chances of escape. There was a gap of about six feet between her and Parker but she had a slight advantage. If she made a run for it, he would have to rise from a crouch position while she had merely to run. She glanced towards the window, her heart thudding. She might have to repeat her earlier leap — *without* the benefit of the piled hay to break her fall. But she would almost certainly break her legs so the escape would be of short duration.

He said, 'Nice little thing, isn't he? He's taken a fancy to me.' He ruffled the fur behind the dog's ear. Max reached up and playfully closed his teeth round the strap of a pair of binoculars which hung round Parker's neck. So he'd been watching for her . . . Parker tapped the dog's nose and Max released the strap instantly.

Dulcie shuddered. Those hands had beaten Clive and smothered Ellen Bly. They had almost certainly held poor Arnold Burnett under the water. And, because of this man, Teddy was gone. Parker was ruthless, vicious and without a shred of conscience. He was a hired killer — and she was alone with him. Terrified, she was determined not to show it.

She said, 'My brother's dead because of you!'

He threw out his hands in a *Don't blame me* gesture. 'Never touched him!' he insisted.

'You didn't need to!'

Parker released the dog who, ignoring Dulcie, wandered away, sniffing excitedly among the dank straw.

Parker said conversationally, 'He can smell rats.'

Dulcie called, 'Max! Here, boy!' Nothing happened.

Parker laughed. 'Never yet knew a woman who could train a dog.'

Dulcie was trying desperately to think of a way out of this dangerous situation but her mind, frozen with fear, refused to function properly. 'He does know some commands,' she told him. 'He's only young. Some dogs mature later than others.' And now he wouldn't get that time. Dulcie felt defeated. Fatalistic. Parker was going to kill her but she wouldn't beg for her life. There was no way she would give him that satisfaction. She forced herself to look Parker in the eye. 'I suppose you're going to kill me.' The words sounded alien.

'That's right. You had it coming.'

'Can't you let Max go?' Maybe he would find his way home. Might even lead the police to her body. *Please God, help me!* she prayed. There must be something she could do. Had the constable told anybody where she was going? Not that it would make much difference. They wouldn't expect her to need help.

Parker said, 'Come here!' He was speaking to her, not Max.

She shook her head. At least when she died she would be with Teddy. The thought gave her a small glow of comfort.

His thin smile was full of menace. Perhaps she could push Max down through the trapdoor, she thought — but he'd probably whine to be allowed back!

'Scared of me?' Parker asked. 'You should be. Too bloody clever for your own good. That's your trouble. And too much lip. Are you coming over here or do I have to come and get you?' He raised himself on one knee.

Dulcie couldn't have answered even if she wanted to. Fear had closed her throat and sapped the strength from her legs.

He said, 'I've been thinking about this moment. Looking forward to it.' He pulled the binoculars from round his neck and with two tugs had freed the narrow leather strap. He held this out straight, testing it for strength. 'I'm going to use this. Once round that pretty little neck and then — Snap!'

Max, sensing a game, began to jump up and down between them, barking excitedly.

'Don't!' she cried.

Parker leaned forward and grabbed the dog by the scruff of his neck and lifted him into the air. His barking changed to a frightened howl.

'No!' screamed Dulcie and hurled herself at Parker, beating ineffectually at his body with her clenched fists. 'Let him go! You're hurting him!'

Parker dropped the dog and swung his fist at Dulcie. She saw it coming but didn't duck in time and it caught her with tremendous force across the right side of her face. She felt a crack and with a cry of pain, staggered and fell. Before she could recover he had thrown himself heavily on top of her, pinning her to the ground with his weight. As he leaned over her she smelled whisky. His expression was full of contempt.

'You stupid bitch! You don't imagine you're a match for me, do you?'

She struggled, tasting blood in her mouth. He had loosened a tooth but for the moment she felt no pain. Perhaps the shock had numbed her jaw. She knew that this was the beginning of the end. An added bitterness involved the suspicion that she had brought the disaster on herself.

He sat astride her, his weight crushing her legs, and grinned down, relishing the power he had over her. At any moment he would put the strap around her neck. Her chance to avenge Teddy would be lost.

She said 'Wait!' How could she distract him? How could she delay her death?

Max sprang forward, intrigued by the situation, and she took a long look at him. His tail wagged, his head was cocked, his small white ears were erect. As she looked at him suddenly, apparently from nowhere, an idea came to her. A very slim chance. Frantically she sought to refine it. There would no room for error. At best it might save them. At worst it would infuriate him.

She said again, 'Wait! *Wait!* You said you like a gamble?'

He wound one end of the strap around his hand, frowning. 'Maybe.'

'What about a wager — with Max's life as the winnings? If you win, you kill us both.' She could hardly believe she was saying such a thing but while there was life there was hope and it just might work. 'If *I* win, you let him go,' she said.

He didn't immediately refuse so perhaps he was interested, she thought, with a flicker of hope. She wiped blood from the corner of her mouth. The pain was beginning but it hardly mattered.

She said, 'Let's see who Max obeys, you or me. You're so sure that women can't train dogs.' He hesitated and she pressed home her advantage. 'Let me get up, first.'

Intrigued, he swung his leg back, releasing

her, watching as she struggled clumsily to her knees.

Dulcie put a hand gingerly to her jaw which ached abominably and she wondered if he'd broken it. It would hardly matter if she was going to die anyway. But if her idea worked . . .

He gave a snort of derision. 'I *know* they can't. They're too stupid. Most of them couldn't climb out of a paper bag!'

Struggling to her feet, she let the insult pass. 'But you're scared to bet on it?'

He looked at her with narrowed eyes, still undecided, obviously trying to figure out if there was something he was missing.

'But if I lose I could kill you both anyway,' he said.

'Not if you're a man of honour.' She almost choked on the words but she dare not let this chance slip away. 'It's a gamble, remember,' she reminded him and waited, fingers crossed. *Agree!* she begged silently.

'OK then.' He looked at Max who was watching them eagerly. 'This'll be a walkover!' Snapping his fingers, he called 'Heel!'

After the merest hesitation, Max trotted forward and sat beside him. Dulcie feigned disappointment but in fact the dog's shift in allegiance was of no real consequence. Success hung on what came next. Briefly, as Parker laughed, she closed her eyes. It was now or never. For her plan to work, she and the dog had to be in front of the window on the far side of the loft directly in line with where Parker now stood. There would be no margin of error. About five yards would then separate them. If she ran across to the window and called the dog to her he might not come. Probably wouldn't.

He said, 'Well? Get on with it, girlie.' His grin was positively wolfish.

Dulcie drew a deep breath. If this went wrong he would know that she couldn't be trusted and she could expect no mercy.

Snatching up an imaginary stick she hurled it towards the window crying, 'Fetch, Max, fetch!' For a second or two Max stared after it and Dulcie's heart almost stopped beating. Then he bounded across the hay in the direction of the window. In a flash, Dulcie ran after him, carefully keeping close to the wall. Max was still sniffing among the hay in search of the nonexistent stick when she grabbed him.

'Good boy!' she whispered. Holding him tightly to her she moved to the window and turned to face Parker.

'Don't come any nearer! If you do I'll jump. Maybe we'll both die but you won't have a hand in it!'

Startled and angry he glared across at her, his face reddening. 'You cunning little bitch!'

Still clutching the struggling dog, Dulcie put one foot on the sill. Please God, let it work!

He shouted, 'You bloody little —'

And then, as she had hoped, he ran towards her. Straight over the cracked beam. There was a snap like a gun going off as the rotten wood gave way beneath his weight. With a startled cry he fell through the floor and disappeared from sight. A dull crash was followed at once by a scream of agony. Dulcie sank to her knees, dizzy with relief. She felt sick from the pain in her jaw but she had done it. For the moment they were safe. It all depended on how badly Parker was injured. When she felt braver she would take a look. For the moment all was quiet down there. She hugged the dog to her, still shaking with fear.

After what seemed like an age, she heard sounds of movement and then a groan. She put Max down and moved cautiously to the edge of the hole through which her tormentor had vanished. As she had expected, he had fallen on to the old tractor and one leg appeared to be jammed awkwardly between the wheel and the body of the vehicle. His left arm hung by his side, apparently useless but with his right arm he was trying frantically to free his leg.

He looked up briefly and now his rage was evident in the grim lines of his face. He knew that his fall was no accident. *If* she had ever had a chance she had now thrown it away. If he *should* free himself — Oh God! She had gained them a little time, but they were still not safe. What were their choices? Think, Dulcie, *think!* Was there time for her to get herself and Max down the ladder? Suppose he freed himself before they had time to run . . . Were they safer up here? She wondered if the ancient trapdoor could be coaxed back into position and if so, would it keep Parker out of the loft? Was there anything heavy that she could put on it to hold it down? A quick glance round the loft revealed nothing of any weight.

Max was scrabbling in the hay and she crawled over to him. 'What is it?' she whispered. Pushing him aside she discovered the binoculars but almost immediately she heard a car pull up in the road nearby. Through a hole in the wall she was astonished to see a Rolls Royce parked by the gate which led to the barn. From it two men emerged, one in plain clothes and one in uniform. The binoculars brought the two figures closer and she saw that one of them was Jack Spencer.

'Dear God, thank you!' she whispered. Her prayers had been answered. She shouted, 'We're up here!' The pain in her jaw had restricted her voice and she could see that the policemen hadn't heard her. But they were on their way and for a moment she watched their approach with relief. An excited bark from Max made her turn. What she saw almost curdled her blood. A furious Parker was pulling himself up the ladder with his one good arm. Blood trickled from a wound in his head and his lips moved in a soundless threat. Already his head had emerged from the trapdoor and as she watched in horror his shoulders followed.

He said, 'You're going to regret that little trick, girlie!'

Max rushed forward with an exuberant greeting and lunged at Parker's head. He ducked back, cursing and for a moment it looked as though he might lose his balance and fall. As Dulcie watched, petrified, he leaned against the ladder and somehow managed to hurl the dog aside. Dulcie realised with a sickening certainty that once in the loft there was still time for him to kill her before Jack could reach them. Looking around in desperation she saw a length of wood. With no time to think she grabbed it, leaned forward and, pressing it against Parker's chest, pushed as hard as she could. For a few seconds their eyes met and his were full of hate.

He took hold of the wood with his good hand but Dulcie leaned her full weight against it. When this failed to dislodge him she abruptly withdrew it. Surprised, he hesitated, fatally giving her a last chance. Using it like a battering ram she thrust it once more into his chest. He gave a grunt of pain and, unbalanced, swayed backwards. His head struck the side of the trapdoor and his eyes rolled suddenly upward. He slithered down the ladder without a sound. Puzzled, Max stared down at him and whined softly.

Shaking violently Dulcie dropped the wood. As she did so she heard footsteps thudding across the grass. Jack was coming. Weak and exhausted, she pulled Max into her arms, pressed her face against his shaggy coat and burst into tears of relief.

Hours later Harriet, dressed in black, sat by Dulcie's bedside in the surgical ward. Dulcie, her face bandaged, was uneasily aware that, elsewhere in the building, Albert Parker was recovering from his injuries. It was the first time Dulcie had been a patient in any hospital and, to her surprise, she found the experience less stressful than she had anticipated. The young registrar had impressed her and the other patients were reassuringly cheerful. Comparing her own injuries with some of their problems. Dulcie considered herself fortunate. Even the combined smell of antiseptic, floor polish and flowers was bearable in the circumstances. Nurse Williams, fussing with her pillows, was young with a friendly face. The blue and white uniform hid a plump figure. The broad white headdress framed an intelligent face.

Dulcie was still trying to relax after her ordeal. Her parents had just left after a sober, silent visit but Jack Spencer had promised to call in as soon as he was free to do so. She was looking forward to that with mixed emotions. She was longing to see him but was hardly looking her best. The left side of her face, discoloured by a large bruise, was badly swollen and bandages restricted her jaw. The results of the X-rays would tell them whether the damage to her jaw was serious. A small dose of morphine had stifled the worst of the pain but talking was difficult.

The nurse smiled. 'Are you quite comfortable, Miss Moore?'

They were all treating her like a heroine and Dulcie was human enough to appreciate the attention. She nodded in answer to the question. Smiling was not much of an option.

Harriet said wickedly, 'I've never known her so quiet, nurse. It's something of an improvement!'

The nurse laughed. 'The doctor will be along shortly with the results of the x-rays. Let's hope it won't be too long before you can talk properly again.'

She moved away to attend to another patient and Dulcie regarded her aunt with deep affection and not a little concern. Harriet had discharged herself from the hospital earlier in the day in order to attend Teddy's funeral. Refusing James's invitation to stay for a few days at Grange Park, she had decided to go home and look after Max, who was temporarily being cared for at the police station. Max had provided Harriet with the perfect excuse to escape from the hospital and to avoid Clarice's well-meant ministrations at Grange Park. The doctor had finally agreed that further progress could be monitored by her attendance as an out-patient.

Harriet said, 'So everything's over bar the shouting. Parker's under lock and key — well, under close guard anyway. After you beat him up!' She raised her eyebrows humorously.

Dulcie shook her head in furious denial but

Harriet patted her knee. 'You were very brave,' she told her, 'and we're all very proud of you.'

It was quite a speech, thought Dulcie and praise from Harriet was praise indeed. Careful of her jaw, Dulcie said, 'The funeral?' She had been unwilling to ask too many questions of her parents. Her mother seemed to have aged ten years and her father had withdrawn into silence. Two traumatic events followed by the funeral had taken their toll on them both.

Harriet's expression changed. She sighed. 'It was very quiet. Serene almost.' She hesitated. 'I saw Teddy before they closed the coffin. I thought you'd like to know how peaceful he looked. Just as though he might open his eyes and smile.' Her mouth trembled. 'Family and close friends. That's what we wanted.' Her mouth tightened angrily. 'But it wasn't to be. The usual ghouls turned up, the way they do but the police were there keeping an eye on things. There are always some people who want to wallow in someone else's grief. I daresay the newspaper coverage didn't help, either.'

In some ways, thought Dulcie, she was glad to have been spared the sight of her brother in his coffin. She preferred to remember him alive. As soon as she could she would go to the churchyard with flowers and say her 'Goodbyes.'

'Annabel?' she asked.

Harriet shook her head. 'No. But her parents were there. He was looking po-faced — been talked into it, I suppose. I spoke to the mother. It seems Annabel's been sent to an aunt in Switzerland. An extended holiday. She's refusing to have the baby adopted but they're hoping she'll change her mind.' She smiled. 'I told her that if they won't take Annabel in with a baby there's plenty of room in my house. That gave her pause for thought! She began to protest but I said the baby was Teddy's and would be *family.*'

Dulcie squeezed her aunt's hand. How like Harriet to fly in the face of convention. And so generous.

Harriet smiled. 'Of course if Annabel comes home at some stage with a young grandchild they might be won over — and you'd be an aunt.'

Dulcie nodded. The same thought had occurred to her. If Annabel kept Teddy's child it would make life bearable. Especially if the child were a boy. It might even bring the Ropers and the Moores together again.

She closed her eyes briefly, worn out physically by her ordeal and bruised inwardly by her emotions. Not least of these was the thought that Albert Parker was not far away. He was hardly in a fit state to go anywhere and a policeman was sitting beside his bed but Dulcie longed for the moment when he was taken back to prison. He had been operated on for a broken arm and injuries to his back and head. For these, Dulcie felt a small twinge of shame. She had never willingly inflicted bodily harm on anyone before and was trying to forget the satisfaction she had felt when she pushed Parker down the ladder. Part of it, obviously, had stemmed from the instinctive need for self-preservation but she knew there had been something deeper. A more primitive aggression fuelled by an uncivilised desire for revenge. The thought lurked uneasily at the back of her mind and one day she would have to confront it.

Perceptive as ever, Harriet said, 'A penny for them.'

She shook her head and said instead, 'Jack Spencer?'

Harriet rolled her eyes humorously. 'He arrived very late — just in time to join us for ten minutes at the graveside.'

'The Braynes?'

Harriet shook her head. 'Gone to stay with Nora's brother in Guernsey to recuperate. I doubt if they'd have come if they *had* been here.'

Dulcie started to say, 'We went to *Clive's* funeral!' but changed her mind, ashamed by the small-minded thought.

Harriet went on. 'The service was very nice, if that's not a contradiction in terms. "Jesu, joy —". The favourites . . . And wonderful flowers. White carnations and blue iris from the family. A wreath from Cornwall. A spray of flowers from the staff at Fellstowe School.'

Dulcie was aware of a moment's bitterness. Fellstowe! In a way, that was where all the trouble had started. She sighed heavily.

Harriet said, 'What else can I tell you . . . ? Oh

yes. Agnes broke down, poor old dear. She was inconsolable. They had to take her outside but by the time the coffin moved to the grave she had rallied a bit. She's no chicken and you know what she's like. She's always been highly strung. Remember when Teddy got himself stung by a bee? She nearly had hysterics. I could never understand why she wanted to be a nanny. All that responsibility . . .'

She broke off as a loud groan came from the bed on Dulcie's left. A quavering voice called, 'Nurse! I want a bed pan. *Nurse!*'

Nurse Williams returned, shoes squeaking on the polished floor. She carried a bedpan under her arm and quickly drew the curtains round the patient's bed.

Harriet shook her head and muttered, 'Being in hospital is so damned undignified — and the food's terrible. Steamed fish, minced beef — Ugh! We'll get you out of here as soon as possible. In time for the Flower Festival, hopefully — and you'll be wanting to see Max again.'

Dulcie tried not to smile. She said, 'Training classes!'

'And about time, too!'

Dulcie sighed. If her jaw was not so painful she would have told her aunt just how good Max had been. He may have been unruly in the past, she couldn't deny that, but when it mattered most he had come up trumps. She was going to buy him a new collar — the best that money could buy.

At that moment the nurse returned. 'There's a young man wants to see you, Miss Moore,' she said, addressing Dulcie. 'He says he's a colleague from the *Standard.* Calls himself Gus and he's —'

Dulcie nodded. Poor Gus. He'd missed the boat again.

Harriet said, 'Only see him if you're up to it, Dulcie. You've been through a lot and you look very tired. The doctor said you weren't to talk too much. I must be going.' She stood up. 'I'm longing for a nice cup of tea in my own kitchen!' Leaning forward she kissed her niece. 'And don't let it get you down. It's not all bad and you *are* still with us.' Then, lowering her voice, she added, 'I think maybe Teddy was keeping an eye on you.'

Dulcie stared at her, startled. For a long moment she watched her aunt until the wide ward doors swung to behind her. She was immensely comforted by the idea that her brother might have been with her in spirit in Sparks barn.

The nurse said, 'What shall I say? If you're too tired —'

Dulcie brushed away unshed tears. She gave the nurse a small nod and watched as she, too, disappeared through the doors at thc far end of the ward. Her aunt was right. She, Dulcie, still had her whole life ahead of her. She must be thankful for that.

Gus arrived looking sheepish with a bunch of pink roses which he thrust into her hands.

Dulcie pointed to her jaw.

He nodded, staring uncomfortably around the ward. Probably never seen so many women, thought Dulcie, amused — and all of them in a state of undress! She indicated the bedside chair and he sat down.

She smelled the roses and nodded her thanks. The nurse swooped on the flowers and carried them off.

He peered at her, fascinated. 'Your face! What I can see of it. Black and blue down that side. You look as though you've gone ten rounds with Joe Louis!'

'I feel it!'

'Can you talk?'

'Just about.'

He cast another nervous look around the ward. 'We're glad you're OK.' An elderly woman in the bed on Dulcie's right caught his eye and waggled her fingers at him. Hastily Gus returned his attention to Dulcie. 'The flowers came out of petty cash on Cobsey's orders. Wonders will never cease!' He grinned cheerfully. 'Actually he can't wait to have you back.'

She raised her eyebrows.

'No, it's true!' he protested. 'Me, too. The fact is, I've come to ask you a favour. A big one.'

She said, 'You want an interview?'

He nodded eagerly. 'An exclusive?'

She pursed her lips thoughtfully and he rushed on. 'Because I know *you* could do it — I mean eventually you could do a personal story but, right now, while the news is hot, *I* could give you a big build-up.' He leaned forward. 'You see, you can't say how brave you were and I can. I'd do a really, *really* brilliant job of it. I know I can do it. Plucky young *lady* journalist — stuff like that. All the nationals would want it.' He stopped and drew a deep sigh.

A sigh that spoke volumes, thought Dulcie. Gus's big once-in-a-lifetime break.

He rushed on breathlessly. 'I can talk about what else was happening such as the policeman going to Scams for a taxi and arriving in one of their Rollers! Well, I know you *could* do it, after a fashion but you'll get your turn later. You'd be doing what happened *to you.* I could prepare the ground for you. Mine would be factual while yours could be emotional first-person stuff. Two very different articles. Mine the news angle — what, when and how. Quote from the police. Stuff like that. Yours a few days later, more of a feature. How it felt, what he said, if you were scared, your fears for the dog. All that stuff. Cobsey thinks you would easily sell it on to a magazine. What d'you say?'

Looking at the freckled face under its thatch of ginger hair, Dulcie discovered that she couldn't refuse him. The *Standard* had cooperated with her when she attempted to offer herself as bait. She, in turn, could be generous.

She said, 'OK.'

Gus gave a whoop of triumph. He grabbed her hands in his, almost kissed them but at the last moment thought better of it.

Beneath the bandages a smile struggled across Dulcie's face. Strangely she no longer felt herself to be his arch rival. The events of the past twenty-four hours made her feel years older and much wiser. Gus, by comparison, seemed young and gauche. Less of a threat. She liked him better.

'Tomorrow,' she suggested, pointing to her jaw.

His broad grin was all the thanks she needed. As soon as he decently could, he made his excuses and said 'Goodbye'.

The elderly lady said, 'Your young man, is he?'

Dulcie shook her head. 'Colleague,' she told her.

'I'm Mrs Denton.' She looked about seventy with wispy white hair and a fluffy pink bedjacket. She pointed to her stomach. 'Ulcer. Nasty things. Milk and more milk. That's all I've been able to drink. And the pain!'

Dulcie nodded politely.

'Course I know who you are,' Mrs Denton continued. 'We all do. I mean, you're famous, aren't you? The ward orderly told us. Nearly got yourself murdered by that wretch who killed poor Mrs Bly. I knew her, God rest her soul. Lived in the same street. I remember her hubby when he was alive . . .'

Dulcie sank back against the pillows. She would close her eyes and, hopefully, discourage conversation. All she wanted to do was sleep . . .

When she awoke it was almost dark. She lay for a moment or two in a state of drowsiness, trying to recapture her dream. Something about a steep cliff and leaves whipped by the wind. She remembered a dog but it wasn't Max . . . and a voice — *Teddy's* voice — shouting 'Don't look back!'

'Don't look back!' she murmured. Closing her eyes she tried to call up his image. Nothing happened.

'Dulcie?'

This time it was Jack's voice. Without opening her eyes she became aware that somebody was holding her hand. Half opening her eyes she saw Jack Spencer. He looked very tired. Very vulnerable, she thought and put her other hand over his. When Parker had been carried away in the ambulance Jack had taken her in his arms. A brief, fierce hug had marked the end of the coolness between them.

He said, 'The doc says you'll make a total recovery. No lasting damage. I'm so glad — was so afraid Parker would — Well, you know. I didn't know what we'd find. When I saw what he'd done to you I wanted to kill him.' He shook his head. 'I've just left him. They say he's not fit to be questioned but he can't hide behind the doctors indefinitely. We're going to throw the book at him!'

'Will he — ?' She left the sentence unfinished.

'Oh yes! They'll hang him this time, thanks to you.'

'Don't!' The thought appalled her.

'He killed three innocent people, remember.' His face darkened. 'He's lying in a hospital bed sipping tea instead of being banged up in a small dark cell. Nothing's too bad for people like him, Dulcie, so don't go soft on me, for heaven's sake!'

'I'm sorry.'

'You're going to have to stand up in court and tell it how it was. Don't you dare start feeling sorry for him. I want you to cook his goose.'

She nodded dutifully. She was ridiculously pleased to see him and so happy that they were holding hands. 'It's such a violent world. I'd never quite realised.' She glanced down at their linked hands. 'Have I thanked you for rescuing me?'

'You didn't need rescuing. He was only half conscious by the time we arrived. You're quite a girl!'

'I was terribly pleased to see you.'

A nurse approached the bed and Dulcie withdrew her hands.

'For you!' The nurse held out a small bunch of carnations.

Dulcie took them. 'They're lovely!'

Jack said ruefully, 'I haven't had a chance to buy you any flowers but —'

Dulcie smiled at him. '*You* are here. That's what matters.'

The nurse said, 'They're from a Miss Hunt. She wouldn't bring them past the front desk in case she met Parker.'

As Dulcie still looked confused, Jack explained. 'It was something Sylvie Hunt said that tipped us off about Parker's whereabouts. She was coming to your house to warn you — to tell you that he was out to get you.'

Dulcie gave the flowers to the nurse. 'Would you mind?'

The nurse laughed. 'We'll be running out of vases soon.'

When she had gone Jack glanced at his watch and then looked at Dulcie. 'I haven't got long — have to report back to Gough. He knows we've collared the blighter but he doesn't know all the ins and outs. I don't want Bridges queering my pitch.'

'You did well, Jack.'

'I wish I could think so. I think the best I can say is that I didn't make too many mistakes. Listen Dulcie, I don't have much time and I must explain about the other night — at the County. Judith and I are finished. I wanted you to know that. It was all rather awful. Rather sad.'

'Oh dear!' Dulcie's heart sank at the thought of inflicting further pain. Why was life so difficult?

He said, 'I wanted you to know that Judith and I have never been officially engaged. Just a — Well, I hadn't proposed.' He shrugged. 'It was a vague understanding. On my part, I mean. Our families lived next door and we grew up together. I suppose neither of us thought much about the relationship.'

'She said she was your fiancée.'

'She'd convinced herself that we were more than good friends. I never thought about marriage — too wrapped up in my career — but, naturally, I was fond of her. We'd been close friends for as long as I could remember. I never did bother to find myself a girlfriend so I suppose it looked — I daresay the parents thought — and Judith, of course . . .' His voice trailed off. 'The last thing I wanted to do was to hurt her.'

Dulcie felt a deep gratitude. 'So it wasn't because of me?'

'No — and yes.' He took hold of her hand. 'It would have happened sooner or later. It just happened to be you. As soon as I met you I wanted to write and tell her. Then she turned up at my digs and it was too late. I'd missed my chance to do the decent thing. She must hate me.'

'No, Jack!'

'She thinks I've betrayed her.' He shrugged wearily. 'I have to accept some of the blame.' His sigh was heartfelt. 'I'm a stupid idiot. Blind to other people's feelings. All in all I'm not such a marvellous catch for any woman. What do you think, Dulcie? Can we start again?'

She nodded. She found herself wondering how it would be to be kissed by this man.

He said, 'I'll collect Max from the station when I leave you and deliver him safely to your aunt . . . I went to the funeral. I'm so desperately sorry about Teddy.'

For the first time that day Dulcie was glad that she wasn't expected to say much. There were no words. She blinked hard but the tears would not be held back any longer. As they rolled down her cheeks he leaned forward and put his arms around her. For a long time she sobbed, her head against the soft cloth of his jacket.

When it was over she said, 'When I'm home, come to supper with us.'

'I'd love to,' he said. 'Dearest girl, I just want to be with you.'

The words and his expression made her feel that someday, somehow, she would be happy again. 'Do you like cassoulet?' she asked.

He said, 'I don't know, but it sounds delicious!'

Then he stood up to go but before he did, he leaned over and kissed her.

The employees of G.K. Hall hope you have enjoyed this Large Print book. All our Large Print titles are designed for easy reading, and all our books are made to last. Other G.K. Hall books are available at your library, through selected bookstores, or directly from us.

For information about titles, please call:

(800) 257-5157

To share your comments, please write:

Publisher
G.K. Hall & Co.
P.O. Box 159
Thorndike, ME 04986